Praise for *Ghost Wood Song*

"What a gorgeous, creepy gem of a book. *Ghost Wood Song* weaves a captivating spell you won't want to break."
—CLAIRE LEGRAND, *New York Times* bestselling author of *Furyborn* and *Sawkill Girls*

"Strikes the perfect balance of atmospheric chills, dark familial secrets, and a yearning for the warm comforts of home." —ERIN A. CRAIG, *New York Times* bestselling author of *House of Salt and Sorrows*

"A high and lonesome love song to family, to place, to music, and to love itself. It will make your heart dance."
—JEFF ZENTNER, Morris Award–winning author of *The Serpent King* and *Goodbye Days*

"These haunted pages are full to bursting with intricate family dynamics, a nuanced queer romance, and a crescendo of an ending readers won't see coming."
—ROSIEE THOR, author of *Tarnished Are the Stars*

"*Ghost Wood Song* is a dusky, haunting daydream of a debut that hits all the right notes." —DAHLIA ADLER, author of *Under the Lights* and editor of *His Hideous Heart*

"When you finish, you'll want to turn back to page one and start all over again." —AMANDA LOVELACE, author of *The Princess Saves Herself in This One*

GHOST WOOD SONG

ERICA WATERS

This book is a work of fiction. Names, characters, places, and incidents are either the product of the author's imagination or are used fictitiously, and any resemblance to actual persons, living or dead, business establishments, events, or locales is entirely coincidental.

HarperTeen is an imprint of HarperCollins Publishers.

Ghost Wood Song
 For information address HarperCollins Children's Books, a division of HarperCollins Publishers, 195 Broadway, New York, NY 10007.
www.epicreads.com

Library of Congress Control Number: 2020933580
ISBN 978-0-06-289422-9

Typography by Jenna Stempel-Lobell
20 21 22 23 24 PC/LSCH 10 9 8 7 6 5 4 3 2 1

First Edition

For my sister, Melinda

ONE

I'm as restless as the ghosts today. The sigh of the trees makes my scalp prickle, my senses strain. There's something waiting for me in the silences between the notes we play, like a vibration too low for human ears. It's been out here in the woods for weeks, just out of my reach.

No one else notices. Sarah leans over her banjo, dark hair falling across her forehead, mouth set in concentration. The music that spins from her fingertips is bright as the sunshine that drifts across the pine needles. She looks soft in this light, her eyelashes downy as moth wings.

The wood behind her glows golden right up to the edge of Mama's property, where the true forest begins. There, the sunlight loses its hold, fading to shadows. Those trees grow tall and close together, clotted with brambles and vines. That's where the ghosts who spill out of Aunt Ena's house like to linger, mingling their whispers with the wind. I can't quite catch their words, but they tug at me, drawing my attention away from the music.

"Jesus, Shady," Sarah says, her voice hacking through the song like a machete. Orlando slaps his hand over his guitar strings to mute the chord he fumbled. "You missed your cue again. Why didn't you come in?" All her moth-wing softness has disappeared.

"Sorry," I say, glancing at the fiddle in my lap. "There's not much for me to do in this song." I pull a loose thread from the fraying hem of my skirt, wrapping it around my finger.

That was the second time I forgot to come in. I'm distracted today, but the truth is, this song doesn't mean anything to me. I want to learn to play bluegrass the way my daddy did—like it's the breath in my lungs, the beat of my heart. And I never will if Sarah keeps picking all these folk-rock songs.

She pushes her short, messy hair back with an impatient hand, revealing her undercut and the cloud-shaped birthmark behind her ear. I've thought so many times about running my lips over just that spot. "The open mic's in one week, Shady. We can play something else, but if we don't decide on a song today, we won't be ready in time." There's an edge to her voice like she's been paired with a lazy classmate for a group project. "You know how badly I need to win this."

"I'm sorry," I say again, louder, taking up my fiddle to show I'm paying attention. I know I'm the one at fault, but the annoyance in her voice makes me glare back at her, all thoughts of lips on skin forgotten. "I want to win, too, you know."

The prize is a free half day in a small recording studio, a

chance to record a song with professional help and equipment. It sounds cool, but I mostly want to win to make Sarah happy. She thinks it would help her get into a good music school.

But we can't even agree on what song we're going to play for the open mic night. Sarah only wants to play newer, more popular folk-rock, Orlando flits from one style of music to another like a butterfly tasting flowers, and I can only really perform if we're playing traditional folk and bluegrass. We're like the leftovers from three different dishes someone's trying to make into a casserole.

"We could do 'Wagon Wheel' instead. It has a strong fiddle part," Sarah says.

"'Wagon Wheel'?" I say, so surprised I flinch. The last time we played "Wagon Wheel" it was just Sarah and me, alone in her room. One minute we were playing and the next our lips were inches apart. Sarah pulled away before we could kiss, but it changed everything between us. We haven't talked about it since. Maybe now she's trying to remind me, to give me an opening?

Confusion passes over her face, followed quickly by a deep blush. She definitely didn't mean to bring up the almost-kiss.

"'Wagon Wheel' is kind of overplayed," I say, glancing away.

"It's a crowd pleaser, though," Orlando offers, oblivious to what just happened. He's stretched out on his belly, wire-rimmed glasses sliding down his nose, which hovers about three inches from a mess of pill bugs he found under a rock. That's always the danger of holding practice in the woods—Orlando will wander off after a grasshopper or get stuck watching the progress of an ant colony for hours on end. His whole absentminded-professor thing irritates Sarah, but you can't blame a person for loving what they love. And Orlando loves bugs.

"Any other ideas?" Sarah asks.

"I've been working on 'The Twa Sisters.' Orlando likes that one too."

"It's too creepy and weird," she says, shaking her head.

I shrug. She's not wrong. "The Twa Sisters" is an old folk song about two sisters who fall in love with the same boy, so one drowns the other. When the drowned sister's body washes up on the riverbank, a young fiddler finds it and shapes her bones into fiddle parts. Her rib cage becomes a fiddle, her finger bones its pegs. But the bone-made fiddle will only play one tune: *Oh, the dreadful wind and rain.*

Daddy taught me "The Twa Sisters" during one of his low times, when his songs all turned dark and drear, as far from the bright notes of bluegrass as a person can get with a fiddle in hand. You'd think he was the one who killed the fair sister from the song, the way his voice got so husky-sad, the way his fiddle cried.

Only tune that the fiddle would play was
Oh, the dreadful wind and rain

I've been practicing it for weeks, but I still can't play it like he did, as if the song's story is my own. My notes come out sweet and bright, no matter how I try to deepen and darken them. But I can't seem to leave this song alone, like it's the only one my fiddle wants to play.

I'd never say it out loud, and even admitting it to myself gives me chills, but if I could have a fiddle made of my daddy's bones, I'd take it. I'd take it and play it and learn all the secrets he kept, all the sorrows he bore inside his breast. I think that's what made his music so good.

"I don't get why you're so opposed to playing new music," Sarah says as if she's reading my thoughts.

"And I don't get why you're so opposed to playing good music," I shoot back, heat spreading across my cheeks.

Sarah's lips part for a retort, but then she closes her mouth, looks down at her lap. She puts on such a tough front, but underneath all that sarcasm and bossiness there's this tender, easily bruised Sarah she tries so hard to hide. And my barb cut right through.

Before I can apologize, she snatches up her banjo and stalks off through the woods, her boots kicking up pine needles. Orlando groans and gets up to follow her, leaving me with only the trees for company. I wish I could make her understand what playing the fiddle means to me—what it used to mean, what it can't ever mean again.

I know that music could be my ticket out of here, out of Mama's crowded trailer, out of Goodwill clothes and food that comes in cans and boxes. It could be an escape from all the memories that never leave me be. But that's not why I play the fiddle. My family history—everything we've lost, all our ghosts and all our griefs—those feel like the truest part of me, the beating heart of my music. Playing Sarah's way is like taking an ax to my deepest, most secret roots.

Bright, soft banjo notes begin to drift through the trees. Sarah's playing a Gillian Welch song, the one about Elvis. Orlando starts singing along, his voice rich and sweet as molasses.

Their music floods me with longing, making me think of ninth grade, when the three of us met. Sarah had just transferred from another county, and Orlando had moved to Briar Springs from Miami the summer before. We were close friends within a few weeks and started playing music together soon after. Orlando was happy to discover that the bluegrass Sarah and I liked reminded him a little of the guajira music—Cuban country—he'd grown up playing with his grandfather and uncles. He taught us a few Cuban songs, and we taught him bluegrass and folk. Music is what made us friends, but now it feels like it's pulling us apart. If we could play together again like we used to, when it was just for fun, when we laughed through half the songs we played—

I grab my fiddle and follow their notes like bread crumbs through the trees.

They both look up, startled, when I reach the small clearing where they sit. "That's the one," I say, pushing down all my doubts. "We'll play that for the open mic night."

I linger in the woods after Sarah and Orlando head home. The sun has gone down, and the woods are hushed, shadows spilling like ink through the trees. The air is cool and sweet with the smells of early spring.

I raise my fiddle and breathe into the quiet, my eyes closed in concentration. A great horned owl hoots gently somewhere nearby, like a chiding mother telling me to get on with it.

Daddy always said twilight was good for ghost raising because it's an in-between time, when the barrier between worlds seems to grow thin as tissue paper and the ghosts are at their lonesomest. This fiddle can't so much as poke a hole in that tissue paper, but it's the only one I've got now.

Daddy's fiddle drew ghosts like hummingbirds to nectar. Mine only reminds me of everything I'm not, everything I'll never be.

My bow slices across the strings, sending a wail into the blue hush and startling the owl, who erupts in a flurry of shocked feathers from a branch high above my head, hooting her displeasure.

I play "The Twa Sisters" over and over again, trying to imagine myself as the drowned sister, watching the world turn to brown river water. Then I play it as the fiddler who finds the body and strings the girl's long, yellow hair into a fiddle bow. But the song comes out the same—sad and sweet, quiet and calm as the river that washed up her bones.

Finally, I let the song fade, its last notes disappearing into the skinny pines. Night settles in around me, the air close and clammy. Cicadas take up where my fiddle left off, and small animals rustle in the brush. The trees sigh and sigh and sigh. This forest feels like an ear that's always listening but never hears what it's hoping to. Maybe it misses Daddy's fiddle same as I do. Maybe it's waiting, like I am too, for a voice of its own.

I turn to put my fiddle in its case, when, like a belated echo, a snatch of music comes back to me from the trees, deep and pure and full of grief, the dark twin of my bow's last arc. A shiver runs up my spine, spreading chill bumps over my arms. Every muscle in my body tenses, waiting for another note.

"Shady," Mama yells from the trailer, making me jump. "It's dinnertime." The door slams, and I shake myself.

I put my fiddle in its case and turn for home, back through the hungry, darkening woods, back toward Mama's trailer, to the life we made inside the emptiness Daddy's death left behind.

TWO

Our trailer always puts me in mind of a tin can with a firecracker that's about to blow. Tonight's no different. My stepdad, Jim, is laid out on the recliner with NASCAR cranked up loud enough to make you think you're on the track yourself, inhaling burned-rubber fumes. Mama's at the stove banging pots and pans and swearing under her breath, while my two-year-old sister, Honey, tugs at Mama's Waffle House uniform. The smells of fried chicken, instant mashed potatoes, and canned spinach make my stomach turn.

"Shady, where've you been?" Mama asks when she catches sight of me standing at the counter that divides the kitchen from the living room.

"I was in the woods with Sarah and Orlando." Honey wanders over, and I start to braid a section of her silky hair. My own hair's so curly and thick you can't run your fingers through it, so I love playing with Honey's.

"They left an hour ago. You been out there by yourself playing that fiddle?" Mama wipes sweat from her forehead with the back of her hand.

I don't answer, so she goes on muttering. "Just like your daddy, too busy playing that instrument to help me."

Mama's in a temper, but I know it's not really about me. It never is. "I'll help you, Mama. What do you need?" I say, touching her arm.

Her eyes soften. "Go tell Jesse to come in here for dinner."

I cross back through the living room, but Jim doesn't even see me, his eyes locked on the endlessly circling cars. His cell phone is ringing, but he ignores it.

I knock at Jesse's door and then poke my head in. "Mama says come to dinner."

My older brother sits on his bed, back against the headboard, with earbuds in, steadily texting. An awful, metallic-sounding music grates from the speakers.

"Jesse."

"What?" he says, yanking one earbud out. He pushes a shock of light-brown hair from his eyes.

"Are you coming to dinner, or not? Mama's in a bad mood, though, so you'd better get in there."

Jesse sighs like I've come to lead him to his death.

"What'd you do now?" I ask.

"Why's it gotta be something I did?"

"It's always you. Can't you find something better to do with your time? You could play with my band and me. It doesn't have to be fiddle—you could learn mandolin or something. Daddy would be so disappointed that you—"

Jesse's face goes hard before I can even finish the sentence. "Fuck off."

I step back and look away, my cheeks flushing with anger and embarrassment. I turn to leave, but Jesse's voice stops me. "I'm sorry. I didn't mean that."

I spin back to face him. "You did, though." Sometimes I look at Jesse and don't even recognize him anymore, but he's still my brother, and I miss him. I miss the way we used to be, before he saw Daddy die right in front of him, before Mama moved another man into Daddy's place.

"Yeah, I did, but I'm still sorry. I just don't want to play music like that, okay?" Jesse's voice softens. "Playing that sad song over and over again isn't going to make him come back, you know. You're only making it harder on yourself."

His words sink like fishing weights in my stomach, landing cold and true. Is that what I'm hoping for, deep down, when I spend hours in the woods, playing for the unreachable ghosts? Is that why I can't stop playing "The Twa Sisters"? These past few weeks it's all I've wanted to do.

I shrug and change the subject. "Will you at least come see me play at the open mic next weekend?"

"Maybe," he says, pushing me forward. "Now get out."

When we trudge into the kitchen, Mama's eyes snag on Jesse, but she doesn't say anything. Jim's glowering at the screen of his phone, which has started ringing again.

I go to the stove and make a big plate of food for Honey and me to share. That way, Mama won't notice if I don't eat any meat. She's dead set against me becoming a vegetarian. Honey's already at the table in her booster chair, and I squeeze past her to the seat between the microwave and window, well out of the fray.

"Jim, turn off that noise and come eat with us," Mama says. "And answer your phone or turn it off."

"Goddamned Frank hassling me about that missing lumber delivery." Jim silences the phone, but keeps scowling at it. "Just bring me a plate in here, Shirley."

"Do I look like your servant?" Mama asks, staring him down.

Writers are always going on about piercing blue eyes, but they must've never seen Mama's brown ones when she's mad. She'll burn a hole through sheet metal.

Jim grunts and turns down the volume on the TV. He plunks himself into the chair next to Jesse, forcing his lanky legs under the table. "Why's your mama in such a bad mood, boy?"

Jesse doesn't say anything. He stares down at his plate, running his fingers over the condensation on his glass of sweet tea.

"The principal called," Mama says, answering for Jesse. "He skipped school all week." She turns to Jesse and levels that metal-burning stare on him. "You trying to get me jailed for truancy?"

"Maybe it's time we pulled him out of school," Jim says, rubbing the back of his permanently sunburned neck. "Let him make his own living. Might teach him a thing or two. He was never going to college nohow, so what's he need to finish high school for?"

"My son is going to finish high school," Mama says, her voice dangerous.

Mama dropped out of high school as a teenager and only went to get her GED after Jesse was born. You mention dropping out of school—even as a joke—and you're in for a three-day lecture about how shameful it feels to go out in the world without an education. Jim ought to know better.

Our stepdad usually keeps his thoughts to himself, at least when Mama's around, but he's like a dog with a bone tonight. Maybe because his boss, his brother Frank, has been riding him harder than usual at the construction company. But more and more, that's just how it is between Jim and Jesse. Each one is an itch the other can't stop scratching, and tonight Jesse's a full-blown rash.

"You keep letting him run around, wasting his life, it don't matter if he finishes high school," Jim says. "He'll be in prison anyway. That's about all he's good for."

Jesse slams back his chair, knocking it against the wall. Honey jumps, her eyes going wide, but no one pays her any mind. Last time Jim and Jesse fought like this, Mama had to pull them apart before punches were thrown.

But Jesse only crosses his arms over his chest. "And what are you good for, Jim?"

"You got a roof over your head and clothes on your back, don't you?" Jim picks a piece of chicken from his teeth.

"So I should be like you, and work a shitty job that barely pays me anything, and make my dead best friend's kids live in a shitty trailer with a shitty stepdad they hate? You think this is what my dad wanted for us?" Jesse laughs, but it's a hard, ugly sound.

"Don't bring your daddy into this. This is about you and your attitude." Jim shakes his head, going back to his dinner. He's trying to seem calm and in control, but his hand tightens around his fork. His job is a sore spot for him. Back before him and Mama got together, his drinking and carrying on got so bad he made a name for himself in town. Nobody but his older brother would hire him, and it kills Jim to work for Frank—probably because everybody loves Frank and thinks Jim's a piece of trash. I can't say I disagree.

When he notices Jim's grip on the fork, a venomous smile spreads across Jesse's lips. He never misses a tell. "You know, Jim," he starts to say, but Mama doesn't miss anyone's tells either. She cuts him off before he can get going.

"That's enough, Jesse Ray. If you can't be civil at the dinner table, you can go to your room. We didn't work all day to listen to you be ungrateful."

Anger flashes into Jesse's eyes again. "He's the one who—"

"Don't talk back to your mama," Jim says, smirking. He's got Mama back on his side.

Jesse studies the two of them carefully, trying to push down his anger and get the upper hand. But when he speaks again, his voice is half strangled with hurt. "You can lecture me all you like, Mama, but I know what you two did, and I'm always going to know it." He pushes off from the table, rattling the dishes, and stomps from the kitchen. "If you wanted me to be a better man, you should've married one," he says before disappearing down the hallway.

Jim makes to follow Jesse to his room, but Mama puts her hand on his arm. "Leave it be, Jim. Leave it be."

I know Jesse is referring to Mama and Jim's relationship, but he's wrong. I asked Mama when Jim moved in if there was something between her and Jim before Daddy died, and she said no, of course not. "Mama, why does Jesse still think—"

"You leave it be, too, Shady," she snaps. "And cut up some of that chicken breast for your sister." I curl my lip at the meat, but I know better than to argue.

Jim's still stewing. "A man breaks his back all day and comes home to this nonsense," he mutters, rising from the table. He takes his plate into the living room and turns the TV's volume up again, filling the angry silence with the monotonous roar of race cars flying around and around and around in circles—a fitting soundtrack for our lives.

Mama stares down at her half-eaten meal, looking tired and sad and guilty. Honey's playing with her food, thankfully oblivious to the rest of us now that the shouting has stopped. I force down a few more bites of watery potatoes, but I can't stand to sit at this table any longer. "I'm going to go get some air," I say.

"All right, baby," Mama murmurs, not meeting my eyes.

I take a huge breath of the pine-scented night air once I get outside and plop down onto the steps, leaning my head back against the trailer's door. But I can still hear the mechanical snarls from the TV, so I wander out to the dirt road that runs past our house, walking along the tree line, where shadows move like the darkness of dreams. I reach the end of our small road and walk for several minutes down the larger dirt road that bumps its way toward the highway.

With the dark pines at my back, I look out over the cow

pasture on the other side, searching for the tree I've come to think of as mine. A blasted oak, twisted like a wrung-out rag, the bark smooth and pale, the limbs reaching up like an old woman's knobby fingers. I guess most people would call it ugly, but I think it's beautiful, even though it's dead and barren and all alone. I like to think it's going to outlast us all; that long after we're gone it will still be standing there not caring it's got no leaves and no acorns, that it can't offer shelter the way other oak trees can. Despite what this tree has lost, it's still standing, a gleam of white against the dark field. Whenever I see it, something in me reaches toward it, like we're kin.

Daddy and I drove past it all the time when he was alive. He'd always start humming an old murder ballad he told me was called "The Old Oak Tree." He would never sing the words for me, though I loved the sad, lilting melody of it.

Tonight, pale, distant stars shine overhead. The forest behind me sleeps, breathing silently, the pine trees' top branches finally at rest. The atmosphere feels the way it did when Daddy played his fiddle—like all creation had gone still and quiet, waiting to see what the music would bring.

I wait with the trees and the ghosts, trembling in the warm spring air, my body tuned to a frequency that only sounds like white noise, empty static to my mind. No matter how hard I listen, the silence never resolves into melody.

As I get ready for bed, I still feel restless and on edge—still caught up in that snatch of music I heard in the woods, the spirits' watchfulness I felt in the trees. I don't think I'll be able to sleep, but I guess all of today's fighting has worn me out. When I fall into bed at ten o'clock, I drift straight from thoughts of the shadowy, restive woods and into familiar dreams.

I'm lying in my little twin bed at the old house—my real home—with the window open to a rare fall breeze. My feet are cold, but I don't want to close the window because I can hear Daddy's fiddle playing from the woods. A low, mournful song I don't recognize drifts in with the usual nighttime creatures' music. It's a sad song, but it comforts me, and my eyes grow heavy.

Just then, my bedroom door creaks open, startling me awake, but it's probably one of the ghosts, nothing to worry about. I pull my quilt higher over my chest, until it's under my nose. Then I hear heavy footsteps on the floorboards, nothing like the soft patter of the ghosts I'm used to. I turn my head toward the door, where a tall, shadowy figure stands, his features obscured by the hall light behind him.

My heart begins to race. "Daddy?" I say, but I know it's not Daddy—his fiddle's still crying in the pines. "Jesse?" I whisper, though the figure's too tall to be my brother.

I already know who's standing at my door.

The figure doesn't speak. He makes his inky way into the room, drawing nearer and nearer to my bed, until he's standing over me, gazing down into my face. I stare up at him as I have a dozen times before, unable to speak or move or even breathe. The figure has no face. He is darkness. He is nothing.

A hand reaches down toward my throat, and I know I should fight, know I should thrash and kick and bite, but my body won't obey me. My limbs lie heavy, useless. Fingertips brush my throat, and finally I work up a scream from somewhere deep inside me. It rips from my mouth, cutting through the shadows in the room, making the dark figure draw back his hand.

I scream until I am no longer a girl, no longer flesh and blood, but only sound and terror hurtling through the night.

Warm fingers close over my arm and shake me. "Shady," someone says. "Open your eyes." And then I'm back in the trailer, in the room I share with Honey, staring into my brother's face. Jesse's eyes soften in relief when he sees I recognize him. I'm still paralyzed, but my eyes flit over the room, searching for a man made of shadows.

"You were screaming," Jesse says. "I thought you were being murdered in your bed."

"I was." A warm tear rolls down my face. When I reach up to wipe it away, I realize I can move again. I sit up, feeling sick and dizzy. "Where's Honey?" She's not in the bed across from mine.

"She probably fell asleep in Mama's room," Jesse says. He studies me carefully. "Are you having the dreams again, like you did before . . . ?" He can't bear to say "before Daddy died."

"Everybody has nightmares," I say. But that fear's still sitting there on my chest, heavy as a body. It's been four years since I've had to fight him off—the dark figure who held me down in the twilight space between dreams and waking, who slipped in and out of the shadows, from choking nightmare to screaming waking. He hasn't visited me since Daddy died.

If he's back now, will the other dreams come back too? The dead girl in my ceiling, the stinging wasps? A shudder runs through me, making me squeeze my eyes closed. And why now? Why has he chosen to come back?

"Shady, are you all right?" Mama says from the doorway. I must have woken up the whole house with my screaming.

I find my voice again. "Just a bad dream. I'm fine. You can go to sleep."

Jesse doesn't speak to her. He gets up and heads back to his room. After murmuring good night, Mama goes too, leaving me alone with the memory of cool fingers on my neck, fiddle music in my ears, a secret I'm half afraid to admit to myself.

The shadow man's back.

THREE

There's still an expectant, uneasy feeling in my chest when I pull up at Aunt Ena's the next morning, a Saturday.

The house where I grew up looks like it always has, like it probably always will. The white paint has peeled and turned the same grayish color as the heavy Spanish moss that drips from the massive oak trees in the front yard. The upstairs windows are dark with dirt, and even from my car, I can see the cobwebs. The grass is overgrown, and cracks vein the bricks of the front stoop like spreading kudzu vines.

You'd think the house was empty of the living if it weren't for the pink azaleas rioting in the front yard, big and fierce enough to make even the oak trees look nervous. Flowers usually cheer up a place, but against the brightness of the azaleas, the house and the woods behind it look more ominous than ever. All shadows and whispers. It doesn't help that the sky's overcast, with big, dark thunderheads rolling in.

I head for the door, my arms loaded with bags. I've been doing Aunt Ena's shopping on Saturday mornings since the first week I got my driver's license. It's not that she can't go out; she just doesn't like to. Crowds make her nervous. And so do open spaces. And fluorescent lights. The grocery store is her idea of hell. Mama says she's always been like that, but it got worse after Daddy died.

Aunt Ena opens the door, still in her nightgown. "Mornin', darlin'." She smiles and stands back to let me in.

Aunt Ena looks so much like Daddy it makes my chest ache. She's got his naturally fair skin, dark curly hair, and snub nose. Her eyes are blue, though, a rarity in our family.

"Your azaleas are going to overtake the house before long," I say as I pass through the door. "What are you feeding them?"

Aunt Ena wiggles her fingers mysteriously and then goes to get some cash from her purse. She always gives me ten bucks for my trouble, the only income I've got. I'd do it even without the money, though. I like spending time with Aunt Ena, and I know she's lonely. Plus, I get to missing this old house something fierce if I stay away too long.

I help put the groceries away in the kitchen, and every drawer and cabinet I open sends a memory whooshing out. Daddy boiling a giant pot of peanuts. Jesse and me eating all the chocolate chip cookies while our parents slept. My homemade volcano shooting red froth up to the ceiling.

There are bad memories here too—waking up screaming from nightmares of the shadow man and, even awake, creeping around dark corners of the house, watching for him. I sat right here on the kitchen floor one night after a particularly scary dream, crying and shaking, until Jesse found me.

I try to push the memory from my mind and let the good things I remember take its place. Whatever Jesse might say to the contrary, I know we were happy here, even with the nightmares, even with the ghosts, though the ghosts are why Mama wanted to move out once Daddy was gone. They weren't her people's spirits. It's one thing to live with the ghosts of your own blood, but other people's—those can be hard to get along with if you don't have the right temperament. They feel all wrong in the air, against your skin. They make your nerves jittery.

Mama could never stand it, and once Daddy was gone, she never slept another night under this roof. We spent a few weeks at her friend's place, and then she used Daddy's life insurance money to buy the trailer on the other side of the woods. She walked away from Daddy's old family home without a backward glance. Jesse turned his back, too—he hasn't set foot in this house since we moved.

"How's your music coming along?" Aunt Ena asks, pouring a bag of dried black-eyed peas into a glass jar.

"It's all right. It's not like it used to be. I don't think I'll ever be as good as Daddy was."

Silence drops and deepens around us. "How's Sarah then?" she says, arching an eyebrow, trying to lighten the mood.

I haven't told many people I'm bi, so I don't know how Aunt Ena figured out about my crush on Sarah. Probably the ghosts whispered it to her. She's always had a better ear for them than the rest of us.

I go to the fridge and pour myself a glass of orange juice to hide my embarrassment. "Sarah's Sarah," I say, but Aunt Ena's not fooled.

"You ask her to prom yet?"

I laugh outright at the thought of Sarah in a prom dress. She'd probably show up in Converse and jeans. Maybe a tuxedo if I could talk her into it.

"Leave me alone," I say, but I smile too.

"All right, all right. I'll make you some French toast." Aunt Ena makes better French toast than any restaurant ever could. She told me once it was her mama's recipe, but she doesn't like to talk about my grandmother, who died right before Aunt Ena started college.

What little bit I know about my grandparents was hard-won, wheedled out of Daddy when he was distracted, pulled like teeth from Aunt Ena's mouth. Neither of them ever liked to talk about the past. Daddy would always say something like, "Don't matter, Shady girl. What's gone's gone," and then he'd go back to painting or hammering or planting. But I do know their mama was Irish and worked as a medium when she was young—helping folks get in contact with dead relatives and lovers.

Daddy got his ghost-raising magic from her, but the ghosts only came to him when he played his fiddle. That came from his mama, too, the instrument passed down through the family for generations.

My grandma stopped working as a medium after she married my grandpa. They settled here in Briar Springs, Florida, in the only house they could afford—a house no one else wanted, on account of it being haunted. Once my grandmother moved in, even more lost souls began to haunt the house and the woods that surround it, drawn to her just like they were to Daddy. I guess the ghosts have been coming ever since.

Our people mostly didn't mind the ghosts, kin or not. Well, maybe Daddy's father did, but poor people can't be too choosy about where they live. I don't know anything about my grandfather, except that Daddy didn't seem to like him much. Maybe the ghosts rubbed him raw the way they did Mama.

Today the ghosts are quiet, listening to Aunt Ena and me chat at the table, Aunt Ena growing steadily more animated. She tells me about the books she's been reading, the plants she's been growing, her blue eyes bright as morning glories in early summer. The tight feeling in my chest starts to fade.

When the faint strains of a mournful fiddle start wafting down from the second floor, we both stop talking. Aunt Ena's smile wavers and then goes out like a spent lightning bug.

"What is . . . ?" I stare at the ceiling, trying to catch the melody, all the hairs on my arms standing on end. "Oh my God, that's 'The Twa Sisters.' I heard it in the woods last night, too," I say, suddenly sure. "I didn't imagine it." The song is distant but unmistakable, and it doesn't sound light and sweet like when I play it. The only person who ever played like that was Daddy.

When Aunt Ena's eyes meet mine, I can tell she's thinking the same thing. Her face has gone pale, her mouth a hard line. "It's just an echo of the past. That's all. Don't mind it. It's an echo. You know this old house is full of 'em."

The music's already gone.

"An echo," I say, but I know she's wrong. Tears stand in my eyes.

"Oh, Shady," Aunt Ena says, reaching for my hand.

I pull it out of her reach and wipe my eyes. "Did I ever tell you about the first time I saw one of the ghosts Daddy raised? He was playing 'The Twa Sisters' that night."

"You shouldn't think about it. The past's the past." God, she sounds so much like Daddy. Everyone in this family's determined to forget.

But the memory crept in with the music, clawed and fanged. I close my eyes and let it rip me open.

I was six years old, upstairs in my bedroom. I was asleep and then I wasn't. I was alone and then I wasn't. From the room below came Daddy's fiddle music, frenzied and wild as a hurricane night. A ghost stood over my bed, staring at me. The louder and faster Daddy's music grew, the more real the ghost became until he looked hardly discernible from a living man. Gray hair, a face lined and hardened. His pants and shirt were made of the same rough, beige-colored material, like a work uniform, a long number stamped across the breast pocket. I was just working up the nerve to scream when he spoke.

"I won't hurt you. I'm looking for someone," he said, his voice a confused old man's. The face that had seemed hard and sinister moments ago became soft, vulnerable.

"Who are you looking for?" I whispered.

His brow furrowed. "I don't know."

The fiddle music downstairs was building and building

until I thought the room Daddy played in would explode. I saw the old man's eyes fill slowly with recognition. He looked down at the floorboards. "I think I'm looking for *him*," he said, pointing at the floor.

"Shady," Aunt Ena says, pulling me from the memory. "This isn't good for you, darlin'." She takes the dirty dishes to the sink and turns on the tap.

"Do you think Daddy's fiddle is really at the bottom of the lake?" I ask, trying to keep my voice even, despite the sharp stab of longing in my chest.

"Where else would it be?" she says, staring fixedly into the soapy, churning water.

I don't answer because I'm picturing Daddy's truck careening off the road, the fiddle sinking into the water. It happened four years ago, and even though I wasn't there, I've pictured it so many times it feels like I was. The truck hitting the lake, sending up a spray of frothy, algae-scented water, his body slamming into the windshield, his blood turning the water red. He was bringing Jesse home from a friend's house, and there was a deer in the road. Daddy died on impact and the fiddle was lost, but Jesse made it out alive.

Aunt Ena turns off the water and leans against the sink, settling her eyes on mine. There is pain and anger and a kind of tenderness in her face, a combination I see there whenever the fiddle comes up. "That fiddle's at the bottom of the lake or broke up and carried off somewhere. Either way, it's gone, just like your daddy."

But what if it's not gone? A thought that's been tempting me for a while surfaces. What if I could find it and use it? I could raise his ghost; I could talk to him again. And with Daddy's fiddle, I could make music worth hearing. I could be everything he meant me to be. Everything I want to be.

"If I could play Daddy's fiddle, it'd be like having him back," I say, but I keep my other ideas to myself.

Aunt Ena guesses my unspoken thoughts, as usual. "Maybe so, but the dead always stay dead," she says gently. "We live with their ghosts, but that's all. Wallowing in your grief will only draw evil. You need to focus on all the good things in your life, not the things you've lost."

"I guess." I rest my chin in my hands and stare at the cracked and faded linoleum floor. Maybe that's what I've been doing these last few weeks, out in the woods playing my fiddle. Wallowing. Maybe that's why the shadow man is back. But if I'm wallowing, Aunt Ena's just as bad—living here alone, the last survivor of her family home, with only ghosts for company.

I leave after a few more awkward minutes, claiming homework. But when I reach the car, I turn and look back, lifting my eyes to the upstairs windows. I don't know what I hope to see there—the dirty windows are empty, except for a few wasps climbing across the glass. Behind the house, the pine forest looms, deep and dark and waiting, always waiting.

The clouds grow heavier and darker as I drive home, and the sky dims like it's twilight instead of early afternoon. When I pull into the driveway, Jim's truck is gone, which I hope means he and Mama and Honey have gone off somewhere.

I climb out of the car and start toward the trailer, but then I hear the fiddle tune again, faint and faded as an old photograph. I stand still in the yard and listen. Only the wind in the trees.

But then a sharp, mournful wail slices through the air, familiar and dreadful at once. I move closer to the woods and listen again. Shadows settle over the golden pine needles, turning the woods dark. The atmosphere feels taut as a bowstring, the storm starting to roll in from across the fields.

And then the fiddle begins to play in earnest, the volume going up and down, swirling through the trees like it's carried on the wind. It's carrying my heart with it.

I walk to the boundary of our five acres and then go deeper into the woods, until the trees grow so close together I have to stop and squeeze through them. My hair catches in hanging vines, and thorns scrape against my skin, snagging my clothes.

The fiddle plays on and on, low and slightly mad, growing into a frenzy wilder than the wind that's whipping through the trees. Rain drops out of the sky without preamble—fat, hard, stinging drops that would soak me to the skin if the trees weren't so thick.

I think of the lyrics from "The Twa Sisters" again.

Only tune that the fiddle would play was
Oh, the dreadful wind and rain

And then the rest of my memory from Aunt Ena's place comes back—what happened after Daddy's fiddle brought the old man's ghost to my room. It was the first time I ever saw a ghost with my own eyes, instead of just knowing it was there or feeling it brushing by. I was so little, but I wasn't scared. I pushed the covers away and got out of bed, my feet cold on the bare floorboards. "Come on," I said, holding out my hand to the man.

His hand felt like a winter chill but was solid enough to hold mine. Goose bumps trickled up my arm from where my skin met his, but I didn't let go. I led him out of my bedroom and down the stairs, into the parlor where Daddy liked to play.

When we appeared in the doorway, a child of six in a pink nightgown and an old man with a lost expression, Daddy looked up, his eyes widening even as his left hand continued to hold down the fiddle strings and his right arm continued to draw the bow across them.

Once his mind took in what his eyes were seeing, he dropped the fiddle and leaped across the room, grabbing my empty hand to pull me away from the man, who cowered away, his solid form already beginning to wane.

"Why'd you come here? I didn't call you here," Daddy said to the ghost, angrier than I'd ever heard him. He glanced back at me as though to assure himself I was all in one piece.

The old man said, "I can't . . . I can't remember." He was hardly a man now, more like a whirl of human-shaped wind.

"Go on home," Daddy said, his voice low and shaking. "Go back to your rest."

And then the man was nothing more than the kind of ghost I was used to—a breath, a memory.

Daddy turned back to me and swept me off my feet and clutched me to his chest like he'd just pulled me out of the ocean half drowned. He sat on a sofa and held me close, his breath in my hair. I pulled my head back to see his face and put one hand on his cheek, which was rough as sandpaper. A tear slipped down from one eye, wetting my hand. I wiped the next one away. "Why are you sad, Daddy?"

He turned his head to kiss the palm of my hand. He stared deep into my eyes, and it was like looking into a mirror, the same soft brown and long eyelashes. "Shady Grove," he said, "I think it's time I laid this here fiddle to sleep."

Of course, that fiddle couldn't be laid down. He took it up again less than a year later. He always took it back up. Maybe he's still playing it, even though he's dead. Maybe that's what I'm hearing now.

The thought speeds my feet, but I run into a patch of trees so clotted with vines I can't find a way through. I have to back-track, looking for an opening, but the woods are so dim now it's hard to see far ahead.

I find an opening and run, full out, until my chest heaves and I'm clutching a stitch in my side. But the fiddle music's all around me now, swirling on the wind, whistling through the tops of the trees. If there's a source, I'll never find it.

Finally, breathless, I drop to my knees on the pine needles, my hair soaked and dripping, my skin marked with scratches. Lightning forks overhead, spreading shadows through the trees. They all look like hulking men.

Oh, the dreadful wind and rain

I lie back on the damp, earthy-smelling forest floor and let the rain pummel me. The thunder has ripped through the fiddle tune, leaving nothing more than half-formed notes fluttering in the treetops, the torn remnants of Daddy's song.

It was Daddy. I don't know how, but somehow, somehow it was him.

"Where are you?" I whisper.

The only response is a low, spine-tingling rattle. I turn my head toward the sound and open my eyes, every hair on my body standing up. The lightning flashes again, illuminating a pair of glittering black eyes and a coiled, sinuous body. Icy fear spreads through me.

A rattlesnake is curled at the base of a tree, its eyes trained on me. Even in the gloom, I can tell it's a diamondback rattler, maybe five feet long. I haven't seen one this big in years. My thoughts turn frantic. If it struck me, sending its poison racing toward my heart, where would my ghost end up? Would Daddy be there to meet me?

Or is he already here?

My breathing is loud and ragged, matched only by the beat of my heart. The snake's tongue flicks out, as though tasting my fear on the air. It shakes its rattle again, a little louder this time.

Every magical kingdom has its monsters.

I should crawl away and run for all I'm worth, but some stubborn spirit has taken hold of me, and I remain where I am, staring into its cold, black eyes.

Thunder cracks so loud it shakes the ground and makes the trees shudder. The snake turns its head and begins to move away, its long body slithering soundlessly over the wet pine needles. I watch until it disappears into a gopher tortoise's hole, its ominous rattle fading into quiet. My whole body feels like a held breath.

When I turn my face back to the treetops, a gust of wind rocks the highest branches, sending pine needles floating down to coat me with the rain. I get to my feet and walk slowly through the storm-whipped woods toward home.

I've lived with ghosts my whole life, but this is the first time I've ever felt haunted.

Another rumble of thunder vibrates through my body a few seconds before lightning scatters across the sky. I'm too tired to run, but I walk fast in the direction of the trailer. I hear Jesse's voice before I see a break in the trees.

"Shady!" he yells from the trailer's front door, his voice nearly drowned out by the wind and rain. He's waiting by the front door when I reach it, a towel in his hands. "One of these days you're going to get struck by lightning, you know." His eyes are wide and worried.

"I'm fine," I say. "I'm always fine." My whole body trembles, but I feel as electric as the sky. I don't know why, but Daddy's out there in the woods, and he's calling to me.

FOUR

One week later, on Friday night, Orlando, Sarah, and I are piled together in his car, driving over to the café in Kellyville for the open mic. Sarah makes us listen to "Elvis Presley Blues" on repeat, as if we can absorb every ounce of Gillian Welch's talent and then spill it out onstage.

Orlando drums the steering wheel with nervous fingers, and I keep turning in my seat to look at Sarah. With my daddy's ghost so close to me, I've barely been able to think about the open mic all week, but now that the night is here, it all feels so much more real. We're going to get onstage for the first time and compete with other artists. I wish my heart were in it the way Sarah's is, but I haven't been able to shake the fiddle in the woods, the shadow man in my dreams, the feeling that something big is coming—something besides a trip to a recording studio. I haven't heard the music in the pines again, but I know it's out there, waiting for me.

Jesse spent the last several days watching me with wary eyes. Each time I came in from the woods with my fiddle, he opened his mouth like he wanted to say something, but instead just closed it and turned away. Sarah and Orlando can tell something is off with me too. At our last practice yesterday, I fumbled so many times that Sarah got angry and Orlando had to make terrible joke after terrible joke to diffuse the tension. They've both started to study me the same way Jesse has, like I'm a string out of tune, frayed to the point of breaking.

Now, as we get closer to the café, I force my thoughts back to the open mic. I need to stay present tonight, need to stay here, with Sarah and Orlando. I can't let them down.

The parking lot is already packed with cars and pickup trucks, and we have to drive way down Main Street to find a spot. The noise inside the café is deafening. People mill around with drinks, yelling to be heard over the awful country pop music pouring through the speakers. This café used to be small, but when the thrift store next door went out of business, the owners knocked down the dividing wall and turned it into a huge event space. The open mic nights attract all kinds of musicians, but there is a heavy country-western influence. There's a girl honest to God yodeling somewhere behind me. I crane my neck to see who it is but can't locate the source. Orlando hears her too and cracks up laughing.

"A little too hillbilly?" I ask.

Orlando shakes his head wonderingly. "My grandpa in Miami would love this," he says. "I wish he were here." His face falls for a moment, but then he catches sight of his family coming through the door. "Be right back," he says, hurrying toward them. I wave at his mom, dad, grandmother, and two brothers, feeling jealous of Orlando's big, close family when my own is so fractured. I know that's not fair—Orlando misses his Miami relatives so much, and his extended family has been fractured too—half of them in Cuba, the rest spread over Florida.

"Did you invite your dad?" I ask Sarah.

"God, no," she says. "I'm nervous enough."

"Yeah," I agree, turning back to the empty stage. My head starts to pound and my hands grow sweaty. I can't believe we're performing for the first time in front of this many people. I need some space, some air. "You try to find seats, and I'll get drinks," I say, handing my fiddle to Sarah. She nods mutely, as overwhelmed by the crowd as I am.

The café side of the building is a little quieter, and my panic starts to fade while I wait in line.

"I swear to God, Cedar, if I hear a single bro country song, I'm gone," a girl's voice says behind me. "I can't believe I let you talk me into this."

I glance back and see Cedar and Rose Smith standing with their heads close together. Rose sees me looking and narrows her eyes, so I turn back around fast.

Cedar and Rose are twins who go to my high school. They're on the wealthier end of the farm-kid spectrum. Rose is probably the most beautiful girl I've ever seen in real life. I mean, most girls are beautiful in their own way, but Rose is ridiculously beautiful. Long, dark, wavy hair, eyes so brown they're almost black. A perfect little nose. A tiny waist even her loose peasant blouse can't hide. I've heard rumors that she's gay, but she's famously ruthless, so I've always steered clear of her.

"We're never going to be able to grow the band if we don't come to stuff like this and meet people," Cedar says. "All the musicians we know are, like, seventy years old."

With his long eyelashes and big green eyes, Cedar's about as pretty as Rose is, but he's also got this tough-guy cowboy act—a combination that makes girls watch him everywhere he goes. Even at school, he usually looks like he just walked off the stage at the Grand Ole Opry, and tonight's no different. He's got on a black cowboy hat and a black, Western-style shirt with red flowers embroidered on the shoulders and pearly buttons running down the front.

"I like old people," Rose grumbles.

I don't hear the rest of their conversation because it's my turn at the counter. But I watch them while I wait for my order. I can't help but shake my head at Cedar's outfit, but I also can't help but smile when he does—I like how his eyes crinkle at the corners. He seems nicer than Rose, even though he hangs out with Jim's obnoxious son—my stepbrother—Kenneth. They're both friends with all the boys who drive giant trucks and wear cowboy boots all the time.

Cedar turns just in time to catch me staring at him, no doubt a dreamy half smile plastered on my face. He winks at me when he and Rose pass by, sending an embarrassed flush straight to my cheeks.

"Shady," Orlando says from behind me, making me jump.

"It's about to start. We're third on the list," he says, rocking on his heels. "Look, our drinks are ready. Let's go." His eyes are bright and happy, his cheeks slightly flushed. His excitement is contagious, and I find myself smiling, despite my nerves. Maybe this won't be so bad.

We push back through the crowd and find Sarah shooting eye daggers at a couple trying to take the chairs she's saving for us, our instruments piled on the table around her. She's wound up so tight I wish I'd ordered her decaf coffee. "This has to go well," she says as she takes her drink from me.

"It's going to be fine," Orlando says. "Chill out, Sarah."

"Shady, you've got to stay focused. You can't doze off or go into a daze or whatever you've been doing lately. Please," Sarah adds.

Weirdly, it's the "please" that pisses me off. "You can play without me if you want," I say, crossing my arms. "If I'm not a good enough musician for you."

"That's not what I meant, and you know it," Sarah says, panic in her eyes. "I just—"

A bearded man who was handing out coffee a few minutes ago jumps onto the stage. "Hey, everybody, welcome to the Main Street Café Open Mic Night," he says. Sarah shakes her head and turns away, wringing her hands. Orlando gives me a sympathetic look and throws an arm over my shoulders. The emcee prattles on for five minutes, introducing the judges, reminding us about the recording studio prize. The other musicians around us lean forward eagerly.

My anger at Sarah was sudden and sharp, but now it's a

knife without a mark. It's just poking at my insides, needling me. Sarah's got no faith in me, that's what it all comes down to. Maybe if I can stay focused tonight, I'll prove her wrong.

The first two performances go by in a blur, and then Orlando's tugging my sleeve and pulling me onstage. So much for keeping my head in the game. I raise my fiddle and look out over the crowd, praying my hands don't sweat all the way through this damn song. Orlando's family yells his name and whoops from somewhere to the right of the stage, earning an enormous grin from Orlando.

Sarah starts playing, and I wait for my cue. When Cedar catches my eye from the crowd, I almost miss it, but then I plunge into the song right on time, closing my eyes in relief. We sound good.

I relax into the song, letting our instruments and our voices fill me up, up, up. This might not be exactly the music I want to play, but it's worth it to see Sarah's head bobbing over her banjo in a beautiful imitation of Gillian Welch's puppet-on-a-string style. The sight makes me forget her annoyance and my anger. The way she lets go when she plays is gorgeous—focused, intense, but free; she becomes more music than girl.

When we finish, the crowd applauds loudly, and a few people whistle. Thank God—Sarah was dreading the polite applause some performers get at these open mics. She says it's worse than being booed.

When she jumps off the stage, she's still high on the music—smiling wide enough to show the little gap between her front teeth she always tries to hide. She even gives Orlando and me one of her rare hugs, leaving me with the lingering fragrance of vanilla in my nose. "You both were amazing," she says. "I think we could win this."

When Cedar and Rose take the stage, the room goes quiet again. Rose's banjo catches my eye. It's small and vintage-looking, without a resonator. I bet it's at least a hundred years old. I glance at Sarah to see her reaction. If the hours she's dragged me through music stores looking at banjos are any indication, she can probably name that banjo's year and maker. But she's only got eyes for Rose, and I can't tell if her expression is love, hate, or some combination of the two. A stab of jealousy goes through me, but then Cedar and Rose begin playing and I forget about Sarah.

The notes are quick and sharp and bright, the melody cheerful as springtime. Yet as Rose's fingers dance over the strings, the hairs on my arms stand on end and my whole body goes cold.

They're playing a song as familiar to me as the rhythm of my breath, the beat of my heart. I think it must be carried along in my bloodstream, singing through every artery and vein.

"Shady Grove," the song that gave me my name.

They're playing it fast, the tempo quicker than how Daddy played it, but the heart of the song's still there. And then Cedar begins to sing, his tenor voice ringing out through the room.

Shady Grove, my little love
Shady Grove, I say
Shady Grove, my little love
I'm bound to go away.

Daddy named me after this song, a hundreds-year-old Appalachian ballad with a thousand variations, though he had Doc Watson's in mind when he decided to call me Shady Grove. He said he knew that's who I was the moment I opened my pretty brown eyes and screamed at the world like my heart was breaking. Of course, now everybody calls me Shady, and most people don't know why.

Daddy sang me to sleep with this song and sometimes he woke me up with it, too. But as the song says, he was bound to go away. Yet here he is again, calling to me, doing everything he can to reach me, even from the grave. What's he trying to tell me?

Cedar's voice draws me in, while Rose's fingers dance over the banjo strings like a spider's legs, spinning a spell that catches me whole. Wrapped up in their song, I can't do anything but listen and breathe and try to keep the tears from my eyes.

But they're already spilling down my cheeks.

Maybe my daddy wants me to know his fiddle's still out there somewhere, waiting for me to play it. Maybe he's been listening to me play in the woods the last few weeks and knows I'm ready now. The thought sends a shiver up my spine.

I feel a gentle pressure on my arm. I'm surprised to see Jesse's beside me, wearing his worried eyes. He must have come to find me because of the song, because he knew I'd need him. A sob is building in my chest, so I lean in to him and bury my face in his shoulder. I'm so grateful my brother came tonight, and that he's here with me for this. Jesse puts an arm around me and holds me close until the song ends. I wonder if the memory of

Daddy's voice cuts through him as sharp as it does through me.

Most of all, I wonder what this song means, what Daddy's trying to tell me. Is he reminding me of who I am or warning me about something still to come?

FIVE

Cedar smiles his cowboy smile and tips his hat, heading off the stage like he didn't just rip a hole in my chest. Rose follows close behind, not even glancing at the cheering audience.

I give Jesse a hug to thank him and head to the bathroom, pushing my way through the packed, noisy crowd. Someone onstage has started singing "Wagon Wheel," which ought to make me smug as hell, but all I can think about is putting a bathroom stall door between me and everyone else.

I let myself into the only empty stall and lean against the door with my face in my hands, my mind heaving. It's only a song, I say to myself. It's not even uncommon. It's in every bluegrass player's repertoire. It's half a miracle I haven't heard it played before now.

But my skin is still tingling, pricked with chill bumps that won't leave.

The fiddle notes finding me in the forest weren't echoes,

and Cedar and Rose's choice of song wasn't a coincidence. The music from the pines has carried all the way to Kellyville.

"Shady," someone says on the other side of the stall door. Sarah. "You all right?"

I open the door after a few seconds and meet her soft brown eyes. We gaze at each other until tears fill my eyes again, and Sarah looks away. Sarah's mom died when she was a toddler. She hasn't said it outright, but I think she killed herself. But even though Sarah's lost a parent too, she always seems embarrassed by my grief.

"Come on, I'll buy you another coffee," Sarah says, her voice gruff. "You're missing all the music." She reaches out uncertainly and takes my hand to pull me from the stall. Warmth spreads up my arm, and I automatically lace my fingers in hers. She doesn't let go.

We leave the bathroom together and run straight into my stepdad. Jim looks down at us, surprise turning his dark, angular face slightly comical. Sarah drops my hand. She's out to her dad and her friends, but she keeps it quiet around other people. And I sure as hell haven't mentioned being bi to Mama or Jim.

"I didn't know you were coming," I say. "Is Mama here?" I didn't invite them.

Jim nods toward the stage. His son, Kenneth, is up there with a guitar singing "A Boy Named Sue," by Johnny Cash, and really hamming it up. He's sweating hard in the overhead lights, his fair skin turning pink from exertion.

"I didn't know Kenneth played," I say. "He's pretty good."

Jim nods again, like he can't be bothered to praise his own

kid. Kenneth lives with his mama and his stepdad and hardly ever sees Jim, which is fine by me. I can't imagine having Kenneth hanging around on weekends. I'm just shocked Jim showed up for this, of all things.

Then I catch a glimpse of Jim's brother, Frank, out of the corner of my eye, making his steady way toward us. He smiles at me and nods at Jim, whose face flushes a deep crimson. Frank looks like Jim, if Jim were about a hundred pounds heavier and sporting a graying beard. His nose looks like it's been broken at least twice. But Frank's the good brother, the one who took over their daddy's business and made it strong, who got married and stayed married, who gave his little brother a job whether he deserved it or not. He's got plans to run for city council next year, which is making Jim even more bitter toward him than usual.

"I'll see you at home," Jim says to me, striding back toward Frank, squeezing his hands into fists at his sides as he goes.

"A real conversationalist," Sarah mutters. She hurries toward the coffee bar, her hands buried in her pockets.

"Better than Kenneth, who never shuts up," I say, trying to act normal, like I don't want to grab Sarah's hand again and never let go. Like my stepdad's not making his way toward his older brother with hatred in his eyes. Like I'm not being haunted by my father's music.

There's a long line, but we finally get our drinks and head back to Orlando and Jesse, who are cringing at the terrible folk singer who just started. They both look up in relief. Orlando's been my best friend for three years, but he's still never learned how to have a conversation with my brother. The only thing they have in common is me.

"You guys were great, but I'm gonna take off," Jesse says, "if that's all right." His voice is gentler than usual, his eyes still worried, expectant.

"Thanks. Did you come with Jim? Do you need a ride?" I ask.

"Shit, Jim's here?" Jesse says, darting looks at every corner.

"Yeah. So?"

"Frank thought I was stoned today and gave me a twenty-minute lecture. Then he made one of the workers drive me home," he says, ducking down into his chair. Jesse's been working for Frank part-time since he turned sixteen. Daddy used to work for the same company a long time ago when he and Jim first became friends, when Jim's father was still alive and running the company.

"*Were* you stoned?" I say, crossing my arms over my chest.

Jesse shrugs.

Kenneth bursts through the wall of people, and I can see at a glance that *he* most definitely is stoned. "Jesse," he yells, so loud people turn to look.

"Shit," Jesse says again.

Kenneth is bouncing on the balls of his feet. "Thanks again, man, for . . . well, you know. I don't think I could have gotten through that without it."

Sarah, Orlando, and I swivel in one motion to gape at Jesse. "Tell me you didn't," I say. "What did you give him? Jim's going to kill you."

"My dad's here?" Kenneth says. He's talking so loud.

"Shut up, man," Jesse says. "Keep it down."

"I bet Uncle Frank guilted him into coming," Kenneth says. "He's here somewhere."

So that explains it. Frank is always nagging Jim about how he's not a good enough dad to Kenneth. I'm glad Frank made him come this time. No matter how much I dislike my stepbrother, I don't like to see Jim hurt his feelings.

"No way, Jim told me he was excited to see you play," I lie. "He said you're really good."

But Kenneth's mind has already jumped to something else. "Shady, you want to dance?" he says, yanking me from my chair. His hand is sweaty and I pull away from him, stumbling into Orlando's lap.

"Oh, so that's how it is?" Kenneth says, eyeing Orlando. "Or is it her?" he adds when Sarah glares at him. His eyes are glassy and strange.

I glance at Sarah, and Kenneth's eyes go ludicrously wide. He lets out a giggle. "Jesus, Shady, are you a lesb—"

Jesse gives Kenneth a warning push before he can finish the question. Jesse barely touched him, but Kenneth is so stoned he stumbles over a chair, falling on his ass.

"Sorry, man," Jesse says, starting to offer Kenneth a hand back up. "You need to watch how you talk to my sister." But Kenneth's already up and swinging like a drunken windmill. He misses Jesse's face and staggers, off-kilter. Guess he inherited Jim's temper, or maybe it's just the drugs.

"You're out of it. Go home," Jesse says, pushing Kenneth

away again. "Go find your old man." But Kenneth grabs his arm, and Jesse's starting to look pissed. I know that look, and I try to step between them, but then Kenneth leans right up in Jesse's face. He says something I can't hear over the music and laughs. Jesse's expression changes from anger to rage as fast as I can blink, and then he grabs Kenneth by the front of his shirt and pushes him backward until Kenneth trips and falls, smacking his head on the concrete floor. Jesse doesn't care. He drops to one knee and drives his fist into Kenneth's face.

"Jesse!" I scream, racing to pull him off Kenneth, but he's strong from all those afternoons and weekends working construction with Jim. He raises his fist again. I pull his other arm as hard as I can, but it's not doing any good. People are beginning to turn their attention from the musicians onstage to the fight, but no one jumps in to stop it. I'm about to yell for help when someone else steps up beside me and yanks Jesse's other arm. Together, we manage to haul him off Kenneth, who's pouring blood from both lip and nose. One eye is already starting to swell closed. But he manages to sit up, so at least he's not unconscious.

Jesse is twisting and fighting against our hold, trying to get back to Kenneth. I finally manage to glance over to see who's helping. It's Cedar Smith, his hat knocked off, sweat gleaming at his forehead with the effort of holding Jesse back.

Jesse twists out of our grasp and lunges for Kenneth again, but Jim's long, wiry arm snatches him out of the air. Jim gets ahold of him by the waist and drags him toward the front door with an iron grip. Jesse fights back, but it doesn't do any good.

"Make sure Kenneth's all right," I tell Cedar and sprint off after Jim and Jesse, the sounds of the open mic fading behind me. I need to make sure they don't start fighting too. One more blowup and Jesse's going to get kicked out of our home. I can't let that happen.

By the time I reach them, they're almost to Jim's truck. Jesse finally wrenches himself from Jim's grip. He starts to say something to Jim, but Jim slaps him flat-handed across the face.

Jesse's eyes clear and then turn cold and hard as two marbles.

I push past Jim and put myself between them before worse can happen. "Don't hit my brother again," I yell at Jim. Then I turn to Jesse. "What the hell is going on with you?" I ask. "Why did you do that?"

"You two get in the goddamned truck," Jim says. "I'm going to get Kenneth."

Jesse gives me a long, angry look and then sets off across the parking lot without a word, disappearing around the side of the building. I wait until Jim and Cedar come out, supporting Kenneth between them. Frank trails behind them, his arms crossed, a look of concern on his face. "You want me to call Gary Jones?" Frank asks. Gary is Kenneth's stepdad and a local cop, not to mention Frank's friend. Probably the last person Jim wants to see now, excepting Frank himself.

Jim ignores him and turns his scowl on me. "I told you to get in the truck."

"Jesse took off."

Jim swears.

"Your friend asked me to give you your fiddle," Cedar says, handing over my case. He offers me a sympathetic half smile.

God, what absolute trailer trash we must seem like right now. "Thank you. And thanks for helping, but I'm not leaving." I turn to Jim. "I'm getting a ride home with Orlando. I want to stay and see who wins." Sarah will be so pissed at me if I bail now, and I definitely don't want to spend my night at the hospital.

But Frank is still watching us like a hawk, and Jim is past caring what I want. "Shady, I swear to God if you don't get into this truck right now—" he growls. He can't stand for anyone to disagree with him in public, and with Frank standing by, he's even more on edge. His tone says I'll end up grounded if I don't go.

The night's already ruined, so I climb into the tiny back seat of the truck, and Cedar helps Jim hoist Kenneth into the front seat. He talks to Jim for a minute and then waves at me through the truck window

Jim gets in and slams the door. "What in God's name was that all about?" he asks once we pull out of the parking lot.

Kenneth gives a broken laugh and then winces. "I was running my mouth like you always told me not to," he says. That's Kenneth's one redeeming quality—he's an asshole, but at least he owns up to it.

"I figured as much," Jim says. "He shouldn't have beat you like that though."

"What'd you say to him to make him go after you?" I ask, leaning around Kenneth's seat. "He wasn't really trying to hurt you at first."

Kenneth looks away, out the window, watching the fast food joints fly by. "I . . . I don't remember."

Jim snorts. "Is that your shame talking, or you got a concussion?"

The hospital is only half a mile away from the café, so we're pulling up to the emergency room entrance before Kenneth can decide how to answer.

"Shady, go get this fool boy a wheelchair," Jim says.

I hop out and run inside, and when I come back out with the wheelchair, Jim's standing on the pavement, leaning into Kenneth's door, holding a balled-up cloth against his son's bleeding face. That's the most I've ever seen Jim act like a father to Kenneth. Still doesn't make up for years of being a shitty dad though.

Kenneth is taken straight back to the emergency room by a nurse, and Jim leaves to park the truck. The waiting room is nearly empty, so I get a chair by the wall and watch the muted TV overhead. I text Sarah. *Sorry I had to go. Jim's being a dick. Did we win???*

Ten minutes go by and I'm starting to think she's decided my family drama isn't worth her time. But then my phone dings. *They just announced. Some basic-ass country pop singer won. Judges were tasteless idiots.* She follows it up with a rolling-eyes emoji.

Sorry, I type back. I am, too. I didn't really care about the open mic like Sarah did, but after how good it felt to play up there, losing stings a little bit. And I can't help but wonder if some part of Sarah blames me.

I'm surprised Cedar and Rose didn't win. They were incredible—even apart from the song they chose. I realize I would love to play with them sometime, might even like to be a part of their band. But even thinking about playing with someone besides Sarah and Orlando makes me feel guilty.

As if she can hear my disloyal thoughts, Sarah doesn't respond to my text, so I put my phone away and watch the local news. Before long, I start to drowse. The stresses of performing, hearing Cedar and Rose play "Shady Grove," and then this nonsense with Jesse . . . After a week of chasing echoes, I'm so tired, worn down to just about nothing.

I'm awake and then I'm not, the sterile hospital atmosphere merging horribly with whatever my imagination is dreaming up. I'm on a stretcher in a dark room, lying on my back and peering up into the darkness, which seems to go on forever, like I'm at the bottom of a well.

But then the darkness starts to move, swirling around me like black smoke. It touches me with the clammy dampness of a frog's skin, making my whole body turn to goose bumps.

I lean away from it, but the stretcher has disappeared, along with the room. A sharp, shrill sound like music from an out-of-tune fiddle begins to play. I try to cry out, but the darkness fills my mouth, stopping up my throat.

I writhe and struggle in its grasp, but I'm bound and gagged and growing more panicked every second. I can't tell the difference between the horrible darkness and the horrible music anymore—they've morphed into a single, inescapable monster.

A hand reaches out of the darkness and shakes me, over and over again. I peer up into a hard, angular face with a heavy five-o'clock shadow.

"Shady," Jim says. "Wake up."

I start out of the chair with a gasp, and Jim catches me before I hit the floor. My heart races, and the blood pounds in my ears.

"Calm down," he says. "You were only dreaming."

There's no *only* dreaming when it comes to my nightmares. I gasp in air, my lungs burning. My eyes are wide open, trying to take in every speck of light. That must have been my shadow man again, just in another form. God, why is he back?

"Your mama used to have dreams like that," Jim says. He's sitting beside me now, with his hands in his lap. "Back before we . . . started up. She thought they were coming from that old house." When I don't answer, he keeps talking, his voice distant and detached. "I had dreams too, when I slept there. Dark, dark dreams."

"When did you sleep there?" I push my hair out of my eyes, glad to be distracted, even if it's by the thought of Jim in my childhood home.

"Back when you and Jesse were babies. I stayed with your daddy and mama for a short while. Round the time my daddy died." He stares at the streaked, dingy floor.

I start to ask another question, but Jim begins to stand. "Come on, we need to get Kenneth home. He'll be out in a minute. They were just wrapping a few things up."

Still reeling from my dream, afraid to be left alone, I put my hand on his arm. The moment my skin meets his, I realize it's the first time I've ever touched him. "What did you dream about?" I ask, pulling my hand away quickly.

Was it the shadow man, or does he only visit me?

Jim settles back into his chair and clears his throat uncomfortably. He shakes his head. "It's hard to say. I don't believe I have the words for it."

"Can I ask you one more thing?" I say, Jesse's outburst from the other night coming to mind. I've never had the courage to ask something like this before, but it's like touching Jim's skin has opened up a well of truth. Besides, after he dragged me out of the open mic, answering my questions is the least he can do. "Did you love Mama before, back when you stayed there? Did you love her before Daddy died? Is that why Jesse hates you so much?" I'm still hearing Jesse's words at the dinner table in my head . . . *I know what you did*. I thought I knew the truth about Mama and Jim, but Jesse's anger makes me doubtful. Maybe I've been naive to take Mama's word for it.

Jim sighs. "Your mama was always faithful to your daddy. But, yeah, I loved her from the first time I laid eyes on her, when she was pregnant with Jesse, her belly out to here." He motions with his hands.

"Did Daddy know?"

Jim shakes his head. "Your daddy didn't notice anything 'cept you and Jesse and that fiddle of his. It was all he had the heart for."

My own heart starts to race again at the mention of the fiddle. "Jim, do you—"

He holds up his hand. "You said one question, and you asked at least three. Let's get on home now. That's enough talk for one night." An orderly wheels Kenneth toward us, and Jim stands and walks away from me.

SIX

Jesse's just coming in the front door when I wake up the next morning. He smells like cigarettes and unwashed clothes, his eyes bloodshot and ringed with dark half-moons. When I try to talk to him, he slams his bedroom door in my face.

I'm the one who should be mad. It was my night he ruined. If he hadn't started a fight with Kenneth, I would have had a fun night with Sarah and Orlando. Maybe I could even have talked to Cedar and Rose. As a way to avoid my worries about Jesse and the shadow man, I've been picturing myself playing music with Cedar and Rose. I've put whole sets together, imagined how the solos would go, how our voices would sound together. Their music has woken up new ideas in me, made me imagine possibilities I hadn't considered.

Still wiping sleep from my eyes, I head for the kitchen, hoping everyone else will stay in bed. But Jim's already up. He bangs out of his and Mama's bedroom, looking mad as hell and way too tall for this trailer. "Did your brother just come in?" he asks, but he doesn't wait for an answer. He stomps into the kitchen, his mouth set hard.

Mama's right on his heels, looking just as angry. "You leave it to me, Jim. He's my son." She snatches at his sleeve.

Jim shakes her off. "And Kenneth is mine. I won't have Jesse getting him all messed up like he is." He pushes past me without a glance.

"Jim, please," Mama hisses. "You don't understand him."

He swivels to face her. "You could be on my side for once, you know. Just once. Jesse's never going to go straight if you don't let me take him in hand. Jesse, get your ass out here," he yells.

Jesse appears at the mouth of the hallway, pushing hair out of his eyes. "What?"

Jim shakes his head. "Don't you 'what' me. I've had enough of this. You want to ruin your life, fine, but you leave my boy out of it."

"He said something rude to Shady. That's why I hit him." Jesse crosses his arms, staring defiantly back at Jim.

"He did," I say. "Kenneth was being a jerk." *Lesbian* isn't an insult, but the way he said it made it sound like one.

Jim ignores me. "I'm not talking about you hitting him. I'm talking about the drugs you sold him."

Jesse opens his mouth to speak but then closes it again. He looks at his feet.

"Where'd you get the Vicodin, Jesse?" Mama asks, her voice tired-sounding, like there's nothing Jesse can do to surprise her anymore.

"From you. It was left over from that time you injured your back. It was just a few pills. Nobody got hurt." He won't look Mama in the eye.

"Nobody got hurt?" Jim roars. "What do you call that beat-up face my son is sporting? What if he had gotten in his truck and drove home like that? What if he had wrecked and died? Could you live with yourself then, you little bastard? Could you live with yourself if you killed my son?"

Jesse's face goes white with rage. He crosses the last few steps to Jim and glares up at him. "You mean like my father wrecked and died? You mean like I—"

"That's not what he meant, Jesse," Mama says, hurrying to put herself between them. "You know it's not. But Jim is right—you need to get your life together, baby."

Jesse shakes his head, his mouth twisted in disgust. "Jim's only mad because Frank was there to see it all, and he doesn't want to look bad in front of him. And you're no better. You're both such fucking hypocrites."

Jim lunges past Mama, but Jesse leaps out of his reach. That doesn't stop Jim's words, which land like punches. "You don't talk to your mama like that. I want you out of this house. Now. Go pack your shit and leave."

"Gladly," Jesse says, turning to go back to his room. My heart drops into my stomach, but Mama snatches Jesse by the back of his shirt and hauls him into the living room. She pushes him onto the couch.

"Sit your ass down," she says, her voice steel. "Jim, you go sit over there. Nobody is moving out, and nobody is leaving this room until we find a solution." She looks at me. "Except you, Shady. This ain't none of your business. Go take a shower or something."

I give Jesse a look that's half scorn and half sympathy, and leave the room. He's being a jerk too, but it hurts to know he still blames himself for Daddy's death, that he thinks he could have done anything to save him.

By the time I get out of the shower, some kind of peace has been reached, though nobody seems happy about it. Jesse's in his room, and Mama and Jim are eating breakfast at the kitchen table, a strained silence between them.

Sometimes I think this trailer's going to crack wide open under the weight of all the words we never say.

Sarah never texted me back last night, but we had plans to hang out today, so I drive over to her house anyway. She lives in a subdivision full of little brick three-bedroom houses that all look the same. Nothing special, but nicer than either of the places I've lived. The other houses have flowers growing in the yard, but Sarah's is plain on the outside, brightened only by some boring green shrubs on either side of the front steps.

"You ready?" I ask when she opens the door. Sarah looks even more disheveled than usual. Her jeans have holes in both knees, and her shirt has clearly never met an iron. I love how Sarah dresses—like she doesn't care what anybody thinks, like she's got bigger things on her mind.

"Yeah, but I'm driving," she says. "You don't have the best attention span."

Ouch. Maybe she does blame me. "Look, I'm sorry we didn't win," I say as I climb into her truck. "And I'm sorry I had to bail last night."

She shrugs. "I guess it was stupid to think we'd win."

"It wasn't stupid," I say as she backs down the driveway. "But you know you're going to get into a good music program without having a song recorded, right? Your grades are good, and you practice harder than anyone I know."

Sarah tries to smile. "What'd you think of all our competition last night? We didn't get a chance to talk."

"Kenneth was actually good," I say. "Funny. Not everybody could pull off 'A Boy Named Sue.'"

"You've got to be part clown to pull it off," Sarah says dryly. She dislikes Kenneth on principle now, even though he's finally stopped teasing her. He spent all last year howling at her whenever she walked by, just because her last name's Woolf. Well, and she kind of looks like someone with werewolf potential.

"I thought Cedar and Rose were the best," I say before I lose my nerve.

"Better than us?" Sarah raises her eyebrows.

"No, they . . . well . . . actually, yeah, they were better than us," I say in a rush. "Their voices are amazing, and their playing. God, did you see how fast Rose's fingers moved? And . . ." Now I'm nearing what I really want to say, but I don't think Sarah will want to hear it.

"And what?" She leans over the steering wheel, eyebrows knit in irritation.

"The music suits them. You can tell they were raised on it,

that it's a part of them. They're performing in a set tradition, and it makes their music feel cohesive."

She gives a grudging sort of "hmm" but doesn't say anything else.

"I think we should see if they'd play with us," I say hesitantly, trying to keep the eagerness out of my voice. "I heard them talking about wanting to meet new musicians."

Sarah shakes her head. "No way. Absolutely not."

"Why?"

"Because I don't want to," she says.

"That's not a reason."

"It is, too," she says flatly.

"Please just tell me why," I beg.

She's quiet a long moment. "Rose and I used to date," she finally says, her voice almost a whisper. She stares straight ahead.

A jolt goes through me. Sarah and Rose? Beautiful, talented, terrifying Rose? I don't know if I can follow that act.

Sarah told me about a girl she dated back in ninth grade, before she transferred to our school, but she never said the girl's name, and I would never have guessed it was Rose. She said the other girl wasn't ready to be out yet, and when things started getting more serious, they decided to end it. That's all Sarah wanted to say about it, and I didn't want to press her. Being a lesbian in a small, conservative town isn't exactly easy.

"How did you even know her?" I ask gently.

"We were in all the same bluegrass competitions. The ones my grandpa made me do." Sarah's voice has gotten quiet and fragile-sounding.

"Have you talked to her since you transferred to Elson County?" I ask, the jealousy in my voice so obvious she must hear it.

"Shady, just forget about it. I don't want to play with them, okay?" She shoots me a glance, eyes pleading.

"All right," I say. "I'm sorry." And I am. Is this why Sarah's so sour on bluegrass now?

I can't blame her for not telling me. There's so much I haven't said either. Maybe it's time for both of us to stop holding back all these hidden parts of ourselves.

The thought gives me an idea.

"Listen," I say. "I want to show you something. Will you—will you come with me to take groceries to my aunt Ena after we eat?"

Sarah seems to hear the resolve in my tone and studies me for a long moment. "Why?" she finally asks.

"Just come," I say. "Please."

By the time we finish scarfing down Taco Bell and about a gallon of sweet tea, things feel good between us again. And I've decided it's time to see what else we can be. Now that she's letting me in, I can let her in too.

"You seriously used to live here?" Sarah says, halting outside the front door, grocery bags hanging off her arms. "This is honestly the most haunted-looking place I've ever seen."

"It is haunted," I say, lifting my eyebrows and making my voice all Dracula-y so Sarah can't tell whether I'm serious or not. "Veeeeery haunted." The door's slightly ajar, and when I push it with my foot, it creaks open as if on cue.

"Aunt Ena," I call once we're in the kitchen.

Suddenly, Sarah stiffens and looks around like she thinks someone's watching her.

"I told you the house is haunted," I say as casually as I can. "All my friends were afraid to come over to play when I was a kid."

"It's just drafty," Sarah says, but her gaze darts around, as if to catch someone looking at her.

To me, the ghosts are mostly gentle presences—light as air, more like familiar smells than menaces, hardly distinguishable from the aromas of honeysuckle and dust. But I can almost imagine what Sarah is feeling as the ghosts move around her for the first time—a shiver in the air, a cool breath against her skin, that eerie, watched feeling I had when the little girl in my ceiling came to visit.

Aunt Ena comes swooshing into the kitchen in one of her long skirts that makes her look particularly witchy, banishing my anxious thoughts. Sarah's eyes widen.

"You must be Sarah." Aunt Ena's smiling way too big.

"Aunt Ena, please don't embarrass me."

"I'm just saying hello," she says, hands up like I've got a gun pointed at her.

"Hi," Sarah says shyly. "It's nice to meet you."

"Yes, it is," says Aunt Ena. She brushes Sarah's arm and looks into her eyes, searching her face like she's reading her soul.

When I see Sarah's eyes go a fraction wider, I know it's time to rescue her. "I'm going to show Sarah around the house," I say, and pull her by her hand, just for a second, to get her away from Aunt Ena. This time I notice how her fingers are soft, except at the tips, which are callused from her banjo strings. Letting go of her hand sends a swoop of longing to my chest.

"I'll show you my old room first," I say, heading for the stairs, trying to keep my embarrassment hidden. Having Sarah here feels a little like being naked, my truest, deepest self on display. It's scary but exciting too.

The stairs are a deep-brown wood, glossy from overuse. The banister is wobbly but the steps will last forever, or at least that's what Daddy used to say. There's a window in the stairwell, but between the dirt and the densely hanging Spanish moss, hardly any light comes in. I glance back at Sarah and see the hesitation in her eyes. The wariness. I don't want her to be like all the neighbors who could see only old wood and chipped paint. I want her to see the beauty of this house, the beauty of its ghosts.

I want her to see me.

The banister leads up to a landing with three rooms. The first is mine—or used to be mine anyway. I guess it still is, but it's half empty without all my things.

Sarah takes a seat in my rocking chair and watches the iron fireplace like she expects a bat to fly out of it. I try to look at the room through Sarah's eyes. The peeling wallpaper, the cobwebs that have formed in the corners at the ceiling. The dead wasps in every windowsill, the ancient hardwood floors that are as much dirt as wood by this point. The whole place looks old and creepy.

That's what Sarah seems to think of the music I love—that it's old and creepy. I worry bringing her here might have been a mistake. I'm only giving her more reasons to think I'm wrong for her.

"My daddy made that chair," I say, just to fill the silence. He worked on it for weeks, as a surprise for my tenth birthday. It's actually one of the newest things in the room.

Sarah studies the armrests, which have floral patterns carved into the wood. She runs her fingers along the grooves with reverence. "It's pretty. You're lucky to have something like this—something he made you," she says quietly, her eyes distant and sad. She must be thinking of her mother. Our parents' deaths might be the deepest thing we have in common. If I can get her to open up, we can help each other.

"Do you—do you have anything like that from your mom?" I ask hesitantly.

Sarah shakes her head. "Nothing she made for me. But all her old stuff is still in the house. Dad never threw out anything of hers."

"Really? You mean all her clothes are still in the closet?"

Sarah nods. "I like having all her stuff. It makes me feel like I know her." She smiles, but I know it's a sad smile because her dimple doesn't show. There's this loneliness at the very center of Sarah—a lack, an empty wanting. I long for something loved and lost, but Sarah longs for something she never really had.

Maybe that's the difference between Sarah and me, the thing that keeps us apart. I want her to see how the music I love is like that chair and this house, like all her mama's old things still filling her home, strange and beautiful and full of memories, a tie to the past. But it's a past she can't ever know.

"Is this what you wanted to show me?" Sarah asks, suddenly shy. "This chair?"

I plop down on the bed, and dust rises up from the old quilt. It's been a long time since I slept here. "No. I guess I wanted you to see all this, where I come from. This is my real home, not that trailer."

"There's nothing wrong with living in a trailer."

"I know that," I say, even though I don't. "But that trailer doesn't mean anything to me. It could burn down tomorrow and I wouldn't give a damn." Sarah raises her eyebrows, but she doesn't say anything. "This house is so much realer, so much more a part of me. It was my daddy's house, and his parents' before him. It's old and it's creepy and it's—"

"—haunted as hell?"

I smile. "And it's haunted as hell. But it's the place I grew up, it's the place where my daddy lived, where he taught me to love music . . ." I can feel the ghosts all around us, their murmurs almost too low for human ears. They seem to be crowding in, waiting.

"What are you trying to tell me?" Sarah says, leaning forward in the chair. Her face is open, interested, like she's seeing me for the first time. Maybe I've been holding back even more of myself than she has.

I brought her here not knowing if I'd have the courage to say what I want to, to confess what I want to confess. But right now, Sarah is leaning toward me like there isn't anything I could say she wouldn't accept as truth. And somehow getting her to understand what I feel for her is all tied up with getting her to understand about the music and the fiddle and—

"What is it, Shady?" she whispers, and my eyes are drawn to her mouth, how her lips are slightly parted, the barest hint of the gap between her front teeth. And I want to tell her about the fiddle, but I want to kiss her, too. I want to run my fingers through her hair and press the truth into her mouth with my lips. Skin to skin, lay out everything I am, everything I feel. It's all too much.

"Sarah," I say, my voice breaking on the second syllable. As if unaware of what she's doing, Sarah leaves her chair and sits on the bed beside me.

After last time, I'm afraid to make a move. I can't stand for her to reject me again. But Sarah's gazing at me and I don't know what to do. I look down at my hands in my lap. Sarah shifts beside me on the bed, but I don't look up until she puts her hand on my knee.

"You're amazing, you know that?" she whispers. "You're beautiful and you're smart. You're talented and you're kind. I didn't need to see this house to know any of that."

"Then why don't you want me?" I ask.

Sarah's eyes are uncertain, questioning. But she puts her hand on my cheek and then slides her fingers gently into the hair at the back of my neck, her thumb brushing my skin, sending a shiver through me. "Who wouldn't want you?" she says.

And then her mouth is on mine.

The room drops away, and I am nothing but skin. Lips and tongue and fingertips. Pulse and breath. Sarah held back so long, but now she is kissing me like she's never going to stop.

I meant to tell her about Daddy's fiddle, the songs in the woods, the shadow man in my dreams, the way I felt when

Cedar and Rose played "Shady Grove." I meant to tell her who I am. But instead I lean into her kiss, wrap my fingers in her hair, and forget that I'm anything except the girl kissing Sarah Woolf.

"Shady," Aunt Ena calls from downstairs, her voice high and urgent. "Shady Grove!"

With a jolt of panic, I untangle myself from Sarah, whose face registers my own shock. I'm out of the room and down the stairs before I even have time to think. Aunt Ena's standing with the landline phone in one shaking hand, her eyes enormous.

"Shady, your mama just called. And, uh . . . darlin', I don't know how to say this. But . . . Jim is dead."

SEVEN

My stomach drops into an icy ocean. "He's . . . dead?"

"He was found at the construction site. The one in that new suburb." Aunt Ena's face is so pale. "Shady, they think he was—they think someone killed him."

"Your stepdad?" Sarah asks, appearing beside me. I nod, but my mind is already throwing up walls on every side. Jim can't be dead. Because if he's dead . . .

"Where's Mama?" I ask.

"She's at the police station, answering questions. She wants you to come get Honey."

"What happened? Who did it? Who—"

"She didn't say. I don't think they know yet, but she was too upset to talk long."

"And Jesse?" I ask. He was in his room when I left, so he couldn't have anything to do with this, right?

Aunt Ena pauses for a long moment. "I don't know. Your

mama said he went to work with Jim this morning, but she didn't say where he is now. She didn't tell me much, mostly that she's going to be at the station awhile, and she needs you to get Honey."

I feel dizzy and sick, and it's a struggle to keep my thoughts in one place. "I left her car at Sarah's," I say, staring at a place on the wall by the phone where the wallpaper is torn. Jesse used to pick at it during his fiddle lessons, back before he finally worked up the courage to tell Daddy he wasn't going to play anymore.

"That's all right," Sarah says. "I can drive you to the station, and then back to my place for the car."

Aunt Ena steps forward and pulls me into her arms. She rubs my back, squeezing me tight against her. "I'm so sorry, darlin'."

"Thanks, Aunt Ena," I say, pulling away. "I'll call you later."

"All right. Y'all drive safe. It'll be okay, Shady."

That's what they said when Daddy died. They said I would be okay, that everything would be all right. They were wrong. It wasn't okay, I wasn't all right. Before he died, I had a sun and a moon in my parents, a balanced world. When he died, he took the sun away with him, left me without anyone to sing the morning into being.

But Jim's not Daddy. He's just Jim. My world doesn't spin around him. He's not even a star. So why do I feel like I'm suddenly drifting?

I tug open the rusted passenger door of Sarah's old green

truck and climb in. We pull away from the house, tires crunching gravel. Her truck is so old it has manual window controllers. I don't even know what they're called. Rollers? I work the one on my side, and the window lowers, the breeze coming in, warm but alive. In Florida, hot air is better than nothing. But there's something else drifting into the open window. From the woods comes a high, wild fiddle tune, so shrill it makes goose bumps erupt on my arms. I glance over at Sarah, but she doesn't seem to hear it.

We drive in silence for several miles, leaving the woods and the ghosts far behind. We turn off the main highway and are halfway to downtown Briar Springs before Sarah says anything. "We'll pick up your sister, and then I can take you back to my house. You can stay with Dad and me if you want, until your mom's done at the station . . ." She throws a worried glance at me but doesn't say anything else. Her lips are still red from our kiss. Now her cheeks are red too.

"Thanks," I say, watching the tire stores and fast-food joints fly by. "I'll see what Mama wants us to do." I can't think. Can't form coherent ideas. Why does Jim's death make me feel so lost?

Maybe anyone's death would.

When we pull into a parking spot at the police station, Sarah turns off the engine and looks at me, biting her bottom lip. "Do you want me to come in, or should I wait out here?" She's so nervous, and I feel bad she's been dragged into this.

"Can you wait out here? I'll try not to take too long." She nods, so I get out of the truck and head toward the door of the station alone, trying to push down my rising panic.

The police station is small, and it only takes a moment before I find Mama in the waiting area. Her eyes are red, and every muscle in her body looks tensed, like she's ready to snatch up my baby sister and make a run for it. Honey is in her lap, playing with the necklace that dangles down Mama's chest, oblivious to everything that's happening.

Honey. My little sister's daddy is dead now. I feel the ache of it, that loss. She's too young to understand it, but she's going to live all her life with that ache too—just like Sarah, just like me. Jim was no saint, but he was better than nothing.

I reach them in a few strides, and Mama leaps up to meet me, putting Honey down into the chair. I pull my mother into a loose hug. She's not a woman anyone would call fragile, but she feels breakable right now, like if I squeeze her too hard she'll crack like an old teacup. She lets me hold her a minute, but then pulls back. "I can't start crying again, not right now," she says, like having a foot of space around her is the only thing holding the tears back.

I remember how that was. How I would stop crying over Daddy, but someone would touch my hand or speak gently, and the well of grief would brim over again. Human touch like a dowsing rod for tears.

"Shady-Shade," Honey says, kicking her legs against the edge of the chair. She looks so little, so vulnerable.

Mama doesn't need my touch right now, so I give it to my sister, who reaches both arms out, wanting to be picked up. I don't tell her she's getting too big for such babying. I hold her close and let her play with my hair, even though I know she's going to make it frizzy.

"Do you know what happened? Who—?" I ask, but Mama shakes her head.

"We'll talk later, when I get home." She takes a deep breath, like she's building a wall inside herself, a fortress made of space and oxygen.

"Where's Jesse? Was he there when it happened? Is he all right?"

Mama shakes her head. "I don't know. He hasn't shown up yet, but I'm sure he's fine. Don't worry."

I'm hesitant to leave her alone here, but I can tell she wants me to go. "Will you be okay? You want me to call anybody?" I ask.

"No, baby, just go home. Make Honey some dinner." She looks so tired, and I remember she's already done all this before. She knows the steps to this dance.

"Give Mama a kiss," I tell Honey, and my little sister reaches out and puts one hand on Mama's face. A tear rolls down my mother's cheek, and Honey wipes it away before pressing her lips to Mama's eyelid.

Then I carry Honey out to Sarah's truck, my whole body suddenly an ache. I yank open the rusty door and plop Honey on the seat.

Just then a huge, shiny blue truck pulls up next to us, its engine an ugly roar. A long, bulky body climbs out. It's Frank. His eyes light on Honey and me and fill with tears. He breathes in so deep his nostrils flare, like he's pushing down some emotion trying to dig its way out. He reaches into Sarah's truck and touches a large, work-toughened hand to Honey's face. I start to ask him if he knows what happened, but he clamps his mouth shut and continues into the station, his work boots smacking against the sidewalk.

"Sarah, will you watch her for one second?" Sarah eyes Honey uncertainly, but she doesn't complain, so I sprint into the station behind Frank. I don't exactly know why, but some uneasy feeling in my gut draws me after him.

He's talking to the officer at the front desk, his voice already raised. "No, I won't take a seat and wait. I want to know what the hell's going on. I got a call from one of my workers saying he found my brother's body in one of our houses. Said he was dead, blood all over. I want to know what's going on here." Frank's voice breaks, a sob pushing against the underside of his words. "He's my brother." The grief in his voice is guttural, ancient-sounding.

I stop by the water cooler and wait to see what will happen.

"Frank," Mama says, crossing the room to him. She eyes him warily.

"Shirley," Frank says, his voice ragged. "What the hell is going on?"

"He's gone," Mama says. "He was hit with a hammer. Killed."

Frank's eyes widen. "No. That's not possible. He wasn't even supposed to be at that site today. Only Jeremy and Brandon were supposed to be working. What was he doing there?"

Mama crosses her arms over her chest. "He took Jesse over there to make up for yesterday, for . . . missing work."

"You mean for showing up high as a kite?" Frank booms, anger cutting through his grief.

Before Mama can answer, a man who must be a detective steps out of a side office. He has dark-brown skin and close-cropped hair, and he's wearing a nice suit. "Frank Cooper?" He reaches out for a handshake, which Frank returns automatically. "I'm Sergeant Martinez. We're doing everything we can to find out what happened to your brother. I'd like to ask you a few questions about your employees, if you have time." He motions toward the office he stepped out of. "If you'll just follow me."

Frank doesn't respond or move at all. The detective tries again. "I'd just like to know who all had access to the construction site, any contractors, vendors, anything you can think of."

Frank's face looks wild now, like he's barely holding himself together. "I don't need to answer your questions. I know who did it."

Mama reaches toward him but stops as soon as she starts, like she meant to slap him or hush him but thought better of it.

But Frank saw. He turns on her. "Apple don't fall far from the tree, does it, Shirley? I told Jim not to get mixed up in your family."

Mama's face twists into an awful, angry smile. "Never could let that go, could you? Never did learn to take your licks like a man."

The detective steps between them. "Sir, ma'am, if we could . . ."

Frank's face flushes a deep, murky red. "That sonofabitch coulda killed me. And now his boy killed Jim."

I'm trying to puzzle out who he means when Mama looks

away from him, laughing bitterly, and catches sight of me. "Shady," she says, stopping short. "What are you still doing here? I told you to take your sister home."

I walk the last few yards toward them. "What's he talking about, Mama?" I glance between her and Frank's hulking form. He's sobbing now, his face buried in his hands and his big shoulders bobbing up and down.

"Don't you worry about it. Your daddy gave him an ass whipping he ain't never got over, that's all. Don't you mind that bag of hot air."

"Mama," I gasp. I can't believe she'd talk that way about Frank—after all he did for Jim. While he's standing there grieving. But if Frank was bad-mouthing my daddy and blaming Jesse for Jim's murder. . . My hand goes to my mouth, and I feel dizzy, so dizzy. Fear settles in my stomach, hard as a peach pit.

"My brother is dead," Frank chokes out.

Mama turns to the detective, who looks like he's about ready to arrest someone, he's just not sure who yet. "Sir, I apologize. Let me walk my daughter out, and I'll come right back."

She grips me by the elbow and steers me to the doorway. "Go on, now."

I peer around her to study Frank. "What was he talking about? Did he mean Jesse?" The pit of fear in my stomach is putting out wicked tendrils, wrapping around my insides.

"Don't you mind it. Just go on home. I'll come as soon as I can." She pushes me out the door and walks quickly back inside, her shoulders squared against the coming storm.

I stumble back outside into the ludicrous sunshine, feeling

like the world's crumbling beneath me. I hold Honey's hand the whole way home, the warmth of her small fingers all that keeps me from falling into the chasm widening under my feet. I tell Sarah the police don't know what happened yet, and she doesn't ask any questions. As we drive on, she grows quiet and distant, and some small part of my mind that's not focused on Jim's death and Jesse's possible involvement worries Sarah is already pulling away from me.

I hear the fiddle again as soon as I step out of Mama's car at home. Did Daddy know what was coming? Is that why he's been playing for me?

I stand and listen so long Honey starts yelling my name from the back seat. It takes all my effort to turn my back on those desperate notes and carry my sister into the trailer.

After I make some butter noodles for Honey and me to share, we lie together on the couch watching whatever's on PBS. It's just noise to me, friendly voices driving away the silence and the fear. Honey falls asleep with her thumb in her mouth. I lie next to her, my mind churning over questions I can't answer, questions I'm afraid to answer.

The trailer door bangs open, and I bolt upright, my heart racing as I peer through the twilight gloom.

Jesse walks in, weaving slightly. I disentangle myself from Honey and lean forward, reaching for him. "Where've you been?"

Jesse pushes past me and staggers to the recliner, sinking into it with a slight groan. "Out."

"Are you high again?" I turn on the light, and Jesse winces away. "You *are* high," I snap, trying to keep my voice low. Honey has seen and heard enough today.

"So what?" Jesse lies back in the recliner.

"Do you know about Jim?" I say, struggling to keep my voice level.

Jesse doesn't say anything.

"Do you know that Jim is dead?" I ask again, then glance at Honey to make sure she's really asleep.

Jesse doesn't open his eyes. "Yeah. I know."

"Weren't you there with him this morning?"

"Yeah, but I took off."

The tightness in my chest eases a little bit. "Was anyone else there with him when you left?"

Jesse gives a slight head shake.

I wait for him to say more, but of course he doesn't. "And you didn't think maybe you ought to come home and help us instead of going out and getting stoned?"

Jesse finally opens his eyes and crosses his arms. "You seem all right to me."

"Have you talked to Mama?"

"Nope."

"The police are going to want to talk to you," I say. "You shouldn't have taken off."

Jesse's almost asleep already. He gives a noncommittal grunt.

Headlights flash across the window, and my stomach twists. "Get up and go to your room. Mama doesn't need to see you like this." When Jesse doesn't move, I kick the recliner lever down, bringing his chair up so fast he nearly tumbles out.

"Damn it," he snarls, clinging to the armrests.

"Get your ass up. Now." I grab his arm and yank him as hard as I can. He staggers to his feet, cursing and grumbling.

"Fine," he says, and stumbles down the hall to his room. I hear his door slam and then his body drop onto the mattress.

Mama comes in with slumped shoulders and red eyes, mascara smudged down one cheek. She puts her purse on the kitchen counter and sinks into a chair.

"Hey, Mama," I say.

"Hey, baby." She rests her chin in one hand, putting all her weight on her elbow. I'm surprised the kitchen table doesn't collapse under all that grief.

"You want something to eat or drink?" I ask, and she shakes her head. I go to the sink and fill a glass of water anyway. When I set it down in front of her, she reaches for it and takes a few sips.

"Thank you."

"I made some dinner for Honey and me. I put a plate in the fridge for you." She doesn't say anything, so I get it out and put it in the microwave. She stares into space, like she forgot I'm here.

When I set the plate in front of her, she automatically starts eating, but I know she's not tasting the food. After a few bites, she pushes the plate away. "Where's Honey?" she asks absently.

"She's on the couch over there, sleeping. I'll put her to bed in a minute."

Mama nods, and I'm afraid she's going to disappear back inside herself, so I force a question out, even though I already heard enough at the police station to know. "What happened to Jim?"

She doesn't look at me, just keeps staring ahead, seeing nothing—at least nothing in this room.

"Mama?"

"Someone hit him from behind with a hammer." Her face pales.

Hearing it again makes me nauseous. "Who would do that?"

Mama shakes her head. Then she looks up at me, her eyes haunted. "Why do the men I love keep dying? You think I'm cursed?"

"Of course not." I sit at the table next to her and put my hand on hers. "You're not cursed, Mama. You've just had some bad luck."

"Ain't that the same thing?" Tears are streaming down her cheeks now, and I feel my own eyes begin to smart. She glances out the window toward the pines. "I think it's these woods. I didn't get far enough away. They came for Jim, too."

"You're not making any sense. It's a coincidence they both died," I say, and I know I'm trying to convince myself, too. I reach over and pull some paper towels from the roll on the table. "Here," I say, handing them to her, though I know I hate wiping my nose with rough paper like that.

"You seen Jesse?" she asks after she blows her nose.

"He's in his room."

She nods. She looks lost, so lost, like she'll never find her way home again. And I can't go with her, can't lead her back to us. Even if I could, I don't have a map to her grief. That's the thing about losing someone. It's a landscape no one's familiar with, and it's never the same for two people. We're all alone in our loss, without a map, without a companion. It's the loneliest thing there is.

"Did Daddy really beat up Frank once? Is that why Frank's nose looks like that?" I ask, trying to change the subject.

Mama nods. "Frank made a pass at Ena, back when she was just starting college. She wasn't interested, but Frank wouldn't leave her be. Your daddy . . . he, he couldn't bear to see her treated that way. Not after his father—" She breaks off and closes her eyes.

"After his father what?"

"Baby, I don't want to dredge up all that ancient history."

A low buzzing against the window catches our attention. A wasp is flying there, fumbling against the glass. Mama shudders. A memory crawls across my skin, but I bat it away.

"I keep thinking about how Jesse beat up Kenneth yesterday," I say. "The way he climbed on top of him and beat him till his face was all bloody." When it happened, I was so busy trying to get Jesse off Kenneth, I didn't really think about how scary and awful it was, but now the memory makes me queasy.

When Mama doesn't say anything, I finally ask the question that's been eating at me all afternoon. "Do the police think Jesse killed Jim?"

Mama closes her eyes, as if against a wave of pain, but then she gazes up at me, her eyes ringed with dark circles. "You gotta stand by your brother. No matter what. You hear me?"

"Are you saying he—"

"Shady Grove. Jesse ain't never done anything but look out for you. It might be your turn to look after him. No matter what. That's what brothers and sisters do." Her lost look is gone now. She grabs my chin and holds my eyes with hers. "You hear me?"

Tears roll down my cheeks, clogging my throat. "I hear you."

Daddy always told Jesse that taking care of me was Jesse's biggest responsibility, the most important job in his whole life.

Mama's right—whether Jesse is guilty or not, it might be my turn to take care of him now.

EIGHT

I step onto the school bus at seven a.m. two days later, and there are already eyes on me, eyes and whispers. Jim's death was on the news last night, along with the reported cause of foul play, which is the strangest expression. Foul play. What's playful about murder? The reporter said the police were considering several possible leads, but I haven't heard any specifics. The detectives questioned me with Mama present, asking what Jim was like at home and how Jesse and I got along with him. I told the truth, but I softened it a little, to make it seem like things weren't quite as bad between Jim and Jesse as they really were.

The police interrogated Jesse for a long time yesterday, and they asked him to come back again today instead of going to school. But I can't let myself believe Jesse had anything to do with it. He and Jim had been fighting a lot lately, but Jesse wouldn't kill anyone, not even Jim. It must have been someone else. Maybe another construction worker—Jim was never well liked at work. Too short a temper, too sharp a tongue.

Orlando called three times to see if we needed anything, but I haven't heard from Sarah since she dropped me at my car after the police station. Maybe she doesn't know what to say or is afraid of trespassing somehow, but her silence feels all too familiar.

I find a seat in the second row of the bus so I won't have to meet all those eyes. I put my earbuds in and stare out the window, anxious about going to school but relieved to be getting out of the house, away from Mama's grief and the people who keep dropping by with casseroles and questions I'm not allowed to hear the answers to. I offered to stay home to watch Honey, but Mama told me to go, said someone else would drop my sister off at daycare.

The field rolls by, a morning mist still on it, the cows not yet out to graze. When the bus passes by my lightning-struck tree, its white, twisted branches seem to reach for me like always. Yet against the watery gray of the sky, the tree looks eerie, otherworldly, like another ghost in my world of lost souls. Maybe it's Jim's death or my fear for Jesse, or maybe it's because the shadow man won't stop haunting my dreams, but today the oak tree isn't comforting. Instead, the sight of it makes me feel lonely and lost and a little bit afraid.

Today, surviving lightning doesn't feel like enough.

The first person I see when I get off the bus is Cedar Smith, leaning against the brick wall like he owns it. Even off the stage he looks like an old country musician—a real one, not like the new ones that are hardly more than pop singers wearing cowboy hats.

I eye him from a distance: brown cowboy boots—not the showy kind, just serviceable work boots—dark Wranglers, a big belt buckle, a plaid button-up with glossy buttons and some kind of star design on the shoulders. I always thought his clothes were all for show, but now that I've heard him play, I see the clothes are well earned.

He probably thinks Jesse and I are trashy after the fight at the open mic, and maybe worse if he's heard about Jim.

The thought of speaking to Cedar makes me want to sink into the earth, but when I get close, I say hello and give him half a smile. To my surprise, he detaches himself from the wall and walks with me. "Shady, right?"

I nod, and he smiles. "I'm Cedar, if you didn't know."

"I know" is all I can manage to say. I suspect he's about to ask about Jim and Jesse, but he doesn't. I force myself to say something else. "Thanks for helping me Friday night—with Kenneth, I mean."

Cedar shakes his head. "That's all right. That boy can't walk five feet without coming across someone who wants to beat his ass."

I laugh—the first time I've laughed in two days. But then I remember how beating up Kenneth makes Jesse look, how it might make him seem guilty of killing Jim.

"Ken is one of my best friends, but God, he's got a mouth on him."

When I don't say anything, Cedar starts talking again. "Y'all were really good Friday night—at the open mic, I mean. You played that fiddle like it was growin' outa your arm," he says with no attempt to hide the drawl we all inherited from our parents.

"Really?" I glance up at him, distracted from thoughts of Jesse. "That's not really the kind of music I like to play. Never feels quite right."

"What kind of music do you like?" Cedar asks, smiling again when he catches sight of the blush spreading across my cheeks. "I always wondered, since I'd see you toting that fiddle around school. Thought maybe you played classical or something."

"I like the same kind of music you do," I say, screwing up my courage. I think his arrogance is making me bold. "That's what I was raised on. Actually—actually, I was named after the song you played. My whole first name's Shady Grove."

"No kidding," Cedar says with a short laugh. His eyes crinkle at the corners. "How'd we do then, playing your namesake?" I can tell he knows exactly how well they played, and if it were any other boy playing any other song, I'd probably put a stop to his peacocking.

"It was almost as beautiful as the way my daddy used to play it," I say. "Almost."

"He died?" Cedar asks, and I nod.

"I'm sorry. That's awful." Cedar clears his throat. "Kenneth told me about your stepdad—about what happened."

There it is. I'm amazed he waited this long to bring it up. "Is Kenneth okay? It's been a rough couple of days for him."

"Yeah. He's upset, but he seems all right. I guess they weren't really close. He's not coming to school today, though."

"No, they weren't close," I say. That probably makes his dad's death even worse.

"Did you like him, or did you hate him like most people hate their stepdads?"

"You met him the other night," I say, as if that's all the answer Cedar needs. A few weeks ago, I would have said I hated Jim—his impatience, his rough manners, his insistence on watching NASCAR all the damn time. But I saw a whole different side of Jim at the hospital on Friday, something soft underneath all those hard angles. "I don't know. He was . . . he could be all right sometimes. I mostly feel bad for my little sister. He's her dad."

"Yeah," Cedar says. But we're at my classroom now, my hand already on the door handle. "Listen," he says, "I didn't really mean to talk to you about everybody dying. I'm sorry about that. I only wanted to tell you how well you played."

I turn to him. "Maybe next time we can talk about something a little happier."

He smiles. "I'd like that. See you later, Shady Grove," he says, and then he winks at me. And despite everything going on, despite the fact that he's a rodeo boy with an ego the size of Texas, I feel that wink all the way down to my toes.

And then I'm watching his very finely made backside wander off down the hall, and I can't find a single mocking thing to say about those Wranglers.

"Hey," I hear, and turn to see Sarah staring at me. She looks between me and Cedar's retreating form, her face unreadable.

"We were only talking about Kenneth," I say, feeling defensive for no good reason.

"Okay." She crosses her arms and glances away. I don't know what I expected after our kiss, but it wasn't this. She doesn't know what to say, where to look. Did she change her mind about me after Jim's murder? Does she regret the kiss? Is that why she didn't reach out to me all weekend? Because her silence felt like it was saying something, even if she didn't mean it to.

I can tell she's about to ask if we know who killed Jim, and I don't want to talk about it—she doesn't really deserve to hear me talk about it after ignoring me all weekend. I yank open the classroom door and head inside, my anger a sudden roar in my head.

Sarah sits in the desk next to mine, and I can feel her eyes on me. When she finally speaks, her voice is tentative. "I thought about texting you, but . . . I didn't want to bother you. I thought you'd be busy with your family and everything." She's embarrassed, maybe a little ashamed of herself.

I'm mad at her, but I give her a weak smile and nod. I know she's doing her best, but it's not enough. Not today. She doesn't try to say anything else, so I stare at the words in my book until class starts, thinking not of Spanish verb conjugations but of Jim's murder and Sarah's silence, the wail of a fiddle in the woods, and—a welcome distraction—the way Cedar's eyes crinkle when he smiles.

The school bus door closes behind me, and I start home with leaden feet. Once the rattling of the bus windows disappears down the road, I can hear the shouting coming from home. Mostly male voices, loud and angry-sounding, but then there's a shrill scream I recognize as Honey's, and I'm running, dirt clods flying behind me. Through the trees, red and blue lights spin lazily, and the world feels like those lights, too bright and dizzying, utterly disorienting.

Two police officers are grappling with Jesse, their limbs tangled with his, all three of them sounding like a lot of bulls trying to kick their way out of a stall. Jesse's fighting hard, but they are big, burly men, and they soon slam him against the car and wrest his arms behind his back, slapping cuffs on his wrists.

Jesse goes limp, like he's given up and given in, resigned to whatever comes next. They slide him into the back seat of the car and slam the door on him. He stares at me through the window, and he doesn't look afraid or angry like he should. He looks ashamed.

"Shady, Shady, Shady, Shady, Shady," Honey is screaming, and I look over in time to see her rip herself from Mama's arms. She runs to me and wraps her hands around my legs, sobbing into my jeans. Mama's face is hard and unreadable as a slab of stone.

One of the officers turns from Jesse, and I realize it's Kenneth's stepdad, Gary. I've seen him drop Kenneth off at school a few times. He probably handled Jesse extra rough for Kenneth's sake. Gary goes over to Mama and talks to her for a minute, puts a slip of paper in her hands. If she understands him, she makes no indication. He pats her on the shoulder and gets back into the car.

They back out onto the dirt road, Jesse still staring out the window, watching his home and family recede from him like the tide. Honey's cries have died to a shuddering sob against my legs, and Mama's still standing where the cop left her, staring at the place the car had been moments before.

Dust is all that's left of what just happened.

I pick up Honey and sling her to one hip, and then walk over to Mama and take her arm. Her eyes clear for a moment, and she lets me lead her up the steps and into the trailer. There's a lamp broken on the carpet, and several books and DVD cases lie strewn around it.

I guide Mama over to the couch and make her sit down, and put Honey next to her. My little sister lies down with her head in Mama's lap. Mama smooths Honey's hair absentmindedly, and Honey puts her thumb into her mouth and closes her eyes. She'll fall asleep if we leave her like that.

I sit down too. "What happened?"

Mama's face looks so tired, like she's living every hour twice. She shakes her head. "They say he killed Jim." She speaks like she's reciting a well-known liturgy, the words flat and empty of meaning. "His fingerprints were on the hammer. Two of the workers saw him arguing with Jim that morning before they left for lunch. He disappeared from the work site and wasn't seen again."

No, no, no.

"So what?" I say, pushing down my panic. "He worked there, so it's not crazy he would have used the hammer. And they are always arguing. It's what they do—what they did.

How do we know those workers aren't lying? Why aren't the cops investigating them? All those guys hated Jim!"

My panic seems to wake Mama up, and she finally talks normally. "The police did, baby. They looked into both of the workers who were there that morning, plus a dozen more. Everything led back to Jesse."

"Well, couldn't there be other suspects? A customer? Or maybe someone who got fired?"

But Mama shakes her head. "Only Jesse. They've dismissed every other lead."

"They're wrong. They'll figure it out eventually. We just need to make them understand." My voice breaks on the last word, a sob lodging in my throat.

Mama's eyes meet mine. "There's too much evidence against him."

I shake my head to clear it. "No. Jesse gets mad, but he wouldn't kill someone. It has to be someone else. He didn't do it."

"I hope not," Mama says, "but even if he did, he's still your brother."

When I don't respond, Mama settles her eyes on mine. "You support your family even when they've done wrong. If you love them, you do. No matter what they've done."

No matter what they've done. The words almost knock the wind out of me. Mama's already given up on Jesse's innocence. I shake my head and back away from her, straight into the trailer's front door. I can't breathe. Can't breathe.

I stumble outside to the edge of the trees, so light-headed I think I might faint. Black dots edge into my vision, and nausea roars in my gut. But the moment I lean against a skinny pine tree for support, the wail of a fiddle cuts through my shock. I snap to attention.

The perfect, hair-raising note sears away the fog in my mind, replacing it with an electric certainty. It wasn't Jim's death Daddy was warning me about, it was Jesse's being arrested. He knew it was coming, he knew I would need his help.

I don't know what Jesse's done, but I know what I need to do.

Once Mama goes to her room to lie down, I take her keys from their hook. I climb into her car and head for Aunt Ena's just as the first star winks in the deep-blue sky.

I'm going to find Daddy's fiddle tonight.

I knock hard at Aunt Ena's door until she opens it, her eyes frightened.

"What is it? What's happened?" she says, standing back to let me in.

I walk deep into the house, all the way to the little parlor off the kitchen, where Daddy liked to play in the evenings. Aunt Ena follows close behind.

I turn and face her. "Where is it, Aunt Ena?"

"Where's what?"

"The fiddle."

"I told you those were echoes you were hearing. It's gone."

"I've heard it, over and over again I've heard it. Here. In the woods. It sounds just the way it did when Daddy played it. I know it's him. I know it's his fiddle."

"Shady, your daddy's dead."

"Nobody's ever dead around here."

"Well, the fiddle's gone, and even if it weren't, I know your daddy wouldn't want you to have it. He wouldn't want you to play it."

"He does. He's been reaching out to me, trying to show me where it is."

Aunt Ena shakes her head. "He wouldn't. I promise you. If I know anything in this world, it's that William wouldn't want you playing that fiddle."

"Aunt Ena, the fiddle was meant for me. Daddy said it would be mine when he was gone. My responsibility."

"Your burden, you mean. That fiddle is nothing but a burden. I'll die before I help you find it."

Her words jolt through me. "So you admit it's still out there? It's not gone?"

She shakes her head.

I try a different approach. "Jesse was arrested today. He's being taken to jail for killing Jim."

"Arrested?" she asks, taken aback, and I realize I should have called her. She's often the last to hear news, cooped up in this house. Her mouth twists with sudden emotion but then settles into a hard line. "That's terrible, but it doesn't explain why you're here. What does Jesse being arrested have to do with William's fiddle?"

"If I can find the fiddle and raise Jim's ghost, I can learn the truth." It sounds outrageous coming from my mouth, but I can't take it back now. I cross my arms and stare at Aunt Ena, masking my doubt with defiance.

Her face registers surprise but she recovers quickly, staring back at me with equal defiance and a lot less doubt. "Sometimes learning the truth doesn't give you what you want."

Her voice is full of pity, but her words make me reel back from her like she's slapped me. "You think he did it? You think Jesse killed Jim?"

She stares at me for a long time. "You do."

I shake my head. I can't let that thought in. Can't give it room to grow. I spin away from her and dart my eyes all over the room. "Where'd you hide it? I'll find it—you know I will. You may as well tell me. Daddy's going to show me where it is anyway."

"You ever think maybe it's not your daddy leading you to the fiddle? You ever think maybe there's a darkness in the woods, or maybe a darkness that's in you?" She's advancing on me now, angrier than I've ever seen her. "Don't you remember your dreams? Don't you remember the dark man in them, the little dead girl in your ceiling? Don't you remember, Shady?" Aunt Ena is shaking.

I step back from her, then turn and pace the room. I don't want to think about the dead girl. She never threatened me like the shadow man does, but she was worse somehow, more unbearable. She clung to the ceiling above my bed, almost featureless except for her white dress. But she gave off fear in waves, filling the room.

The memory of her makes my chest feel tight, so I turn my thoughts back to the fiddle. I run my hand over the walls of the parlor, searching for I don't know what—a hidden compartment? I pick up a child-sized teapot from the fireplace mantel, checking the wall behind it.

"You think I'd keep a cursed thing like that fiddle in my house?" Aunt Ena spits, snatching the teapot away from me and cradling it in the crook of her arm. "The fiddle's not here."

"Tell me where it is," I say. "If you love me at all, you'll tell me."

"I do love you. That's why I want you to leave this be. Go home, help your mama, take care of your baby sister—while you've got her." Aunt Ena's voice cracks.

"And what about Jesse? Who's going to take care of him?"

"I don't know," Aunt Ena says tiredly. "The Lord, I guess, if he looks after any of us."

I turn on my heel and stalk from the parlor, straight to the front door. I slam it behind me as hard as I can, so hard the windows rattle in their frames. The ghosts press up against the house, spilling into the driveway and the forest, thick as the humid night air. They'll wait around until the Second Coming, but me, I'm done waiting. I won't wait around for justice to be done, for Jesse to be proved guilty or innocent. I'll find a way to learn the truth.

NINE

The viewing room is surprisingly crowded. I guess in the South even people like Jim get large turnouts when they die. We're all too polite to stay home.

Well, that's the generous answer. A more accurate answer might be that people are here to gossip, to whisper, to speculate.

Sure, some are here to grieve—Mama, in the same black dress she wore to Daddy's funeral; Jim's mother, who clutches the edge of the open coffin like a captain clutching the helm of a sinking ship, her knuckles bone white; Frank, who looks angry now rather than sad, as if he can shout Jim out of the coffin. His face softens only when someone comes to shake his hand or hug him. It's strange how well liked he is in town when you consider he's related to Jim. Men look him in the eye like he's someone important, and women smile at him like he's a catch, while his wife looks on, quiet at his side, a perfectly demure Southern lady.

Several guys from the construction company came to pay

their respects, and I wonder if they're here for Jim's sake or for Frank's. Pedro Flores, a contractor who installs HVACs in Frank's houses, came and brought his son Juan, who's a friend of Orlando's. Mr. Flores hugs both Mama and me and says Jim was a good man. I thought everyone at work hated Jim, but Mr. Flores seems sincere.

"We can only stay for a few minutes. Will you be all right? Is Orlando here?" Juan asks.

I shake my head. "He offered to come for moral support, but I told him I'd be fine on my own. I guess I thought I'd manage better that way." If Sarah had asked, I might have said yes, but she didn't offer, which really shouldn't surprise me at this point. But it does, and my anger at her boils quietly underneath everything else I'm feeling.

Juan seems to sense my misery and gives me a quick hug. "Take care, Shady," he says. "See you at school."

I wave goodbye to Mr. Flores and turn back to survey the room, loneliness settling over me. Everyone here looks natural and at ease, as if milling around a dead body while exchanging pleasantries happens every day. But to me this is a creepy and unnecessary funeral tradition. Why would you want people to have to look at the empty shell who used to be a person they loved? I suppose if it's someone you hated, looking at them defeated and empty in a coffin might offer a sort of pleasure, but what good is there in it for those of us who just lived with the person, shared a home, moved in each other's orbit not because we wanted to but because that's where our orbits happened to be?

I wish I had taken Orlando up on his offer to come. He could have been a kind of buffer for me. Instead, I take Honey from Mama's arms and make her my buffer, trying to keep her entertained and safe from the overly tearful old women who want to shower her with kisses and germs.

I try not to think about it, but this wake reminds me horribly of Daddy's—of seeing his body laid out, unnaturally still, looking all wrong in a suit when he only ever wore jeans and work boots. I wanted to scream at him to wake up, to get out of that coffin and go home with us, but all I could do was sit in a chair and weep until my eyes were nearly swollen closed, feeling more alone than I ever had before.

I wonder if that's how Kenneth is feeling now. I think about going to talk to him, but I can't bring myself to walk over there. He sits in a corner with his hands in his lap, for once too stunned to speak. His mother sits beside him, messing around on her phone, like she'd rather be pretty much anywhere else on earth. She doesn't look the least bit sad. I guess her and Jim's divorce was pretty nasty. I heard him refer to her as a grasping shrew on more than one occasion, although I don't imagine he behaved much better himself. Still, you'd think she'd try a little harder for her son's sake.

Her new husband, Gary, has been standing out front smoking all morning like he's afraid to come inside. I was surprised he came at all since he and Jim despised each other, but I guess he is Kenneth's stepdad, as well as Frank's friend, so it makes sense. Plus, he's a police officer, so he's going to lead the funeral procession to the graveyard later. But having the cop who arrested Jesse here really isn't helping me and Mama.

At least Honey's too young to know what's happening. I've kept her away from the coffin because no little kid needs a memory like that buried deep in their mind, a memory they'll dig up one day in therapy or unexpectedly when their dog dies or something. It's bad enough that people keep coming over and touching her face or shaking her little hand, their faces full of pity.

I remember them all from Daddy's funeral and hate them even more than I did back then. I hate their cliché "in a better place" speeches and their Sunday-best clothes. I hate their talk about God's love and forgiveness. Most of all, I hate their unwavering belief in Jesse's guilt.

I'm wrapped in my own web of anger when Cedar walks in. At first, I don't even recognize him. He's bare-headed and wearing a dark suit, without a single embellishment on it. He looks stripped down somehow, pulled out of context. I stare at him for a long time, trying to process it.

But he's looking around and catches sight of me, and a blush spreads up my neck. Mama thinks she's cursed with dead husbands, but I know I'm cursed to blush every time I get near this fool boy.

"Hey, Shady," Cedar says when he reaches me. "Sorry about all this." He doesn't say anything about Jesse. I could hug him for it. "Is this your little sister?"

Honey's head is against my shoulder, her arms wrapped around my neck. She's almost asleep. "Yeah, she's about tuckered out."

Cedar smiles at her. "She looks like Kenneth a little bit." He glances back at me with a sly smile. "Thankfully, though, she looks more like you."

Is Cedar Smith seriously flirting with me at a funeral? "Thanks" is all I say. "Kenneth's over there in the corner." I motion with my head. "It was really nice of you to come and be with him."

Cedar ducks his head. "I'll go find him. See you later." He touches my arm as he passes by, and it's the first thing I've really, truly felt since the police dragged Jesse away yesterday.

I watch as Kenneth's eyes brighten when he catches sight of Cedar. He stands and grips him in a bear hug, almost lifting Cedar off the ground.

Once Honey finally falls asleep, I pass her over to Aunt Ena and go to the bathroom to escape the whispering voices, red velvet, and the coffin at the far end of the room that draws people like moths to a front porch light. They can throw themselves at it and feel the electric zap if that's what they need, but I want some quiet and solitude.

But of course there's a line for the toilet. I'm about to turn around and find another place to hide when I hear Jesse's name. Two elderly ladies in line are talking about him. I edge a little closer without letting them notice me.

"You know what I think?" says a voice like the creak of a screen door. "I think if it turns out he really did kill Jim, they ought to reopen William's case. Maybe he killed him, too."

"William died in a car accident."

"So? The boy was with him, wasn't he?"

"But Jesse would have only been a kid."

"He was a strange child. The way he stared at his daddy sometimes." She fakes a shiver, and I recognize her—our closest neighbor growing up, Miss Patty, who seemed old even back then. She's ancient now, but still every bit as vile. She was always coming around the house with pamphlets from her Pentecostal church—usually with flames on the covers. She'd talk to us about heaven and hell and fighting off demons. Daddy would get so mad at her he could barely hold his temper.

Now my own temper is rising. Daddy's death was an accident, and Jesse was never a suspect because there was nothing to be suspected of. It was a deer in the road. Jesse might have survivor's guilt, but that's all. I can't believe she would say such horrible things.

"Oh, that house was full of sin, full of the devil," Miss Patty goes on. "I don't know how many times I told them—they needed an exorcism. Of course, it started years ago, when William and Ena's parents first moved in. It was his mama that started it all—she was some kind of psychic. I told her it wasn't good Christian spirits she was consorting with—it was devils. Oh, that house was so dark, so wrong."

"I've heard stories about that place," the other woman whispers. I don't recognize her, but that's the way things are around here—people always seem to know you even if you haven't the faintest idea who they are.

Miss Patty shakes her head. "I swear I saw a pair of red eyes looking at me from a top window one time. It's no wonder their boy Jesse turned out so wrong."

"What about the girl, the one with the strange name?"

"Shady Grove? She's a good girl from what I hear. Her

mama must've gotten her out of that house just in time, before the devils got hold of her."

I've heard about all I can stand, so I clear my throat, and both ladies look up. Miss Patty isn't the slightest bit embarrassed to have been caught talking about my family, but the other woman goes rigid.

"I'm so sorry for your loss," she says in a sugar-sweet voice.

I'm not even going to try to be polite. I turn the full force of my pent-up fury on Miss Patty. "My brother did not kill *anyone*," I say. "And our house was *not* awful. You are, you bitter old hag." I spin on my heel and stalk back into the crowd before she can answer.

Aunt Ena catches my arm as I pass. Honey is draped across her chest, asleep. "Funeral gossips getting to you?"

I haven't talked to her since our fight. My voice comes out brittle when I speak. "How'd you know?"

"I hear 'em too. All kinds of rumors flying around. Folks think this is *CSI*."

"I don't know what that is," I say, and Ena rolls her eyes.

"Darlin', I'm sorry about our argument. I don't want to fight with you," Ena says, reaching for my hand. Aunt Ena is one of the most important people in my life, and I should never have spoken to her the way I did, no matter how upset I was.

I squeeze her fingers. "I'm sorry too."

Aunt Ena smiles up at me, her blue eyes glistening. "Can we leave that subject be then? Can we forget about it?" Her voice trembles.

I can't forget about it, but we don't have to talk about it

now. I nod and change the subject. "I just heard Miss Patty say she thought Jesse killed Daddy, as well as Jim, and that our house was evil."

Aunt Ena shakes her head. "She still comes around the house with her tracts sometimes. Loves talking about the devil so much, it makes you wonder."

"But why would she say that about Jesse?" I don't want to let everyone else's doubt—Mama's, Aunt Ena's, now Miss Patty's—chip away at my faith in Jesse, but maybe my faith was shaky to begin with. After all, he was the first person I thought of when Aunt Ena told me Jim was killed.

All those fights he had with Jim. How Jesse snapped when Kenneth whispered something to him.

Aunt Ena gazes at me, studying my face. "You know your daddy and Jesse didn't have an easy relationship."

"But that doesn't mean—"

From behind me comes a loud, anguished voice. I turn and see Frank looming over Mama. I don't know what he just said, but his arms are crossed and there are tears on his face. Mama's leaning away from him like a skinny new tree bending in the wind—nothing like how she was at the police station the night Jim died. Jesse's arrest and all the police tramping in and out of the house took more out of her than I realized. They only questioned me once, and that was bad enough. Mama's been through hell.

I guess Frank isn't faring much better. He's never acted like this before.

"Go rescue her. I'll keep hold of Honey," Aunt Ena says.

I cross the room and head straight for Mama, who I can see is crying, the tears leaking from her eyes, forming rivulets of mascara. I don't think she even knows she's crying anymore. She doesn't try to wipe them away.

". . . that piece-of-shit son of yours killed my brother and all you've got to say for yourself is that you're sorry," Frank bellows before he catches sight of me heading their way. He has the decency to look ashamed of himself. "I'm just talking to your mama, Shady. It's not your concern," he says gently.

"You're yelling at my mama, so it is my concern," I say, coming to stand next to her.

"Shady," she says, "don't—"

"No," I tell her. "Your husband just died, and he has no right to be yelling at you a few feet away from Jim's body."

"He was my brother," Frank growls, but his voice breaks on the last syllable. A few heads turn to look at us, but I don't care.

"And Jesse is mine. And he didn't kill Jim," I growl right back, my anger displacing my doubts. "I know you're upset about Jim's death, but if you don't get out of my mama's face, I'm gonna call security."

Before Frank can respond, Kenneth is standing between us, one hand on his uncle's chest. He's nearly as tall as Frank is, his hands almost as big as his uncle's. "Please don't make a scene at my daddy's funeral," Kenneth says quietly, more seriously than he's ever said anything in his life. He looks between Frank and me, and I almost regret losing my temper.

"Don't you care he killed your daddy?" Frank asks Kenneth, his voice hoarse with grief and anger. "You that sorry you don't even care?" A tear trickles down Frank's cheek.

Kenneth's cheeks flush red, and he wipes the back of his hand over his moist eyes. I wince, wondering if his bruises still hurt. "Whatever Jesse did or didn't do ain't their fault, Uncle Frank. They're just here trying to grieve, same as you."

"I wish we still hanged people," Frank mumbles before Kenneth pulls him away, their arms wrapped around each other. His words knife through me. I haven't really let myself consider all the consequences of Jesse being blamed for Jim's murder. Florida doesn't hang people anymore, though we do still have the death penalty. But not for teenagers, right? He's safe from that at least.

Frank is so sure it was Jesse. So sure he wants to see Jesse die. What if I'm the only one who's wrong to trust in Jesse's innocence?

Now's not the time for these thoughts. Mama's body sags with relief once Frank leaves the room, and I put my arm around her.

"I can't believe we haven't even made it to the service." She drops her face into her hands and rubs it tiredly.

"It's only another half hour. We're almost done."

"Come on with me, and we'll look at Jim's body one more time," she says, squaring her shoulders. When I don't move my feet to go with her, Mama gazes at me. "You haven't paid your respects yet?"

"I didn't want Honey to see," I say, avoiding the truth.

"Come on, baby. This is part of it. You can't turn your face from death 'cause it's always gonna find you."

I let her lead me toward the casket, and the crowd parts around us. Even Jim's mother moves away from the coffin when we approach. Jim was her favorite son. In her eyes, nothing he did was ever wrong and no one gave Jim half of what he deserved. So of course, she doesn't think Mama deserved Jim, and Mama can't stand the woman for it. She doesn't even glance at her mother-in-law now.

"Look," Mama says. She reaches into the coffin and touches Jim's hand.

I force my eyes to his face.

People always say the dead look like they're sleeping, but Jim looks like nothing. He is a wax figure of his former self. His hands are folded across his chest, and his eyes are closed, but if you look carefully, you can tell they are glued.

I feel bile rising up my throat, but I force it back down. I try to cover up the revulsion I feel before Mama sees it.

But when I look over, her eyes are locked on Jim's face, like she's searching the body for traces of the man she loved. Maybe the body means different things to some people than it does to me. Maybe one day I'll love someone romantically and they'll die, and I'll want to touch their corpse; I'll still love the body even though it's empty.

But I have lived all my life with the whispers of the dead, so I'm not fooled by the embalmer's tricks.

Jim's body doesn't matter now. Only his ghost could tell us what we need to know.

Mama asked me to play my fiddle while the pallbearers bring Jim up the aisle. She requested "Go Rest High on That Mountain," probably because every local funeral anyone's been to since 1995 includes it.

I stand alone at the front of the funeral home chapel, close my eyes, and play. I don't care anything about this song, but I want to do right by Mama. As the song soars across the chapel, making old ladies weep, I remember how it felt to watch Daddy's coffin borne up this same aisle, with Jim and Jesse at the front, each bearing Daddy's weight with a skinny arm. They both looked guilty, shamefaced, like it ought to be their bodies going up the aisle.

I thought maybe people at funerals always looked like that, half guilty to still be alive while the one they love isn't. But when I open my eyes, I see Jim's pallbearers. Most of them look stunned, as if Jim's murder has reminded them of their own waiting deaths, their own inevitable fates. Kenneth's face is only lost and grieved, Frank's grim and determined.

When the coffin reaches the front of the church, Frank glares at me for a moment before he turns. There's so much accusation in his gaze, I feel a stab of shame, as if Jim's blood is somehow on my hands. Is everyone going to look at me like that now, with either pity or suspicion, as if I'm either a victim or an accomplice in my brother's crimes?

I don't know what's true, who's to blame. But I do know that despite what this song's lyrics say, Jim's work on earth isn't done, and there won't be any rest for him—or for me, especially once Daddy's fiddle is in my hands.

When I left Aunt Ena's house after our argument, I swore to myself I wouldn't wait around like the ghosts. I'd find the fiddle and learn the truth on my own. But in the time that has passed since I made that promise, I keep wondering if I'm no better than the ghosts. Maybe I'm waiting for someone else to do justice, someone else to prove Jesse's innocence, to set him free. Because no matter how many times I insist Jesse isn't guilty, maybe deep down I'm afraid justice might not be in Jesse's favor. Maybe I'm afraid to be the one who ties the noose around his neck.

TEN

I don't see Cedar again at the funeral, but the next morning I hear him shout my name from down the hallway between classes. I turn at his voice, and he comes running up to me, smiling that cocky smile of his. He throws an arm over my shoulders like we're old friends.

"Listen, your fiddle playing was amazing yesterday—even better than at the open mic night."

"Thank you."

"Rose will probably kill me for asking you this before checking with her first, but we've been talking about adding some more instruments—trying to get up a proper bluegrass band, I mean. And I'd love it if you'd play fiddle for us."

I pause for a long time, trying to make sense of what he's saying. My thoughts are all tied up in Jim and Jesse, and his meaning doesn't register at first.

"What do you think?" Cedar asks when I don't answer. "You want to play with us?"

When I finally realize what he's asking, I gape at him in surprise. "A bluegrass band? *Just* bluegrass?"

"Just bluegrass," he says, laughing.

I want to say yes. I can't think of anything I'd rather say yes to. But Sarah . . . "I would love to, but Sarah and Orlando and I play together. I can't bail on them. Sarah would murder me in my sleep."

He laughs and leans toward me, and I notice his stubble's heavier than usual. He looks like such a cowboy it's ridiculous. "Let's me and you get together and play sometime then."

"The two of us?"

"Why not?"

"That's not much of a band. Sounds more like a date." The moment the word *date* leaves my mouth, I regret it. I blush to the roots of my hair.

When Cedar sees how red my face is, he barely smothers a laugh. "Would that be so bad?"

I don't say anything for awhile, and Cedar's still got his arm around me, which I have no idea how to respond to. Two drama club girls pass by and shoot us curious looks, and I stare at my shoes. I don't know if they're whispering because of Jesse's arrest or because of whatever's going on between Cedar and me. I hope it's on Cedar's account, because I'm tired of being haunted by whispers in the hallway and cafeteria. Being haunted by a phantom fiddle's bad enough.

"So how 'bout that date?" Cedar says, trying to sound cool, but his voice breaks a little.

This time I laugh. "We can play together if you want."

Sarah and I kissed, but that doesn't mean we're a couple. It doesn't mean I should feel guilty for playing music with Cedar. Especially since Sarah's gone back to ignoring me. If anyone should feel guilty, it's her.

"If you really don't wanna be alone with me, I'll invite Kenneth." He looks at me sideways, a smile lingering around his lips.

"I'll risk it," I say quickly. This isn't how I should be spending my time right now, not with Jesse in jail and Jim freshly buried, but the thought of a break from all the grief and the worry is too tempting to resist. "Tonight?"

"I'll pick you up. Here, I'll put my number in your phone so you can text me your address," he says, his hand brushing mine as he takes the phone from me.

"Where are we going to play?"

"It'll be a surprise," he says before tweaking one of my curls and winking at me. Then he's off down the hallway like it's his stage.

"What the hell was that?" Sarah's voice sounds behind me.

I startle and turn around, trying to cover my smile when I spot Orlando and Sarah.

But Orlando shakes his head. "Many a girl has fallen for Cedar's country-boy charms," he muses, using the ridiculous accent of a rich plantation owner from a Civil War–period movie.

But Sarah's not laughing.

"Are you seriously going behind my back, after I told you I don't want to play with them?" she says. Anger and hurt strangle her words.

My guilt and embarrassment turn to irritation, making my voice sharp. "I didn't go behind your back. He came up to me."

She crosses her arms. "What were you talking about?"

On another day, I might enjoy her jealousy, but not now, not with everything that's going on. It takes all my effort to keep my voice even when I answer. "Sarah, I spent all day yesterday fighting with people at Jim's funeral. I don't have the energy for this. I'm so tired of fighting, especially with you."

Her eyes soften. "I'm sorry—it's just that you've been so difficult lately, and—"

"*I've* been difficult lately? Me? Are you kidding? You're the one who kissed me and then pretended it never happened." Out of the corner of my eye, I see Orlando flinch. I guess neither of us had the courage to tell him. But I keep my eyes on Sarah. "You haven't even tried to be there for me after Jim got killed or after Jesse got blamed."

Sarah flushes, but ignores everything I just said. "Were you asking him to play with us?"

"For your information, *he* was asking *me* to play with him and Rose. He said they needed a fiddler for a bluegrass band."

Sarah looks like I punched her. "And what'd you say?" She's trying to sound angry, but fear is creeping into her voice now.

"I told him no, but you know what—since I've been *so difficult* lately, I'm going to go find him and tell him I will."

"Shady, that's not fair," Orlando says.

"No." Sarah speaks over him. "If she wants to play with them, let her. That's fine." Now she looks more like she's hugging herself than crossing her arms. She's hurt, jealous. But she'll never admit it. And her feelings really don't matter right now—mine do.

All my simmering anger at her boils over, and suddenly I'm yelling.

"God, you're supposed to be my best friend. And you don't even care that my brother is in jail, getting charged for my stepdad's murder. All you care about is that I'm talking to Cedar? Are you serious?"

"It's not my fault Jesse killed your stepdad," she spits back.

"Shit," Orlando mutters.

Sarah has always been blunt, but she's never gone this far. She looks as stunned by her words as Orlando is. She opens her mouth like she's going to apologize, but then she closes it again. It wouldn't matter if she apologized, anyway, because she meant it. She thinks Jesse's a killer. No kiss can make up for that.

My fingertips tingle, longing to slap Sarah's face. I take a step toward her, but Orlando throws an arm between us, his eyes pleading. "She didn't mean it, Shady."

Sarah doesn't say anything. She stands there looking lost, like she doesn't know how she got here.

"We're done," I say, and stalk away down the hallway, tears gathering in my eyes.

By the end of the day, I've mostly managed to put the fight with Sarah out of my mind and am looking forward to seeing Cedar. I wait at the end of the road, my fiddle case in hand. I feel foolish standing on a dirt road like this, but I panicked. I tried to wait for Cedar's truck on the trailer steps, but as the minutes ticked by, my fear and shame grew until I decided I'd just meet him up the road. Whenever a friend sees the trailer for the first time, I see it for the first time too. And through their eyes, I see every ugly thing. The aluminum steps, the antenna on the roof, the poor stupid ugliness of it all. I can see the words "trailer trash" dancing in their eyes.

And now that Jesse's in jail, what if Cedar pulls up and sees where we live and thinks, "Well, no wonder"? Again, the gnawing thoughts about Jesse's innocence rise in me. I've been denying Jesse's guilt since the moment he was arrested, telling everyone they're wrong, refusing every bit of evidence that Jesse could have done it. But what if I'm the one who's wrong? What if Jesse really did kill Jim? When Sarah said it in the hall, without a shred of doubt in her voice, it was like she slapped me. But it stings worse knowing a part of me believes it too. A small, disloyal part of me thinks Jesse could have killed Jim. Like Mama said, there's too much evidence.

When Cedar's truck comes barreling down the road, throwing up dust, I put out my thumb like a hitchhiker, pushing my hateful thoughts away.

Cedar slows down and pulls the truck up next to me. When I climb into the high cab, he smiles and turns down the radio. It's the local country station, all top-forty stuff.

"You're gonna have dirt in your hair standing out here like that."

"I got tired of being home."

Cedar nods. I figure everyone understands the desire to get away, even if they don't share my reason for it.

The inside of his truck cab is spotlessly clean. There's a half-finished Red Bull in the drink holder. A pair of sunglasses dangles by one arm from the passenger-side sun visor. Otherwise, this truck could have just rolled off a showroom floor. There's not even dust on the dashboard.

Cedar does a three-point turn and heads back for the highway, dirt flying up behind us. "We actually live pretty close to you," he says, pointing across the fields. "Out that way. We've got a farm."

"Peanuts or cows?" I ask, my eyes fixed on my blasted oak in the distance, which glows pink and orange in the fading sunset, like its heart still burns with the lightning that bleached its bones.

"Cows. And my dad breeds horses for the rodeo."

I wrinkle my nose at the mention of rodeo. But Cedar's looking ahead at the road and doesn't notice. "You still do calf roping?" I ask. I heard about Cedar's rodeo exploits last year, which is probably why I haven't had a crush on him like every other girl in school. I guess if I decide I don't like him after all, at least I've made Sarah jealous. At least I've hurt her a little bit like she's hurt me.

"Moving up to bronco riding now," he says, the barest note of pride in his voice.

"That's where you try to stay on a bucking horse?"

"Pretty much."

"Well, I guess that seems like more of a fair fight."

He cuts his eyes at me. "You don't like calf roping?"

"Seems mean," I say, shrugging. "Unnecessary."

He's quiet for a while, and I think I've offended him, but

when he speaks, his voice is thoughtful. "I used to think so, too, when I was a kid and I first started learning. I was afraid to hurt them." He glances at me to see my reaction.

"Why'd you do it then?" I sound more confrontational than I mean to. "Sorry, I mean, if it seemed wrong, why did you want to do it?"

Cedar rubs the back of his neck and stares at the road ahead. "I didn't. Not at first, but my dad . . . well, he didn't make me, but . . ."

"But he wanted you to, and that's as good as making you," I say. It's not a question. I know what men are like with their sons. Even Daddy was a lot harder on Jesse than he was on me. Aunt Ena was right when she said Jesse and Daddy didn't have an easy relationship. They were always rubbing each other wrong, especially where the fiddle was concerned. I don't think Jesse ever really wanted to learn to play—he was just trying to make Daddy happy.

Cedar nods. "But, I mean, I like the rodeo. It's different than anything else in life. It's not safe. It doesn't happen on a screen. It's real, you know?"

"I guess," I say, watching the fields and trees roll on forever. I wonder if Daddy's fiddle plays on in the pine woods, even without me there to hear it.

We're quiet for a long while, just the low noise of the radio—the DJs talking about a local barbecue place. I feel like I should try to break the silence between us. "What would your cattle-farming daddy say if he knew you were driving around with a vegetarian?"

Cedar looks at me sharply. “Girl, I will turn this truck around and take you home.” He tries to look serious and stern, but the corners of his mouth betray him. “Why on earth would you want to be a vegetarian?”

I sigh. I’m still not good at explaining my reasons. “Just seems like there’s enough death in the world without me adding to it,” I say. “Enough loss.”

Cedar’s smile turns soft and understanding. “That’s all right so long as you don’t try to keep me from ribs and hamburgers. Man’s gotta eat.”

I study Cedar. This is a boy wearing leather boots and a leather belt, driving a truck paid for by the sweat and blood and meat of animals, who spends his spare time roping baby cows and subduing horses.

Why don’t I hate him?

He was born into all of it, I guess. That’s part of it. We can’t help what we’re born into—I know that better than anyone. There’s also that sly smile and those slender hips. And there’s a kindness about him. He’s not what I expected.

“All right” is all I say.

“All right.”

“Where are you taking me anyway?”

“It’s a surprise.” He smiles that eye-crinkling smile and glances at me again.

“Looks like we’re heading for the springs.”

“Maybe so.”

The dirt road that winds up to the springs is lined with oak trees with more Spanish moss than leaves. The road’s always getting washed out when the river floods, so it's full of potholes big enough to rip off an exhaust pipe. When we pull into the parking lot, there's only one other car.

We head down toward the water. There's no stairs here like at the bigger, more popular springs. This place isn't well known, so it's pretty quiet, except on the weekends in the summer.

I stumble over a root, and Cedar catches my arm to keep me from falling. He runs his fingers down my forearm until they reach my hand, where he laces his fingers in mine like it's the most natural thing in the world. His fingers are rough and callused and still cool from the truck's AC.

I start to pull my hand away but then realize I don't want to. Mama would say he's being too forward, but I think touch just comes to him by instinct, like how he hugged Kenneth at the funeral. And I like the way his skin feels against mine—comfortable, easy. He's not asking anything of me. And it's reassuring after the week I've had.

"Thanks," I say, and Cedar smiles. He doesn't let go of my hand until we reach a sandy spot where there's a picnic table. Then he climbs up on the tabletop and pats the space beside him.

Side by side, we look out over the water, which is a deep blue, and glittering with the late afternoon sun. Springs are about the only natural feature our part of Florida can really brag about. The water's so clear you could drink it, and ice cold, which means it's about the only place around here you won't find alligators. There aren't any manatees either; you've got to go a little farther south for them. But that means the tourists don't flock here, don't fill up the banks with their sun chairs, don't clog the shallows with their floatie-wearing kids. This place, Little Spring, is just for the locals, and we love it the way it deserves to be loved. I spent all the summers of my childhood here, swimming in the shallow parts, away from the sharp, slippery rocks that warn you you're about to plunge into the cold, dark caves at the bottom of the springs.

It's still the most beautiful place I know, though I can't come here without thinking about Jesse, how he used to pull me through the cold water, closer and closer to the caves. I would scream, but I was never scared. He always stopped before we got close enough for him to throw me in. But Jesse always dived straight into the deepest water the moment we got here. He always seemed so fearless. Maybe that's why I felt safe with him, even when he was pretending to drag me to my death.

That's Jesse, though. He's always made me feel safe, even when he wasn't acting like himself. That's why the thought that he could do this monstrous thing—bash in Jim's head with a hammer—is too horrible to believe. If Jesse could kill Jim, he's not the person I thought he was. Everything else I know and believe about him stops being true. Doesn't it?

Cedar leans toward me, bumping my shoulder with his. "Whatcha thinkin' 'bout?" He's got those green eyes locked onto my face, and they flit toward my mouth.

I look away, my mind spinning with a sudden panic. "My daddy," I lie, because I don't feel like talking about Jesse. I can't talk about Jesse. "We came here a lot when I was a kid. He loved it here."

"He died when you were younger, right?" Cedar clears his throat nervously.

I nod. "Car accident. I was twelve."

"I'm sorry," Cedar says, and he sounds it. I hear more than sympathy in those two words. There's fear, too, and knowing. But he doesn't offer up any stories of his own.

I take a deep breath. "Thanks. You want to start playing?" I was trying to avoid talking about Jesse, but I don't want to talk about Daddy either.

"All right." His mandolin is out of its case and in his hands before I have even finished opening the clasps on my fiddle case.

"Eager," I say, teasing.

He cocks one eyebrow at me. "Always."

I laugh. "You're ridiculous."

"What's ridiculous is this song I'm about to play," he says. And then his fingers are flying over the strings and my heart is filling up, bigger and bigger, until I can't keep the grin off my face anymore. Cedar plays with this perfect blend of deliberateness and abandon, like he's bound to the music but as free as it's possible to be.

Watching his brow contract with concentration as he leans over his mandolin, playing fast enough to impress Ricky Skaggs or one of those other old famous bluegrass mandolin guys, I try not to fantasize about what else he might do with those hands.

I am getting pulled in, sucked in like a swimmer caught in a tide pool. I might still be able to scream and kick my way out, but I'm not sure I want to.

He looks up and catches sight of me, and I swear I must

look like a cartoon with enormous eyes and giant red hearts hovering over my head. Twitterpated, to quote *Bambi.* His eyes search my face and he leans toward me, and for a moment I think he's leaning in to kiss me, but he whispers, "Your turn." I'm relieved and disappointed at once.

I shake myself a little and then pull my fiddle up, its solid weight under my chin like a life preserver yanking me out of my own foolishness. Drawing the bow across the strings settles me even more, and I remember why I was interested in Cedar in the first place—and it sure wasn't for his cowboy charm. It was this music—this music I've been longing for, music that sent Daddy's messages swirling on the forest wind, that found me even in an open mic night in Kellyville.

I close my eyes and pull all my concentration into the fiddle. Cedar's playing again too, and we sound pretty good for just a mandolin and a fiddle, our instruments weaving and dancing like they've been playing together since they were slabs of wood. This is what I wanted—to play like this, to get wrapped up in music I love with someone else.

I open my eyes on the last note, and Cedar's staring at me, and I can see the little red hearts hovering over his head, too, unbelievable as that seems. I'm about to speak when someone starts clapping.

ELEVEN

We both whip our heads around, but it's only Kenneth. "What're you doing here?" Cedar says with a laugh, a cool cowboy again.

"Rose told me you'd be here. I brought my guitar." The head of a black cloth case sticks up over one of Kenneth's shoulders. "I didn't realize what I was walking in on though."

"That's all right. Isn't it, Shady?" Cedar asks uncertainly.

I give a resigned shrug, and Kenneth sits on the bench near my feet and unzips his case. He's got a Martin made of light-blond wood. It looks new.

"I gotta audition for this band?" Kenneth asks, squinting up at me, sun in his eyes, the afternoon light making his red hair blaze.

"Yeah, show us what you got," I say. I don't want to treat him any differently than usual—I hated how people did that to me after Daddy died, like I was suddenly breakable. And the way Kenneth handled himself at the funeral was actually kind of impressive.

"I'll play 'Rolling in My Sweet Baby's Arms' for you two lovebirds," he says. And then he's playing and singing, and I can see his "A Boy Named Sue" performance wasn't just because of the Vicodin—he's got one of those naturally drunk and raucous-sounding voices, like Roy Acuff.

"See, I'm not so bad," he says once he finishes with a G-run flourish.

"You sound better when you're not stoned," I say.

Kenneth shakes his head and gingerly touches a yellowing bruise under his eye. "That was a stupid night."

"I'm sorry Jesse beat you up like that." Jesse's anger, Jesse's strength—they've taken on a whole new meaning since his arrest.

"I left my phone in the truck," Cedar says. "I'm going to go get it and let y'all talk."

We watch Cedar sprint away. Kenneth looks back at me. "I shouldn't have said what I did. I can't believe I spent my last night with Dad like that."

"Kenneth," I say, my voice careful, "you don't believe Frank, do you? That Jesse killed Jim?" I just need one person who knows Jesse to say he didn't do it.

Kenneth looks away for a long moment and then meets my eyes. "I don't know what you want me to say. He was arrested. The police think he did it. And I don't really know Jesse all that well. I just bought pills from him a few times. Do you think your brother could have killed my dad? You know him better than I do."

Kenneth's gazing at me, his face open and vulnerable. He really barely even had a dad—Jim wasn't much of one to him after the divorce. And now whatever hope he had of a relationship with Jim is gone forever. But Mama told me to stand by Jesse, no matter what. And I know Jesse would stand by me.

"No, Jesse has his problems, but he's not a killer," I say as firmly as I can. "The police are going to figure it out."

Kenneth doesn't look convinced, but all he does is sigh. "I know I'm supposed to be angry and out for blood or whatever. But all I feel is sad. I feel so damn sad he's gone. I don't want to see Jesse get charged for it if he's really innocent. I'm sorry he's in jail."

I gaze back at him for a moment, stunned, and the tiniest bit lighter. "You're a good guy, Kenneth. You should stop trying to hide it all the time."

Kenneth looks down at his hands in his lap. His brow furrows as he turns his hands over and stares at his palms like he doesn't recognize them. Unease starts to spread through my chest, but then his face clears and he's his usual, goofy-looking self again. "You're just mad 'cause I kept howling at your girlfriend."

I laugh and slug his shoulder, already dismissing my moment of disquiet.

Cedar saunters back over. "Kenneth, me and Shady's going to play 'Blackberry Rag.' You think you can keep up?"

"Boy, I'll turn you into jam," Kenneth says.

I laugh and bring my fiddle up, ready to play again.

We speed through the rag so fast, our fingers are all fumbling on the strings, struggling to keep up. I'm almost panting by the end. I haven't felt this excited about music in so long. Haven't felt *happy* about it in ages. "Another!" I yell.

"Let's play 'Salty Dog,'" Kenneth says, and it takes all I have not to roll my eyes. I see exactly what kind of musician Kenneth is. "Come on, it's funny."

"Fine," I say with a sigh.

We play until the sun has almost set and the sky is shot with pink and red, until the buzz of mosquitoes and the drone of cicadas have joined our song. Kenneth says he'd better get home before his stepdad does, and takes off at a trot, leaving Cedar and me sitting here, holding our instruments but not playing, just staring at the spring, watching its surface darken with the sky.

"I should get home too," I say, smacking away a mosquito. "Honey will be wondering where I am." Having both Jim and Jesse gone has been hard on her. She's used to having a house full of people to dote on her.

Cedar nods, and we go back to looking at the water, neither of us moving to leave. There's a single pale star shining high in the dark-blue sky. The cicadas have amped up their electric singing, as if we were the opening act and they're ready to have the stage to themselves. But I'm still full of the music, the strings still vibrating from my fingertips to my heart.

"Shady," Cedar says, turning to look at me. I meet his eyes and almost wish I hadn't, because I'm getting pulled in again, drawn almost against my own will. "I like you. I know you've got a lot going on with your family right now, and I don't really know what's between you and Sarah." He blushes ever so slightly. "I don't want to make things more complicated. But I want to tell you I like you, and there's no rush at all, and no pressure. But . . ." His lips quirk into a smile. "But I really wanna kiss you right now." His ever-so-slight blush deepens. "Is that awful?"

All the air leaves my lungs, and I just stare at Cedar, taking in every detail of his face. He's not the one I've been longing for, but all the same, I really wanna kiss him too.

"So kiss me," I say, and he smiles, not the sly kind, but a new kind of smile I haven't seen yet, shy and sweet and wondering.

He leans in and cups my cheek with one hand, his face inches from mine and his eyes searching, questioning. I fill the space between us, and then our lips are touching. I can feel the prickliness of his stubble against my face, and I'm breathing in the smell of him—and he doesn't smell like cloves or starlight or any of the other nonsense boys smell like in romance novels—he just smells like a boy, but it's nice.

We kiss with only our lips at first, soft and sweet, and then he opens his mouth wider, and his tongue is in my mouth, and then his hands are in my hair, and I'm worried our instruments are going to go crashing to the dirt because it's like we've been caught up in a wind, and that wind's going to carry us wherever it's already going. I wrap my arms around him and feel the hard muscles of his back, the broadness of his shoulders. I run one hand up the back of his neck, across the short, sharp hair at his nape, fresh from the barber's shears. He shivers and kisses me harder, and it's like we're not two separate bodies anymore but a collection of atoms trying with all their might to join into one great big giant atom.

My phone rings, jolting me back to reality. The ringtone is

loud in the still twilight of the open springs, the sound echoing across the water. Cedar laughs against my mouth. "Better answer that."

Honestly, my first thought is that it's my daddy calling me from the grave, telling me to get away from that boy before his hands start wandering. But more likely it's my mama. I break away from Cedar and fish around in my bag until I find the phone.

It's a number I don't recognize, but I answer anyway. An automated voice comes on telling me I'm receiving a call from an inmate in a correctional facility. My heart starts to race.

I set up my phone so Jesse could call me from the detention center days ago, even though I figured he wouldn't want to talk to me. When the voice asks if I'll accept the call, I practically shout, "Yes." Then there are some mechanical clicks on the line, followed by a hollow space.

"Hey, it's me," Jesse says, his voice gravelly and tired.

"Oh my God, Jesse." Relief floods me at the sound of my brother's voice. "Jesse," I say again, a lump rising to my throat.

Cedar's eyes get big, and I turn away from him, a twinge of guilt in my stomach. Jesse's in jail and I'm kissing a boy at the springs.

"Are you okay?" I jump down from the table and start pacing by the edge of the water.

"Yeah, I'm fine. I'm calling to see if you and Honey are doing all right."

"We're fine too. But are you really okay? Are you safe?" I want to cling to the sound of his voice.

Jesse laughs. "I'm about to be a convicted felon, but otherwise I'm all right."

"Why do you say that? You're innocent," I say, but my voice wavers so much I might as well have added, *right?*

"If my own sister doesn't believe me, why should a judge?" Jesse says, sounding hurt.

"I do believe you. It's just . . ." I rub my eyes. How can I explain what's happening inside my head, my heart? "Anyway, you're only seventeen, so even if they charge you, you'll only go to juvie."

"They want to charge me as an adult. The world thinks I'm trash, Shady. I already have a record. My public defender is a joke. There's no way I make it out of this without going to prison."

The thought of Jesse in prison—locked away behind bars with dangerous men—turns my will to iron. "I'm going to make sure you go free."

"What's that supposed to mean?"

I walk away from Cedar, down around the side of the spring, so he can't hear. "I'm going to find out the truth."

"No, you need to stay the fuck out of this. You're forgetting that someone literally smashed in Jim's head with a hammer."

I pause, screwing up my courage. "Aunt Ena told me Daddy's fiddle's still out there, that it wasn't really destroyed when he died." The challenge hangs in the air.

"That fiddle can't help anyone," Jesse says coldly, no trace of surprise in his voice.

"Wait, you knew. All this time you knew what happened to

the fiddle. You knew it wasn't lost." If he lied about the fiddle, what else might he be lying about?

A man's voice in the background says something I can't hear. There's a sound like someone scuffling for the phone. "Just give me a fucking minute," Jesse growls at the voice, making me jump. "Shady," he says to me, fast and low, "you've got to leave it alone. Just leave it be."

"I heard it in the woods, Jesse. It's been calling to me."

There's a long silence. When he speaks again, his voice cracks with fear. "I knew there was something weird going on with you. I shouldn't have—"

"You shouldn't have lied to me."

"I don't have time for this. Just promise me you'll leave it alone."

I squat down at the spring's edge and trail my fingers in the cold water. A shock runs up my arm, like the night when I was little and held the elderly ghost's hand. "Don't you want to know what really happened to Jim?"

"It's not worth it."

"Your life's not worth it? If we know—"

Jesse's voice cuts across my question. "Promise me you're not going to mess around with the fiddle. It's not safe." When I don't answer, he starts swearing. "Promise me, right now, or I make a full confession saying I killed Jim and I planned it for weeks."

"What?" I bite out, splashing the water, startling an inch-long fish. It darts away like a stream of melted silver. "You can't do that."

"I will. I'll call my public defender right now if you don't promise me."

"Jesse, that's ridiculous."

"Promise me," he says, his voice desperate. I've never heard him so afraid.

What if Aunt Ena's right, and Jesse is too? What if the fiddle . . . ? Maybe I should leave it alone.

"Fine, I promise," I say, my voice still hesitant.

"Swear it. Swear it on Dad's grave."

"I'm not doing that."

"Swear it right fucking now."

I let out an enormous sigh. "I swear. But I don't understand why you won't—"

"I gotta go. Someone else needs the phone. I love you," Jesse says. Then he hangs up.

"I love you too," I whisper to the air. Because I do, no matter what he lied about, no matter what he did. Like Mama said, that's what you do for family. You love them and take care of them, not because they are always good or right, but because they belong to you.

TWELVE

Sarah slides into the desk next to mine in history the next morning and clears her throat. "Shady."

"Yeah?" I say without looking up. My head aches from thinking nonstop about Jesse and the fiddle. I don't have the energy for Sarah's hot-and-cold act today.

"I'm sorry. I've been a bad friend. I'm really, really sorry."

When I finally glance at her, her face is tense and full of guilt. Her eyes search mine, desperate to see forgiveness. My anger cools just a little. Can I really hold this against her when I've had the same thoughts about Jesse? After all, he's not her brother. He's mine.

Guilt makes me more forgiving than I would have been, but I'm still not going to make it easy for her.

"What are you sorry about?" I say, making my voice hard.

"What I said about Jesse. That was messed up." She bites her lip, and I can tell she's fighting not to defend herself. "And

I'm sorry for jumping on you about Cedar and everything. I guess—I guess I was worried you were going to bail on me, on Orlando and me, I mean."

When I don't say anything, she presses on. "And Orlando and I have talked about it a lot, and if you really want to play with Cedar and—and Rose, that's fine with us. You can be in two different bands if you want to."

"Really?" This isn't what I expected. Surprise softens my tone, and Sarah's voice sounds more hopeful when she speaks again.

"Yeah, or maybe—maybe we could all play together sometime. Just to see how it is."

My mouth almost drops open. "What about Rose?"

Sarah shrugs, flashing a dimpled, embarrassed smile. "That was a long time ago."

"I don't know," I say, excitement and dread swirling together inside me. A band like that is what I've wanted, but what about Cedar and me? Will Sarah still feel this way once she finds out there's more to us than just music?

"But I thought this was what you wanted," Sarah says, her smile faltering. Her brow knits, hurt showing in every line. "If playing with them is what you want . . . I—I don't want to lose you. As a friend, I mean," she adds hurriedly.

But her eyes say she didn't just mean as friends.

"Okay," I say, pushing through my confusion, my doubts. "Okay, yeah, let's do it."

And then she's smiling that dimpled smile again, and the longer I look at her, the more I wish she was the one I spent last night kissing. I really like Cedar, but Sarah . . . I've wanted to be with her for so long.

"You want to hang out this weekend?" she asks, pretending to pick a piece of lint off her T-shirt.

If I'm staying true to my promise to Jesse and leaving the fiddle alone, I need to find something to do besides worry. And spending time with Sarah again, like things are normal, feels like the best distraction I could ask for.

"I'll probably have to babysit, but you can come over—and Orlando. We'll watch a movie." Despite all the pain and doubt and anger I've been carrying around all week, a tiny seed of hope is bursting to life inside me. Maybe there's still a chance for Sarah and me.

I'm still smiling when I bang through the front door after school, but then Mama looks up from the cell phone in her lap, her face filled with a brand-new grief—something besides missing Jim. My little seed of hope's green shoots wither and die.

"What is it?" I say, my heart freezing.

Mama looks me in the eye. "I spoke to Jesse's public defender today."

Every last hopeful thought leaves me in a rush, like the time a boy at school punched me in the stomach and every ounce of air fled my lungs in a second, leaving me gasping on the ground, unable to draw a breath. I sink to the sofa. "What'd he say?"

"The state is offering Jesse a plea deal. If he confesses to the murder, he'll be tried as a juvenile."

"And if he doesn't?"

"They'll charge him as an adult and go for the maximum prison sentence. He could spend his whole life behind bars."

My hand goes to my mouth, thoughts already spinning through my head. "What does the public defender want him to do?"

"He thinks Jesse did it, so of course he wants him to plead guilty and take the deal. The thing is, he'd be transferred out of the juvenile center and into the adult prison as soon as he turns eighteen, so it doesn't mean he'll be safe." She crosses her arms like she's cold, but nobody's ever cold in a trailer in Florida.

"Do you know what Jesse's going to do?"

"If I were him, I'd probably take the deal."

"But he didn't kill anybody," I say, loud. Maybe if I keep saying it loud enough, I'll even convince myself.

"Shh, your sister's napping," Mama says, glancing down the hallway.

"Do you really think he could have done it, Mama?" *Please say no. Please.*

She closes her eyes, looking worn and ancient as the earth. "I honestly don't know. No mother wants to believe her son could do something like that. But Jesse's been out of my hands for a long time now. He's angry; he can't control himself."

Like when Kenneth whispered something, and a thread inside Jesse snapped. Like when he punched Kenneth, over and over again, smacking Kenneth's head against the floor.

He wasn't like that before Daddy died. When we were kids, he was gentle and sweet. I hurt him more often than he hurt me.

One of my earliest memories is sitting on the front porch of the old house crying over a skinned knee, and Jesse sitting with his arm around me, blowing on the stinging wound.

But I've got another image of my brother now, one I never saw but still can't quite shake: Jesse's hands around the handle of a hammer, his eyes wide as the metal comes arcing down.

I put my head in my hands, and the tears rise up out of me, hot and irrepressible. I'm crying for Jesse, but I'm crying for myself, too, for all I've lost and all I'm losing. Daddy's death blew a hole right through our lives. What will Jesse going to prison do to us?

Mama gets out of her chair and comes to sit beside me. She puts her arm around me and lets me cry until I'm done. She doesn't try to comfort me or tell me things are going to be okay, because she knows they won't be. All we can do is get through everything that's coming.

When I look up at her, her eyes glisten with tears, and I realize they aren't for Jesse or even for herself. They're for me, for the pain I feel. I hug her hard, and I don't let go.

I know I promised Jesse I'd leave the fiddle alone, but sitting here with Mama, I also know there are things more important than promises.

That night, I toss and turn in bed for hours, agonizing over what's happening to Jesse. When I finally slip into dreams, the shadow man comes too, with his freezing, choking grasp. Sometimes his face changes and he looks like Jesse, standing over me with hatred in his eyes. Twice I wake up coughing and gasping, trying desperately to take in air. After the second time, I stop trying to sleep. I climb out of bed and dress quietly, shivering, even though the room is warm. I go into the living room and pull on a pair of tennis shoes, lacing them with shaking fingers. While Mama and Honey sleep quietly in their beds, I let myself out the front door, into the warm spring night. Without a flashlight, I slip into the pines, following my usual path by habit.

I can't wait around any longer for the fiddle to find me. I can't let my doubt and my fear keep me from finding the answers that could bring Jesse home. I can't lie in bed doing battle with my nightmares while Jesse sleeps across town, probably doing battle with worse ones.

Daddy's done his part—now I have to do mine. I was getting distracted with Sarah and Cedar. But Jesse has to be my first priority now. I have to get him out of jail before he's sentenced. And I don't see any way to do that except with Daddy's fiddle.

THIRTEEN

The pine woods carried the fiddle's music to me, so that's the only place I know to look. It's about two in the morning, and the forest is black as pitch, the air close and clammy. Every step I take sends small animals scuttling out of my path. Wings brush my face and hair. My heart beats fast, the rush of blood in my head louder than my footsteps on the soft, springy ground.

I should be afraid, but there's no more room in me for fear, at least not of these woods and what they hold. Losing Jesse is all I fear right now.

So I walk and walk, deeper and deeper into the woods, but I hear no fiddle, no music—not so much as the wind in the trees.

I begin to sing—the first song that comes into my head—"Ain't No Grave," hoping that my voice will draw the fiddle out. The words swell and fill the forest night, and chill bumps erupt on my arms.

There ain't no grave can hold my body down

When I hear that trumpet sound
I'm gonna rise right out of the ground
Ain't no grave can hold my body down

It's a song about the Resurrection, but right now it feels like it's about Daddy's fiddle—and even buried under the ground or drowned in a lake, it can't be silenced. I throw my voice out with abandon, letting it waken every ghost in these trees.

I sing through the song twice before the fiddle answers, sliding over my voice with a long, drawn out note. I shiver and press on through the forest, following the sound.

Moonlight filters through the trees in fits and starts, spreading like quicksilver over the shadowy ground. The fiddle plays and plays and plays, until I expect all the ghosts in the forest to grow solid around me.

The fiddle's music builds in intensity until it's as frenzied as the night Daddy raised the old man's ghost, the night I realized what his music could do. My pace picks up too, until I'm running through the trees with abandon, not even worrying where I place my feet. The trees are little more than black columns, obstacles between the fiddle and me.

I run until my muscles are burning and I can barely catch a breath, and then I stumble on, unable to stop putting one foot in front of the other. The fiddle seems impatient, like it's dragging me behind.

And then, far ahead through the gloom, the world grows bright. I break through the trees, into the open air, and the moon stretches out across the lake, turning it into an enormous reflection of itself. The sky is pricked with thousands of stars.

After the darkness of the trees, it feels miraculous. I drop to my knees in the damp grass, chest heaving, breathing in the smells of mildew and lake water, grass and rotting plants.

This is where Daddy died, where his truck ran off the road and crashed into the water, killing him on impact. Where his fiddle supposedly sank and drowned, lost forever in the murky water.

The music beats against me, relentless, opening me up. I push to my feet, muscles weak and burning, and trudge down the long perimeter of the lake toward the road, where there's a dock and boat ramp. Water fills my tennis shoes, making every step heavier. I finally reach the dock and take my shoes and socks off to let them dry. Barefoot, I walk down the dock, my eyes on the center of the lake, where the moonlight glows brightest and the fiddle music seems to have concentrated.

I drop to the dock and wait, exhausted but exhilarated, every cell of my body tuned to the fiddle's music. The song has changed from frenzy to a low, almost unbearable wail, deep and mournful, the pain in it so evident tears burn my eyes.

The song shivers through me, an empty, aching melody I know, though I haven't heard it in four years. I won't find this song on Spotify or even on an old, forgotten album stashed in someone's basement. This song was never recorded. It was never heard outside our house.

It's one of Daddy's songs, probably the last he composed before he died. The music itself is almost unbearable—I think it would have made even Jim weep. But the look on Daddy's face when he played it was worse, a horrible mingling of grief and regret and rage. He played it over and over and over again in the days before he died, mostly out in the woods, but sometimes I'd catch him at it in the parlor. And then he'd look up at me but not see me, lost to emotions I couldn't comprehend.

I understand the song better now that I've lost him. I hear echoes of it in my own chest. If you could distill the feeling of losing the person you love most in the world down into a single song, this is what it would sound like. Anger and despair and something like betrayal. I wonder who Daddy lost to make him write a song like that.

Now I know without a doubt that the fiddle's here, beneath these waters, waiting for me to bring it back up. And Daddy's brought me here, led me straight to it. I stand to my feet and strip down to my bra and underwear. My muscles are shaking with fatigue, but that's nothing to me now.

I dive into the water the way Daddy taught me when I was a little thing, and dart through the murky depths like a fish. I let the momentum carry me far, far out into the lake before I shoot to the surface again for a breath of air. The fiddle plays on, its notes closer than ever, so close I can feel the vibration of the metal strings on my skin.

I cut through the water with swift strokes, heading farther out, until it feels like I'm inside the music, swimming in fiddle notes instead of lake water. And then, at the crisis of the song, when the highest note hangs trembling like a feather in the wind, I dive, straight down to the bottom, my eyes open but blind in the dark water. I kick harder, going deeper and deeper.

Finally, I touch the lake bottom and feel its sandy, slimy

silt running through my fingertips. I reach around, searching for the fiddle case, but my hands find only what feels like dirt and weeds and rocks. I keep searching until my lungs are so starved of air I'm getting light-headed. Then I push off the bottom, rocketing back up toward the light.

When I break the surface, gulping down air, the music stops. It doesn't even fade out like before, it simply cuts off like someone's thrown a power switch. Now I can hear the ghosts. Their murmurs reach me from shore, a tumult of whispered voices, lonesome as the moonlight on the lake's face. I can almost make out their words, like voices trying to press through radio static. They are troubled. Treading water, I feel suddenly how tired I am, how weak. The shore looks a thousand miles away.

One voice breaks from the throng of ghostly murmurs, a honey-gravel baritone as familiar to me as my own voice. I only catch one word—*Shady*—but I swim toward it, each stroke of my arms feeling like it's going to be my last. I'm nearing the dock, my strength almost gone, when I sense something behind me in the water. A lurking, silent something.

I pause and turn my head, catching movement in the silvery water. A long, heavy body cuts slowly and sinuously through the lake. At first it's only a shapeless mass, but then light glints off two black eyes, and a scream bursts from my mouth, scattering across the lake's surface.

Panic floods me, but I try to remember everything Daddy ever taught me about alligators, on all the afternoons we'd see them from the dock or drifting by us in the water while we fished. There are ways to behave around alligators, but I can't remember any of them now. Do I stay still or swim? Fight or flee?

Every nightmare I've ever had about the beasts races through my mind—finding myself in a gator-infested swamp, with hundreds of the reptiles between me and dry land. Walking by one unsuspecting, and having it lunge out of the vegetation-choked water with jagged mouth wide open. Being grabbed by one in the water and drowned in its death roll. I dreamed those dreams over and over again as a child, a recurring nightmare I couldn't shake.

The alligator swims steadily toward me, picking up speed, and my body takes over my mind, propelling me through the water as fast as my tired limbs can carry me. I swim faster and faster and faster toward the dock, and I'm so close, so close, so close—

The gator grabs me by the leg, biting into my calf. "Daddy," I scream, right before I'm yanked down into the water. Down, down, down, spinning through the dark. My mouth was open and now I have a mouthful of dirty lake water. I swallow it and try to hold my breath, but there's no air left. No air, no air, no air. The pain in my calf is a distant ache compared to the burning in my chest. I'm fading.

Is this what I get for promising Jesse I'd leave the fiddle alone? I swore it on Daddy's grave, and now I'm drowning in the place he died, my life coming to a close in the murky depths where his blood spilled out.

The police said he died on impact, so he didn't drown, but

did he feel this afraid, so afraid his terror became all that was left of him? My mind goes dark and blank and silent.

Then a melody pours through the blackness, carrying a wave of pain so strong I can coast on its back. It's Daddy's song again, that haunting, miserable tune that turned him from my daddy to someone strange and distant, unknowable.

A breeze blows over the water and hits my bare skin, making me shiver. And then Aunt Ena is looking down at me, her eyes wide and frightened. The melody drifts off with the breeze. I'm lying on the dock now, and I can feel every inch of my body. There is no wound in my calf. My lungs don't even hurt.

I would think I dreamed the whole thing if I weren't stripped to my underwear and soaking wet, my muscles like limp spaghetti. Aunt Ena must have dived in and rescued me.

"Do you see?" she says, her voice shaking. "Do you see now, darlin'?"

"What happened?"

"You almost drowned," she says, her voice so husky and low it's almost not her own. "You almost drowned for that—for that—for that goddamned fiddle."

"The alligator—you chased it away?"

"There wasn't any alligator, Shady."

"It dragged me under."

Aunt Ena shakes her head. "That fiddle dragged you under. Just like it did William. Why won't you learn?"

"Is it here? In the lake?"

"No," she says, loud. "No, it's not here. All that's here is your own grief, and mine."

"You were humming Daddy's song."

"The ghosts were humming it. The whole goddamned world was humming it. That's how I found you."

"He's here," I say. "I heard his voice, right before the alligator dragged me under."

"There wasn't any alligator."

"I drowned."

"You didn't. But you would have if I hadn't come and pulled you out. Don't you see? That fiddle's all darkness, all the way to its core."

"No," I say. "No. I heard his voice."

"You heard my voice, yelling from the dock."

I sit up and my head spins. Aunt Ena grips my elbows. "Did you inhale any water? Do you need to go to the hospital?"

"No," I say, though it makes no sense. I felt myself drown. I look back at the water. "It's still out there."

"Shady," Aunt Ena says, shaking me, hard, her fingers like iron digging into my skin. "The fiddle's not out there. That's not where we put it. You won't find it in this lake."

"Where *we* put it? Who's we?"

"Never you mind. We put it back where it came from, back where it belongs. So don't come here again, don't come back to this lake." She shakes me again.

"But Daddy—"

"Don't you remember the way that fiddle sucked your daddy in, how dark he got when he played it?"

"It wasn't always like that," I say. "And he wanted me to play it. He said he was going to teach me one day . . . before he died."

Aunt Ena shakes her head. "Sometimes even the people who love us most do us hurt."

I can't say anything else for another minute, but finally I ask, "You really don't think it's Daddy who's been drawing me to the fiddle?" Saying it out loud makes me feel so hollow, so lonesome.

If it wasn't Daddy . . . He admitted the fiddle had its dangers, that it laid the player open to ghosts, gave them more power over him than they normally would have. But to think there's something out there that means me harm, and that it could be using Daddy's fiddle to hurt me . . . My mind flits to the shadow man, his hungry, reaching hands.

"Aunt Ena?"

But she's not listening. "I've lost too much, Shady. Too much. Do you hear me?" she says. And then she's weeping, her body shuddering.

I put my arms around her and draw her close. We're both soaking wet and smell like lake water. But she clings to me all the same, clings to me like I was dead and came back to her, like if she can keep hold of me, I'll stay with her. And I cling to her too because my daddy was here, and now he's gone, and it's never going to stop feeling like my heart's been ripped from my chest and buried in this lake.

"Don't leave me again, Brandy," she sobs into my hair. "Don't leave me again."

I pull away. "Aunt Ena, who's Brandy?"

Her face is pale and washed out by the moonlight, but I see her features freeze. "I said 'Shady.'" She pauses, and then her voice grows surer. "Shady Grove."

Aunt Ena's had a bad scare, so I let her slip go. Whether there was a real alligator or not, I would probably be dead now if Aunt Ena hadn't come in time to rescue me. I'd have drowned, if only from my own fear. And that thought terrifies me worse than anything. What sort of being has the power to warp your thoughts so terribly that you'd drown out of pure fear?

I thought Jesse was the one in danger, but maybe he's not the only one. Maybe I am too.

FOURTEEN

I'm dead tired when I get to school the next day. Every muscle in my body aches from last night's . . . haunting. That's what I'm calling it. It was a haunting and there's no other word for it. If it wasn't Daddy drawing me, then who was it? And if not to help Jesse, then why? To hurt me? I feel more alone than I've ever felt before, empty and lost and scared. More like a ghost than a girl.

I trudge past the office building, dreading sitting through a day of classes that are meaningless compared to what's going on with Jesse and the fiddle. Then someone reaches out a tanned, freckled arm and snags me by a belt loop. I startle, ready to fight off whatever nightmare's come after me this time. But it's only Cedar, and he's smiling and pulling me gently toward him.

"Hey," he says, flashing a smile that makes me feel a little more tethered to this earth.

"Hey yourself," I say, eyeing him uncertainly. We lean

against the brick wall side by side, watching kids pour off the yellow buses.

"You're quiet. And I know I'm not supposed to say this to girls, but you look tired. Did you have a rough night? Or were you up thinking about me?" he asks, smiling that sly smile.

I almost roll my eyes, but I don't have the heart for banter today. "A rough night, yeah. It looks bad for Jesse," I say, tears starting again. And bad for me, too, but I don't know how to explain that to Cedar. I don't even know how to explain to myself what happened last night at the lake and what it means.

"I'm sorry." The moment he sees my tears, he pulls me against him with gentle hands.

I had planned to tell him our kiss was a bad idea, but instead I rest my cheek against his neck, and he lays his face against my hair. I feel rather than hear him sigh. We barely know each other, but already this feels natural and easy. Like slipping into a favorite pair of shoes—familiar, comforting, safe. Not because he's a boy and I'm a girl. But because he's Cedar, I guess. And right now, with everything that's weighing on me, a little safety and comfort is exactly what I need.

I try not to think too hard about how being with Cedar means whatever chances I might have with Sarah will disappear, even though the idea sends a tiny shot of panic straight to my heart.

"Well, *I've* been thinking about that kiss," he whispers into my hair, his voice drawing me back to him.

I lift my head and look at him, and he's so beautiful and solid and *here* that I can't help but rise up on my tiptoes and kiss him on the cheek. He lifts one side of his mouth into a smile and turns his head, lowering his face until we're nose to nose. He kisses me lightly on the lips, and that cold emptiness inside me warms.

"You smell like coffee," I say, wrinkling my nose and pulling away. That's when I catch sight of Sarah, standing stock-still on the sidewalk staring at us. My heart drops into my stomach, and I take a step away from Cedar.

She shakes her head and walks off fast, eager to put some distance between us.

"Shit," I whisper. I should follow her, I should explain. But Cedar's still got a hand wrapped around my arm, and I'm not ready to let go of this warmth, this safety. I'm not ready to throw myself into another battle.

He glances between Sarah and me, unsure. I can almost see the questions forming behind his lips, but he doesn't ask any of them. "You should go talk to her" is all he says. When he mentioned my relationship with Sarah that night at the springs, I didn't tell him what's between her and me. He still doesn't know how much I feel for Sarah, or what she feels for me. But he has probably guessed.

The thought of facing her right now, facing all that anger and betrayal I saw in her eyes . . . "I'll talk to her tonight. She's coming over with Orlando to watch a movie."

"Am I invited?" he asks lightly, but there's a smidge of jealousy in his voice.

"Probably not a great idea," I admit, watching Sarah disappear around a bend in the hallway, taking a little chunk of my heart with her. I thought I'd have more time to make up my mind, but I guess it's made for me.

That lost feeling settles into my chest again.

As soon as I step off the school bus at home, the fiddle's wild cry catches my ear, saying *follow, follow, find me*. But I ignore it, hurrying home up the dirt road, like the alligator's on my tail, my pulse pounding a steady rhythm in my head. I slam the front door and turn on the TV to make sure I drown out any notes that followed me inside. I don't trust that sound anymore.

Mama leaves for work at six, and I manage to get Honey in bed before eight, right before there's a knock at the door. Orlando's standing outside gazing up into the sky, holding a Tupperware container. "Thunderstorm's coming," he says.

"Where's Sarah?" I ask, even though I knew deep down she wasn't going to come.

Orlando squeezes past me into the trailer. "She said she wasn't feeling well."

"And you actually bought that?"

"Why wouldn't I?" He pushes up his glasses with his ring finger, the gesture as familiar to me as my own face in the mirror. Suddenly, I want to confess everything.

"She saw me with Cedar today."

"So?" he says, sprawling on the couch, long, lanky limbs filling every inch of furniture. He holds out the container. "Pastelitos, from my abuela."

"Thank you," I say, accepting the food. I open the lid and inhale the sweet smell of pastry. "Ooh, guava and cheese. I love these. Give Mrs. Ortiz a kiss for me."

Orlando reaches into the container and swipes a pastry, shoving it into his mouth with a groan.

"Anyway," I say, "about Cedar. We were together, you know, *together*."

Orlando's eyebrows rise toward his hairline in a perfect imitation of Sarah. He swallows the sticky pastry and wipes his mouth. "You and rodeo boy, huh?"

I shrug and take a bite of a pastelito, closing my eyes at the heavenly taste. It's almost good enough to make me feel less miserable about Sarah. I should save one to take to Aunt Ena.

"That's good. It was never going to happen with you and Sarah anyway."

His words sting, but Orlando doesn't know everything. I push the remark away, clinging to my stubborn hope. "It could happen. We kissed, remember? It was a really good kiss," I add.

Orlando snorts, and my desire to confess everything disappears. I throw a pillow at his head. "Let's just watch the movie." Maybe there's no use talking about it. Sarah's never going to open up to me like that again. Anyway, this isn't what I should be thinking about—I should be thinking about Jesse, and finding a way to get him out—without the fiddle's help, I guess, since I nearly drowned going after it. Since Aunt Ena's probably right, and it wasn't Daddy drawing me.

But if it wasn't him . . . I think I know who it might be, and the thought turns my worries about Sarah and Cedar to nothing. If it's him, if he's found a way out of my nightmares . . . I shiver and drop into the recliner, hugging my knees to my chest.

We're halfway through a mediocre fantasy movie when the storm outside kicks up in earnest. The power flickers in and out, in and out, reminding me horribly of my dreams. Lightning flashes in between rumbles of thunder.

I want to hide under a blanket, but instead I go to the window and peer out. A strike of lightning illuminates the trees, which are tossing in the wind. I can hear them rustling in the quiet spaces in the movie, when the actors stop speaking, the weapons stop clashing.

"Does the same tree ever get struck by lightning twice?" I ask Orlando, but he's asleep, his mouth hanging open. If my favorite tree goes down tonight . . . If that tough old tree falls, what chance do I have to stand against everything trying to tear me down?

Without thinking about it, I start to hum "The Old Oak Tree," as if my music can keep it safe from the storm. I tried to find the words to the old murder ballad a few years ago, since Daddy would never sing them. I had to search for hours, sifting through obscure ballads on useless webpages until I found it on a university website. The ballad tells the story of a girl who sneaks out on a cold, dark, rainy night to meet a man and then goes missing. Her mother searches and searches for her, but she's vanished without a trace. Her mother dies of a broken heart. Weeks later, a squire and his dog find the girl's body, stabbed and buried, under an old oak tree. When they confront her killer, he shoots himself and dies. He's buried right there where he killed her, and no priest will bless his grave. It's no wonder Daddy would never sing it for me.

It was a struggle to put the lyrics to the melody. But I managed it, and I sing the words to myself now, though sometimes the thunder roars so loud it drowns out my voice. As I finish a verse, I trail off in thought.

Beneath the old oak tree . . .

After what happened at the lake, I should do like Aunt Ena said—get on with my life. But as I stand at the window watching lightning scatter across the heavens and rain drive through the trees, the thought draws me as surely as Daddy's fiddle. "What if . . . ," I whisper to myself.

Aunt Ena said they put the fiddle back where it belonged, where it came from. But surely she didn't take it back to Ireland, back to Daddy's ancestors. She must have meant something else. Somewhere else.

She thinks the fiddle is death and darkness. She thinks it's rotten to its core. And yet I'm drawn to it just like I'm drawn to that old lightning-struck tree that made my daddy hum a murder ballad every time he drove by . . .

I open the trailer's door and peer out into the storm. Rain dashes against my face, wind hurls back my hair. The forest is full of shadows, and the trees toss and moan. I shouldn't go out in this storm, but an idea has taken hold of me, the rightness of it running like static electricity through my limbs, popping in my muscles, making me unable to keep my seat.

My good sense finally kicks in and I close the door, but then I open it again, listening for the fiddle. When I finally catch it between rumbles of thunder, I could swear it's playing "The Old Oak Tree."

I make sure Honey and Orlando are still asleep, and then, like the girl from the song, I put on a raincoat and slip out the door into the dark, stormy night. The rain is beating down hard, the driveway already turning into a river. I run around to the little shed behind the trailer and search for a shovel. All I can find is a small hand spade Mama used once for planting flowers, but I take it and set off down the road, dodging puddles.

The lightning illuminates my path every few minutes, but I know the way without it. I try to walk fast, concentrating on not falling into a rainwater-carved rut, but between the expectation thrumming through me and the roar of the storm, I can't help but run. My tennis shoes smack the road, sending splatters of mud halfway up my back. Soon, my chest is heaving, but I can't stop.

Finally, in a flash of lightning, the oak tree looms ahead of me. I run past it to find a gate, and let myself into the field. It's more like a marsh now, the high grass sodden and treacherous. I trip twice, falling to my hands and knees, but finally I fight my way to the lightning-struck tree that stands bare and white in the midst of the darkness like a beacon in a storm-tossed sea.

Of course. It's always been a beacon. I haven't loved it all these years for nothing.

I put my hand on the trunk and feel my way down to the roots, searching the ground for a soft place. Once I find a space free of roots, I start digging like the squire and his hounds from the ballad. Water fills the hole as fast as I can empty it, and after a few minutes, I abandon the spot and try another, and then another.

But then lightning and thunder meet above my head in a

roar of light and sound that makes me scream and fall to the muddy ground, shielding my head with my arms against the blue-white glare, waiting for tree limbs to fall on me. The thunder cracks again, and the backs of my tightly squeezed eyelids flash white. If I were brave enough to lift my head, I'd see clear across the field, the lightning is so bright.

But the tree is still whole, and I'm not dead, so I pull myself from the mud and pick up my spade, trembling against the assault of wind and rain, any bravery in me shattered. The only thing that keeps me from flying back to Mama's trailer is the thought of Jesse in a jail cell across town, listening to a storm he can't see.

I keep digging, and finally, long after my arms begin to ache, long after my knees feel bruised, my spade strikes something hard. It could be a rock, but I know it isn't. Carefully, carefully, I dig around it with my hands, trying to ignore the lump forcing its way up my throat. This could be Daddy's fiddle, the answer to all my questions.

With shaking arms, I unearth the object, which is encased in plastic, and hold it up to the light. It's the right size for a fiddle case, but it's too wrapped up to be sure. But it must be. Of course it is.

I tuck it under my arm, my heart thundering in my chest, and start for home. The rain starts to let up as I near the trailer, but the lightning still forks across the sky. I let myself into the trailer quietly. The movie's over, the credits rolling down a dark screen. Orlando is still asleep, snoring quietly.

I throw my raincoat over a chair and kick off my muddy

shoes, but I'm too excited to bother changing out of my wet clothes. Instead, I take the parcel down the hallway to the bathroom and sit on the floor with it, waiting for the trembling in my limbs to stop. The plastic is thick and tough, but after a few tries I rip it open and pull it off, mud and grass falling away with it.

And there is Daddy's fiddle case, black and battered, covered in scratches.

But whole.

A sob catches in my throat but I force it back down. With trembling fingers, I unlatch each of the rusting clasps, half afraid some dark creature's going to come leaping out at me. But when I open the lid, only the smell of home wafts out—must and dust, Daddy's aftershave, and the barest hint of cigarette smoke.

The fiddle lies against the green velvet, its bow clipped into the top of the case, as quiet as if it's just been lying there forgotten all this time. As if its music hasn't been chasing me through forests and lakes, drawing me and drowning me, threatening all I am.

I pull it out of the case like it's a newborn baby I might drop, fragile and dangerous at once. I lay the fiddle in my lap and stare down at it. Daddy's fiddle. Not lost, not dark. The wood still gleams, and the strings aren't rusted. It looks exactly like it did the last time Daddy put it away. After all this time, it's whole and bright and beautiful.

Do the strings remember the last notes he played? Is the music still trapped inside the wood?

After so long underground, the fiddle's strings should be loose and out of tune. But when I touch the A string with one finger, it gives out a single, soft note. A shiver runs up my arm.

Someone says my name, startling me. It must have been Orlando. I get up and listen at the bathroom door, to see if he'll call again.

Shady Grove, the voice says, light as a breeze drifting through a window. *My little love.* It's a man's voice, but not Orlando's.

It's a voice as familiar to me as the fiddle in my hands. A voice with the timbre of a Johnny Cash album dipped in honey.

"Daddy?" I whisper, disbelief and longing at war in my chest.

His words pour out, from a source I can't see, can't find. *Shady Grove, don't you forget what I taught you. Ghosts aren't all gentle and innocent. Some of them have got murder and vengeance on their minds, and some are so bitter they'll try to pull you back down to hell with them. Don't you go playing that fiddle until you're ready, baby. And I can tell you right now, you're not ready.*

Daddy.

There's a long pause filled with the rustle of a pine-scented breeze. *Be careful, Shady Grove. I miss you and I love you.*

Before I can speak, the voice is gone, the room is still. A swoop of grief goes through me.

Then Honey lets out one long, terrified shriek from our room on the other side of the wall. I drop the fiddle in its case and scramble out of the bathroom.

When I flip on the lights in our room, she's sitting up in bed, her eyes open and staring, her mouth open in a never-ending scream.

I rush to her and take her in my arms, sitting down on the bed. "Shh, Honey girl. Shh, I'm here," I say, but she goes on screaming.

Orlando comes thundering down the hallway and peers in. "What's wrong?" he yells, eyes darting around the room, looking for an intruder.

"I don't know." I turn Honey so she's facing me, and she keeps screaming, right into my face, her eyes open and staring.

"Oh my God," Orlando yells. "Get out now, get out."

I leap to my feet and race for the door with Honey in my arms. Orlando slams it behind us. The moment the door shuts, Honey stops screaming.

"What was it?"

"Wasps," Orlando says. "A bunch of them. There must be a wasp nest in the room somewhere."

Honey's quiet now but shaking in my arms, her eyes still staring straight ahead. There's a growing red welt on one of her cheeks. "I want Jesse," she whimpers.

Orlando touches her face with gentle fingers. "Looks like one of them got her. Is she allergic?"

"I don't think so."

"Check her for more stings," he orders, leading us to the living room.

The rest of Honey's body is unmarked. Her eyes have cleared.

"You okay, Honey girl?"

She nods, but her bottom lip trembles. "Bad dream. I want Jesse," she says again, wringing my heart.

"Jesse's on a trip, remember?" That's all we could think to tell Honey—that Jesse was traveling. "But I'm here. You had a bad dream?" I ask, my voice gentle. Honey's always having vivid dreams that she struggles to put into words. Her vocabulary hasn't caught up with her imagination.

She nods. "Bugs. Lots of bugs with wings." She whimpers.

Orlando's brow scrunches together.

"And dark. It was dark," she says, her voice tinged with hysteria. I hold her close to my chest until she seems calm, and then I sit next to her on the couch. She slumps against me with her thumb in her mouth, exhausted.

Now that Honey's calm, Orlando's worried expression is turning to curiosity. "I'm going to go take a look," he says, slipping down the hall.

"Orlando, be careful," I call.

I hear the bedroom door creak open, and then silence. "Huh," Orlando finally says.

"What?"

"They're all dead."

I jump off the couch and join him in the room. There are dozens of dead wasps scattered over the carpet. Orlando lifts one carefully into his palm and studies it. "It's an eastern yellow jacket," he says. "I don't understand what happened. Wasps don't just fall dead out of the air."

"Is there a nest in here?"

Orlando runs his hands along the walls and gazes up at the ceiling. "No, not that I can see. It could be inside the wall, I guess. You guys should get it checked before you sleep in here again." He puts his ear to each wall and listens for a long time. "The natural history museum in Gainesville had an exhibit on Florida wasps. Yellow jackets are really, really aggressive, and their nests can be huge."

My skin tingles like the wasps are buzzing over my arms. I felt the same thing a few weeks ago but couldn't place the sensation. But now I know what my skin remembers.

"Do you mind if I take these home?" Orlando asks, going back to the living room with dead wasps cupped in his palms. "I want to study them a bit more."

"Fine," I say. Sarah would make a sarcastic comment now, but my mind's not on Orlando—I'm thinking of something that happened in the weeks before Daddy died. I kept dreaming about wasps, and finally one night the wasps came out of my dream and chased me from my bed. I ran downstairs to get Daddy, who was playing his fiddle, and when he went upstairs, all the wasps were dead.

Later, I decided the wasps had already been in my room and that's why I dreamed about them, like when you need to pee at night and dream you can't find a bathroom. I figured I'd still been dreaming when I ran downstairs.

But now I know, it must have been the fiddle. The fiddle must have brought the wasps, and the music gave them life. It doesn't make sense, but they came when Daddy played, and then when I plucked a single note they appeared for Honey.

I shudder. This means Jesse wasn't overreacting, and neither was Aunt Ena. I can't believe I didn't realize it before.

What else can the fiddle bring?

I gaze at my little sister's bed.

I did this, with one flick of the fiddle's strings.

I rush to the bathroom and lock the fiddle in its case. I slide it under my bed, slam my bedroom door, and hurry to the living room to take my sister up in my arms. I hold her close and feel our hearts beating together. "They won't hurt you again," I promise, but Aunt Ena's words ring in my ears. Sometimes the people who love us most do us hurt.

"Wait, why are you all muddy and wet?" Orlando asks once Honey wriggles her way out of my arms. He cocks his head at me, taking in my bedraggled appearance and the fear in my eyes. "What's going on?"

How do you tell your best friend you just dug up your dead father's fiddle in a thunderstorm? You don't. Especially if your best friend is a science-loving agnostic. Orlando doesn't like to talk about the supernatural. His grandma is very superstitious, but he has tried hard to distance himself from anything science can't explain.

"I took out the trash, and fell in a puddle," I say. "I'll go change." I leave the room before he can ask more questions, but I feel his eyes follow me down the hallway. There's another pair of eyes on me, keener than Orlando's, seeing deeper than he ever will, but I don't know whose they are.

I hope they're Daddy's, but I don't think so. Not anymore.

Because I know that was Daddy's voice in the bathroom, and

he came to warn me. I might not listen to Jesse or Aunt Ena, but I have to listen to him. He said there were spirits who would drag me down to hell. He said I wasn't ready to face them.

The same spirit who led me to a rattlesnake, who tried to drown me in the lake, who sent wasps to sting my baby sister—he's the one who's watching. He's the one who's been playing Daddy's fiddle. Who's been playing me.

If I let him, he'll take all I have.

FIFTEEN

I don't pull the fiddle out again all weekend. I want to—my fingers itch for the strings—but I leave it where it is, no matter how desperately it calls to me. No matter how badly I want to prove Jesse's innocence. I ignore Aunt Ena's phone calls, and on Saturday morning, I drop her groceries on the front porch so I won't have to see her. I don't tell anyone about the fiddle or the wasps. I try not to think about Jim's ghost or Jesse in his cell. Daddy said I wasn't ready—and he was right.

But by Sunday evening I can't stand it anymore. I can't keep anything fixed in my mind except that velvet-lined case underneath my bed. My desire to play the fiddle has turned from want to need. I know it's dangerous and I know I should put it back in the ground it came from, but all I want is to hear it sing. The craving thrums through me, stronger than my desire to kiss Sarah, stronger than the urge to wrap my body around Cedar's.

I pace my tiny bedroom, back and forth, back and forth, my mind wavering with my steps. What did my daddy mean when he said I'm not ready? That I'm not strong enough? That I'm too weak to rule such a powerful instrument? Or that I'm not ready for what will come when I play?

All the answers I need lie just underneath the fiddle's strings, waiting to be released. But more than that, some part of me that has been sleeping all these years is awake now, and it's greedy for the fiddle's music.

But if it's a dark spirit doing all this, if it's something Daddy doesn't want for me after all, I have to resist, don't I? I can't put others in danger to satisfy my own cravings, my own needs. I have to think of Honey.

I leave my room in a rush, before I do something stupid. Before I give in to the dark spirit trying to drag me down with him. I'm halfway down the hallway when someone knocks on the front door. I didn't hear anyone pull up outside, and it's just Honey and me at home.

Mama doesn't like me to answer the door to strangers when she's at work, but when I glance out the hallway window, Frank's truck is parked out front. A crash of conflicting emotions hits me—anger, annoyance, worry, but underneath all that there's the old familiarity of Frank. Solid, dependable, everyday Frank. So I take a breath and pull open the front door.

I have to crane my neck to meet his eyes, he's so tall. Frank gives me a grim smile, and I step back to let him in. Honey jumps up from her coloring book with a squeal. "Uncle Frank!" She launches herself into his legs, and he bends down and lifts her, drawing her close to his chest.

Honey wraps her arms around Frank's neck and squeezes tight.

"Hey, sweetheart," Frank croons into her hair. The knot of worry in my belly loosens.

"Your mama here?" Frank asks me.

"She's at work. She's had to pick up extra shifts since . . ." I don't know how to finish the sentence without bringing up Jim.

Frank nods and squeezes his eyes shut. He puts Honey down and goes to sit at the kitchen table. Honey follows him and crawls into his lap. She must be missing Jim more than I realized.

"I came by to apologize," Frank says, rubbing a hand over his face. His wedding band flashes in the light. He looks down at it and sighs. "I shouldn't have said what I did at the funeral. I was angry and looking for people to blame." He meets my eyes. "I'm sorry. Will you tell your mama that for me?"

"I will," I say, taking the chair adjacent to him.

"Are y'all doing all right?" Frank asks.

I nod. "Honey is confused and sad sometimes, and it's been hard on Mama. But we're getting by."

"If you all need anything, anything at all, you know you can call me, right?" Frank says. He gives Honey a hug, and she burrows into him.

"All right," I say, softening toward him. "Thank you." Maybe Frank really does regret what he said to Mama, maybe he's even sorry for how quick he was to blame Jesse for Jim's death.

“I’d hate to think the way I acted at Jim’s funeral made y’all think I don’t care about you,” Frank says carefully.

Now I have to ask. “Does that mean you don’t think Jesse—”

Frank shakes his head. “No, I still do. I know it was him. But your mama didn’t deserve how I acted at the funeral. It’s not her fault.”

“Why are you so sure it was him?” I ask, my temper flaring.

But Frank doesn’t notice my anger. He runs his fingers absently over Honey’s hair. “Jim and Jesse were a time bomb, just waiting to go off. I saw it every day at work, Shady.”

I clench my jaw. “I just don’t believe my brother could do something like that.”

“I used to feel that way about Jim, too,” Frank says, his voice quiet. “I used to think better of him. Before he started drinking and carousing. But after he showed his true colors one too many times, I had to accept who he was.”

“Jim wasn’t that bad,” I say. I don’t know why I suddenly feel the need to defend him.

Frank smiles sadly. “There’s a lot you don’t know, Shady. You’re too young and sweet to know half of what’s in men’s hearts.”

“I might not have known Jim as well as you did, but I know Jesse. He’s innocent. And that’s going to come to light, one way or another.”

Frank sighs. “You’re a good sister. But soon you’re going to find out—”

My stomach tightens. “What? Did something new happen?

What do you know?" I lean forward in my chair, squeezing my hands so hard it hurts.

"You shouldn't have to hear about this," Frank says.

"Just tell me."

Frank picks Honey off his lap. "Go draw me one of those pretty pictures, baby," he tells her.

Once Honey's out of earshot, Frank leans toward me. The anger in his eyes is still there, sharp and true, but there's something more now, too—regret and heartache. "There was a man from the power company working on the electrical lines. He had pulled up near the construction site just as Jesse was running out the front of the house where they found Jim. He came forward to the police this morning."

"So?" I say, even though the knot in my stomach is so tight I can hardly breathe.

"So, he saw that Jesse had blood on his hands. The man thought it was just paint, but looking back, he realized it was blood."

I push my chair back and spring to my feet. "No. No, he was wrong. Or he's lying. Jesse would never—" A sob crawls up my throat.

"I'm sorry, sweetheart." Frank stands and puts a hand on my shoulder, but I shake it off.

"Please go," I say, looking toward the front door. "I've got to get dinner ready for Honey. It's her bedtime soon."

Frank sighs and walks past me. "I really tried to do right by Jim, you know? He made it almost impossible, but I really tried. Some people are just determined to tie their own noose."

"Sure," I say. "See you later." I close the door behind him. Maybe I should have been kinder, but all I can think about is Jesse with blood on his hands. Jesse with another damning piece of evidence hanging over his head. And it's yet another person saying I'm wrong to believe Jesse, yet another voice trying to break down my confidence in my brother.

The moment Mama gets home and goes to her room to change, I snatch the fiddle from underneath the bed, tuck it under my arm, and march into the woods, far, far away from the trailer.

That will keep Honey safe. Or at least I need to believe that it will because I've got to play this fiddle, not for my own sake or any evil spirit's. For Jesse. For my brother.

Daddy didn't say I couldn't ever play the fiddle. He said I shouldn't play it until I'm ready. But what if Jesse doesn't have that long? This is the only way I have to help him. I open the clasps and lift the lid, sucking in my breath when the wood gleams in the fading light.

Gingerly, gingerly, I lift it from the case and bring it up to my chest. With a racing heart and trembling fingers, I tune the instrument, thinking how Daddy's were the last hands to turn these pegs, his fingers the last to hold this bow.

And then the instrument is ready and waiting for me to play. It's not too late—I could still put it back in the case and close the clasps. But instead, I take a deep breath and draw the bow across the strings.

The notes pour out like a dark-brown river, carrying a drowned girl away. My breath catches in my chest. I'm playing

"The Twa Sisters" exactly the way Daddy played it, as if I carry every ounce of the drowned sister's fear and shock, every ounce of the killer's shame. It's beautiful and haunting, exactly how it's meant to be.

I am tensed for wasps or worse, but I make it through the whole song. The music fades into the forest, and nothing happens. The cicadas pick up where my fiddle left off, the sun goes down, and no ghosts appear. Daddy didn't raise a spirit every time he played either. There must be some secret to it, a secret I'll learn soon. A secret I have to learn.

My cell phone dings in my pocket, and it's a text from Sarah. Orlando must have been working his peace-making magic on her.

Band practice soon? You can invite Cedar and Rose.

I can't imagine what it cost her to send this text, to let me have the band I want when it's bound to be painful for her. Her history with Rose is bad enough, but now with me and Cedar . . . This is the most selfless thing Sarah's ever done for me. Maybe for most people it wouldn't be a big deal, but it's a huge thing for Sarah, giving ground like this. I blink away the tears that try to start in my eyes. I can't let myself go weak now. Not when there's this much at stake.

All that matters is learning to play Daddy's fiddle—to play it for what it's made for, to use it to raise Jim's ghost. No matter how dangerous, no matter what it costs.

Maybe with my band's help, I can learn to make the fiddle do my bidding. Maybe if I love it enough, play it enough, I can burn the darkness right out of it. And then I'll set Jesse free.

⁂

I get to Sarah's early, and Orlando's Honda is already in the driveway. Sarah's black Lab, Trouble, jumps all over me when I let myself in.

"You are a terrible guard dog," I tell her. She keeps licking my hands.

"Shady?" Sarah calls from the kitchen, and I find her pouring bags of chips and pretzels into serving bowls like a hostess, which makes me laugh. Orlando's sitting on a stool beside her shoveling the food into his mouth as fast as she can get it into the bowls.

"What?" Sarah knits her eyebrows.

"Nothing," I say, eyeing her. We still haven't talked about the day she saw Cedar and me together. I think she's choosing to pretend it never happened, just like our own kiss.

But I'm not being particularly forthcoming either. I know I shouldn't be bringing everyone here without telling them what my fiddle is, what it does. But if I tell them, they might not want to help me. And Sarah might reject me once and for all. Might decide that my family and I are too much, too strange, too complicated to fit into her world.

Besides, this isn't a haunted house or a forest filled with ghosts. It's an ordinary house in suburbia, and I've never felt a spirit here. It's a safe place—far from all the ghosts I know. Sure, some ghosts can travel, but I need to believe that the dark spirit won't follow me here. That there's somewhere I'm safe from him. A place I can learn to use Daddy's fiddle, to master it, before I go looking for ghosts to raise.

The thought of Jesse and that witness who said there was

blood on Jesse's hands, that's enough to push my guilt and misgivings away. I have to use the fiddle, no matter the risks.

The doorbell sounds, pulling me from my thoughts, and I go answer it. Cedar's standing at the door with Kenneth and Rose.

"This is my sister, Rose," Cedar says unnecessarily.

"Hey, I'm Shady. Sarah's in the kitchen."

Then Rose does that thing girls do where they flit their eyes from your shoes to your hair, sizing you up, or judging your outfit or whatever. Her mouth tightens, so I guess she's not impressed, but she says, "Nice to meet you." Kenneth winks at me as he comes inside. I didn't know he was coming, but after our jam at the springs, I'm not surprised Cedar invited him.

When I lead them into the kitchen, Orlando's eyes catch on Rose and stay there a minute. Then he seems to realize he's staring, and he waves both hands awkwardly. "Hey," he says shyly. "I'm Orlando Ortiz." Sarah barely glances up from the bowls of food.

Introductions go around, everyone nervous and jittery, feeling each other out. Sarah sticks close to Orlando, and gets a weird look on her face every time Rose glances her way. An awful, achy jealousy fills me, and I know it's wrong, but I'm tempted to flaunt my new relationship with Cedar, just to get a rise out of Sarah.

But then Rose settles her eyes on me again, appraising. "So you're the one whose brother killed Kenneth's dad."

Kenneth's mouth drops open, and Cedar swears under his breath. "I'm sorry, Shady," Cedar says. "She's—"

"That's okay," I say, even though everyone is standing

around wide-eyed and gaping. "My brother was arrested for Jim's murder, but he didn't do it." That's why I'm here. That's what this is all for—to get to the truth. I have to hold on to this goal.

Rose cocks her head, disbelieving.

"Even Kenneth doesn't think so," I say. He looks at me uncertainly but doesn't say anything. Jim's death is probably the only thing Kenneth has never been able to make into a joke. He's barely mentioned Jim since that day at the springs.

"Leave her alone, Rose," Sarah says, and Rose flashes her a glare, which makes Orlando step closer to Sarah. A flash of triumph fills my chest, followed by doubt. Has Sarah confided in Orlando? Does he know what she feels for Rose, what she feels for me?

God, this petty jealousy is stupid, considering everything else that's on the line. This is the band I've wanted for so long; this band could help me become the musician I've always wanted to be. And maybe if I'm finally good enough, the ghosts will follow my playing. If I'm good enough, I can control the fiddle's power. I can bring Jim back long enough to save Jesse. Not tonight, but soon.

"Forget it. Let's just play." I've got to pull us all together or this band will fall apart before we've even played a note. I reach for Daddy's fiddle case, ignoring the creep of fear that makes my fingertips tingle. "Where should we set up?"

Sarah points wordlessly to the living room.

Everyone sits down and starts pulling out instruments, eyeing each other warily.

"Nice guitar," Cedar says to Orlando. "You been playing long?"

"Like seven or eight years. I played Cuban country with my abuelo and tíos in Miami." Orlando looks down shyly at his Gibson. You can tell he loves it by the way he holds it, how his fingers caress the wood. His love for his family is wound in its strings, just like my fear and hopes are strung through my daddy's fiddle.

While everyone tunes their instruments, I survey our new band. There's my fiddle, Sarah's and Rose's banjos, Orlando's and Kenneth's guitars, and Cedar's mandolin. Not bad.

"It would be good to have an upright bass," Cedar says, "but this will do for now. Should we start with something simple?" He tries to look innocent, but everyone knows what he means. He doesn't think we're up to snuff. Bluegrass musicians usually start learning their instruments before they can walk, and it makes them think of anyone else as a beginner. Typical Southern macho shit. But Orlando's mouth curves into an amused smile, and Kenneth tells Cedar where he can shove that mandolin of his. Everyone laughs and the tension breaks.

"We should play some Gillian Welch," Sarah says.

Cedar whips his head around. "That's not even bluegrass. It's folk."

"So?" Sarah bristles.

"Rose and I play bluegrass."

Sarah scoffs. "This is what's wrong with bluegrass players. You're too traditional. That's why bluegrass is going to die out one of these days."

"I don't see any point in starting a bluegrass band if we're not even going to play bluegrass," Cedar says, shaking his head.

They both look at me, expecting me to resolve the argument. I open my mouth and close it again. "Well, what if—"

Rose interrupts. "Cedar, you're such a fucking purist. Stop acting like you're Bill Monroe." Kenneth supports her with a dramatic "mm-hmm" like a Southern grandma.

"I'm a bluegrass player," Cedar says stubbornly. "I didn't come here to play 'Wagon Wheel' or whatever other nonsense people are always trying to bring into bluegrass."

Sarah shoots me an angry look, probably thinking this is a dig at her on my behalf. Orlando clears his throat nervously.

"Look, I'm not trying to be an asshole," Cedar says, "but I play bluegrass mandolin. I thought that's why you invited me. If you want to play something else, you'll need to find yourself another mandolin player."

"How about we focus on bluegrass tonight? See how we sound together?" I say, giving Sarah a pleading look. "We can argue about this more later."

"Fine," Sarah says, glaring at Cedar. He nods, ignoring her.

"How about 'I'll Fly Away'?" I suggest, relieved. "It's an easy song everyone knows." I turn to Sarah. "You want to get us going?" This was my idea, but I've never played with so many people. I'm hesitant to take the lead, especially with Daddy's fiddle in my hands.

"All right," she says. "Key of G?"

"Throw us some taters," Cedar says. Sarah rolls her eyes at

the bluegrass jargon, but picks out the first four notes.

And then we're playing. It's jumbled-sounding at first, everyone trying to learn each other's rhythms, but soon it smooths out. Orlando's providing a good rhythm on guitar and singing baritone, a perfect complement to Cedar's higher tenor voice. Rose adds her voice, a rich, deep alto. Her banjo's quiet since it's open-backed, but it's a nice contrast with Sarah's noisier one. Even Kenneth holds his own.

My fiddle blends perfectly with the other instruments, lending the song a longing quality I've never managed before. Sarah and Orlando keep darting me surprised looks. I must sound different even to them.

This is my first taste of belonging to a real band, and already I love it. I think it must be impossible to feel lonely while playing music with other people, the way your minds and hearts and bodies all sync up, bound by the music you're building together. It feels like I'm soaking up everyone else's talent and passion and pouring it into my fiddle. This is everything I'd hoped it would be. My fear of this fiddle and all it can bring fades away into the back of my mind.

When we finish the song, I turn to Cedar, carried by the music into a more lighthearted mood. "Well, are we good enough for a busy guy like you to stick around for? Everyone know their way around an instrument to your satisfaction?"

Cedar ducks his head in a show of bashfulness, but his eyes tell me he's not the least bit cowed. "Y'all'll do," he says, smiling, and Orlando barely contains a laugh, probably at Cedar's unapologetic drawl. But Sarah only glares at Cedar, while Rose eyes her uncertainly. This is a strange and tangled sort of band we're forming, but it's working.

Cedar leads us into "Bury Me Beneath the Willow." We play it a few times until everyone's got the hang of it, and then move on to "I Am Weary." Cedar and Rose do most of the singing, but Orlando sings too, and I sing during parts where I'm chopping the rhythm instead of playing. Sarah clearly has no intention of ever singing a word in this band. But she looks like she's having a good time, despite all her former protests about boring traditional music.

When we finish playing through "I Am Weary" for the third time, Kenneth says, "Are there any bluegrass songs that aren't about dying?" and everyone laughs. You'd think all these songs about death would remind him of his dad, but if they are, he's not showing it. Maybe he's just determined to be cheerful.

"I know one," Cedar says, and he launches into "Shady Grove" with a flirty smile. Sarah's eyes go wide and she looks at me worriedly, but I shrug one shoulder and start playing. It was bound to happen, and after the shock of hearing it the first time, I'm ready to start enjoying the song that gave me my name again. And I'm ready to play it with Daddy's fiddle.

When he sings the line "A kiss from little Shady Grove is sweet as brandy wine," Cedar quirks his eyebrows at me, and something inside me loosens, like my grief for Daddy's been caked against my ribs, but this song's breaking it apart.

I am never going to be able to hear or play this song without hearing Daddy's voice in it. Every lyric is written on my heart in his handwriting. Every note carries a memory of him.

As we play, I close my eyes and let the memories wash over me—Daddy singing me awake with this song, his hands brushing my hair. Daddy climbing into his truck, waving at me from the window. Daddy's coffin being lowered into the ground, his voice buried by six feet of earth.

I let my fiddle fly, losing myself in its frantic wails. As I pick up speed, everyone else does too, as if they're drawn into my energy. We get faster and faster, till we're playing quicker than I've ever heard anyone play this song. My fingers should be cramping up, but I feel almost detached from my body, lost in the music. I close my eyes and all I can hear is music, until that hearing becomes feeling, and the music is deep inside me, pulsing like waves. If I open my eyes, I'm convinced I'll look down to see a yawning ocean.

Cedar has stopped singing because my fiddle's too loud to sing over, so it's just the instruments now, the frantic pinging of the mandolin, the howling of my fiddle, two banjos twanging for all they're worth, and Kenneth's desperate attempt to keep up. The only instrument I don't hear is Orlando's guitar. When I open my eyes, he's staring wide-eyed and shocked at something behind me.

I swivel my whole body to look so I can keep playing, and as I do, I see a woman standing at the door, her dark hair tousled, her eyes long-lashed and brown like Sarah's. I recognize her from the framed picture Sarah keeps by her bed. It's her mother.

Her dead mother. A flash of feeling goes through me—fear and regret and joy and hope all in one.

"Sarah," I manage to croak, but I don't stop playing. She looks up at me, not noticing her mom. "Behind me," I say, stepping out of her line of sight.

When Sarah sees her mother, her mouth falls open and she drops her banjo. The carpet muffles its thud, but Cedar and Rose startle and stop playing. I don't stop moving my bow partly because I don't want to and partly because I can't. I'm locked in this song.

"Mom?" Sarah says, rising slowly off the couch. She pulls each of the picks from her fingers, leaving a trail of them on the carpet. She crosses the room, stopping a few feet from her mother. The two of them stare at each other, their faces so full of emotion it's hard to look right at them.

Finally, Sarah reaches out to touch her mother's cheek, and I can imagine what she feels when her skin meets her mother's, that tingly cold I felt the night the old man's ghost came to my bedroom.

"But you're dead," she says, though my fiddle nearly drowns out her voice.

Cedar puts a hand on my shoulder, and I know he means for me to stop playing, but if I do, Sarah might not get to hear her mother's response. I change songs, playing as softly as I can. Cedar looks at me questioningly, but when I shake my head, he leaves it be.

"I'm so sorry I left you," the ghost says, her eyes luminous and haunted.

"Why'd you go?" Sarah asks, hugging herself, and there's this desperate note in her voice, like it's a question she's asked a hundred times before.

Her mother searches her eyes, like she's deciding whether she's brave enough to tell the truth, or whether Sarah's strong enough to hear it.

"I was so sad," she says. "So sad. Everything was too hard. Taking care of you was hard. Getting out of bed was hard."

Sarah backs away a few steps, and her mother moves forward, filling the space. Her hands go to Sarah's cheeks, and to my surprise, Sarah doesn't flinch. "I loved you so much," the woman says. "You were the most perfect little girl, and I didn't deserve you, not one single inch of you. You needed better than I could give you. I thought I was doing the right thing, leaving you."

"I missed you so much," Sarah says. "I still do."

"Can you forgive me?"

Sarah nods, her eyes filling with tears.

The ghost pulls her into a hug so fierce I can almost feel it. Then the woman looks over Sarah's shoulder and locks her eyes on me, her face imploring. She wants me to let her go.

Something snaps in me, like a rubber band stretched too tight. I stop playing, and the moment I take my bow from the strings, I drop to the floor and into darkness.

There are things in the darkness. Dark, angry, hungry things. I can't see them, but they flit around me, all wings and want. I don't know what they are, but I bet Miss Patty would call them devils.

I try to move, but I'm paralyzed, numb. The wind from the devils' wings brushes my face.

I gaze up into inky blackness, terror rising in me like a

flooded river. This isn't a dream. I know without a doubt I'm inside the shadow man, chained up in the festering blackness of his heart.

A scream rips from my throat, a pulse of energy hurtling into the darkness.

And when my scream hits it, the darkness breaks, shattering like a mirror, letting the light in. The devils cry and wail, bursting into puffs of ash.

But I don't stop screaming until I feel the carpet of Sarah's living room underneath me, until the electric light turns my closed eyelids red.

And then there are hands on me, rough hands on my arms and my shoulders, shaking me.

"Shady," Cedar says, over and over. "Shady, Shady, Shady."

I open my eyes and gaze up into his face. His mouth is open and he's breathing heavy, his nostrils flaring. He's so afraid.

"Shady," he says again, but this time it's a statement and not a plea. "Shady."

When I sit up, the room spins and I'm afraid I'm going to drop back into the darkness. But Cedar holds on to my shoulders, and then my head, like he's trying to make the room go still for me.

"You all right?" he asks, his voice shaky.

"Yeah."

"What happened?"

I meet his eyes again. Blink and then look away, passing a hand over my face. "I guess I passed out."

"Cut the crap, Shady," Rose says from the couch. She

doesn't look scared or worried like Cedar; she looks mad. She looks like a tiny pirate who wants to rip out my heart and feed it to the sea.

"What?" I ask, my voice hoarse, not quite meeting her eyes.

Rose gestures angrily at Sarah, who's kneeling on the ground a few feet away, weeping into her hands. Orlando is kneeling beside Sarah, rubbing her back. I remember her mother's ghost, and the thought chases away the shadow man from my mind. I've never seen Sarah cry before.

I push off the ground and go to her. "Sarah, are you okay?"

She looks up at me, tears running down her cheeks, and opens her mouth to speak, but only a sob comes out. And then she throws herself into my arms, nearly knocking me over. She wraps her arms around my neck, pulling me into her. She lays her head on my shoulder and cries, just like Honey has done a thousand times.

I hold her close, running my hand over her hair. My thumb brushes her ear and the cloud-shaped birthmark behind it. All I've longed for is to be this close to Sarah, to hold her in my arms, but this isn't how I wanted it to happen. I hate to be the reason she needs comforting.

"I'm so sorry," I say. "So sorry." I rock her gently as she weeps into my hair, guilt and shame flooding me. "I didn't mean to."

Finally, Sarah pulls back and looks at me, her face a mess of tears and anguish. Orlando hands her a tissue, and she wipes her face. "Didn't mean to *what*?" she asks, hiccuping down her sobs. "You didn't do anything."

"It was my—" I pause, not sure I'm ready to confess everything. "Was it awful to see her like that?" I ask instead, and Sarah's eyes fill with fresh tears.

"Not completely," she whispers. "It was . . . a lot. A lot to process. I'm not sure what I feel."

"Jesus Christ. Tell us what the fuck is going on here, right now," Rose says.

Sarah glances between us, and understanding fills her eyes. She stares at me, shocked. "You—you . . ."

"You brought that ghost here." Rose's voice is so matter-of-fact I wonder if her little banjo has a history like my fiddle's.

"Yeah, I did." I look back at Sarah. "I'm so sorry."

Sarah leans away from me. "How?"

I get up and pick my fiddle off the floor and show it to them. "It was my daddy's. We thought it was lost or destroyed when he died. But, well, I found it, and it . . . it, um, brings the spirits of the dead to the person who plays it."

I expect the room to burst into angry noise, but everyone just stares at me.

"That's ridiculous," Orlando says. He's holding Sarah again, his hands tight around her arms.

Rose turns on him. "Didn't you see the fucking ghost?" Orlando flinches back from her, mumbling about carbon monoxide poisoning. He doesn't want to accept what happened, doesn't want to believe that all the stories his grandmother told him about wayward spirits and family curses might be true.

"Where did the fiddle come from?" Cedar asks, his voice surprisingly calm now. "I mean, why did your dad have it?"

"It's been in the family a long time. It doesn't look like much, but it's old. Really, really old. Someone buried it, but then I found it."

"The other night. You came back all muddy," Orlando says. "That's when you—"

I nod, but I don't meet his eyes.

"Can I look at it?" Cedar asks, and I hold the fiddle out to him, though the moment his fingers touch it, I feel a hunger to have it back. He takes it in his hands and studies it, turning it over. I cross my arms to keep from snatching it away. Cedar doesn't handle the fiddle like it's a ghostly object that was recently dug out of the ground. He holds it like any other instrument, a collection of wood and strings, and it hurts me to watch him turn it over so roughly. Kenneth peers over Cedar's shoulder to see the fiddle, too, his expression a mingling of curiosity and fear. But Rose is looking at Sarah—strangely, almost longingly, like she wishes she were in Orlando's place, holding Sarah close.

Finally, after a long silence, Sarah speaks. "Why would you want to raise my mother's ghost?"

I push my hair out of my face and sink into the recliner, as far from Rose as I can get. She's a tiny girl, but she's radiating anger. I thought she was a jerk, but maybe she's just protective, the way Jesse is of me.

"I didn't mean to," I say. "She's not the one I—"

"How does it work?" Cedar asks.

"Like I said, the fiddle attracts ghosts, and it can let them take solid forms, at least long enough for them to speak, to say their piece, whatever."

"Why would you want to do that?" Orlando asks, horrified. If Orlando's brother was wrongly jailed, I know his response would never be something like this. He'd find a safe, logical solution that didn't involve summoning ghosts.

But there isn't one. This fiddle is all I've got. I'm not sure any of them are capable of understanding my reasons, but I have to try to make them see. Words don't seem like enough, but they're all I've got.

"For Jesse," I say. "I need to talk to Jim—to find out what really happened. I've been trying on my own, but it's not working. I just want to get Jesse out of jail."

"Jesus Christ," Kenneth says. "You want to raise my daddy's ghost?" His face is pale and shocked. I can't bear to look at him.

"Oh my God," Sarah says, her grief turning to anger. "This was practice. You were using my mom as practice."

I jump out of my chair. "No, no, I swear. I didn't mean to bring your mom here."

Everyone's staring at me, and I don't know how to explain myself. I'm not sure I even understand my own reasoning. "It's just that the fiddle isn't . . . I don't really know how it works, but I thought playing with y'all would make me strong enough to play it, it would help me play well enough to make it do what I want. I haven't been strong enough to do it myself. I'm sorry. I didn't plan this. I just wanted . . ."

"You wanted to use us like some kind of freaky ghost-raising amplifiers," Rose says. "That's all this is about." She turns to Cedar. "She's probably not even really into you."

Cedar's eyes fill with hurt. "You're just using us?"

"No. I wanted this band before the fiddle—from the first time I heard you guys play at the open mic. But then, after I found the fiddle, I guess I thought having a band would help me get control of it. I thought playing with you guys would make me strong enough to raise Jim. And I have to—I have to help Jesse."

I turn back to Sarah. "I'm so, so sorry. I really didn't think anything like this would happen. I don't even understand why it happened."

She won't meet my eyes.

"You should go," Rose says. She swipes my case and bow from the floor, and throws them into the recliner next to me. "Cedar, give her that fucking fiddle."

"Rose," he says, his voice a warning, but he hands me the instrument. Having it back in my hands floods me with a moment of relief, but I turn my attention to Sarah.

"Sarah," I whisper, and she looks up at me, her eyes unreadable.

"Just go," she says. "Everybody, go home." She turns and walks quietly down the hallway and into her bedroom and shuts the door, leaving us standing in the living room.

"I'll stay with her until her dad gets home," Orlando says absently. I can almost see the struggle going on inside him, between his family's beliefs and the science he loves to cling to.

"I'm out of here." Rose starts for the door, Kenneth trailing behind her, still lost and stunned by the thought of his father's ghost. He shoots a furtive look at me over his shoulder but doesn't say anything else. Guilt turns my stomach sour.

Rose turns, with her hand on the doorknob. "Are you coming, Cedar?"

Cedar looks at me uncertainly. "Are you okay to drive home?"

When I nod, he follows Rose and Kenneth out. I watch from the doorway as they get into a pickup truck parked across the street and drive away.

I look back at Orlando. "Take care of her."

"I will," he says more gruffly than I've ever heard him speak. Is he thinking of the wasps? Does he think I did this on purpose? Does everyone think I did this on purpose?

I leave Sarah's house feeling like the worst person alive, my head aching and my heart matching it beat for beat.

SIXTEEN

When I get home, I park Mama's car and head into the woods. Despite everything that just happened, I already want to play the fiddle again.

This instrument has nearly drowned me, filled the trailer with wasps, and transported me to a dark and hideous hell dimension. It called up my best friend's dead mom and almost hurt my little sister. Jesse and Aunt Ena were right to keep it from me—to keep it from the world. There's a darkness at its core, something beyond its ability to draw out spirits.

But my fear of it is still less than my wonder—I raised a ghost. With my fingers and the fiddle's strange magic, I brought a ghost to life. I let her move and speak. I gave her a chance to tell her daughter she loved her, even if it did hurt my friend. Exhilaration is slowly pushing my doubts and even my guilt aside.

I understand now why Daddy was always picking up the

fiddle again. Some things are worth the dangers—like Cedar said about rodeo, it doesn't happen on a screen or to someone else. It's real life, and that makes it worth the risk.

These trees are full of spirits. How many stories do they have to tell? How many of them are longing to be seen, to be heard as more than a rustle of wind in the pines?

I was born to play this fiddle, to make this ghost wood sing.

My heart races as I push through the trees, deeper into the woods, as far from Mama's trailer as I can get. That will keep Honey safe. The only person I can hurt out here is myself.

I find a clearing where the moonlight is bright enough to let me see any ghosts I might raise. I sit on the blanket of pine needles and wait, listening.

The ghosts are here, practically pressed against my skin, drawn to the fiddle's power. They murmur and sway like dry leaves, their presence comforting, familiar. They aren't evil; they aren't trying to pull me down to hell. They're just lonesome.

I bring up my fiddle and begin to play an old Everly Brothers song, "Here to Get My Baby Out of Jail." It's about an elderly woman who wants to bail her son out of jail. She brings her watch and her chain, even her wedding ring, ready to offer anything for his release. The moment she embraces him, she dies. The song seems right somehow, a way to tap into the ghosts' longing, into the ties that keep them bound to this world.

In this moment, I wish Daddy's ghost would come. I wish he would appear and tell me what to do, how to help Jesse. I wish he would hold me and tell me everything will be okay. But

I'm also not ready to see him yet—I might only get one chance to raise his ghost, and I want to make sure I know how to keep him as long as possible. I want to be ready to say all the things in my heart.

The fiddle warbles into the night air, making goose bumps erupt on my arms. I play the song all the way through, but nothing happens. No ghosts appear.

When the notes fall silent, the forest sounds fill the night again. The ghosts are still here, closer even, more eager. But they remain quiet, invisible. The fiddle hasn't touched them, hasn't drawn them out.

I play a few more songs, but the ghosts don't speak or show themselves.

Frustration wells in me, making me play wrong notes, making my bow screech. How could I raise Sarah's mother's ghost, but these ghosts, *my* ghosts, are unaffected? What am I doing wrong now? Why did it work before? Was it really because the band played with me? My heart starts to beat faster. If I can't raise a single ghost in these woods, how will I raise Jim?

Daddy told me all kinds of things about ghost raising, except the one thing I need to know now: exactly how to do it.

I have to figure it out, if I'm going to find out what really happened to Jim. If I'm going to clear Jesse's name.

The only person who could help me won't want to, but I have to try.

Early the next morning, I'm standing on Aunt Ena's porch, waiting nervously for her to answer my knock. She lets out a sigh the moment she opens the door, like she knows why I'm here and what I came to ask. "A gift," I say, shoving a white bakery bag into her arms.

"More like a bribe, I'll wager," she says, already pulling a doughnut hole from the bag. "Now what do you want?" she asks through a mouthful of pastry. "I know you didn't bring me this out of pure sweetness."

"Let's go inside," I say, leading the way to the kitchen. Aunt Ena pours herself a cup of coffee before she sits across from me, her eyes wary.

I could lie, but she'd see right through me. Besides, she deserves the truth.

I take a deep breath. "I found it. I found Daddy's fiddle."

Her face blanches. She opens her mouth to speak, but I interrupt her.

"I know this isn't what you want for me, and I know it's dangerous. But I had to find it, Aunt Ena. I had to. And I'm going to use it." I hold my hand up when she tries to say something. "For Jesse. That's all. I have to do it for Jesse. You know you would have done the same for Daddy."

Aunt Ena crosses her arms, her mouth going tight. I could argue with her all day, but something in her eyes tells me I won't have to. She must know as well as I do that this was inevitable.

"What do you want to know?" she asks. Her voice is tired, defeated-sounding.

Guilt and relief both flood me. "I want to know how Daddy did it. How he raised the ghosts."

"I don't know, darlin'. I really don't," she says. "Your daddy never told me. He just did it. That's all."

I squash down my frustration. "Okay, well, is there anything else you can tell me? Anything to help me raise Jim? You live in a house full of ghosts. I know there's something you can say to point me in the right direction. I've been playing in the woods . . . practicing on our ghosts."

Aunt Ena sighs. "The ghosts here—some of them died in this house or in these woods. But most of them didn't. Most of them are old, old ghosts, gone for a long time. Their families have died, or their old homes have been torn down. They've got nothing left to hold them to one place. So they chose to come here."

"What's that got to do with Jim?"

"He's a new ghost, so he's probably still hanging around where he was killed. You know they do that, for a while, until they get used to things. If you're really going to try to raise him, maybe it should be at the construction site."

It's sad to think about Jim haunting that empty, half-built house, lurking all alone at the scene of his murder. Maybe if I can raise his ghost, he'll be glad for the chance to speak, to connect with someone alive, even if it's just the stepdaughter who never liked him.

But Jim as a ghost? I've been so focused on figuring out *how* to raise his ghost that I hadn't really considered what it would be like to face him, to speak to him. Going over the specifics with Aunt Ena, saying it all out loud, makes it feel real in a way it hadn't before. If I'm successful, I'm going to face down my stepdad's ghost. The thought sends a shiver down my spine.

Aunt Ena seems to sense my fear. "You don't have to do this, you know," she says, her voice pleading. "There's all kinds of ways to take care of people, and this isn't the only way you can do that for Jesse."

I hesitate, thinking over her words. But I shake my head. "He's running out of time. Every day there's more evidence against him. There's nothing else for me to do. I have to try this."

Aunt Ena reaches across the table and grasps my hand in hers, warm and alive in a room full of ghosts. "Just don't lose yourself, Shady—while you're trying to save your brother, don't lose yourself, too."

On Monday, Orlando catches my arm as I pass his table in the cafeteria. He's sitting with his younger brother, Carlos, and their friends Juan and Shane from the Latin language club, a group known for their love of D&D and LARPing. "We need to talk," Orlando says.

"Thank God. I thought you were going to ignore me like Sarah," I say in a low voice. It's been three days since I raised her mother's ghost, and Sarah hasn't answered any of my texts or calls. I couldn't bring myself to reach out to Orlando after the way he glared at me, and Cedar was tied up with rodeo stuff. It was a long, lonely weekend that mostly involved trying (and failing) to raise a ghost with Daddy's fiddle. I know where to raise Jim's ghost, thanks to Aunt Ena, but I haven't been out there yet because I still don't know how to do it. The dead aren't talking to me either.

Before Orlando can answer, Juan gets my attention. I haven't seen him much since Jim's funeral, and I've been meaning to thank him for coming.

But he's already talking before I can get a word in. "Shady, I heard you were dating Cedar Smith. So, uh, how do you feel about space cowboys? I cosplay a mean Malcolm Reynolds." He gives me a huge wink and a flash of two dimples, then shoots me with finger pistols.

"I'll keep that in mind," I say with a laugh.

"Sorry, but we gotta go," Orlando says, gathering up his bag and empty tray. He ruffles Carlos's hair and waves farewell to Shane and Juan. I smile at them and hurry after Orlando. Once we're out of earshot, Orlando turns back to me. "You really can't blame Sarah for being pissed. You lied to us."

"I didn't lie. I just didn't tell you."

"That's the same thing." He shakes his head, but it's not in his usual wondering way. It's full of hurt and disbelief. "You didn't trust us."

We push through the crowded room and out into a little courtyard lined with concrete benches. Orlando settles onto a bench. I turn to face him, sitting cross-legged, but he doesn't look at me for a while. Instead, he stares back toward the cafeteria, chewing on his thumbnail.

"Please just say what you want to say." I can't take his silence anymore.

He turns toward me, annoyed that I'm rushing him. "You know I've never believed in ghosts. I thought all that stuff my abuela says about spirits was superstition. But I've been thinking about it for days, and there's not a logical explanation for what happened."

"Duh."

"But I do know you're being stupid. You're doing something dangerous and selfish that's going to hurt you and everybody else."

"I'm not doing this for me. It's for Jesse."

Orlando stares at me. "Is it though? Would Jesse be really okay with everything you've done while trying to help him? Because those wasps could have hurt your sister, and who even knows what kind of lasting damage you've done to Sarah. And the way you passed out . . . If everything my abuela has told me is true, then you put all of us in danger the other night. You shouldn't open doors you don't know how to close."

"I'm sorry. I really am. But I have to get Jesse out of jail. I can't stand for him to be in there, Orlando."

His eyes soften. "I know. But is this really the best way? Can't you . . . I don't know . . . ask some questions? Look for information—discreetly, I mean?"

"I'm not Veronica Mars, teen detective," I say, crossing my arms.

"Even if you do raise Jim's ghost and he tells you who did it, then what? Are you going to go to the cops and try to convince them a ghost told you Jesse's not a killer?"

"Of course not," I snap. "But it will be something more to go on. I can at least point them in the right direction. Give them another suspect." And then *I'll* know for sure, I think, but I don't say that part.

Orlando sighs. "Just please don't do this, Shady. I'm worried about you. I know you love your brother, but this doesn't seem like the way to help him. Like, at all."

The bell for our next class rings, and Orlando gets to his feet. He gives me one final, serious look. "I know you've lost a lot, and I can't begin to understand that. But there's a lot you haven't lost. Maybe if you remember that, you can stop this before things get more out of control." He doesn't wait for me to answer before he strides away.

I'm watching Orlando lope down the hallway when Cedar bumps into me accidentally. "Hey," he says, surprised. Then he follows my miserable gaze. "Is he mad at you?"

"Yep. Everybody's mad at me."

Orlando disappears around the corner, and Cedar puts his arm around me and pulls me forward. "I'm not mad at you. I'm not," he insists when I give him a skeptical look. "I think we all just need some time. This is . . . wild."

"But you don't regret . . . you and me?"

Cedar looks at me with that sly smile of his. "Uh-uh. Girl kisses you like that, you'll make allowances for a little bit of spookiness."

I smack his arm and he laughs, but then his face turns serious again. "You think you're going to be able to do it? Bring back Jim's ghost, I mean?"

"I don't know. I'm not sure how I did what I did at Sarah's house. And I probably need to find out more about the particulars of Jim's murder. Like, which house it was in, which room." I told Orlando I wasn't a teen detective, but he was right that I needed to learn more. I'm just going to apply his advice a little differently than he intended.

"Well, Kenneth might be able to help, at least about the

house, since he saw Jim that morning," Cedar says.

"Kenneth was at the construction site? I don't remember hearing that."

Cedar glances at me, surprised. "His dad wanted to talk to him about what happened at the open mic night, I guess. Asked him to come by."

"Oh, how'd you know that?"

"Kenneth texted me that morning saying he was going over there." Cedar hesitates. "You didn't know?"

I shake my head. "I think he said something to me about how he felt bad he spent his last night with his dad acting stupid. I assumed that was the last time he saw him. No one ever mentioned Kenneth being there that morning."

I guess Orlando was right about asking around for more information. Kenneth might be able to help fill in some gaps for me. Unless maybe he doesn't want me to know. Unless he's hiding something. Because I'm pretty sure the police don't know he was at the construction site the morning Jim died. Either that, or his stepdad asked them to keep quiet about it.

The memory of Kenneth staring at his hands like they didn't belong to him that day at Little Spring floats through my mind, but I dismiss it. He's a grieving son, that's all. Maybe the police did know and already looked into it—it's not like anyone's been willing to tell me much of anything.

"Will you tell him to call me later?" I ask as I head toward my next class. With that new witness and more evidence against Jesse, I need any help I can get.

SEVENTEEN

Having Cedar back on my side makes me feel a little less lost, but I want Sarah back too, even if it's just as my friend and bandmate. With Jesse in ever more danger and the shadow man dogging my dreams and now my waking hours, I need to feel less alone in this world. I need people to keep me anchored here, to the living.

I tried to apologize when I saw Sarah in American history, but she wouldn't even look at me. I can't blame her. First, I threaten to go off and play with Cedar and Rose, then she catches me kissing Cedar, and then I bring back her mother's ghost . . .

And it isn't just that I raised her mom's ghost—I exposed Sarah's deepest vulnerability to a room full of people. I exposed her. That's going to be hard to forgive, impossible to forget. She might never come out from behind her defensive walls again.

I keep seeing her shocked face in my mind, the open,

defenseless look there. I've been wanting her to show her feelings for so long, but now that she has, it makes my chest ache. Knowing I put that expression on her face. Knowing I'm the cause of all her hurt. That was never what I wanted.

Whatever might have been happening between us, whatever relationship was growing up slow and sweet in its own time, has been hacked down like stalk of sugarcane. You can't tape a stalk of severed sugarcane back together, can't return it to its roots. It's done and over with, and you've got to make it into something else. I at least have to try.

So after Mama gets home from work, I borrow the car and drive over to Sarah's house. Her truck's in the driveway, right next to her dad's.

Sarah's dad, Tom, answers the door, still in his oil-stained uniform from the auto repair shop he owns, with Trouble on his heels. She slips out the front door and circles me, barking and jumping, licking whatever body part she can reach. I squat down and try to hug her, but she's too excited and knocks me over onto my butt.

Tom grabs her by her collar and pulls her back inside the house, beckoning me in. "Sarah's in her room. Did she know you were coming over?"

"No," I say, suddenly nervous. What has she told him?

"She's been in a funk for a few days. You know anything about that?" Tom narrows his eyes.

"It's my fault. She's mad at me."

"Well, go fix it then," he says.

"Yes, sir."

At the door to Sarah's room, I take a deep breath and knock.

"Come in," she says, so I turn the knob, my heart hammering in my chest.

Sarah's sprawled on her bed with a math textbook open, writing in a notebook.

"Hi."

She looks up quickly but doesn't speak right away. "I thought you were my dad."

"He let me in," I say, just to fill the awkward silence, and Sarah looks back down at her book, not even trying to pretend she's glad I'm here. I close the door behind me and slide down it to sit on the floor. I lean my head against the wood, trying to keep my eyes from the framed picture of Sarah's mom by her bed. Trying not to think about the relief on her ghostly face when I let her go.

"I'm sorry."

"For what?" Sarah still won't look at me. Her hair falls across her eyes, obscuring her expression.

"For everything. For your mom, for . . . Cedar."

Sarah presses her lips together. I wish she'd open them instead, maybe yell at me a little bit. At least then I'd know for sure what she's feeling.

"I didn't know that would happen with your mom. I didn't even think about it. I never would have brought my daddy's fiddle here if I thought that were even a possibility. I swear."

Sarah's silent so long I think she's not going to say anything. "It wasn't just . . . practice? For Jim?"

"Oh my God, no. No. I wanted us all to play together. I

thought your house would be a neutral place, away from ghosts. I forgot about your mom. I shouldn't have forgotten."

Sarah finally looks up, but her expression is unreadable. I catch her eyes and try to keep them on me. "I never meant for you to get hurt, Sarah. I swear. I should have been honest with you, but I didn't know if you would believe me. If you would think I was crazy. And I was afraid you wouldn't want to play with me anymore if you knew. I was wrong, and I'm sorry," I say, tears rising to my eyes. "I put you in danger and I hurt you, and I hate myself for it."

Sarah stares at me for a long time. "It's okay," she finally says. I venture a smile, and her eyes soften, one corner of her mouth turning up. I can see she doesn't want things to be like this between us either.

"Thank you." I want to ask her more, whether seeing her mom was all bad or if she was glad to speak to her, but I know Sarah's not going to tell me anything anyway, not this soon. And I don't deserve to hear it.

"About Cedar," I say, but Sarah holds up her hand, her mouth turning to a hard line again.

"That's your business."

"Sarah, let me explain. It's you I—"

"What's there to explain?" she says, her voice tight, like she's on the verge of tears too. "You like him, he likes you."

"But—"

"Shady, I've got homework to do. Would you please go?"

I stare at her, but she won't look at me, her eyes fastened firmly on her notebook, hair falling over her face again. She even starts writing.

I want to tell her I have feelings for her, explain how much I want to be with her, but the confession lodges in my chest.

"I didn't expect it to happen. He wasn't the one I . . . God, if you would just . . . if you would just open up a little," I say, suddenly angry. "That's why Cedar and I are . . . at least he didn't just disappear after he kissed me."

Sarah acts like she doesn't even hear me, but her hand tightens on the pencil.

"Fine," I say, knowing even as my voice rises that I have no right to be mad at her now. I came here to apologize, but now I'm as furious as she's been for the last week. "I'll leave you alone since that's apparently the way you like to be."

I open the door and slam it closed, and then bolt from the house before Tom can see the tears running down my face.

I snatch up Daddy's fiddle and head into the woods before Mama even knows I'm home. Raising Sarah's mom was a mistake and a setback, but there's still Jesse to think of, still this fiddle to master. I won't try to raise Jim until I know I can do it right.

In the bluish hues of twilight, surrounded by the whispering pines, I play through all the songs I know so well I don't have to think about them. The music that pours out sounds like every feeling in my body I can't put into words. All the anger and the hurt and the fear. I feel so lonely, so weighed down.

If Daddy were here . . .

But if Daddy were here, I wouldn't need helping. Jesse wouldn't be in jail right now, and I wouldn't even have this fiddle. Daddy would still be playing it, filling the woods with his songs, waking all the ghosts. Maybe now that I'm older he'd trust me with the fiddle's secrets. Maybe he'd teach me to play it, just the way he taught me to play my ordinary one.

The memory of his fingers guiding mine across the strings cuts through me. Some girls have memories of dancing with their daddies, their little feet on top of their fathers' as they whirl. But my memories are of playing the fiddle with my fingers beneath Daddy's, his hand guiding my arm to draw the bow across the strings.

I transition into the easiest, simplest song, the first I ever learned—"You Are My Sunshine." Most people only know the chorus, but Daddy taught me every verse. I whisper the words to myself as I play.

The other night, dear
As I lay sleeping
I dreamed I held you in my arms

A voice behind me sings the next words.

But when I awoke, dear
I was mistaken
And then I hung my head and I cried

I drop the fiddle and the bow as I spin to see who's there. I was thinking of Daddy while I played, but it's not him. Instead, a woman stands behind me, her face lined more with regret than age. "Who are—" I start to say, but she's fading. I scramble for my fiddle and start to play again, but it's too late. By the time I start the song again, she has disappeared back into the pines.

"No, no, come back," I call. "Please, come back. Let me

help you." But she's gone now, and no matter how long I play, she doesn't reappear.

But a slow, sure knowing fills me. I know now how this fiddle works. I finally understand how it brings the ghosts across the veil. It doesn't have anything to do with luck or skill or the songs I choose to play.

I know now why Daddy looked so stricken when he played, why he was always getting lost in the darkness.

This instrument runs on grief and regret and rage; it only works if its player gives herself over to grief, lets it fill her like the music, every nook, every cranny of her soul. The same reason the ghosts are chained to this world, unable to pass on, is why Daddy's fiddle can raise them. Grief is what binds the living and the dead.

He couldn't have taught me to play this fiddle even if he'd wanted to. Only his death could teach me.

EIGHTEEN

I tiptoe up the trailer's aluminum steps and gently turn the doorknob. It doesn't budge.

"Shit," I whisper. It's past midnight, so Mama must have thought I was already in bed and locked the door. I'm locked out of my own house.

I knock, preparing myself for a proper tongue-lashing.

Feet thunder to the door and then someone fumbles the lock, and the door swings open. Mama is a dark silhouette against the bright lamp behind her. "Where the hell have you been?"

She lets me into the trailer, glaring at me all the way.

"I'm so sorry, Mama. I was in the woods, practicing—"

She gasps. "Is that—what is that you're carrying?"

"It's just my fiddle," I say, tucking it under my arm so she can't see it. Why isn't she yelling at me for waking her up?

"Oh. For a second I thought—I thought . . . Never mind,

Shady. I got some upsetting news today, that's all." She rubs her face tiredly, her hand trembling. Then she takes a few steps back and sits down heavily in the recliner.

"What is it? Is it Jesse?" I ask, panic rising up my throat. Is there even more evidence? Another witness?

Mama nods. "He's all right, but he was in a fight today. His lawyer said he got jumped by a couple of other boys." Her voice cracks on the last word.

Relief and worry flood me at the same time. "I'm sure he's all right, Mama," I say, dropping to my knees beside her chair. "Jesse can hold his own in a fight. I've seen him."

"But there were two of them—and who knows what kind of boys they are, what they've done," she says, her voice wavering.

"He'll be all right. He'll be fine."

"But I can't . . . I can't even call to check on him," she says, her voice breaking into an anguished sob. "I can't help him or do anything for him."

"It's all right," I say, rubbing her back. "It's all right." But my mind is spinning off into horrible directions, imaging what could happen to Jesse in a place like that. Something worse than a fight.

"He seems so tough, I know, but he can't go to prison. He won't make it there—his heart's too tender. He's too young."

"I know, Mama," I say. But there's something I can do for Jesse, even if she can't.

I can find out once and for all whether or not he killed Jim. Daddy said to wait until I was ready—well, I know now how the fiddle works, so I'm as ready as I'll ever be. Once I talk to

Kenneth and learn what I can about the house where Jim died, there won't be any reason left to wait.

But my stepbrother doesn't call or answer my texts, and the next day at school he seems to disappear every time I catch sight of him. He's avoiding me. Did Cedar mention I was looking for him and scare him off? Is he upset about my plans to raise Jim, or is there some other reason?

Finally, at the end of the school day, I spot him across the parking lot. He's surrounded by a group of his dip-chewing, truck-driving friends. They're sitting on tailgates and lounging against the sides of other people's cars. When I call Kenneth's name, the boys whistle and say things I'm glad I can't quite hear, but the open, friendly look on Kenneth's face disappears.

"Shut up," he says, shoving one of the boys half-heartedly as he makes his way toward me.

"Hey, Shady. What's up?" he says, darting a look back at his friends.

"I missed my bus, and I was hoping you could give me a ride home," I lie.

Surprise flits across his face, followed by something like fear. "I think Cedar's around here somewhere. You could text him."

"Well, I also wanted to talk to you. Please," I say.

"About my dad?" Kenneth looks down at his feet.

I hesitate, afraid to say the wrong thing. "Yeah. I wanted to know how you feel about . . . what happened the other night. What I'm planning to do."

"I haven't wrapped my head around it yet, I guess," Kenneth

says to his boots. "But I don't think you should do something like that. It's not right."

"You could help me if you want to," I say. "You could see him, talk to him again."

Kenneth's head shoots up, terror on his face. "What? No, no way."

I put my hand on his arm, but he steps back like I burned him. Is he actually afraid of me? "Please. I need your help. I just want to get Jesse out of jail."

"I have to go home," Kenneth says, glancing around for help. Like I'm going to beat him up. Like he needs to be rescued from a girl half his size. "I'm not going to help you with this. I've been trying to be nice to you about Jesse, but now you're taking it too far. I'm—I'm leaving now."

"Hang on, please. I wanted to ask you a question about that day—at the construction site, since you were there with Jim."

Kenneth startles and his face bleeds white as my meaning sinks in. "I don't know what you're talking about."

I thought it was strange I never heard about Kenneth being at the construction site, but now that he's acting so shifty about it . . . maybe he really did hide it from me on purpose. And if Jesse and Kenneth were both with Jim that morning, why wasn't Kenneth ever a suspect? Why's my brother sitting in jail while Kenneth's walking around free?

"I'm raising Jim's ghost tonight," I say, "whether you like it or not." It sounds brutal, bare, said like that, but I can't afford to hold back any longer, not with Jesse's safety and freedom on the line. "I know how to do it now. So either you can tell me why you lied about being at the construction site that morning, or your daddy will."

Kenneth looks like he's going to be sick, all his anger dropping away. "Okay, I'll talk to you, but not here. Come on."

He leads me out of the parking lot and around the side of the building, watching for teachers. We walk out toward a utility shed and then sit on empty paint buckets behind it. Kenneth pulls out a pack of cigarettes and lights one with a shaking hand. There are cigarette butts all over the ground, so this must be a regular smoking spot.

"Shady, you can't tell anyone. I'll get in so much trouble. Please," he says around the cigarette.

Fear squirms in my stomach. "What did you do?"

"I didn't do anything. That's the problem. I was there that morning. Dad called and asked me to meet him and Jesse at the construction site. He wanted to talk about the pills and the fight and all that."

"That doesn't sound like Jim," I say. "When has he ever wanted to talk about anything?"

"I know. I thought it was weird too. But I went because . . . because it's the kind of thing I've always wanted him to do. Be my dad. Lecture me about drugs. Whatever. And, I mean, he came to see me at the open mic night, didn't he? I thought he was trying."

"Okay, so what happened when you got there?"

"Nothing. He went off on me about how I was following in his bad footsteps and yelled at Jesse a lot. Jesse was pissed and went downstairs for a smoke or something. I left. That's it. That's all that happened."

I gaze back at him, not even trying to pretend I believe him. "So why were you hiding it then?"

"My stepdad. He's a police officer, you know?"

"Yeah, I know. He arrested Jesse."

"Shit. Yeah. Well, he didn't want me to say I was there. He said it would make me a suspect. So my mom lied for me and said I was home all morning."

I shake my head, and a bitter laugh leaves my mouth. "But you were fine with making Jesse the only suspect, I guess. You could have given evidence in Jesse's favor, you know. You still can." Wouldn't Jim's son's evidence count for more than some stranger's?

But Kenneth's eyes are bright with fear. "Gary would be so pissed if he knew I was telling you. Please don't tell anyone else. Please. He could lose his job. And he and my mom are already having problems."

I'm still not convinced. This sounds like a lot of bullshit to me. "But how did you know Jesse wouldn't say you were there?"

Kenneth looks down, shame in his eyes. "My stepdad said not to worry about it because no one would believe Jesse after he beat me up the night before."

I'd like to beat him up myself. "*Did* Jesse tell anyone you were there?"

Kenneth shakes his head. "You believe me, don't you, Shady?" he asks, his eyes pleading.

"Do you—do you believe Jesse killed Jim?" I say, lifting my chin. "You were there that morning. Did Jesse seem like someone who was about to murder his stepfather?"

"Maybe nobody ever looks like who they are," Kenneth says, and there's so much sadness in his voice it makes my heart contract, no matter how mad I am at him right now, no matter how much I doubt him. "But if I thought he was going to kill my dad, I wouldn't have left them there alone together. I keep thinking that if I'd stayed, if I'd helped them work on the house like Dad wanted me to, he'd still be alive."

Or maybe Kenneth would've gotten killed too. Jim's the only person who can answer that question.

I don't try to offer Kenneth any comfort—nothing I say will make his what-ifs easier to bear. But my voice grows gentler as I turn the conversation to the specifics of the house where Jim died. We talk for another five minutes, and Kenneth seems relieved to be hiding his secret from one less person.

Once he has told me what he knows, I realize I've gotten all the information I can from the living—now it's time to ask the dead.

NINETEEN

"You sure you're ready for this?" Cedar asks, glancing at me for the millionth time in ten minutes. "This is really what you want to do?" He grips the steering wheel so tight his knuckles are white.

"Yes, I'm sure. If you don't want to—"

"I said I would. I don't want you to do this alone, but I still think you should have asked Sarah and Orlando to come too." He glances at me again, hesitant, anxious, trying to pretend he's not scared out of his mind that we're about to raise Jim's ghost.

"I can't ask Sarah; I can't even talk to Sarah right now."

"But Orlando's your best friend, right? I can't believe he won't help you," Cedar says.

"He is. But he was pretty clear that he didn't want to get involved with this." I lean back in my seat and close my eyes. I do wish Orlando were here. And Sarah. As much as I'm trying to pretend otherwise, I'm scared. I'm scared of what will happen, scared of what I might learn from Jim's ghost.

Cedar's quiet for a few minutes, but then he starts up again. "Are you sure Kenneth didn't want to come? I mean, it's his dad."

"No, he was totally freaked out by the idea," I say, "and I don't blame him after what happened with Sarah." The memory of her sobs is still too sharp in my mind. Plus, ever since I found out Kenneth was there the day Jim was killed, I can't rule him out as a suspect. However unlikely it is that he could kill his dad, I can't let myself trust him until I hear what Jim has to say.

"Now stop talking and let me think." I turn the radio back up. Jason Isbell's music fills the cab, his familiar voice settling my nerves.

We drive past the dark woods and the shuttered houses, past the convenience stores blazing their light into the blackness, past the silent, sleeping churches. Finally, we near the road that leads to the place Jim's life ended.

"Turn here," I say, pointing at the sign for the new neighborhood.

It's past midnight when we approach the half-built house where Kenneth said Jim was working the morning he died. Cedar's about to turn into the driveway when his headlights illuminate another truck parked there. A big, shiny blue truck.

"Shit, keep going," I hiss. We coast past the house and stop at the cul-de-sac several lots down. "That's Frank's truck. Jim's brother. He's going to notice if we park here. Turn around and go back the way you came. Maybe if he saw us, he'll think we got lost."

"What's he doing here at midnight?"

"I don't know. It's weird."

We go back the way we came. I try to peer inside Frank's truck, but I don't see Frank. That doesn't mean he hasn't seen us, though. We turn onto the main road and park on the shoulder after a few yards. There's nowhere else around here to leave the truck.

Cedar pulls the key from the ignition, plunging us into darkness. Even though I can barely see him, I feel his eyes on me, and I swear I can hear the beat of his heart.

"Let's come back tomorrow night, when he's not here," Cedar says.

"No, it has to be now. I need to do this while I've got my nerve up." Before Jesse really gets hurt. Before he's been sentenced and it's too late. "And Frank might not even be here. Maybe he just left his truck or something. Let's at least go see. It'll be all right."

Cedar hesitates, but then he opens his door and climbs out.

A few cars blow past us as we walk back toward the neighborhood, but no one stops. The moon is full tonight, though it's almost completely hidden by clouds, casting the world in gloom. We keep to the shadows once we get closer to the construction site, both of us watchful, almost holding our breath.

The whole neighborhood is deserted, littered with the usual trash of an active construction site. Tractors loom up out of the darkness, promising holes for unwary bodies to fall into. Even the finished houses are still empty. Nobody has moved into the new subdivision yet, and there's no other houses for at least half a mile. Based on all of Jim's complaining at home—about how hard Frank was driving them—this should all be much closer to done by now. The site seems not to have been worked on since Jim died.

I brought a flashlight, but I don't dare use it. Instead, I grip Cedar's hand and walk carefully along the newly paved street, grateful to have another warm body beside me, especially one as steady as Cedar's. His hand is sweaty, but it's warm and firm.

As we near the house, a man's voice punctures the silence. He swears loudly, his words slurred and angry. We both duck, thinking he's seen us. But then he swears again, his voice fainter. He's not yelling at us, but no one else responds.

I wait for my heart rate to slow before I start to creep along again. I wish there were more places to hide. I feel exposed and vulnerable out here.

When we're as close as I dare go, I crouch behind a tractor at the edge of the yard, pulling Cedar down beside me. I peer around the tire and into the darkness. Frank slouches on the front stoop, a bottle of Jack Daniel's in one hand and a cigarette in the other.

"You sonofabitch," he slurs. "Why would you stay here, why would you stay here, why would you stay? You knew, you knew. You goddamn sonofabitch."

Beside me, Cedar's hand grips mine more tightly.

There's a brief silence while Frank drinks. Then he starts back in, ranting at the empty night. "It's him—he's the one.

That lying, conniving worm. He was sorry—everyone knows that. He was a sorry waste of space. Let him rot! Let him rot in there. It's his fault."

I had hoped Frank might soften toward Jesse after seeing Honey and me that day he came to the house, but it sounds like he's out to get my brother as much as ever. Fear opens up in me like a gaping black hole, but before I can give in to it and go home, Frank's moving.

He climbs to his feet shakily. "No, I won't—I won't, God damn it," he roars, throwing the whiskey bottle off into the darkness. It smashes against something. "I won't," he yells one more time, before stalking across the yard to his truck.

"What's wrong with him?" Cedar whispers.

"I don't know." Mama said grief affects everyone differently. Maybe it's turning Frank into a drunk. I almost feel sorry for him, despite how he acted at the funeral, despite how hard he's working to send Jesse to prison.

We hunker down in the shadows until Frank's headlights point away down the road. He weaves the truck along the empty street.

"We should call the police—he could kill someone driving like that," Cedar says.

"Call if you want. But don't give your name or say where you are. We could get in trouble for being here. And do it fast." Being found in the place where my brother supposedly killed our stepdad won't do me any favors, especially considering Kenneth's stepdad and Frank's friend works for the police department.

Cedar speaks to a dispatcher for a few minutes before hanging up. I doubt it will do any good. Frank could be anywhere by now. And even if they catch him, they'll just slap his wrist and tell him to get his act together before the city council elections. Small-town good ol' boys and all that.

As we approach the dark house, a horrible thought grips me. What if Frank wasn't just drunk and raging at the night? What if he was raging at someone else? Someone only he could see?

A cold weight settles in the pit of my stomach, sending a painful shiver up my spine. Before the fear can paralyze me, I pull the flashlight from my pocket and use it to find our way to the front door, then let myself inside. Something small rustles in a corner, but I don't have the energy to worry about what it might be. Cedar and I walk softly through the house, listening, but the only sound is the blood pumping in my temples. We climb the stairs and open the door to the master bedroom. It's right where Kenneth said it would be. Just as we step inside, the moon comes out from behind the clouds, pouring its silver light into the windows.

This is the room where Jim died, where someone bashed in his head with a hammer and sent his blood spilling out on the floor. Thankfully, someone has cleared away the bloodstains.

Now, only moonlight puddles on the hardwood floor. I go and sit in it, let it wash over my skin. I feel a little safer sitting in its glow. Cedar hovers near the door, all his rodeo arrogance gone. Even he can probably feel that there's a ghost here—one with ties to this earth so strong it might never get free. It makes my skin crawl.

"Come here," I say. "It's all right." Cedar walks slowly toward me and sits, looking helpless and unsure what to do with himself. "Just stay with me," I say. "That's all I need." And that's all he can offer me now. Where I'm going, he can't follow.

I'm pretending to be braver than I feel. I don't know if I'll fall into that dark, shadowy place again like I did after Sarah's mom. But my hands shake as I take out the fiddle and start to tune it, flinching at every half note and squeak.

As I raise the bow above the strings, I hesitate. The fiddle is dangerous, but what I might learn from using it—that feels like a ticking time bomb. What if Frank's right and it was Jesse? What do I do if I learn he—

"Just breathe, Shady," Cedar says, like he's coaching me through a recital. But he doesn't know what's required of me.

Breathing carefully in and out, I close my eyes and focus on the feel of the strings beneath my fingers, cast my mind back to the first time I felt them, to how Daddy laughed at my clumsy attempts. The memory of that laugh—deep and big and honest—is all it takes to send me spiraling into my grief. Will it be enough? Do I need to tap into my anger, too? That helpless rage I feel when I think about his truck crashing into the lake? The despair of seeing him lowered into the ground?

I can almost feel it when my grief's power meets that of the fiddle—like to like. As I draw the bow over the strings, every hair on my arms stands on end. My scalp tingles. My heart beats so hard and fast I'm surprised it doesn't overpower the sound of my fiddle.

I take a deep breath, and then I plunge into "Omie Wise,"

a murder ballad about a man who tricks a woman into meeting him at a river and then drowns her there, leaving her body behind. Of course, I don't sing it; my fiddle's all the voice Jim's ghost will need. Unlike a lot of other sad bluegrass songs, this one's got a mournful tune to go with mournful lyrics.

As I draw my bow back and forth over the strings, I imagine Jim's ghost materializing bit by bit, building itself up like an intricate Palm Sunday cross woven from palm fronds.

I play the song slow and low, sensing that Jim doesn't need frenzy to call him forth. Since he's been murdered, he's probably simmering at the surface like a pot of water about to boil. This fiddle's just a dash of salt to hurry him along.

I close my eyes, and the song's story dances through my mind. I can see little Omie Wise, desperate and trusting, daring to hope, darting furtively through darkness to meet John Lewis, who waits by the spring on his tall, dark horse. Then the quick flight of the horse, its hooves pounding into the damp mud of the riverbed, Omie's hair whipping behind her, her suspicions rising to equal her hopes. And then the boat, and the drowning, a strong hand pushing her down into the cold water. John Lewis's strange, hateful face her last sight.

Despair and terror and betrayal mingle in my chest and flow from my fingertips. A cool breeze from nowhere rustles my hair. I swallow down my fear and open my eyes.

My stepfather's ghost is staring back at me.

TWENTY

"Jim." My voice comes out weak, barely more than a whisper, so I clear my throat and try again, pitching my voice above the fiddle. "Hey, Jim."

My stepfather, whose body I saw laid to rest in a coffin only days ago, blinks at me like I'm the ghost. As scared as I am, I've never been more relieved to see him. Even after Sarah's mom and the woman in the woods, I still wasn't sure I could do it. But here he is. Triumph surges through me, tempering my fear.

"Shady," he says, his voice a rasp. He looks puzzled, lost. He eyes Cedar uncertainly.

My heart pounds, and my hands have gone clammy. It takes all my effort to keep the bow moving over the strings. I don't know how long Jim will stick around, so I get straight to the point.

"Who killed you, Jim?" I ask, gazing up at him. My whole body trembles, including my voice. Jim cocks his head at me, and I think maybe he didn't understand, so I ask him again. "Who hit you with the hammer?"

Jim's eyes clear slightly. "The hammer," he says, licking his lips.

"Who was it? Who hit you?"

Jim's lips start to form a name, but then he stops and studies me, like he's taking my measure, deciding what I can handle. That lost look is gone.

Panic surges through my veins. "Tell me," I say.

"How's your mama?" he asks instead, and I'm wound so tight I want to cry and scream and throw my bow at him, but I keep playing—steady, steady—a power source that can't spark or wane.

"I don't have time for this," I say. "Mama's fine, Honey's fine, Kenneth's fine. But I need to know who killed you." My throat goes dry, so I don't say anything more. Instead, I stare at him, taking him in. He looks like the Jim I always knew, dressed in his company's collared work shirt, jeans, and heavy boots. He's too thin, unhealthy, scruffy. Jim's all angles, no soft places. Even his eyes are sharp.

Sharp and considering, deliberating. I thought the truth would come bubbling out of him, irrepressible as the springs that bubble up from the ground, flowing into rivers. But I can see him working at it, cutting a little off here, sanding down an edge there. Making it into something—something that will fulfill a purpose. I hadn't considered that his answer might not be the truth. Or at least not the whole truth.

"Jesse's in jail," I say in a rush. "He's being charged with your murder. It's bad enough you're dead, but now Jesse . . ." I shake my head. "Haven't you hurt him enough?"

"I hurt *him*?" Jim says, disbelieving. "I never did anything to that boy. But he . . . Well, now, that's another story."

A wave of nausea smashes into me. "What did he do?"

Jim cocks his head at me, looking for all the world like a rangy bird. "It'll be better for all of you if he goes to prison. One less thing for your mama to worry about. He's only gonna bring her pain, but at least if he's in jail, he can do it on someone else's dime."

"But he didn't kill you," I snarl. "He's innocent."

"Ain't nobody innocent, Shady, least of all your brother. Sometimes the judgment that falls on us ain't for the crime we did, but it's owed us all the same."

"What's that supposed to mean?"

Jim rubs the back of his head. "I didn't deserve that particular hammer that bashed in my brains, but I ducked plenty of ones before it. And there was gonna be another hammer, sometime, someday, so why not this one?" He smiles, showing a flash of tobacco-stained teeth.

"Just tell me who did it. Stop talking riddles and tell me who killed you." He'd never protect Jesse like this and wouldn't care about my feelings if Jesse were the murderer. There's only one person he'd protect so fiercely. Kenneth.

Jim's voice draws my attention back to him. "I got myself killed, girl, like we all do. Everybody wants to be a victim, but even if we're victims, we're the executioners, too. I've been putting the knots in my own hanging rope for a long, long while."

That sounds like something someone else said to me recently—but who?

"What did you do?" I ask, my curiosity pushing the thought from my mind.

"You want me to confess my sins?" he says wryly. "Fine. I lied to you at the hospital that night. Your mama and I were together before your daddy died."

"You what?" I should have known, but I guess I didn't want to. Jesse was right, and Mama and Jim both lied to me. I shake my head. "I don't know what Mama ever saw in you."

"She saw somebody who'd pay mind to her instead of that goddamned fiddle in your hands." He nods at Cedar. "You remember that, boy, if you're starting up with this one here. She's her daddy all the way through."

Jim laughs bitterly. "Now put that fiddle down and go home, and leave me to my afterlife."

"Not until you tell me," I say, gritting my teeth. "I need to know who killed you." My arms are aching from holding up the fiddle, and the music's starting to sound shaky and shrill. Sweat beads at my temples. I don't know how much longer I can keep this up. But Cedar's thigh moves to touch my knee, making me feel a little more anchored to this realm.

Jim squats down until he's nose to nose with me, his eyes boring into mine. I resist the impulse to cringe away.

"I'm dead, and it's Jesse's fault, and there ain't nothing you can do about that. I don't know where in God's name you got that magic fiddle, but you better put it back where you found it, and leave dead men be."

"Are you really going to do this to Daddy's—to your best friend's—family?" Another question creeps into my head like a dark fog, and before I can think, it's out of my mouth. "Or—or were you glad Daddy died? So you could have Mama?" I'm as surprised by the question as Jim is, but I keep my gaze fixed on him, an anger that doesn't even feel like mine radiating from me.

Jim looks rattled for the first time. "Glad he died? Me?" He leaps to his feet, looming over us, seeming bigger and darker than he ever was in life. "You want to talk about William dying, you go see your brother. Now drop that goddamned fiddle and leave me be," he roars, lunging for my instrument.

Cedar throws himself in front of me, knocking the bow from my hand and bringing "Omie Wise" to a sudden end, cracking our connection right down the middle. Jim reels back, but Cedar kneels between us, his arms spread out to protect me.

Jim looks at me as if from the other side of an abyss, all impotent rage. And then he's gone and there's just the moonlight pouring through the window.

"Why'd you do that?" I yell.

"He was coming after you—I thought . . . I just acted. I'm sorry. Let's get out of here, please," Cedar says, his eyes wide with fear.

I start to stand, but then a cold, strong hand grips my wrist, and an eerily familiar voice rasps, "Pick up your fiddle. Play me a tune." When I don't move, the hand tightens its grip, each finger pressing a bruise into my skin. "Now."

I turn and see darkness in the shape of a man, a festering blackness without a face. This is what crawled out of the crack I made when my music stopped. A monster climbing out of a rent between worlds. I think it was his anger I felt before, his voice whispering that question about Jim being glad of Daddy's death. But now the monster isn't just in my head.

I open my mouth to scream, but no sound comes out.

"Shady," Cedar says, backing away toward the door. "Shady, let's go. Come on, let's go." But I can't. I know what comes next. I know it with the dreadful certainty that usually only comes in dreams. In nightmares.

I didn't know he could find me here, in the waking world.

It's the shadow man who haunts my sleeping hours. He visited me in the hospital—the night Jesse beat up Kenneth. He stopped up my throat with his darkness. And it was his darkness I fell into after raising Sarah's mom.

But this is different. Somehow, Daddy's fiddle has given him shape, form, power. Instead of being paralyzed, my body is in his control, my limbs moving against my own will. I keep telling myself to move, to fight, to run, but nothing happens.

My throat closes up as I retrieve my fiddle from the floor. Will the music make him stronger? It must, or else why would he make me play? I need to stop him, need to get back control of my limbs and my fiddle. But no matter how hard I try to rip myself from his control, I can't break free. I am twelve years old again, a phantom hand at my throat, my body turned traitor against me. Only this time it's not a dream.

If I could scream, I could banish him, send him hurtling

back into the darkness he oozed out of. But my voice is locked up tight, so this fiddle's the only voice I have, and now it's his weapon instead of mine. Tears burn at the corner of my eyes, the only outward sign of my struggle against the shadow man.

Cedar's still beside me, pulling at my arm, but he seems as distant as if he's in another house, on another block. He yells, but I can't hear him. It's just me and my fiddle facing down the darkness. And I'm not ready. I'm not prepared.

"Play," the shadow man says. "Play."

As if my hands aren't mine anymore, I dive into "The Twa Sisters," the song that started this whole business. The song that drew me into the woods and made me find this fiddle. Anguish and sorrow and regret flow from my strings.

I thought nothing could be worse than lying on my back in bed, helpless against the hideous shadows hovering overhead, but this is worse. To see the music that belonged to Daddy put in service of this monster, to see Daddy's fiddle twisted to its evil purpose.

I glare at the shadow man, my nostrils flaring, my jaw clenched, but he only laughs. And then he swirls around me, making the whole world go dark.

My mind fills with fear, until every terror I've ever had is pressed inside, one against and atop the other, and my breath comes short, and sweat coats every inch of me, even though I'm freezing. But I can't stop playing. Now "Anna Lee" pours from the fiddle, beautiful and haunting.

While I make music, the shadow man makes nightmares. The worst dreams in my memory, the ones that left me gasping, cold and shivering in my bed, play over and over in my mind. The wasps chasing me down the stairs, their stingers like fire. The dog leaping at my face. The old man in the jogging suit choking me across a fence on a dusty road. The little dead girl in my ceiling gazing down at me with a face I can't see, her white dress billowing around her legs. Being sucked into the Atlantic undertow and drowned. And, of course, the alligators.

Then my nightmares shift, mixing horribly with my daytime terrors: Daddy's coffin. Jesse's rages. Mama's blank, tired face. Sarah turning her back on me forever. The dreams and the fears merge, forming nightmares my subconscious could never have dreamed up. Horrible, grotesque images flit behind my eyes, fast and merciless, seemingly endless.

Fear fills my whole being, until there's nothing left.

And the shadow man grows and grows, spreading through the room, gaining substance and power from my fear. Wings brush the walls and flutter fitfully in my hair. Stingers scrape against my skin, leaving burning trails. I should pass out from pure terror and exhaustion; I should fall into darkness and disappear, but I can't. The music has me rooted to the spot.

I don't know how many songs I've played, how long this has gone on.

I'm surrounded by my own terrors, my nightmares made flesh. But I'm already awake, so there's no hope of rescue. He will keep me here until I die. That's what he wants from me—I see that now. All along, he's been trying to kill me. He couldn't kill me in my dreams, so he used the fiddle to lure me into danger. He's greedy for my death, but I don't know why.

When a banjo starts playing, I think it's another nightmare come to get me, a dream I must have forgotten about in the crowd of lurking monsters. At first it's faint as my breath, like it's coming from another room in the house. But then it gets louder, more insistent, demanding to be heard. Soon, the banjo's tempo matches mine, but where my music feels forced, drawn out of me like blood from a vein, this music is alive in the way only bluegrass can be, the notes bright as sunshine.

Sarah.

As the music fills the room, overpowering my fiddle, slices of moonlight break through the darkness, like sunlight between the slats of a blind. I catch glimpses of Sarah, sitting cross-legged across from me with the head of the banjo resting in her lap, hair flopping over her eyes, bare fingers dancing over the strings. My heart gives a rebellious thump against the shadow man's prison walls.

As if she hears it, Sarah looks up and locks eyes with me. Her eyes seem black and glittering and . . . powerful. Normally, Sarah breaks eye contact after a few seconds, but now she's staring into me, like she's searching inside my body for the real Shady, shackled up somewhere inside this automaton playing a fiddle.

Her eyes are worried but filled with something I haven't seen there before. Excitement? Triumph? I don't know. They shine out at me, and all I can think is that I have no idea who she is, or what she might become. But I'm certain the darkness is no match for her.

And then she starts singing. Sarah Woolf is singing. She

doesn't have an amazing voice, but it's hers and she's using it. I feel the darkness breaking up around me, like a tree's being pulled up by its roots in a storm, and the darkness is breaking away into clumps, crumbling into nothing.

A guitar joins her, and then two other voices—Cedar and Orlando. I didn't even realize I was playing it, but they're all singing "Shady Grove." As the words wrap around me, I feel my daddy's presence here, too, all the love he had for me pressed into these syllables and notes.

The shadow man snarls and clutches at me, but his fingers are only vapor when they touch my skin, his strength is almost gone. He lets out a frustrated roar and falls back, shrinking to his usual shape. Moonlight floods the room again.

Finally, unbelievably, my fingers stop moving, and the fiddle falls into my lap, mute for the first time in what feels like a million years. It must have been hours, if Cedar had time to get Sarah and Orlando here.

The shadow man swirls away, like water down a drain, back into the hole my music made. And then there's Sarah, her banjo, her voice, her eyes. The whole world—all the worlds—narrow to a girl-shaped form made of bluegrass.

She finishes the song with a flourish and holds my gaze. I can't look away, not because I'm trapped again, but because my heart won't let me. I feel like I've been born again, like I finally know what my Baptist relatives are always going on about. I've been saved by a girl with a banjo, baptized in her song.

And then she's holding me, so close I can feel her heartbeat against my own skin. She has her arms wrapped around me like she just rescued me from the edge of a cliff, and she's afraid if she lets go I'll plunge down into the abyss, which maybe isn't that far from the truth. So I cling to her, too, burying my face in her neck.

I'm shaking, my whole body racked with chills. Sarah chafes my arms, as if to warm me with her own energy. "It's all right," she murmurs into my hair. "It's all right."

Finally, she pulls back and looks at me, studies my face, my shoulders, my arms. She gasps when she turns over my left hand. My fingertips are dripping blood. The shadow man's hold made me rip right through my calluses. "Oh, Shady," she whispers.

"I'll go get my truck," Cedar says, running from the room.

Orlando kneels beside me, fear and worry in his eyes. "Let's get you home," he says, and his voice is the gentle one I know, not the hard, brittle one he's been using all week.

When Cedar gets back, he and Sarah lift me to my feet. Cedar pulls me to his side and helps me down the stairs and out of the house, taking half my weight. He settles me into the cab and goes around to his side, talking to Orlando.

I turn to Sarah, who lingers beside my open door. "I thought . . . I thought you'd never talk to me again."

"I would have come if you'd asked," Sarah says gently. "I'll always come." She looks like she's daring anyone to say otherwise. She means it.

Sarah holds my gaze, but I can't tell what she's feeling. Her eyes search mine. Finally, she says, "I forgive you. For what happened at my house. And . . ." She lowers her voice so only I can hear. "And for Cedar. He's—he's a really good guy."

I stare at her. It sounds like she's giving me her blessing to be with Cedar. Does she think I *want* her to hand me over to him? I need to make her see how much I still feel for her, that even though I like Cedar, she's the one I want. The one I've always wanted.

I probably shouldn't be thinking about my love life after what just happened—actually, no, I should. The shadow man feeds on my grief and my fear, but he can't touch what I feel for Sarah. She just proved that to all of us. "About Cedar," I say, but she cuts me off.

"Not tonight. You've been through enough. We'll talk tomorrow, okay?" She turns away and calls for Orlando to follow her. Frustration and disappointment fill my chest as I watch her walk away. I almost call after her, but what's the point?

After how she fought for me against the shadow man, how she clung to me once he was gone—I thought this was going to be another chance for her and me, but just like that, the brief opening is gone, vanished. My mind spins and sputters like tires stuck in mud.

Cedar climbs in next to me and starts to drive. He's so still, tense and silent. After everything I put him through tonight, at least he didn't overhear the exchange Sarah and I just had. At least I don't think he did. I can't think too hard about it. Exhaustion hits, and all I can do is gaze out the window at the construction site. It looks forlorn, half formed. Not a place anyone would want to die or haunt. I almost feel bad for whoever moves in here. Their brand-new house will already be haunted.

"Bye, Jim," I whisper as we pull away and speed into the humid Florida night.

Cedar doesn't say anything about Jim or the shadow man. He grips the steering wheel even harder than he did on the ride over, darting worried glances at me every few minutes the entire ride home.

When we near my home, I don't ask him to drop me at the end of the road like the last two times he's driven me; I don't think he would anyway. But when we pull up to the trailer, I wince as the headlights hit the siding, more out of habit than any real embarrassment. Going up against an evil darkness that wants to trap you inside every nightmare you've ever had has a way of putting things in perspective.

Cedar's eyes glance over the trailer, but he doesn't look surprised or dismayed or resigned. It's like he doesn't see it. He jumps out of the truck and comes around to my side, helping me down from the cab. I'm weak and aching and hollow-feeling. When he pulls me into a tight hug, I rest into his chest, laying my head against his neck and breathing in the salt-sweat smell of him. I wish he could come inside and spend the night. I'm afraid to go to sleep.

But he helps me to the trailer steps, kisses my forehead, and starts toward his truck.

"Thank you," I say, and he turns back around. "Thank you for helping me—for coming with me and for calling for Sarah and Orlando. For keeping me safe. If y'all hadn't come . . ." The thought is too horrible to finish.

Cedar looks troubled and exhausted in the glare from the

front porch light, but he gives me a small smile. "You're welcome, Shady. I'm just glad you're all right."

"What did you see, while it was happening, while he was . . . hurting me?" I ask.

Cedar shakes his head. "Not much—mostly shadows moving around. But you were frozen and you looked so scared. And I could feel him—his darkness, his evil." Cedar shivers. "I can't imagine what you went through." He takes a few steps toward me and cups my cheek. "Get some rest," he says. He kisses me lightly on the lips and then watches me thoughtfully as I unlock the door and disappear inside.

Mama has been waiting up for me, so I don't have a chance to hide the state I'm in. She takes one look at me and sends me to bed, saying we'll deal with it tomorrow. The sight of her face sends a stab of anger to my stomach. After everything else Jim said, their affair should hardly matter, but what if it matters more than all the rest? It seems to be the main cause of the rift between Jim and Jesse, the thing that led to their troubled relationship. I still don't think Jesse killed Jim, but all that anger he held against Jim is what led us here. It's why Jesse was the primary suspect, why he's sitting in jail right now. I can't help but wonder how different things would be if the affair had never happened at all.

But I'm too tired to think through it all tonight. I go to the bathroom to bandage my fingers, wincing each time the fabric touches my skin. When I drag myself to the bedroom, Honey's in my bed, curled like a little bean at the edge of the mattress. I lie beside her and listen to her breathe, trying not to fall asleep, trying not to think about everything that happened, trying not to think about the shadow man. Trying not to think about how I failed.

Because what's even worse than the shadow man's attack is what happened before, or rather what didn't happen. I didn't find the answers to Jesse's freedom or gain any real clues to help prove his innocence. I only unearthed more questions.

TWENTY-ONE

I wake to pain. My shoulders, my arms, the tips of my fingers. My back, my neck. I don't think there's a part of my body that doesn't hurt. But it's my insides that suffered the most damage last night. Everything Jim said, and then all the shadow man put me through, it all pulls at me. I don't know what to think, what to do. I'm never going to be the sort of person who lets life happen to her, who coasts along with events, accepting what comes. But today I want to be.

I lie in bed and stare at the ceiling, pretending its pebbled white surface is an early morning beach, the sand fresh from the receding tide, unmarred by feet or tires. Today waits for me like that flawless stretch of sand, untouched by my decisions or mistakes. If I stay in bed, it can remain perfect, a clean plane of possibility.

But then I hear Mama rattling around in the kitchen, talking in a low voice to Honey, who is singing the alphabet song in between bites of her breakfast.

So I drag myself out of bed and kick the imaginary sand under my feet. If I don't get out there, Jesse will be stuck in prison forever. I might not be much, but I'm all he's got.

"Mama, I want to visit Jesse," I say once I work up the courage to enter the kitchen. "Why haven't we been yet?" I know why I haven't asked before—because I've been afraid he'd see the doubt on my face, or that he'd give me even more reason to lose my trust in him. But why has Mama stayed away?

She blinks at me tiredly from behind a steaming mug of coffee. She's still wearing her fluffy blue robe. "He said he didn't want to see me."

And now I know why. He's been angry at her all this time about her affair with Jim. What would Mama say if she knew I raised Jim's ghost last night? If she knew all he told me? I'm not sure if anything he said about Jesse was true, but I know he wasn't lying about him and Mama. I should probably be mad at her, too, but with how tired and grieved and lonely she looks this morning, the thought of her cheating on Daddy only makes me sad.

"I bet Jesse'll see me." I use my uninjured hand to pinch pieces off a powdered doughnut on her plate.

"You can't go alone. I have to be with you." She sets her coffee down and smacks my hand. "Quit picking at my breakfast. There's a box on the counter."

"What about Aunt Ena?" I ask, dusting off my fingers.

Mama tilts her head and gives me that "don't kid yourself" look. "Your aunt Ena can't even go to the grocery store."

"Let me ask her. Is she on the visitor's list?"

"No, but we can get her on it."

"Will you, please?"

"All right," Mama says, pushing her bangs off her forehead. "Now leave me alone until I have my coffee. And eat some breakfast. You look like hell."

I guess she's decided not to ask me about last night. Or maybe she's too tired now and she'll launch into it once she's caffeinated. I'm not waiting around to find out.

I kiss the top of Honey's mussed head and retreat down the hall to do something about my own wild hair.

When the bus pulls up to school, I look for Cedar, and instead find Sarah. She's leaning against the wall outside the office, one blue high-top Converse flat against the bricks. She's got on a T-shirt from a kids' summer camp, which seriously detracts from her moody expression and crossed arms. I can't help but smile at the sight of her, though it also makes my stomach rumble. She saved me last night, saved me when no one else could, and that has to mean something.

"Hey," I say.

"Cedar will be right back," Sarah says in a rush.

"Oh. You guys . . . talked?"

"A little," she says, and shrugs.

"About last night . . . thank you for coming," I say, meeting her eyes. Sarah looks tired and worried. But whatever stronger emotion I saw in her last night is gone today.

"I'll always . . . come," she says haltingly. The promise doesn't sound as fervent as it did last night, but I can tell she means it. "You're my best friend."

Her best friend. I should be grateful to have her as a friend at all, but it's hard to let go of what we might have been, if things had been different. Even with the weight of the shadow man dragging me down, my fear for Jesse, all of it—knowing I'm losing Sarah still manages to feel like a punch to the gut.

Then Cedar comes around the corner, followed by Rose and Orlando and Kenneth. I eye my stepbrother, feeling awkward about seeing him after raising Jim's ghost, and more uncertain than ever if I can trust him. I wonder if Cedar told him what happened last night.

Orlando bumps his shoulder against mine, a simple touch that means all is forgiven. Rose is scowling, but I wouldn't expect anything different. She stands next to Sarah and says something to her, but Sarah steps away and looks at the ground.

Cedar slips an arm around my waist and smiles at me. "Hey. You all right?"

I look from him to Sarah, and then to the others. "I'm fine. Why's everyone here?"

Rose rolls her eyes. "For you, dummy. So you don't get yourself killed or lost in hell or whatever the fuck happened last time. You obviously can't handle this ghost crap on your own."

"But I already raised Jim's ghost. I already talked to him," I say, glancing at Kenneth. I expect to see fear and guilt in his eyes, but he only looks uncomfortable. He crosses his arms and clears his throat.

"Cedar already filled me in," he says. "Maybe I should have gone, but I . . ."

Sarah, of all people, puts a hand on Kenneth's arm. "Trust

me, Kenneth, you're better off leaving things as they are. It's not like you think it would be."

But I'm still upset at Kenneth for lying all this time, and he also hasn't done anything to convince me he shouldn't be a suspect too, so I don't really care how he feels about it. Maybe I'm being unreasonable, maybe it wouldn't have made a difference if he'd told the truth, but it would have been something. It would have been the right thing to do.

"I was just trying to get information to help Jesse. That's the only reason I did it."

"And?" Kenneth says, his voice expectant. "What—what did Dad say?"

Everyone's staring at me, waiting for an answer, but I'm not sure what the answer is. "Jim . . . he wasn't really clear. I don't think he wanted to tell me the truth." Cedar cocks his head at me, like he took away very different information from Jim last night.

I can't tell if Kenneth is relieved or disappointed. "You could . . . you could bring him back again," he says, his voice wavering, "to ask him more when he's ready." Is Kenneth bluffing now, trying to make himself seem less afraid of being accused?

"I don't think he'll come. He's not interested in helping me."

Sarah's voice catches my attention. "Do ghosts have a choice? Can they choose not to come?" she asks, her voice throaty, heavy. I know she's thinking about her mom.

I nod. "Some of them can, especially the ones who have been around a while. Daddy said the fiddle just sort of opens a door, and ghosts have to decide whether to walk through it."

Sarah's eyes go bright with tears she won't let spill, and she looks away, toward the PE fields.

A bell rings, and Orlando looks at his watch. "We should get to class." But instead of going, he turns to Cedar. "What's the plan?"

"Let's meet and play tonight," Cedar says to the group. "Seven o'clock."

"Why?" I ask. "I already—"

"Just bring your regular fiddle this time," Rose interrupts.

Cedar smiles at me. "We're your band. We want to support you. Make sure you're okay. A band practice will be a good chance for us all to talk."

I look to Sarah, and she nods. "We can't play at my place though," she says hurriedly, crossing her arms again.

I don't know that I can play again after what the shadow man did to me, but I offer up Aunt Ena's house for the meeting. I can call her after school to make sure she doesn't mind, but she'll probably be thrilled to meet my friends. Besides, I need to talk to her. After she helped me, she deserves to know what happened. And I want to be in the place I feel closest to Daddy. After last night, I'm longing to hear his voice again.

As the others file away, I pull Kenneth to one side. "Hey," I say.

"Yeah?" He glances at me with nervous, wary eyes. His face is built for honesty—wide and freckled, with that shock of red hair. But he said himself that people aren't ever who we think they are. Maybe he's not either. I still can't help but wonder if his resentment of Jim finally broke open on his daddy's head. If he's not speaking up for Jesse because he's the guilty one.

And yet he's not acting like someone who's guilty. I search his face for the truth, but I don't see anything except sadness and weariness. The only person acting guilty is Frank, I realize—drinking alone in the place Jim died, railing into the night.

The thought pushes whatever I had planned to say to Kenneth from my mind. Instead, I ask about Frank. "Before I raised Jim's ghost last night, I saw your uncle Frank there at the construction site. It was midnight and he was drunk and yelling at no one. Do you think maybe he might be—"

Kenneth recoils, his pale skin flushing red. "Now you think Uncle Frank killed my daddy? What the hell, Shady?"

Before I can respond, Kenneth shakes his head and stalks away, but then he turns at the last second. "You know, Uncle Frank has always talked to me a lot about forgiveness. He was always telling me I needed to forgive Dad for not being there for me, that I should give him another chance. Uncle Frank said he forgave Dad even though he was the reason their daddy died. Did you know that? My dad was supposed to watch Granddaddy when he was so sick, and instead Dad took off to buy a bottle of Jack and Granddaddy died. But Uncle Frank forgave him and gave him work, no matter how bad Dad treated him, and he made sure I was always taken care of. Uncle Frank's a good man. You could take a page from his book."

"I wasn't accusing Frank—I just thought you should know how he was that night—so you could check on him." My cheeks flush with the lie.

"Yeah, right," Kenneth says. "You gonna accuse me next?"

I square my shoulders. "Why shouldn't I?"

Kenneth's mouth twists. "You're not the person I thought you were, Shady." He spins on his heel, and I practically sink to the ground under the weight of his anger. Under the weight of my own shame. Maybe he's right, and I'm just looking for anyone to blame, anyone except Jesse.

I thought getting the fiddle would solve all the mysteries and make clear all the secrets, but instead it's like a letter opener sliding under an envelope's flap. I'm half afraid to know what's going to come springing out of the unsealed paper. I still don't know who killed Jim or why, but I'm more unsure of Jesse than ever, and nowhere feels safe—not the woods, not Mama's trailer, not even my dreams. Aunt Ena's house feels like my last refuge.

I get to Aunt Ena's half an hour early, and before I've even turned off the engine, the knot of anxiety in my belly starts to loosen. The house looks bigger than usual in the deepening twilight, the azaleas faintly glowing in the gloom of the oaks and hanging moss. No one passing by would see safe refuge here, but as I walk up the steps, my protective walls fall down, one by one.

When Aunt Ena pulls me into a hug, I finally let go of the burden of unshed tears I've been carrying around since last night. Ena holds me and croons into my hair the way I do for Honey when she's sad.

After I've gotten all the tears out, I tell her everything—

about raising Jim, what he said, the shadow man, Sarah's rescue. Her eyes light up when I talk about Sarah, but I quickly change the subject to what I came here to ask.

"Will you take me to visit Jesse on Saturday?"

"To the jail?" She leans back. "Why?"

"The juvenile detention center. It's just teenagers there," I say. "I need to talk to Jesse, to find out if all the stuff Jim said about him is . . . if there's any truth in it. Look, I was wrong to use the fiddle. I see that now. I should have tried to talk to Jesse first, to see if I could get him to tell me what happened. That's what I want to do now."

"I don't know, Shady . . ."

"Please, Aunt Ena. I know it will be hard for you, but he won't see Mama, and anyway I wouldn't want her to hear what we talk about. It's important. Please."

Aunt Ena's eyes fill with dread, but she nods. "All right."

"Thank you," I say, wiping away the last of my tears. "And thank you for letting us play here tonight. I know it was short notice."

Aunt Ena waves away my thanks. "You know this is still your home. You can always bring your friends here. But are you going to play again . . . so soon? Look at the state of your hand."

My fingers are covered in Honey's cartoon-themed Band-Aids, which will make it hard to play. But more importantly, I'm not sure I'm ready to pick up even my ordinary fiddle again, not after last night, not after my encounter with the cold, insatiable shadow man. But I know I need to be here, in this house full of familiar ghosts.

"I'll be all right," I say, but Aunt Ena doesn't look convinced.

Cedar and Rose are the first to arrive, and Cedar laces his fingers in mine almost as soon as he's in the door. Aunt Ena raises her eyebrows at me, and I shoot her a look worthy of my mama.

"This house is a fucking nightmare," Rose says before she notices Aunt Ena. "This is the most haunted-looking place in the whole goddamn South." Cedar clears his throat, and Rose says, "Oh, sorry, I—"

Aunt Ena laughs. "It is haunted. Very haunted. But I like it here."

Rose's eyes widen with appreciation, and she disappears on a tour with Aunt Ena before I've even introduced them.

Now that I'm alone with Cedar, I pull him into the living room, onto an ancient couch. He doesn't let go of my hand, and his other one is already caressing my face, stroking my hair. His thumb settles into one corner of my mouth, which draws my eyes up to his.

"There she is," he whispers. "My Shady Grove. I was so scared for you last night."

At his words, I feel the shadow man's hideous presence again, so I push myself closer to Cedar. God, his eyes are so green, his lashes so black. I want to swim in those eyes, bathe in them, stay there, away from all the troubles of my life. I lean forward and kiss him, breathing in the smell of him. When I pull back, he smiles sleepily, like I'm a drug sending him off to his dreams. "Mmm," he says.

Someone knocks at the front door, and I reluctantly get up to answer it. Sarah and Orlando stand on the porch in the twilight. Orlando is mesmerized by a brownish-colored moth fluttering around the porch light, but Sarah finds my eyes right away.

"My valiant rescuer," I say in an attempt at a joke.

She quirks her lips into a shape that could almost be called a smile, then turns to Orlando. "Come on, you can bring the moth if you want," she says, pulling him by the arm.

"It's a tulip-tree beauty," he says. "Quite common." But all the same he cups his hands around it, drawing it away from the light. He carries it inside, and Sarah picks up the guitar he left, shaking her head with an indulgent smile.

We all settle down together in the living room, Cedar and I on the couch, Rose, now returned from her ghost tour, in an overstuffed chair, Sarah and Orlando on the floor. Aunt Ena is in the kitchen, pretending to bake but probably just eavesdropping.

Rose pulls out her little banjo and starts an idle sort of alternating roll, her fingers dancing over the strings. No one speaks.

"Well," Cedar finally says, but then there's another knock on the door.

Rose sighs dramatically, rising to her feet. "Will that bastard ever be on time?"

When Rose walks by her to get the door, Sarah starts shifting her weight around, crossing and uncrossing her arms. Just being in the same room with Rose makes Sarah fragile as an autumn leaf. I leave Cedar's side and sit next to her on the floor, my shoulder close but not touching hers. Orlando is on her other side, watching the moth traverse the back of his hand.

I don't see Kenneth until he plops down in my place next to Cedar, looks around at everyone except me, and says, "Well, this looks fun. Who needs ghosts when you guys can make a room feel so dead?"

No one laughs, except Aunt Ena from the kitchen. Why did he even come here? He must hate me now. What's he trying to prove? Maybe he just wants to hear exactly what his father said. I can't blame him for that.

"Anyway," Cedar begins, "we're here because Shady raised her stepdad's ghost last night, and . . . it didn't go well." He settles worried eyes on me, waiting. "I think you should tell us what happened."

"She doesn't have to tell us anything she doesn't want to," Sarah says. "It's her business." You can always count on Sarah to be the defender of privacy.

"It stopped being her business when she dragged us all into this shit," Rose says, turning her scowl squarely on me. I don't know why Rose is here either. It's not for my sake. Maybe for Cedar's, or maybe Sarah's. She is clearly no fan of mine. "Spill, Shady. Now."

Orlando looks up from the moth and smiles at Rose like she's some rare butterfly that's floated in from South America. She sees him looking at her and spits out, "Forget it, dude. You're not my type." Her eyes flit to Sarah, and instinctively, I move a little closer to her. Cedar follows the movement with his eyes, his brow furrowed.

This is not going well.

"Fine, here's what happened." I launch into the events of last night, trying to repeat Jim's words exactly as he spoke them. I'm doing all right until I get to the shadow man, and then my breath starts to feel tight and I can't go on.

Oddly, it's Kenneth who jumps in, although his words aren't comforting. "Shady, I know you don't want to believe Jesse did it, but you just told us Dad said it was him." He stares at me, certain now that Jesse's guilty. I guess his anger at me has made him sure.

"Not really though," I say. "Jim wouldn't tell me the whole truth. He kept talking in riddles. I don't think he wants me to know what really happened. He said it was Jesse's fault he's dead, but he didn't actually say Jesse killed him."

Kenneth shakes his head. "Dad was always straightforward. That was, like, his one good quality. You always knew where he stood."

"Did you know he slept with my mama before my daddy died? Is that straightforward?" I shoot back.

Rose's mouth drops open, and Orlando looks like he wants to climb under a rock and never come back out again. Kenneth flushes. "Yeah, I knew," he says. "I thought you knew too. Jesse did."

I guess I was the only one of us naive enough to believe our parents.

"Jesse was really touchy about it. That's why—that's why he beat the shit out of me at the open mic. I said something about that."

"So you all think Jesse did it then?" I ask, gazing around the room. Everyone shifts uncomfortably. Dread pools in my stomach.

"Shady," Cedar says, his voice gentle. "We're all on your side. You know that."

But Rose cuts across his reassurance. "Have you considered that maybe your brother doesn't want you to save him? That maybe it's better if you stay out of it?"

"Rose—" Cedar says, his eyebrows raised in warning.

"Honestly, I don't care what Jesse wants," I say. "I'm not going to leave him in jail. No matter what Jim said Jesse did."

"You're not going to try to raise Jim's ghost again, are you?" Orlando asks, unable to keep the disapproval from his voice.

I shake my head. That's the only thing I'm sure of. "I'm going to visit Jesse on Saturday, and I'll see if I can get anything out of him. That's all I know to do now." I slump forward and hide my face in my hands. I didn't want to be alone in this, but maybe having everyone involved isn't helping either.

Maybe Rose is right, and I can't help Jesse. Maybe Jesse has to help himself. That's what I have to make him do tomorrow.

"Why don't we play?" Orlando says. "For fun, I mean. That's kind of what bands do, right?"

"Great idea," Cedar says, already lifting the clasps on his mandolin case. "It will do us all good." Everyone else starts pulling out instruments and tuning them. The room fills with discordant, intermittent music that actually makes me want to play, to be a part of it.

I put one hand on my old pawnshop case, and my fingertips

throb. I lift each latch slowly, carefully. Even though I brought my ordinary fiddle, it feels like a snake, waiting to sink its fangs into me. I pull it out and bring it up to my chin, but the moment I touch the bow to the strings, the room starts to spin. Black dots pinprick my vision, and my chest feels tight.

I put the fiddle back in its case and close the lid on it. "I can't."

"We won't let the shadow man get you," Kenneth says, a nasty sarcasm lacing his voice.

"Shut up, Ken. Shady, you don't have to play tonight," Cedar says. "Come here and sit by me. We'll play and you sing. Or just listen." His eyes are tender, protective.

I nod and go back to his side, and he pushes Kenneth off the couch. I settle into Cedar's warmth and closeness, glad to leave the fiddle on the other side of the room. Sarah's looking at me, worry in her eyes and something else, jealousy maybe. Resignation? I don't know, and I don't want to think about it. I lay my head against Cedar's shoulder, accepting the shelter he's offering.

They start playing "Wildwood Flower," and I can feel the ripples of Cedar's muscles against my face as he plays. As I breathe in the smell of his deodorant and laundry detergent, the black at the edges of my vision recedes. My chest loosens up again.

"Orlando, will you teach us some Cuban country?" Cedar asks once they finish the song.

Orlando grins and launches into one of his favorite songs by the Buena Vista Social Club. He plays smoothly, showing off his finger work with tremolos. No one understands the words since they're in Spanish, but everyone is tapping their feet and clapping.

Kenneth starts trying to sing along, and they all laugh. I wish I could join in, wish I could share their joy tonight, but I feel unmoored, set adrift on an unfamiliar sea. So I lean back against the couch and close my eyes, letting their music and their laughter wash over me. I won't worry about the shadow man tonight—he can't possibly slip into all this noise and joy.

I wake to silence and the warmth of a blanket. Everyone except Cedar's gone. He's laid out on the couch with me, his back pressed against me, our warmth making the blanket like a nest I never want to leave. I put one arm over his side, and he grasps my hand, bringing it up to rest on his chest.

"How long was I asleep?" I ask, hoping he's not about to tell me I was snoring.

"An hour or so. Everybody packed up and left twenty minutes ago. I guess your aunt went up to bed. I thought you needed some sleep."

"You thought right," I say through a yawn, and snuggle against his neck.

He's quiet so long I think he's fallen back asleep, but then he speaks again, his voice wavering. "Shady, I feel like a jerk even bringing this up right now, but . . . what's between you and Sarah? Do you still have feelings for her? Rose says you do, and it seems like she's right."

Fucking Rose. I sigh. "I don't know. She's my best friend,

except for Orlando. I guess, yeah, I do have some of those feelings, and maybe she does too, but . . ."

"But what?"

"But Sarah's so closed off. She won't let anybody get near her. Just when I think there's an opening, it's gone again, that fast."

"So you're settling for me?" he asks with more than a little hurt in his voice.

"It's not like that."

"It feels like it."

"I like you," I say. "I like spending time with you. You make me happy."

"I'm afraid you're going to change your mind," Cedar says. "I'm afraid I'm going to . . . get attached . . . and then you're going to decide you'd rather be with Sarah."

I don't know what to say to that. I can't promise I won't change my mind. But right now, I'm tired of talking about Sarah, tired of everything except the warmth of Cedar's body, the nearness and safety and goodness of him.

I pull his arm, making him turn over to face me. He looks tousled and sleepy, unbearably lovely. I put my hand against his face, run my fingers through his hair and curl them at the nape of his neck. He closes his eyes and purrs like a cat.

I laugh, but then I'm kissing him, kissing him like he's the sun and I've got a whole world of darkness that needs lighting.

We kiss until we're gasping and our hands are wandering of their own volition. I hope to hell my daddy's ghost isn't here to see this.

Cedar finally pulls back, his pupils enormous, his lips red and slightly puffy from my kisses. "Wait," he says, breathing hard. "You didn't answer. Are you just killing time with me until Sarah decides she wants you?"

"It's not like that. I . . . I care about you," I say. "I like being with you."

Cedar's quiet until his phone buzzes in his pocket. He pulls it out and squints at the screen. "I gotta go home." He gets up, untangling his limbs from mine, fighting his way out of the twisted blanket.

"Don't go," I say, making to get up. But he has already turned away from me. "Cedar."

He turns back around, his face half longing and half anger. "Just—just make up your mind. And don't take too long. I'm not waiting around forever."

He's out the door before I can say anything else, the heat of his kisses still on my lips. I shouldn't have let him go.

When the door closes, I hear Aunt Ena's footsteps on the stairs. "What the hell is that all about?" she calls down. "I thought you liked girls."

"I do," I say, "and I like boys too. You knew that."

"I guess I was hoping you'd swear off the boys," Aunt Ena says. "Girls are a lot less trouble."

She's got that dead wrong, but I don't want to talk about it. Any other time, this push and pull between Cedar and Sarah would take up all my headspace, but right now, with everything else going on, it's just a distraction from what matters. It's just one more hurt in a parade of hurts.

Aunt Ena seems to sense it too. "You worried about seeing Jesse?"

All I can do is nod.

She finally comes downstairs and sits under the blanket with me. She's wearing pajamas printed with yellow stars and crescent moons. "I know, darlin'. Jesse's so much like William—I spent half my life worrying about your daddy."

"If they were so alike, why did they fight so much?"

"They both love too deeply. Feel too much."

"That doesn't sound like a bad thing."

She gazes at me. "Shady, the way you love people is sweet and openhearted and easy. But love's not like that for everybody. Some people love until it hurts, until it's more pain than anything else. That's how William was, and that's how Jesse is, too. That kind of love can break a person in half."

I sigh. Maybe she's right and I do love easy. But lately it feels like my love for Jesse won't only break me—it might also get me killed.

TWENTY-TWO

I'm getting ready to go pick up Aunt Ena for our trip to see Jesse when my cell phone rings. It's a local number I don't recognize, so I ignore it, sending the call to voice mail. Several minutes go by and I think it must have been a wrong number or a scam, but then the voice mail notification dings. No one leaves voice mails anymore, so I'm curious enough to listen.

A man's rumbling voice plays in my ear. "Shady, this is Frank Cooper. I'm calling to talk to you about what you said to Kenneth, though maybe it's better I got your voice mail, because I need to talk and you need to listen." His voice sounds so authoritative I automatically stand up straighter. This isn't the angry man from Jim's funeral or the gentle man who came to my door to apologize or the drunk man screaming into the empty night. This is Frank the Boss, Frank who could run for local office and win by a landslide. This is the Frank Jim despised.

"Kenneth lost his father, and he is grieving. How dare you accuse him of killing his own daddy. How dare you imply that he is anything but a victim in this crime. How dare you, Shady Grove." My cheeks begin to burn with shame.

"I always thought you were a good girl, better than the stock you came from . . . I know you can't help your breeding, but you can choose how to behave in the world. You can choose to accept the truth and move forward. But this—accusing an innocent boy, threatening him, implying that anyone except your sorry brother had anything to do with Jim's death—it's disgusting."

Now my cheeks burn for a different reason. A white-hot rage licks at my insides as Frank speaks on.

"You will drop this nonsense right now, or I swear to God I will go after Jesse even harder than I already am. I will not rest until he gets life in prison. I will make him a roach beneath my boot and I will squish his guts into the ground.

"So, unless you're ready to see that happen, unless you're willing to do that to your brother, you'll leave my nephew alone. You'll stop sticking your nose where it doesn't belong. You'll stay at home like a good girl and try to make something better of yourself than the rest of your family ever did."

He goes on, lecturing me about his family name and his power in the community, the weight and influence he wields. With every word, I squeeze my phone a little tighter, all my shame gone. He doesn't ever say the words "trailer trash," but they are implied in every syllable he speaks. He thinks my family is nothing, is garbage, is weak. He thinks we will lie still while he destroys us. Well, he's wrong about that.

Frank is still talking when I press the End button with shaking hands and save his message on my phone. He meant to intimidate me, but all he's done is light a fire under my feet. The Frank I know—the Frank this town knows—would never speak to a teenage girl like that. He's showing a side of himself only Jim seemed to know about. And that means he's got something to lose.

Anger keeps me going all morning, until Aunt Ena and I pull up to the juvenile detention center. Only then does my rage begin to sour, turning bitter in my mouth. The place looks like an elementary school surrounded by barbed wire, which is quite possibly the most depressing thing I've ever seen. I wonder if the smell of crayons lingers in the air alongside teenage sweat and desperation.

As we walk through the gate, my mood plummets even further. Everything here is cold and mechanized, almost inhuman. It's hard to believe Jesse lives here, day in and day out, locked up like a dog in a cage. Tears rise to my eyes, but I choke them back down.

We pass through a metal detector, and then a female guard checks us for weapons or drugs or whatever else we might try to bring in. We have to remove our shoes. Then she asks me to take my hair down so she can check it for contraband too.

We're waved on by a bored-looking officer in a glass booth. Automated clicks and buzzes shepherd us through the mazelike hallways. Aunt Ena is pale, and when she reaches out for support, her hand is clammy. I feel like a monster for making her bring me here.

Finally, an officer ushers us into a large visiting room that looks less menacing, despite the uniformed, baton-wielding officers standing at attention by every door. There are tables and chairs, drink and snack vending machines. Teenage boys in blue uniforms sit with their parents and siblings, some laughing, some in heated discussion. A few play cards. There are drink cans and empty wrappers on every table.

We find a table shoved up against a wall and sit to wait for Jesse. I concentrate on the institutional gray walls and instructional posters, trying to resist the dread that's swirling around me like fog.

"You want to get Jesse something from the vending machines?" Aunt Ena pushes a clear plastic bag full of dollar bills toward me. It's pretty much all we were allowed to bring in. I'm glad Aunt Ena remembered to bring cash for the machines. I can't imagine the cafeteria food here's any good; Jesse will be glad for something different to eat.

I go to the machines and get Jesse a root beer and a Snickers bar, my peace offerings. And then I hurry back to Aunt Ena, who is leaning against the wall with her eyes closed.

"You all right?"

She opens her eyes. "Yes, it's not so bad." But then she closes them again, so I doubt that's true. It took a lot of courage for her to come here with me, to face her fears of the outside world. I hope I've got some of that courage too. I'm going to need it.

Aunt Ena's about to speak again when Jesse appears at the table. "Hey," he says, his voice deeper than I remember.

The first thing I notice is his black eye, then his busted lip. My eyes fill with tears again, and Jesse thumps down into the empty chair. "See, this is why I didn't want you to come," he says. "I didn't want you to see all this."

I reach out to touch his face, but he pulls away. "What happened?" I ask, wiping my eyes.

Jesse tosses one shoulder. "Got in a fight." By the look of his knuckles, he did his own share of damage.

"Over what?" Aunt Ena asks, though her tone says she already knows it's something stupid.

Jesse smiles and then winces at the pain in his mouth. "I told a guy his girlfriend was ugly. He's got her picture taped to the wall by his bed."

"Jesse," I say, "why you always gotta make life so much harder than it needs to be? Mama's worried sick about you."

"Look who's talking. I assume you're here because of the fiddle."

I glance at Aunt Ena nervously, and she excuses herself to go to the bathroom. I push the soda and candy bar toward Jesse, and he goes straight for the Snickers. Once his mouth is stuffed with gooey chocolate, I take my chance.

"I raised Jim's ghost," I say in a low whisper. No use dancing around the subject.

Jesse slaps his palm against the table, making me jump. He swallows down a bite of candy so fast it must hurt his throat. "Jesus, Shady, I told you to leave it alone. After everything I went through to—"

"I wanted to get you out of here."

"How did you find the fiddle? Did Aunt Ena tell you where it was?"

"No, I figured it out on my own. Why'd you hide it under the oak tree?"

"That's where she said to put it. She wouldn't tell me why." Jesse shifts in his chair and worries the tab on his root beer can. At least I'm not the only one Aunt Ena's keeping secrets from.

"What did Jim say?" Jesse grinds his back teeth, making a muscle in his jaw twitch. With his blue uniform and his beat-up face, he looks scary, angry. No wonder they want to try him as an adult. But his eyes don't look angry—they look like a little boy's, lost and scared.

"He . . . he wouldn't tell me anything—not really. He kept talking in circles, making metaphors."

"Jim's not capable of literary language." Jesse rubs his jaw, which boasts only a light dusting of fair hair, nothing like Cedar's dark stubble.

"I think he was trying to protect someone. Kenneth maybe."

Jesse starts. "Kenneth? What do you mean?"

"I know Kenneth was there that morning. He told me. Why didn't you tell the police that?"

Jesse puts his head in his hands and groans. "Damn it, just forget about Kenneth, okay?"

I lean forward. "Frank called me this morning and threatened me, saying I need to leave Kenneth alone. Does that sound innocent to you?"

Jesse looks up and his face turns pale as oatmeal. When he speaks, desperation laces his words. "Kenneth doesn't matter. He didn't do anything. Leave him out of it. Leave everybody out of it."

I change tactics. "Jim didn't say you killed him, but he said you're the reason he's dead. He said you deserve this." When Jesse doesn't respond, I finally squeak out, "Well, do you?"

Jesse brings his eyes up slowly to meet mine. "I do."

The world tilts and sways. "Why?"

Jesse looks away, rubbing the back of his neck. He lets out his breath in a sigh of exasperation, or maybe regret, I don't know.

"Is this about drugs?" What else could it be? What other thing could Jesse be mixed up in?

"It's not about drugs, but that's all I can tell you. Anything else would—" Jesse makes a sound like there's something stuck in his throat. He sniffs a few times, looking down at the table. I realize he's trying not to cry. I put my hand on his forearm, and he looks up at me, eyes rimmed red. "I didn't mean for him to get killed, I swear. It's not what I wanted." His expression is earnest, sincere.

"But you know what happened to him?" Relief makes my voice hoarse. Jesse did something, but he didn't give Jim the blow that took his life. He's not a killer. I've been doubting him all along, but I believe him now. Looking in his eyes, I know for sure Jesse didn't kill Jim. And knowing that changes everything.

Jesse nods. "I didn't kill him, but I may as well have."

"You know who did this," I say. "You're sitting in here while Jim's murderer's out there."

Jesse looks down at his hands, fear and shame and exhaustion playing over his features.

"Then why aren't you fighting this? Why are you letting yourself get sent to prison?" I can't keep the impatience from my voice.

Jesse puts his face in his hands again, and I can barely make out his next words. "No one would believe me. Why should they, with my record, with everything I've done?"

"I'm going to figure it out," I say. "I'm not going to let you stay in here."

Jesse looks up, his eyes pleading. He's afraid. "Shady, I've caused enough trouble and pain for one lifetime. I don't want to cause any more. If I go to prison, at least you'll be safe and everything will be all right, and no one else has to suffer. Please."

I start to ask him who he's so afraid of, but then something else Jim said hits me. "Jim said sometimes you get punished for a crime you didn't commit, but you were owed punishment for something else, so it's the same thing."

"So?" Jesse says.

"Is that what this is about? You think it's your chance to pay for something else you did?" I ask, my face burning. I didn't come here to accuse Jesse, but ever since Jim said I should talk to Jesse about him wanting Daddy to die, I've been hearing Miss Patty's voice in the back of my head, saying they ought to reopen Daddy's case. Saying maybe Jesse killed him. I hate myself for thinking it, but I guess her words climbed into my brain like ticks in a dog's fur, and they've dug their suckers in.

"What's this really about, Jesse? Because I don't think it's just about Jim."

My brother looks like he's struggling between nausea and anger, like some deeply buried thing is trying to burn its way out of his belly.

"Just tell me," I say.

I don't want him to tell me. I finally know he's not Jim's killer. The relief of that certainty—having my faith in him back again . . . I can't have it snatched out from under me.

"You'll never forgive me if I do," Jesse says, and I can already feel the ground starting to fall away beneath my feet.

My stomach twists. It's all too much. I don't want to find out if it's something I could never forgive him for. I don't want to dig up these secrets. I've already lost too much. I want to keep what little I still have. Jesse didn't kill Jim. I should've left it at that.

"Aunt Ena's been gone a long time," I say, pushing away from the table. "I'm going to go check on her, make sure she hasn't passed out somewhere. Finish your candy."

Jesse nods, relief spreading across his face.

I stride across the room, trying to ignore how the eyes of the inmates follow me. Some of them give me the leer that usually accompanies a catcall, but most of them just look like they envy my freedom to get up and leave.

I find Aunt Ena sitting on the bathroom sinks, her head bowed, hands gripping the edge of the counter. "You all right?" I ask.

She looks up. "Yeah. You get what you need?" I nod, so she hops down and we go back to our table in the visitor's room.

But when we get there, Jesse's gone.

TWENTY-THREE

It's raining when we make it outside, coming down so hard and fast it's bouncing back up from the pavement. Aunt Ena and I race to the car but are soaked by the time we get in, water dripping from our hair and clothes.

As I drive back down the highway, I stare straight ahead at the road, chewing the inside of my cheek. The road's half flooded, but my mind is like a barn on fire, all panic and flames.

"Did he kill Jim?" Ena asks quietly, barely loud enough to be heard over the rain.

"No," I say, my voice firm and certain for the first time in weeks. "He didn't, but he knows who it was. He knows what happened."

"Then why the hell's he sitting in jail? Stupid boy."

"I think Jesse's trying to protect me and Mama and Honey. He said if he stayed in jail, we'd be safe, that no one else would have to suffer." I don't tell her about the rest of that conversation. In fact, I decide I'm going to let it burn to ashes, to be forgotten and dispersed on the wind. What matters is that Jesse didn't kill Jim, that he's being punished for a crime he didn't commit.

Aunt Ena doesn't say anything, so I keep talking. "Jesse said that no one would believe him because of his record. I wonder if that means the person who really did kill Jim is someone people trust, or at least someone whose word would be believed. I thought it might be Kenneth, but Jesse was so sure it wasn't him. And honestly I find it pretty hard to imagine too."

Aunt Ena makes a sound of agreement.

We drive in silence for a while, my brain spinning through possibilities. But the pieces won't come together, won't make a whole—at least not one that makes sense. "Damn it," I yell, slapping the steering wheel. "If Jim would've just told me, instead of talking in riddles, this would be so much easier."

Aunt Ena lays a hand on my shoulder, her touch calming. "Tell me again what Jim's ghost said," she prompts

I sigh, but I walk her through Jim's ghost raising step by step, trying to get every word right. ". . . And then he said he'd been putting the knots in his hanging rope a long time, or maybe he tied his own noose, something like . . ."

Where else have I heard that before? It sounds so familiar. "Is that a thing people say, tying their own hanging rope? Like, an expression lots of people use?" A memory hovers just out of my reach.

"I haven't heard it before, I don't think," Aunt Ena says.

There's something here, but I can't grasp it. I think and think until I feel a migraine starting at the back of my skull.

Then it hits me. "Oh, oh my God."

Aunt Ena's head snaps toward me. "What is it?"

"Frank." In my mind, I hear his voice, rumbling at me as he left the trailer that day. "I remember when Jim said that about the noose, it sounded familiar, like I'd heard it before. Frank had said almost the same thing when he came to the house to apologize to Mama. He said that some people were determined to tie their own noose."

Frank's drunken words, screamed into the darkness on the night I raised Jim's ghost, come back to me, too—"It's him—he's the one. That lying, conniving worm." He was talking about Jesse, but I didn't realize there might be any truth to his words. What exactly did Jesse do, and what does it have to do with Frank?

That last puzzle piece clicks into place. Frank's insistence that it was Jesse, how strange he acted at the construction site, the voice mail he left me.

"I'm not saying he hit Jim with the hammer, but he's involved somehow. He has to be." I think I knew it all along but couldn't quite believe it.

"I don't know, Shady," Aunt Ena says. "It's possible."

I take a steadying breath. "I want to go see him. I want to find out why he's so sure Jesse did it. Why he didn't suspect anyone else. Lots of people had access to that house, and I'm sure plenty of those guys hated Jim. It could have been someone else on their crew. Frank would know that. But he went straight for Jesse without a second thought. He's hiding something, and I want to find out what it is."

Aunt Ena pauses before she answers. "I don't think that's a good idea, Shady. You shouldn't be confronting Frank. You're a sixteen-year-old girl and he's a grown man. And he's not the saint people around here think he is. I knew him when we were young."

Kenneth believes Frank is Jesus Christ in Levi's, and I've never heard anyone except Jim and Mama say a word against him. But I know he's no saint. I've had two glimpses of his darkness—that night he was drunk at the construction site and the hateful message he left on my phone. But just how unsaintly is he?

"What do you know, Aunt Ena?"

She only sighs in answer.

"Mama told me about that night Daddy beat him up," I prompt.

"She told you that?" Aunt Ena's voice is a mingling of surprise and embarrassment.

"Only that he made a pass at you and you weren't interested, and Daddy got mad and hit him."

She pauses and I think she won't say anything, but then she murmurs, "Frank Cooper isn't a man who likes to hear the word no."

"So he—he tried to . . . ?" I can't finish the question. The idea makes me feel sick.

Aunt Ena clears her throat, and when she speaks, her voice is shaky. "Yes, but he didn't get very far. Your daddy took care of it, and I never—well, I never had the guts to report it. The town loves him. I figured they'd never believe me." From the corner of my eye I see her pass a hand over her eyes, the way she does when she feels overwhelmed. "I've always been ashamed of that—that I haven't been braver."

The thought of Aunt Ena feeling guilty about something that wasn't her fault makes my heart ache. I put my hand over hers and squeeze.

Frank and Jim, light and dark, good and bad. But what if all this time, we were wrong about which of them was the good brother and which one the bad? What if Jim was right all along, and Frank's the wolf in sheep's clothing Jim always said he was? Jesse and I could never quite believe Mama would marry someone so awful—maybe she didn't.

"Aren't you tired of it, Aunt Ena?" I say.

"Tired of what, darlin'?"

"Tired of letting the Franks of the world make us scared?" I glance at her and see her shudder, wrapping her arms around herself.

"What are you going to do?" she asks.

There's a roar going through me, made up of rage and fear and hope. I'm close now. Close to the truth. I just have to find a way to make Frank talk.

"Jim knew about Daddy's fiddle. Did Frank?"

"Shady, you can't play your daddy's fiddle again. Not after what happened."

"Did he know?"

Ena sighs. "Not completely. But I think he guessed. He called William unnatural, warped—that night of the fight."

Then maybe I already have a way to make him talk. That makes up my mind. "I'm driving over to see Frank now. Should I take you home first, Aunt Ena?"

She's quiet a long time. "No, don't take me home."

⁂

I pull into the parking lot of Frank's office, a low-slung brick building with scraggly bushes out front. His truck is there, like I knew it would be. Jim always said Frank's too greedy to take a day off. I figured he was just jealous of his older brother because Frank was more successful, more respected. I don't know what to think anymore.

I don't know who Frank really is, but I guess I'm about to find out.

Daddy's fiddle's on the back seat, where I stowed it this morning, afraid to even leave it in the house with Honey. I turn and stare at it for a moment, considering. Aunt Ena turns too, and her eyes go wide when she sees it. "Shady," she says, her voice low and warning.

How many more times can I play it before the shadow man kills me? I don't know, but I have to take the risk. I'm too close to Jesse's freedom to let my fear win.

I take a deep breath and grab Daddy's fiddle.

I put my hand on the door handle. "You can stay out here," I say, but Aunt Ena shakes her head. We run through the pouring rain to the front door. It's not locked, and a bell dings as we enter. The reception desk sits empty.

The moment I step into the building, the hair on the back of my neck stands up. Aunt Ena shivers and then puts her arm out in front of me, like she's stopping me from stepping out into traffic.

"You feel that?" she asks.

I nod, fear creeping up my spine. But before I can speak, Frank pops his head out of his office. His beard is longer and thicker than usual, his eyes bloodshot. "Can I help you, ladies?" he says before realizing who we are. He strides to the front desk, a look of annoyance on his face. "Shady, what are you doing here? I told you to stop bothering my family."

"We went to see Jesse today," I say, squaring my shoulders, meeting his eyes. I'm not a roach to be squished.

A breeze from nowhere drifts across my face, making me shiver.

Frank lumbers around the counter and looms over us like a grizzly bear. "And?"

My knees tremble, but I hold his gaze. "I know Jesse didn't kill Jim. And I suspect you know it too. Why have you been lying?"

He takes a step back and licks his lips. "I don't know what you're talking about. What I do know is that you need to get on home now, leave this matter to the police and the grown-ups." He's trying to act commanding, but he's off-center, agitated. And that chilly breeze on my face tells me why. He's being haunted.

If Jim's already moved on from haunting the site of his murder to haunting his brother, what does that mean? Nothing good—that's for sure. Daddy always said the only ghosts with power like that had made roots in the world from their fear and rage. Those are the kinds of ghosts you have to worry about.

I lay my fiddle on the counter. "Do you remember this?"

"It's a violin," he says dismissively.

I throw open the clasps and lift the lid. "It was my daddy's.

You remember how he used to play it?"

"So?" Frank says, stepping back again.

"Well, I play it now," I say, letting his answering silence deepen for a moment. "Do you want to know what happened when I raised your brother's ghost?" I gaze at him, waiting. "Do you want to know what he said?"

Frank tugs at his beard, glancing sharply to his right. "You ain't never . . ."

I pull the fiddle from the case and raise the bow above the strings. "Should I call him back now? Don't you want to say goodbye? Don't you want a chance to tell him you love him?"

I gently touch the bow to the strings, and the fiddle emits a high, shivery note. Frank takes another step away from me.

The fading note pulls at me, urging me to call it back. But I have to stay focused.

"Jim's haunting you, isn't he?" I say. "You know, ghosts never stop haunting once they get started. They're like a stuck record, playing the same note over and over again. They can't help it. They'll haunt you until you join them."

My heart races, and goose bumps prick my entire body, but I keep talking. "I feel him here now. I can let you see him if you'd like." I was planning to bluff my way through this, but now I don't need to. Jim is here, and his ties to this world are even stronger than they were the night I called his ghost.

I raise the bow again, and Frank strikes, slapping it out of my hand. "You little bitch," he screams, all of his calm bravado gone. "You little bitch." I'm so shocked I don't move for a few seconds. Even after the voice mail he left me and the story

Aunt Ena just told me, it's still hard to believe this is the person Frank's been hiding all these years. This must be the Frank Aunt Ena knew back when she and Daddy were young. The Frank Jim knew.

Ena steps in front of me, cringing away from Frank's raised hand. She's been silent all this time, but now she speaks to Frank. "Why don't you go to the police? Maybe if you tell them what you know about his murder, Jim will give you some peace."

"I'm not to blame for this," Frank says, but not to us. He's looking over our heads, as if out the window, though the draft on my neck tells me what he's actually seeing. *Who* he's actually seeing.

"We didn't say you are, but there's a reason your brother's ghost is in this room. He's been haunting you for weeks, hasn't he?" I ask. I realize now that Frank wasn't just raving that night at the construction site, he was arguing—with Jim.

Frank snatches a heavy glass bowl full of mints off the receptionist's desk, scattering the candy across the floor. He grips the bowl in one hand, lurching toward me. "Did your brother tell you I did it? He's a liar, you know. He tells all kinds of lies."

I step back instinctively. "What kind of lies, Frank?"

"Of course, I believed him," he roars over my head. "I saw how you looked at Marlene."

"What's your wife got to do with this?" Ena asks, but Frank's not listening. He's still advancing toward me, the bowl lifted in one meaty fist, his eyes focused on Jim's ghost.

"Shady, go get in the car," Ena says, her voice shrill.

Slowly, I pick up my bow and put it in the case with the fiddle.

"Don't touch that," Frank yells. His eyes are dark and wild and lost. "It's your creepy, freaky family that cost me my brother. That's why I—" A strangled sob stops his words.

I slam the lid down and snap the clasps. "That's why you killed him?" I ask, the truth settling into my chest with a horrible certainty. "That's why he's haunting you?"

Frank moves toward us again. "I—"

"You killed him," I interrupt, fear filling my entire being. I'm face-to-face with the man who bashed Jim's head in with a hammer. My eyes take in the heavy glass bowl in his hands, the horrible strength of his arms.

My legs feel numb, but I back toward the door with the fiddle held to my chest. My heart beats hard against the case, and I swear I feel another heart inside the fiddle, matching mine beat for beat. "If you killed him, you'll never be free until you confess, until you're punished. He'll cling to you until you die. That's what ghosts do to their murderers."

But now Frank's eyes are locked several inches above my head, his face pleading. Then his features twist with rage. "Get out," he screams, so loud his vocal cords must burn inside his throat. He draws back his arm and hurls the glass bowl in my direction.

Aunt Ena and I throw ourselves to the floor as glass rains down on our heads. He wasn't aiming for us; we aren't the ones he's trying to drive away. But that doesn't mean he won't hurt us. Not in the state he's in. I grab Ena's arm and we scramble from the building, Frank's screams propelling us forward.

The rain's still pouring, the gravel parking lot turned to gritty puddles. We splash through them, and I yank open the driver's-side door and throw myself in, fumbling to latch my seat belt with shaking hands. Frank is running toward the car, so I back out before Aunt Ena even has her door closed. We shoot backward from the parking lot and squeal onto the empty road.

I don't know if he's coming after us, but I'm not waiting to find out. This is the man who murdered my stepdad. Who killed his own brother and then blamed it on mine. I can't take any chances.

As I'm speeding away, the car hits a stretch of standing water at the bottom of the hill, and my tires lose traction, making the car skid across the drenched pavement into the other lane. I yank the steering wheel to pull it back, and the car swerves into the correct lane and then keeps swerving. Aunt Ena screams and reaches for the steering wheel, but we plow into the ditch with a roar, heading straight for a stand of trees.

The world shatters into glass and blood and finally into darkness.

TWENTY-FOUR

When I come to, sirens are wailing around me, shrill and insistent. A wave of pain makes me close my eyes again.

After a few moments, I remember where I am. In my mama's car, surrounded by glass and twisted metal, wet tree leaves brushing my face.

Blood drips down my cheek. With agonizing slowness, I turn my head to the right.

Aunt Ena is unconscious, her face nicked with a dozen tiny cuts, her head slumped against the passenger-side window, which is cracked but not broken. I watch her chest to see if she's breathing. I whisper a relieved prayer when I see it rise and fall.

We're alive.

I lay my head against the headrest and wait for the sirens to reach us. The rain falls and falls and falls. Frank's nowhere to be seen. I don't know if he was even chasing us. Maybe he was running too.

Somehow, despite all the blood and glass and smashed metal, I walk away with only a fractured rib and a nasty laceration across my forehead, courtesy of a branch that smashed through the window when we hit the trees. I get eight stitches and some ibuprofen, and the doctors say I can go home. The fiddle is unharmed—I made the EMTs put it on the stretcher with me before I'd let them take me from the wreck.

But Aunt Ena has a concussion. It turns out her head is what caused the crack in the passenger-side window. The real problem though is that she can't stop panicking. She's wild with fear, and they can't sedate her because of the concussion. They gave her something for anxiety, but it's not working. She's stuck in a tortured panic, and the hospital is a thousand times worse than the grocery store. I've tried holding her hand, talking to her, even singing, but she doesn't even seem to recognize me. She keeps whispering to herself. I can't make out most of what she's saying, but she has mentioned a tea party a few times, which makes no sense to me.

I dash to the door of the examination room when her doctor walks by. "Dr. Yamamoto, please let me take my aunt home," I beg. "She'll feel better once she's out of here. She's afraid of the fluorescent lights and all the space and noise." What she needs is the quiet of her house and the comfort of her ghosts.

The doctor gives me a sympathetic smile. "I'm sorry, but I can't release her to you. You're a minor. You'll have to wait a little longer." Dr. Yamamoto has been really kind to us even though the ER is so busy, so I just nod and let her go back to her other patients.

Mama's car is totaled, but even if I did have a vehicle, would Aunt Ena get into it? I texted Mama but haven't heard anything. What if Frank decides to go after Mama now? Or Honey? What if he—I won't let myself think it. But he's out of his mind, and Jim haunting him isn't helping any.

I turn off the lights in the room and sit next to Aunt Ena on the bed. She's lit by the glow of various machines, her hair long and wild, freed from its pins. Her eyes, when she looks up at me, are like a cornered animal's.

When I put my hand on her shoulder, she shudders. But at least she has stopped gasping for air like a fish on a hook.

"It's all right," I say. "You're safe. It's okay." I repeat the words over and over again, until they have lost their meaning, until they're just sounds, a shushing lullaby. Aunt Ena stops shaking.

"I want to go home," she whispers.

"I know. We'll go soon," I promise. "You were really brave," I add.

She reaches up and touches my bandaged forehead. "I won't let him hurt you again, Brandy. I swear it."

That's the second time she's called me Brandy, but this doesn't seem like the right moment to ask about it. "It's Shady, Aunt Ena," I say, "and Frank won't hurt me. The police will catch him."

I've already given them my statement about Frank and the crash. I told them Frank threatened me and scared me, and that's why I ran off the road. I told them some of the things he said to us made me think he was involved in my stepdad's murder. Aunt

Ena was still unconscious when they came by, and I was too worried about her to say much more. They dutifully wrote down my statement, but they didn't say what they would do about it. They probably thought I was the one with a concussion.

My phone vibrates in my pocket. When I pull it out, the screen illuminates Aunt Ena's face, and I can see she's much calmer than before. She's almost herself again.

"Look, Mama's calling," I say, trying to keep my voice steady. With a shaking hand, I accept the call.

"Shady," comes Mama's tremulous voice. "Thank God. The hospital was trying to reach me, but I didn't hear my phone. They said you were in a car accident. Are you all right?" Her words come out in a panicked rush. I can hear the engine of Jim's truck in the background.

"Yeah, I'm okay. Just some stitches. But Aunt Ena has a concussion, and the doctors won't let us go. Are you—are you okay? Is everything—"

"Don't worry, I'll be there soon," Mama says. "I'm on my way. Stay right there." Her voice is laced with fear, but it's fear for me, not anything to do with Frank.

"All right. Love you."

"Love you, baby," she says before hanging up. I imagine her flooring the truck's gas pedal, desperate to reach me. Poor Mama—how many more calls like this can she handle?

But when Mama bursts into the hospital room, with Honey on her hip, I put on a brave face for her. I let her hold me close and fuss over me. I promise her I'm all right. I say all the things she needs to hear.

And then I pull back from her and meet her eyes. "It was Frank, Mama. Frank killed Jim."

"What?" she says. "What are you talking about?"

I tell her about our confrontation—how out of control he seemed, how guilty and lost. Her eyebrows furrow as she listens, like she's trying to find some sense in my tale. When I get to the part where Frank throws a glass bowl, her eyes go wide.

"That son of a bitch, I'll kill him," she says, clenching her fists. "Threatening my child."

"Then . . . I thought he was chasing us," I say. "That's why we wrecked. I thought maybe he was trying to keep us from telling the police what he did."

"Shady, Frank might be an angry drunk, but that doesn't mean he killed Jim," she says, once I finish. "Did he actually say to you that he killed him?"

"Mama, you can't be serious. It's so obvious that he did it."

She shakes her head. "He's grieving. People do strange, scary things when they grieve."

"The day Jim died, at the police station, you told Frank that he had never loved Jim."

"Sometimes the worst grief comes from not loving people the way we should," she says, her voice sure.

"But Jesse—"

Mama holds up her hand. "We need to get Ena home. We'll talk more in the car."

But once we get into Jim's truck, Mama doesn't speak again. Aunt Ena's panic grows as we drive, and she grips my hand hard, singing and muttering to herself. Most of it is incoherent, but I catch phrases here and there. "One day . . . we'll grow up . . . never hurt us again . . . never never neverland. Here, I'll . . . cup of tea. Shhh, shhh, shhh."

Mama glances at her nervously, but doesn't say anything.

The fiddle lies silent in my lap, but it doesn't feel like an instrument at rest. It's longing to be played—I can feel it, its need the same as the need in my chest. We're like two magnets being drawn together. The shadow man is what stands in our way, but there has to be something I can do, a song I can play or sing or something—I'll find a way around him. If Mama's not going to listen, and Frank's not going to confess, and Jesse's going to keep hiding all his secrets, leaving the rest of us to suffer . . . the fiddle's the only one on my side.

We get Aunt Ena settled into the downstairs guest room, and Mama turns to me. "Is there someone we can call to come stay with her? Does she have a friend who would come?"

"We can't leave her here alone. And I don't want to go home. Frank might come looking for us there."

"Baby, Frank's not coming after you. He just wanted to scare you."

"Why won't you call the police?" I burst out. "He killed Jim. He did it—I know he did. They won't listen to me because I'm a teenager, but they'll listen to you. You were Jim's wife."

"You're overexcited from the wreck. You need to calm down," Mama says, her voice firm.

"I'm not," I yell. "Why won't you listen?"

"Shady, you can't prove anything. They'll think you're trying to get Jesse out, and you might even get in trouble for harassing Frank. He has friends on the police force—Gary Jones for one."

"Yeah, and he's the one who arrested Jesse. Kenneth told me he—his stepdad made him lie about where he was the morning Jim died. Kenneth was there, at the construction site that morning. His stepdad made him say he wasn't."

"I already knew that," she says. "Jim told me he was having Kenneth come by there."

"Why didn't you say anything?" I yell, throwing out my arms.

I'm staring her down, my eyes as steely as hers for once, when my phone starts ringing.

"Answer that goddamned phone. It's bothering my nerves," she says, turning away from me. I could scream.

Instead, I hit the green icon to accept Cedar's call. "Shady," he says, his voice relieved.

"What's wrong?"

"Kenneth told me you were in an accident. Are you okay?"

"How'd he know?"

"His stepdad responded to the 911 call."

"Of course he did," I spit, glaring at Mama's back.

"Are you okay?" he says again.

"I . . . I went to see Frank, and . . ." My mind stutters. Why is Cedar calling me? He's supposed to be pissed off.

"What happened?"

"I'm fine. I'm at Aunt Ena's," I say, my head throbbing. If Kenneth's stepdad responded and Frank is his friend . . . maybe Mama's right. Maybe there's really nothing I can do. Frank has everybody in this town on his side, including the police. "I have to go, sorry," I say. I hang up before he can try to stop me.

I walk back into the guest room, and Mama stands up. "I'm going to call Miss Patty and see if she'll come stay with Ena. I want to get you home."

"No," I say. "No. I'm not going anywhere, and I'm not leaving Aunt Ena here with that horrible woman. Frank is out there and he's dangerous. He might want to kill us like he killed Jim," I say, beginning to shake again. Today has been too much. Too much. How can Frank—the one who gave Jim a job, who was always so sweet to Honey—how can he be the murderer? And if Frank's a murderer, what does that make Jesse? Another innocent victim.

Mama's eyes soften. "Okay, we'll stay," she says. "Is there a teapot around here somewhere? Ena's been going on and on about it. Maybe if she holds it, she'll calm down."

I stride to the parlor and grab the chipped and yellowing tea set off the mantel. The cups are so small, I can fit two in one hand.

When I settle the teapot in Aunt Ena's lap, her eyes go distant and calm.

"Honey, you want to play tea party with Aunt Ena?" I ask, hoping my baby sister's soothing superpowers will work on Aunt Ena as well as they've always worked on me. I set her on the bed and give her one of the teacups. She holds it in one little hand, and Aunt Ena automatically reaches out to pour her some invisible tea.

"See," Aunt Ena says. "I told you we didn't need any cookies."

Mama shudders and then strides from the room. "I'll be back in a few minutes. I'm going to get some clothes and things for all of us."

When a knock sounds on the front door, I assume Mama must have locked herself out. But instead it's Cedar standing on the front porch. He steps back in surprise when the door swings open, like a ghost's going to come jumping out at him.

"Hey," I say, squinting at his silhouette against the glare of late afternoon sun.

"What's going on?" he asks, but then he catches sight of my bandage and the blood on my clothes. His hands immediately go to my face, his eyes searching the rest of me for more injuries. "Shady," he whispers in the tenderest voice I've ever heard, and I feel the tears I held off for Mama's sake start to come.

So I pull away and tell him to come inside, blinking away my tears and trying to make my lips stop trembling before he sees.

I head to the living room, and Cedar follows, shutting the door behind him. Before I can reach the couch, though, he pulls me back toward him by my waist. He cradles my face, studying my forehead. I try to avoid meeting his eyes, try so hard to hold back the tears, but then they are spilling over my cheeks, and there's nothing I can do about it. So finally, I just let them fall. Let the sobs escape my chest.

Cedar doesn't say anything; he pulls me gently against him, his hands soft against the back of my neck and hair. I lay my cheek against his chest and breathe in his smell, wrap my arms around his waist, twist my fingers into his shirt. He holds me and lets me weep. Every shudder makes my fractured rib scream, but all this fear and rage and anxiety needs to leave my body somehow.

When I finally pull away to wipe my eyes, he kisses me gently at the corner of my mouth, just once, and then leads me over to the couch.

His eyes glimmer strangely, and I realize he's struggling not to cry too. That makes me smile a little, knowing a rodeo boy like Cedar is brought to tears by a girl's crying.

He touches my cheek again. "Did Frank hurt you?" he says, his voice husky.

"Mostly it was the tree we hit."

His eyes go even more glimmery, and I'm afraid he's actually going to start crying. "I'm fine," I say. "Just some stitches and a fractured rib."

Cedar touches my side with feather-light fingers. "Is Ena all right?"

I nod. "A concussion and a lot of little cuts all over her face, but she's fine too."

"I don't understand what happened. I thought you were going to see your brother today. How did you . . . why'd you go see Frank?"

"We went to confront him after seeing Jesse."

"You did what?" Cedar says, leaning back from me. "Why would you do that? You knew he wasn't in control of himself—after we saw him at the construction site. You knew there was something off. You should have asked me to come. I would have helped you. I would have kept you safe."

I wave away his concern. "He did it, Cedar. He killed Jim. It wasn't Jesse," I say.

Cedar can't seem to take his eyes off me. "But he didn't get arrested yet?"

"Mama doesn't think the police will believe us. I guess I don't think they will either."

Cedar's eyes widen. "So he's still out there? He could come back and look for you? You shouldn't be alone in this house. I'm going to stay here tonight. I won't leave you alone until he gets arrested."

I start to say no, but I'm scared and exhausted, and having a rodeo boy watching over me actually sounds pretty good right now. When I nod, Cedar puts an arm around my waist and pulls me against him, gentler now that he knows about my rib. We sit, side by side, in silence for a long while, our beating hearts the only sound.

As I sink into the comfort of his touch, I think how strange it is that here I am being comforted by Cedar, the rodeo boy. Even a week ago, I'd have only wanted it to be Sarah sitting next to me. But then I realize the person you choose to love isn't the one who shows up when you ask them to. It's the person who shows up even when you don't. Maybe even when you don't want them to. Sarah would have come if I'd asked, but I didn't have to ask Cedar.

"I was so scared," I say, and then the words are tumbling out of me—the whole story of what happened at Frank's office and then the wreck. And Cedar listens quietly, his eyes tender and his mouth set firm, like he's never going to let anyone hurt me again. When I'm done talking and all my tears are spent, he holds me to him and rests his head against my hair. We sit like that until Mama comes through the front door.

"Who's this?" Mama asks when she pushes through the door with two duffel bags.

"My boyfriend, Cedar," I say. "He's going to help you with those bags."

Cedar's head swings around so fast it makes my own neck hurt. "Boyfriend?" he says at the same time Mama does, his expression so hopeful I can't help but smile.

I give him a wink I hope he feels all the way down to his toes.

Cedar jumps up and takes the bags from Mama's hands, his face a little red. "Nice to meet you, ma'am," he says, smiling a little wider than the occasion would seem to warrant. But now he knows—I made my choice, and he won't have to wait around anymore.

Honey runs in from the bedroom and gazes up at Cedar, starstruck. "Are you a cowboy?" she asks, a grin starting over her face.

Everybody laughs, and Cedar bends down to shake Honey's hand. "I am," he stage-whispers, and she giggles.

"Cedar, you want to stay for dinner? You're not a vegetarian, are you?" Mama asks, giving me an appraising look.

After dinner, he gets his mandolin out of his truck and performs "Froggie Went A-Courtin'" for Honey, complete with all the voices and sound effects. She cackles all the way through the song and gasps when the frog gets eaten by a snake at the end. I smile, watching them together, but my mind's on Frank and Jesse and the fiddle that longs for my touch.

Mama agrees to let Cedar stay the night as long as he sleeps on the couch and I promise not to leave my old bedroom. I agree, mostly because knowing he's downstairs between the front door and everyone I love is the only reason I'll be able to fall asleep.

But when a scream tears through the house, I know a hundred Cedars wouldn't be enough to make us safe.

TWENTY-FIVE

I dash into the room where Honey and Mama are sleeping and flip on the lights. Honey sits ramrod-straight in bed, the way she did the night of the wasps, her little chest heaving. I check the air and her skin, but there are no stinging insects.

Mama's eyes are open and staring, but she's still lying down, as if she can't move.

"Mama," I say. "Mama." I reach out a hand and shake her, and she bolts upright, gulping air like she's just surfaced from underwater. Her eyes dart around the room in panic before settling on me.

"What is it? Why are you in here?" Mama says, putting a hand to her chest.

"Honey was screaming," I say. Mama looks sharply at my sister. "She was dreaming."

Mama's quiet for a long moment. "Shady, will you take her downstairs and give her some juice or something? I'll be down in a minute," she finally says, her voice distant and strange.

"What is it? Were you dreaming, too?" The hair at the back of my neck prickles.

"Just . . . go downstairs," she says. "Please."

Honey wraps her arms around my neck and buries her face in my hair. I carry her from the room but glance back when I reach the doorway. Mama pulls her knees to her chest and wraps her arms around them, rocking herself.

A chill shoots through me, but I take Honey downstairs.

When I reach the stairwell, Cedar waits at the bottom, gazing up at me in the dark. "Everything all right?" He must be scared too, the way he's gripping the banister.

"Bad dream," I say, passing by him to get to the kitchen. He stops me and kisses my cheek, and then kisses Honey's too.

"I haven't slept much either," he admits.

"Because of the ghosts or because of Frank?"

"Both," he says with a sheepish smile.

We go into the kitchen together, and soon Aunt Ena and Mama join us.

"What did you dream about, Honey girl?" I ask, my heart racing. "Was it wasps again?"

Honey rubs her eyes and nods. "They hurt a little girl. Up there." She points at the ceiling. Mama shivers and then takes Honey in her arms, holding her tight. Is it the same little girl from all my dreams when I lived here, the dead girl in the ceiling? The thought makes me shiver too.

Aunt Ena glances up, her blue eyes wide and frightened. "I told Brandy not to take the cookies for the tea party," she says, her mind not in this world. She begins to hum the low, mournful song the fiddle was playing when I dived into the lake. Daddy's song, the one that turned him darker than "The Twa Sisters" ever could. My skin tingles.

"This is why I moved y'all out of here. This house isn't good for a child," Mama says. "Or an adult for that matter," she adds, looking meaningfully at Aunt Ena, who stares at her folded hands on the table while she hums.

Mama's face is pale with fear.

"What is it, Mama?"

She shakes her head. "I'm going to take Honey back to bed, but then we're leaving in the morning. We won't spend another night here. I can't stand it." She carries Honey from the room. Cedar gets up too and goes back to the couch, probably trying to stay out of our family business.

But I trail after Mama up the stairs, a horrible thought forming into a question in my mouth. "Does this house have an attic?"

"It's blocked up," she says, "and for good reason." Halfway up the stairs, she stops and stares into space, as if she's listening. When I put a hand on her arm, she flinches. "Let's go home tonight. I don't want to stay here anymore. This house isn't fit for the living."

"I won't leave Aunt Ena alone here," I say. "Not like this. And we should stay together. Frank could come—"

Mama swivels to face me. "Don't you see—Frank's the least of our worries right now." Her eyes are pleading.

"No, it's all connected somehow," I say, the knotted threads of the last few weeks beginning to come unsnarled in my head. "Frank and whoever Brandy is and Jesse and Daddy. It's all connected somehow."

"Shady, get your head out of the goddamned past. What's done is done. All we can do is live now. Because *we* are alive." She sets Honey down gently on the bed.

"If you care so much about the living, why don't you fight for Jesse? Call the police and tell them to arrest Frank."

"I'll stay tonight, but tomorrow we're gone. Ena can come stay with us if she wants to." Mama crawls back into bed, pulling the covers over herself.

"You had the same dream Honey did, didn't you? Who's Brandy, Mama?"

She rolls over to face the wall. "Just go to bed, Shady."

"Is she the dead girl in the ceiling?" I ask, but Mama won't answer.

"Shady-Shade, sleep here," Honey says, pulling at my pajama pants. "Sleep with me. I'm scared."

"Shhh, Honey girl, don't be scared," I say, sliding into bed beside her. I pull her against my chest, and she snuggles into me. But I'm scared now too.

Honey is breathing steadily after a few moments, and even Mama falls back to sleep. But I lie in bed and stare at the ceiling, listening to the moans and creaks of the old house.

It has always felt most haunted at night here—the patter of footsteps across the floorboards, sighs pulling doors closed, unidentifiable smells floating through rooms. As a child I found it comforting, signs that our ghosts were nearby, watching over me while I slept. But tonight the ghosts are silent, the only sounds from the house itself—ancient wood settling and creaking. I'd almost say the ghosts are afraid to move, afraid to breathe.

But what are they afraid of? What's left for a ghost to fear after death?

I can feel the secrets in every corner, spun like cobwebs. Are they holding this house together? If I begin to untangle them, will the whole place fall down around our heads? Maybe I should try to find the attic and discover what it's hiding. Because Brandy and a little dead girl in the ceiling, the shadow man, Daddy's fiddle and Honey's dreams—right now they feel like single threads, but I sense that there's a larger pattern.

I thought Daddy's fiddle would solve our problems, but it's only made more trouble. It didn't make Jim tell the truth or get Jesse out of jail. It only brought me more enemies—Frank and the shadow man and the wasps.

I'm tired of wondering about everyone's secrets, sick to death of waiting for the pattern to be revealed. I'm going to get the answers I need. I've failed at everything else I've tried, but I won't fail at this.

I throw the covers off and creep from the room, back into mine. I turn on the light and pull Daddy's fiddle case from beneath the unmade bed. I'll take it out to the woods, I'll walk the paths Daddy walked and play the songs Daddy played. For me, for Jesse, but for all the rest of my family too—for Aunt Ena, for Mama, for Honey.

Just as I start to stand, a floorboard creaks behind me. I whip around. Cedar's eyes widen when he sees me on my knees, the fiddle case clenched tightly in my hands.

"No," he says, shaking his head. "No, I won't let you play it again. Not after what happened. You could have—you could have—I don't know what would have happened, but it was bad. You weren't in control of yourself. Your mama's right. You need to leave it be."

I try to brush past him, but Cedar's hand closes over my wrist. His eyes are determined. "No. I won't let you do this. Not again."

"Let go," I say, but his fingers stay wrapped around my wrist.

"I need to find out what's going on in this house. Everyone's dreams—the things Aunt Ena keeps saying. I can't do anything about Frank tonight, but I can find out what this house is hiding. I can find out what's causing so much pain to everyone I love."

"There are other ways," he says. "We can search the whole house for clues if you want." His green eyes are wide and pleading and resolute. The light dusting of freckles on his cheeks and nose stands out starkly against his skin, which is uncharacteristically pale. He must be more frightened or angry than he's letting on. "Please, Shady."

With agonizing effort, I make myself release the fiddle case. I push away the voice that says Cedar's just another person trying to get in my way. When I nod, his fingers relax against my wrist. "Then I want to find the attic," I say.

"All right," he says. "All right."

It takes a long time for us to find the entrance to the attic, and we have to be quiet so we don't wake anyone. We check the ceilings and the walls, searching everywhere for the outline of a door beneath the plaster and wallpaper. Finally, Cedar thinks to push the heavy dresser in my old bedroom to one side. We pause to listen for Mama, in case we woke her up, but if she hears us, she stays in bed and pretends she doesn't. Then I run my hands along the wall, feeling for a place where the door should be. The wall is smooth, but I find a dip in the plaster. I trace it with my finger and wonder who sealed it closed, locking my family's secrets inside.

After a half hour's quiet work, Cedar uncovers the attic door and pulls a heavy tape from around its edges, unsealing it for the first time in decades. Plaster and splintered wood litter the floor around it, and the wallpaper is torn around the edges. But it's there—an attic door just big enough for us to fit through.

It doesn't have a doorknob or even a latch; that must have been removed when it was sealed. Cedar pries his fingers into the edge, pulling at it. After a few moments, it pops open with an ominous creak. I swear every ghost in the house sighs—with relief or fear, I can't tell.

The light bulb doesn't come on when I pull the hanging string, so I send Cedar to the kitchen to get flashlights from a drawer by the stove. I stand waiting at the entrance, goose bumps covering my arms. I expect the air to feel cool and musty like a forgotten library, but it's like most Florida attics: hot, humid, and rank. My stomach feels sour and my head slightly dizzy, like my body knows better than to climb these stairs and is trying to stop me.

As I stare into the yawning blackness, the house seems to grow even quieter, the silence practically humming around me. I can't shake the feeling that I'm about to travel into the decayed, worm-eaten center of my family's secrets, and every ghost here knows it. But Cedar comes back with two flashlights, and I cross the threshold into the waiting, silent darkness.

Once inside, we have to step more carefully, shining the flashlights down to find our way. The floor's rotten in places, hardly an inch of it stable. We cast our flashlights around the walls and ceiling, revealing old boxes, broken furniture, and forgotten tools.

"I know it's just an attic, but it doesn't feel right," Cedar says, his voice husky. "Let's do this fast."

We separate, shining our flashlights in different areas, searching through the jumble. For what, I don't know. What are we hoping to find here? A dead girl's body? After twenty minutes, our efforts turn up only junk—old insurance papers, magazines, and ancient, moldy clothes. Despite this, I sense that we'll find the answer I need here, the one that makes everything fall into place.

We've looked through so many boxes and trunks that in my desperation, I'm starting to think of sneaking off to play the fiddle again. With a sigh, I pull out an unsealed cardboard box that once held bananas. At the bottom of a pile of dusty papers rests a heavy book, an old family photo album. I turn my flashlight on it and begin to turn the pages, my hope quickening. I don't recognize any of the faces—the pictures are old and yellowing, belonging to another time.

But then my flashlight illuminates a crumbling, water-stained family portrait of two parents with two young children.

I recognize Daddy first, perhaps ten years old. He's not smiling, just staring at the camera with deep-brown eyes that look exactly like mine. Aunt Ena's next to him, maybe six or seven, smiling nervously. Their mother is thin and pretty, her hair feathery and strange, her clothes even worse. She seems familiar somehow, but it's the man in the portrait that stops my breath.

"Him."

"What?" Cedar says, coming over to squint at the page.

"He's the ghost that came to my room when I was little. He's younger here, but that was him. The first ghost I ever saw Daddy raise."

My vision goes spotty at the edges, and my fingers ache with a familiar pain.

"Are you sure?" Cedar asks.

"He seemed like a confused old man who'd lost his way. I didn't understand why Daddy was so afraid. Why he cried." I look up at Cedar, but he's hardly more than a silhouette in the darkness, his face blue shadows. I touch his arm to make sure I'm still in this world.

"The ghost was my grandfather. My daddy's father. And Daddy was scared of him."

Of course he was. What little bit I know about who he was in life would have made me afraid to meet his ghost.

Cedar puts a protective hand on my lower back. "That's your dad there?" he asks, pointing at Daddy's face.

"Yes, and that's Aunt Ena." I shift the flashlight to get a closer look, searching her young face for clues of the woman she would grow up to be. Her head is tilted away from the rest of the family, as if she's leaning toward another person. I tilt the picture and gasp. "Look, there was someone else here, in the portrait."

Cedar reaches a tentative finger and scratches at the paper. Part of the built-up residue flakes away, but the image is no clearer. Water stains and mold branch out from that side of the portrait, reaching hungry fingers toward the young family. It's like they're being eaten up by time.

I don't know what the mildew is hiding, but I feel it in my gut, know it as sure as I know the words to all the songs Daddy ever taught me: This is what made Daddy play the way he did. This is the reason for his dark moods and rages. This is the reason for everybody's pain. This little patch of mold-stained paper could answer all my questions.

I fold the picture up and put it in my pocket, ignoring the unpleasantly damp smell it leaves on my fingers, the unnatural weight of it in my hands. Maybe it won't bring Jesse home, but it could help me lay some ghosts to rest.

TWENTY-SIX

I wait until dawn, when morning just begins to break over the horizon, casting pale shafts of light into my bedroom, illuminating the dusty dresser that we shoved back into place last night. Cedar is asleep beside me in bed, his hair sticking up like duck fluff. Mama would have a heart attack if she knew he slept the rest of the night in my bed, but all he did was hold me. All he did was help keep the darkness at bay.

It was a late night, and he's not waking up anytime soon. So I tiptoe past him and out of the room, stepping carefully down the stairs and avoiding the creaky ones. He'll be mad I left without him and put myself in danger without him there to protect me. But there are some things even cowboys can't protect you from.

I grab my fiddle on the way out.

I cut through the woods to get to Miss Patty's house, a half-mile walk from Ena's. She's the last person I want to talk to, but she's the only one who knew Daddy's family back then, the only one except Aunt Ena who can explain the picture I found in the attic. And Ena is too fragile right now for me to bother her with questions.

Church music rumbles out of an open window, but not the nice kind of church music. It's repetitive and overly emotional, and all about blood and sacrifice. I have to knock three times before Miss Patty shuts it off and comes to the door. She peers out at me suspiciously.

"Good morning," I say.

Miss Patty opens the door all the way but doesn't invite me in. "Come to apologize?" she says in her creaky voice.

"For what?" I ask, even though I'm breaking about thirty Southern ideals by speaking to her that way, even if she is a bitter old hag.

Miss Patty raises her eyebrows and I gather up all my anger and stuff it into some dark pocket of my heart. I don't have time for it today. "Of course, Miss Patty. I apologize for being rude to you at Jim's funeral. It was an emotional day."

"Well, all right then. I wouldn't be a Christian woman if I didn't forgive even the worst of sinners."

I somehow manage not to roll my eyes as she steps back to let me in.

She shuffles to the kitchen and turns on the light. "Well, what is it? You're interrupting my praise time."

I pull the picture from my pocket and hand it to her. "I was wondering if you could please tell me about this picture. It's my daddy's family."

Miss Patty puts on a pair of ancient reading glasses and peers at the picture for about a hundred years. "What about it?"

"Is there someone missing from it? There, beside my aunt?"

"Well, I don't see anyone—oh! Oh, oh, I had forgotten about the other little girl."

A bolt of lightning runs through me. "What girl?"

"The other sister, the one who died so young. She broke her mama's heart, wrecked that whole family. A wicked child."

A shiver starts working its way up my spine with tiny, chilly fingers. "What was her name?"

"I'm an old woman now. I forget so many things. But she was a terror—always into trouble, always driving her poor parents mad. No discipline could stop her. That's how she died—up to some mischief or another, and it ended badly for her. When you invite the devil into your home, you shouldn't be surprised when—"

I try to bite down my impatience, but I can't help but interrupt. "You can't remember her name at all?"

Miss Patty goes back to staring at the picture. "Brenda? Belinda? Who can say?"

"Was it—was it Brandy?" I hold my breath.

Miss Patty snaps her wrinkled fingers. "Brandy! Yes. What a child, named after the devil's drink, no wonder, no wonder. A trashy name."

"Thank you," I say, before she can launch into another one of her evil speeches. I pull the picture from her hand. "Have a nice day," I add, rushing for the front door.

Miss Patty is still muttering about the rudeness of wicked

children when I close the door, collect my fiddle from the porch, and bolt back into the trees. She might have been able to tell me more, but I don't want to hear her warped version of my family's history.

Brandy was Daddy and Aunt Ena's sister. A sister who died young, a sister whose name they never spoke. She's the source of all their guilt and their pain. She's the secret our family's been sinking into for thirty years or more.

She's the next ghost I need to raise.

When I'm out of hearing range of Miss Patty's, about halfway back to Aunt Ena's, I stop and lean against a pine tree. The ghosts whisper and stir around me, drawn by the presence of the fiddle. Is Brandy here, too, waiting for someone to help her? Waiting to tell someone what happened to her all those years ago?

I'm about to unclasp Daddy's fiddle case when a twig snaps under someone's boot. I swing around, my heart in my throat.

"What the hell, Cedar?" I say, automatically hiding the fiddle behind my back.

"I could say the same to you." There's no flirtation in his voice, no laugh on his lips. "You took off—with everything going on, you took off. And here you are out here with that fiddle again."

"How did you even find me?"

"I've been hunting since I was five. It wasn't any harder to track you than a deer." When I don't say anything, he comes closer. "What are you doing, Shady?"

"I went to see this old neighbor of ours, to ask her about

the picture. And I was right—there was someone else in it. Her name was Brandy. She was Daddy's sister. And she died when she was a kid."

"Okay . . . That's really sad, but—"

"I just have this feeling, like Brandy's the answer to everything—to Jim and Jesse and Frank, to Daddy and this fiddle."

Cedar's eyebrows knit. "That doesn't make sense. What could a girl who died decades ago have to do with Frank killing Jim?"

I shake my head. "Maybe nothing, but she's still important. There's something here." I feel it, a bone-deep knowing, a recognition. "I have to know what happened to her."

"So you came out here to raise her ghost? What about the shadow man?" Cedar's voice is strained and taut as a bowstring.

"You don't have to help me. You can go home." I turn away from his anger, looking out into the trees, which are just beginning to glow golden with the early morning light.

Cedar closes the distance between us in a few steps. He wraps his arms around me from behind and nuzzles his unshaven face against my neck. He sighs into my hair. "You really don't understand how this works, do you? I can't ever just go home again."

The part of me that has fallen for this rodeo boy melts a little. But there's another part of me, too, a part that is eaten up with grief and fear and darkness. That part of me has to fight the urge to run off into the trees by myself, to open the case and play the fiddle and raise Brandy alone. I want to. I want to so badly. But that's not what Daddy would want for me—to carry this burden all by myself. And I wouldn't have survived the shadow man last time if it weren't for my friends. If Cedar hadn't been there to call for help. If Sarah hadn't found a way to step inside the shadow man's darkness and break me free.

So even though it about tears me in two, I take Cedar's hand and lead him back toward Aunt Ena's, ignoring the lure of the fiddle in its case. "Let's call Sarah and Orlando," I say.

"They're already at the house. I called them as soon as I knew you were gone. I knew you'd want Sarah there since last time she . . ." Cedar trails off, embarrassed.

I guess it wasn't enough to call him my boyfriend and leave it at that. He needs to know that Sarah and I are done, that I'm not settling for him. Even a rodeo boy's ego has its limits.

I stop him before we reach the front porch. "Listen, just in case I wasn't clear before, about me and you. I made my choice. You're the right person for me. If you still want to be with me after all this is done, you're the one I want. The one I want to be with. My mind's made up and I won't change it again."

Cedar meets my eyes. "You're sure?" When I nod, he breaks into a toothy smile that makes the fiddle in my grip and the secret in my pocket feel just a little bit lighter. He catches my cheek in one gentle hand, running a callused thumb over my bottom lip. "I swear to God, Shady Grove, if that devil comes sneaking 'round here again, I'll knock him back to hell myself." And then he kisses me good and thoroughly, just in case I don't believe him.

When I finally open the front door, there's a huge clatter

coming from the kitchen. There's no sign of Mama, Honey, or Aunt Ena, but our entire band is sitting at the table, eating cereal. Orlando is doing one of Aunt Ena's crossword puzzles, tapping a mechanical pencil against his chin.

"Well, help yourselves," I say.

Rose mumbles something unintelligible around a mouthful of Raisin Bran, but I suspect it's as crass and rude as usual. She's sitting next to Sarah, who shrugs at me with a half smile.

"Where's Mama and Honey?" I ask.

"Your mom said to tell you she'll be back to pick you up this afternoon," Kenneth says.

That little bit of happiness I just found with Cedar on the front porch evaporates in an instant. "Why are you here?"

Kenneth flinches and rises from the table, his face red. "Shady—"

"Did you know all along it was Frank?" I ask, ready to punch his stupid face. "Were you covering up for him?"

"Can we talk in private?" Kenneth asks, gesturing me toward the living room. I stomp ahead of him and wait just outside of the kitchen. Kenneth shuts the door, but everyone can probably still hear us, not that I care. I've got nothing to hide.

Kenneth faces me. "We still don't know for sure it was Uncle Frank. You don't really have any proof," Kenneth says, crossing his arms over his chest. "I'm sorry, but you don't."

"Are you kidding me? He's being haunted by your daddy, and he threw a fucking glass bowl at my head. I could have died trying to get away from him."

"He's my uncle. He's my stepdad's best friend," Kenneth

says. "He never did anything to hurt me. He always tried to make Dad be better to me. He was always a good man." True pain makes his voice crack. If Frank goes to prison, Kenneth will lose a father and an uncle all at once.

But I don't have time for Kenneth's pain, not when my brother's life is on the line. Not when all our lives are. "You knew," I say, fuming. "You knew he was involved in Jim's death all this time. I thought you were hiding something, but I didn't think it was something that big."

"Of course I didn't know! It was *my* daddy who got killed," Kenneth says, anger making his cheeks go even redder.

"But you were hiding something," I say. "Something that proves Frank could have done it."

Kenneth bites the inside of his cheek. "I saw his truck coming into the construction site when I was leaving that morning. But I didn't have any reason to think he killed my dad. And my stepdad said to leave it alone. I wouldn't say I saw Frank, and he wouldn't say he saw me."

"And you didn't think there was anything wrong with that? You thought lying was the right way to respond to your daddy's death?"

Kenneth stares at the floor, his anger giving way to shame.

He should be ashamed. "If you'd been honest, Frank would have been investigated. That could have changed everything. He might be in jail right now instead of Jesse. I wouldn't have these stitches in my forehead. And my aunt"—I point angrily toward her room—"wouldn't be lying in there with a concussion."

"I'm sorry," Kenneth whispers.

"Give him a break, Shady," Rose calls from the kitchen. So they've all definitely been listening in. "He'd just found out his dad was killed. And his stepdad's an asshole." I guess her protectiveness extends past Cedar and Sarah.

"He is," Kenneth says, finally finding the courage to look at me. "And I've felt weird about it for a long time. When you said you were raising my dad's ghost, I just . . . I was so scared of what he'd think of me. Of what a coward I am. How I let my stepdad push me around."

"You're not a coward," I say, all my anger used up. Staying mad at Kenneth won't help anything. And I did accuse him of murdering his own dad. "It's . . . it's all right. Let's just forget about it."

Kenneth's face fills with relief and he starts toward me, prepared to give me the same bear hug I saw him give Cedar at Jim's funeral. How did I ever think this goofball could hit Jim with a hammer? He can barely hold a grudge for more than half an hour.

"Fractured rib," I warn him before he can get his paws all the way around me. He gives me a small hug and we head back into the kitchen, where everyone looks at us expectantly.

"We're good," I tell them. Rose pumps her fist and Cedar smiles, clearly relieved that his best friend and his girlfriend are done fighting.

I look around the table again. "Wait, do you guys all know why you're here?"

"We're here for the ghost raising," Kenneth says. And then he goes back to his seat and slurps up more Cheerios as if we

didn't just enact a scene from a soap opera, as if we're n
to enact one from a horror movie.

I wrap my arms around myself. "You understand hov
gerous this is, right? None of you should feel like you hav
be here."

"Do I look like I'd do anything for you I didn't want to?
Rose asks.

"We're helping you, okay?" Sarah says, side-eyeing Rose. "We're your friends, and we're helping you. So just shut up and let us."

Orlando leans down and rummages under his chair, then drops a small bag on the table. He pulls sea salt and a bundle of sage from it. "I didn't tell my abuela what we're up to because she would skin me alive. But I asked her some questions about ghosts, and she said these are used for protection from spirits. Maybe they'll protect us against the shadow man." Orlando gives me a sheepish smile.

I drop into the chair next to him and put my head on his shoulder, wrapping my arms around his bicep. "Thank you" is all I can say, amazed that he's willing to meddle in the supernatural for my sake. He lays his head against mine, and I feel like maybe we're all going to make it out of this all right.

After breakfast, we trudge up the stairs to my bedroom. Sarah sits in my old rocker again, reminding me of the last time we were here and how badly I wanted her. It was only a few weeks ago, but it feels like years. That desire for her is still there, but what I have with Cedar is lessening it to hardly more than a dull ache. Besides, as much as I hate to admit it,

didn't just enact a scene from a soap opera, as if we're n
to enact one from a horror movie.

I wrap my arms around myself. "You understand hov
gerous this is, right? None of you should feel like you hav
be here."

"Do I look like I'd do anything for you I didn't want to?
Rose asks.

"We're helping you, okay?" Sarah says, side-eyeing Rose. "We're your friends, and we're helping you. So just shut up and let us."

Orlando leans down and rummages under his chair, then drops a small bag on the table. He pulls sea salt and a bundle of sage from it. "I didn't tell my abuela what we're up to because she would skin me alive. But I asked her some questions about ghosts, and she said these are used for protection from spirits. Maybe they'll protect us against the shadow man." Orlando gives me a sheepish smile.

I drop into the chair next to him and put my head on his shoulder, wrapping my arms around his bicep. "Thank you" is all I can say, amazed that he's willing to meddle in the supernatural for my sake. He lays his head against mine, and I feel like maybe we're all going to make it out of this all right.

After breakfast, we trudge up the stairs to my bedroom. Sarah sits in my old rocker again, reminding me of the last time we were here and how badly I wanted her. It was only a few weeks ago, but it feels like years. That desire for her is still there, but what I have with Cedar is lessening it to hardly more than a dull ache. Besides, as much as I hate to admit it,

Orlando was probably right—Sarah and I weren't ever going to happen.

But my longing for Daddy's fiddle, the longing to put my fingers on its strings and draw the music out of it, feels almost overwhelming. Despite the damage it can do—what it's already done to me—it's a part of me now, and I need it.

When I pull the instrument from its case, everyone eyes it warily. Orlando sighs and begins scattering the salt in a circle around us. He burns the sage bundle and waves it around, spreading the acrid smell throughout the room. He circles me with the sage, and I notice he's wearing the azabache bracelet his grandmother gave him when he was little. He's always kept it on his bedpost, but now the jet-black stone catches the overhead light, promising protection.

I tune my fiddle quickly and carefully and wait for the others to finish tuning too. "The Twa Sisters," I say automatically, and Sarah groans. Rose elbows her in the side, and Sarah smirks. All that autumn-leaf fragility between them has turned to something new, something like springtime.

"Try to stay with us," Cedar says, his eyes worried. "Don't go off on your own." He turns to the others. "No one stop playing, no matter what."

I nod and begin to play, concentrating on the instruments around me. I feel us sync up, as if we share a single heartbeat. The ghosts, who were so still last night, so hushed, seem to perk up. I can feel them swarming around me, hoping for release, but I push them away and focus on Brandy. I focus all my thoughts onto a little blond-haired girl.

But when I open my eyes, the ghost who stands before me

isn't Brandy. It's the woman whose ghost I raised in the pine woods, who sang a snatch of song with me. I understand now why she looks like regret distilled into human form.

She's the woman from the picture—Brandy's mother. My grandmother, who died before I was born. She's older and sadder now, middle-aged, her brown hair turning gray, her face prematurely wrinkled. Her eyes are hollow and empty, her mouth hard. She radiates loneliness and longing.

The ghost stares at me vaguely until her eyes catch on the fiddle. "Is that William's?" she asks. "William's fiddle? Who are you?" She doesn't remember me from the woods, from before. She's lost, drifting through this world like a plastic bag on the wind. I shouldn't be able to hear her over so many instruments, but her voice penetrates the noise, as if coming from inside me.

"Where's Brandy?" I ask, ignoring her questions. "I wanted Brandy."

"William made that fiddle, you know," she says absently. "I never heard anything so beautiful."

"No, you gave it to him. It was your ancestors'."

She shakes her head. "Brandy had a lovely voice too. She sang like a nightingale. But he took her voice—he took everything from her."

"Daddy?" I say, a pit of ice forming in my stomach. It's an awful thought, but it would explain his dark moods, his guilt.

"He finally got what he deserved," she says as if I hadn't spoken. "If only I'd lived to see it."

Are all ghosts incapable of giving a straightforward answer? Is this some maddening condition of the spirit world?

"I never did though. I never got what this world owed me."

She shakes her head. "I should have stopped him. I should have—"

She grabs her throat, the words strangled there. Darkness pools around us like tar. Her eyes grow wide with terror. "I should have—"

I'm still playing strong, but she begins to fade as darkness fills the room. A distant buzzing reaches my ears, pulling my eyes from her transparent face. By the time I look up, it's too late. The wasps are already flying out of the fireplace and swirling around us. They pour down the chimney and over the hearth like a funnel of darkness, their wings whirring the air. They flit and dive in circles around my room, flying faster and faster around my head, the sound of their wings as sharp as their stingers.

Around me, my bandmates falter at their instruments, ducking to cover their heads. Their startled cries and screams fill the room.

I drop the fiddle, cutting off the music before the shadows can get hold of me, and then I curl into a ball and cover my head against the encroaching darkness. I won't let the shadow man take my voice this time—I scream like my voice is a tornado that will pick the wasps out of the air and toss them into another state. I scream all the rage and grief that's taken up residence in my bones; it pours out of my marrow and into my blood and is pumped through my heart straight into my voice.

When I finally stop screaming and open my eyes, morning light floods the room and dead wasps lie so thick you can barely see the floorboards. Cedar kneels next to me, eyes wide,

Kenneth right beside him. Orlando sits up and blinks like an owl, stunned. Sarah and Rose cling to each other, their arms around each other's necks, their faces pressed together.

"Holy shit," Kenneth says. He turns to Orlando. "Good salt, man," he adds.

"Thank you, Abuelita," Orlando whispers.

After we make sure everyone is okay, we all file back down the stairs together into the living room. Everyone's talking, but my head is too full to follow their conversation or answer their questions, so I wander off to the kitchen. Meeting my grandmother's ghost again has unsettled me and raised even more questions I don't have answers to. I'm definitely not hungry, but I pour myself a glass of orange juice and sit at the table, staring at the violet wallpaper pattern over the kitchen sink and thinking about what I'm going to do next.

"Hey," Sarah says from the doorway. "Can I come in?"

I nod, and she sits in the chair next to me. Silence pools between us, but it feels restful now, like we're finally going to be able to be real friends again.

"So, Rose, huh?" I say, startling her. It hurts, but the hurt doesn't make it to my voice.

Sarah almost smiles, but she's holding back. "Are you mad?"

I shake my head. "How could I be? I'm dating Cedar. But I wish you'd talked to me. You said we'd talk, that night at the construction site. But then you disappeared on me again."

She fiddles with the lid on a plastic jar of honey shaped like a bear. "I know. I'm sorry. I didn't know what to say."

"Anything would have been good. One single word."

Sarah looks up. "I do care about you. And I did—I do—have feelings for you, but . . ."

"But I'm not Rose?"

"It's not that. I mean, yeah, I've always been hung up on Rose, but it wasn't because of her."

"Then why? Why wouldn't you ever trust me? Why wouldn't you let me in?"

"Because I knew I'd let you down," Sarah says. "I'd never be enough for you. I'd never be able to be there for you the way you need. We're just not right for each other. No matter how much we like each other, sometimes it's not enough to want to be together. You need someone like Cedar."

"And you need someone like Rose?" I ask, holding her eyes.

Sarah sighs. "Maybe. I don't know yet. But you did help me. I thought I'd never be able to let anyone in again, and maybe I still haven't, but you made me feel like I can. Like I need to."

None of this is what I wanted to hear, but at least Sarah's finally talking. At least she's finally opening up and telling the truth. At least I can have some closure.

"Are you happy . . . with Cedar, I mean? I know everything else right now is crazy, but is he making it better?"

"Yeah," I say. "He is."

She nods and gets up to go. When she's at the doorway, I call her name, and she turns. "I know you're scared to lose people, after your mom . . . but I'm not going anywhere. I'm always going to be there for you."

"I know," she says. And then she heads back into the living room, where Rose is probably waiting on pins and needles.

And that's the end of Sarah and me, of whatever lingering dream of us I'd held on to in the back of my mind. I'm with Cedar and she's probably going to be with Rose, or with someone else who isn't me. I know deep down that it's for the best, but it still hurt a little to hear her say it, to have the truth laid bare.

I wish that was the hardest conversation I would need to have today, but there's one more waiting for me.

TWENTY-SEVEN

After I convince everyone except Cedar to go home, I make my way to the guest room on the first floor. Aunt Ena lies propped up on pillows, staring out the window. She looks awful. Bandaged cuts cover her pale face. Her hair still has bits of glass in it, which catch the light like crystals.

She turns worried eyes on me. "What happened? I heard all the noise. I felt—I felt—I would have come, but . . ." She gestures to her pitiful form. But I know that's not why she didn't come.

"How are you?" I ask, forcing myself to be patient and gentle when all I really want to do is shake the truth out of her.

"I'll be fine. Just got my head knocked around a little." Her voice is finally normal, and she is firmly in our world, in the present, if unwillingly. "It'll heal."

I finger the hem of my shirt, unsure how to begin.

"Come here," she orders. I sit at the foot of her bed, and she runs her eyes over me, searching for injuries. "Lucky girl."

"We're both lucky, I guess." She's speaking of the accident, but I'm not.

It feels cruel to do it, but I ask anyway. "Aunt Ena, what happened to Brandy?"

She blinks at me for few seconds. "Hmm?"

"All this family's secrets almost got us killed. Isn't it time to tell the truth? What happened to your sister?"

Aunt Ena blanches. "That's . . . How did you . . ."

"Just tell me. Please. I've already figured out most of it anyway." I pull out the creased picture and place it in her lap. "I know it's painful for you talk about it, and I can't imagine what it was like for you to lose her. But I'm losing Jesse, I'm losing my brother, and I can't seem to do anything about it. Nothing I do is helping. Maybe . . . maybe somehow Brandy can."

Ena gazes down at the portrait, pain filling her eyes. She touches the moldy growth that obscures Brandy's form. She looks like it nearly kills her to do it, but she finally speaks. "Brandy was my little sister. *Our* little sister, mine and Will's."

"What happened to her?"

"Please don't make me, Shady," Aunt Ena says, meeting my eyes. "Please, it will destroy me."

"It won't, Aunt Ena. Maybe . . . maybe it will help you. All this family ever does is bury its secrets, and yet they keep climbing out of the dirt and sneaking up on us. Maybe if we just dig them up and face them, they can't hurt us all so much. Maybe if we speak them out loud, they won't have so much power over us."

Aunt Ena squeezes her eyes shut tight, but a tear escapes and rolls down her cheek. "She was allergic to wasps."

"That's how she died?" I say so quietly I'm not sure Ena hears me, but then she nods.

"That's what killed her, yes, but not who."

"Who was it?" I ask, my heart constricting, but she looks away, not speaking. "Was it . . . was it Daddy?"

Aunt Ena startles. "No, of course not. Not *your* daddy."

I hear the emphasis on *your*—slight, but there. "It was yours," I say. "Your daddy."

She nods, the tears spilling from both eyes now. A fear as old as this house twists her features as she looks up at the ceiling. But she takes a deep breath and goes on. "He used to lock us up there when we were bad. In the attic."

"When you were bad?"

Aunt Ena stares ahead, not seeing anything, or maybe seeing a whole lot I can't. "When we got in fights or broke things. Childish stuff. The day she . . . Brandy stole some cookies from the cabinet for our tea party. She didn't ask."

"And he locked her up there?" God, for taking cookies. What else might a parent like that do? It's too horrible to think about.

Mama might have slapped my hand once or twice, but I never even got spanked when I was little. Jesse didn't either, no matter how much he misbehaved. Even that time he got caught playing with matches, all Daddy did was send him to his room.

Aunt Ena nods. "When we heard Brandy screaming, he said she was acting out. We didn't know there were wasps up there. But then when she went quiet . . ." Aunt Ena can't go on.

"Why didn't you or Daddy ever tell us?" I ask, a tremor

starting deep inside me. This house was my home, the place where I was loved. I had no idea it held so much trauma.

Aunt Ena wipes her eyes. "Some stories hurt too much to tell."

"What happened to your . . . father?" I can't call him her daddy now. He's not worthy of the name.

She sighs. "He went to prison. He died before they let him out—another prisoner stabbed him. But Mama died first, I think at least partly of grief. She was never the same after. . . And Will and I stayed here. To be close to Brandy."

"Is that why the fiddle meant so much to Daddy? Because of Brandy? He wanted to see her again?"

"That was a lot of it, I think," she says vaguely, noncommittal. Then she's quiet for a while, as if she's steeling herself. What else could be left to tell after this?

I think I know. "How did Daddy really get the fiddle? It wasn't from your mother, was it?"

She wrings her hands over the covers. "He came home with the wood for it the night Brandy died. Later on, he had a luthier make the fiddle special for him. But he's the one who made it what it is."

"How?"

"I don't know exactly."

"Aunt Ena," I prompt.

She shakes her head. "Grief, guilt, longing. He played it until it started bringing the ghosts to life. And then he kept on playing, found a purpose in it. Well, at first. But later I don't think he could help himself. He was bound to it somehow. He always meant for you to have it once he was gone, but Jesse was determined to keep you from it."

That's why grief makes the fiddle do its magic, I realize. It's a fiddle made of grief.

"Did Jesse know Daddy made the fiddle?"

Aunt Ena shakes her head. "No, I don't think so. I never told him. Will didn't want you kids to know. He wanted you to love music."

It's no harder to believe Daddy's grief made our fiddle than it is to believe our Irish ancestors gave it ghost-raising magic. I know how powerful grief is. I've felt it pound through my body like ocean waves, leaving me half drowned. Of course grief could shape a fiddle into an instrument for summoning the dead. Of course the player's grief could make it stronger. That doesn't surprise me one bit.

But that Daddy would lie to me like this, that he would draw me into his grief and make it my responsibility . . .

I've never felt sorry for Daddy before—he always seemed so far above all that—but now I do. I feel pity for him, which is not a way a girl ever wants to feel about her father. I've held this perfect image of him for the last four years, an unbreakable source of comfort and support, this deep and unshakable knowing—and it's starting to crack right down the middle.

"Let's go for a walk," I tell Cedar when I leave Aunt Ena's room.

"What did she say?" he asks, jumping up from the couch. But when I shake my head, he follows me onto the front porch.

I need to move, need to feel the ground under my feet. I grab Cedar's hand and lead him around the back of the house and into the woods. I can feel him practically vibrating with questions, but he doesn't ask a single one. Instead, he laces his fingers in mine and follows me through the dark woods, as if I'm leading him down a beach instead of into a haunted forest.

We walk in silence, the pine needles soft and spongy under our feet, shafts of sunlight illuminating patches of moss across the forest floor. There are no birds singing, no squirrels leaping from tree to tree. The woods are empty and hushed, waiting. Every ghost for ten miles is holding its breath.

I want to scream my rage into the silent trees, and I want to fall to the earth and ask it to hold me. I want to cut down every tree in this forest and burn down the house that is the wood's beating heart. I want to . . .

I snatch up an old limb from the ground and slam it into the nearest tree as hard as I can. The shock reverberates up my arm, and I feel it in my teeth. I hit the tree again and again until the limb snaps.

I sink to my knees and let the emotions well up and then surge out of my body, leaving me shaking and weak. My fractured rib aches and makes my breath come short.

"Shady," Cedar croons, touching my back. "What's wrong?"

"Jesse is in jail and Frank is out free, and I can't do anything about it," I say, my words barely coherent. "And my daddy was a liar and so is pretty much everyone else I love." I break down weeping again, the hurt of it too much for words.

My family's history is a dark stream that flows through my veins. I can't escape it—it's as much a part of me as my DNA.

Is that all we're here for? To hurt and then to die?

And despite everything I've learned—despite the shadow man and the wasps—I still want to play Daddy's fiddle. I need it. The depth of that need scares me worse than anything.

Jim was right about me. I'm my daddy all the way through.

TWENTY-EIGHT

When we get back to Aunt Ena's, Mama and Honey are there. "Where've you been?" Mama says, her voice frantic. She clutches her cell phone tightly in one fist.

"We went for a walk. What's wrong?"

She squeezes Honey to her chest. "I called Frank this morning."

"Why?" I ask, startled.

"To give him a piece of my mind. You don't treat *my* child like that," Mama says, her anger flaring up for a moment. Mama has always defended Jesse and me against the slightest offense, like a bear when her cubs are threatened. But this time I wish she hadn't.

"You knew he was dangerous," I say, exasperated. "What if he comes looking for us?"

"I thought you were exaggerating," Mama admits. "I'm sorry, baby. We'll stay here at Ena's."

"He'll probably just come here next, since she was with me yesterday," I fret. "What did you say to him? What did he say?" I ask, my panic rising.

She shakes her head. "Something is wrong with him—he's not right in the head. When I think how close you were yesterday to—" But a sob escapes her throat and she can't go on. "I did what you wanted and called the police. I told them he threatened you and that I thought he was unhinged. They didn't take it seriously. I'm still not sure Frank had anything to do with Jim's death, but I don't feel safe having you out here away from me right now. Not with Frank wandering around like that." She turns to Cedar. "You can't leave her alone. Promise me you'll watch out for her."

"Yes, ma'am," he says and puts an arm around me. I shake him off.

"We can't wait around. We have to do something," I say, my whole body trembling. I'm sick to death of crying and waiting and talking.

"Here, take your sister," she says, handing Honey over to me. I wrap my arms around her and feel our hearts beating together, and I wonder if this is how Aunt Ena felt about Brandy. But Honey's restless now, and slithers out of my arms to the floor and shoots into the room where Aunt Ena's sleeping.

"Come on," Cedar says, pulling me toward the kitchen. "I'll make you and Honey some lunch. You'll feel better after you eat."

But then Mama cries out, and by the time we turn around,

Frank is already barreling through the front door, just like I knew he would. We should have left here the moment Mama told me she called him.

"Call 911," Mama yells, and Cedar has his phone out of his pocket before I can even think to reach for mine. "Shady, take Honey upstairs. Now."

I start across the room to find Honey, but Frank's screams stop my feet. "I'm going to kill them all, Jim. Is that what you want? You want your whole family dead?" He pulls a black handgun from his waistband and points it at Mama. "I'm going to kill them all."

"Shady, go," Mama yells again, staggering away from Frank.

"No, you stay, girl," he yells, pointing the gun at me. Cedar leaps in front of me, still frantically speaking into his phone.

"Hang up that phone right now," Frank growls, pointing the gun at Cedar. His eyes are bloodshot and wild, scanning the room frantically. He looks like he hasn't slept in days, weeks even. Cedar puts the phone in his pocket and backs me toward the kitchen. "Stay right there," Frank screams.

This isn't the same man I saw yesterday. Yesterday he was half mad from being haunted, but now he's lost, practically a ghost himself

A motion out of the corner of my eye catches my attention at the same moment it catches Frank's. He swivels the gun, pointing it at Honey and Aunt Ena, and a wave of terror washes over me. "Your baby girl, Jim. Your baby girl. Is that what you want?"

Mama runs past Frank, heedless of his gun. She snatches Honey up into her arms. "Get out of here, Frank. Right now," she says, her voice shaking hard. She stands next to me, pulling Aunt Ena beside her. Mama doesn't understand why this is happening; she has always managed to ignore the ghostly parts of our family. But Aunt Ena knows how much danger we're in. Her eyes look like a rearing horse's, the whites showing bright.

Frank settles his gaze on me again. "Shady, go get your fiddle. I want Jim to watch me kill you all, and I want to see his face while I do it."

I don't need to be told twice. I race up to my bedroom and pull the case out from under the bed. Luckily, Frank doesn't know what he's asking. This fiddle is the closest thing I have to a weapon right now. I run back down the stairs so fast I stumble on the last step and nearly pitch into the wall.

Back in the living room, I rip the case open and pull out the fiddle. "Play," roars Frank. "Isn't that what you threatened me with? My brother's ghost? Bring him then."

Mama's eyes grow wide. She grips Honey to her chest and watches me in silent confusion. Aunt Ena backs against the wall and slides down it, hiding her face in her hands. Cedar drops to his knees beside me. "Shady, you can't do this."

"He's going to kill us all if I don't," I hiss back, my hands shaking as I tune the instrument.

"Play!" Frank screams. For good measure, he fires into the wall behind my head. Honey yelps and begins to wail. Mama puts her palm over Honey's mouth and shushes her. My hands are trembling so hard I can barely hold the bow, but I have no choice but to play.

I play "Omie Wise" again, since it worked the first time I raised Jim's ghost. The notes come out crooked and shrill but loud enough to drown out Honey's cries. But as I play, I grow more confident, pouring my fear and rage and shame into the fiddle. It melds to my emotions like melted plastic, and I lose track of the difference between wood and skin.

I close my eyes and forget about Frank and Cedar and Mama and even Honey, focusing all my thoughts on the grief that can draw Jim back to our world. He's already here anyway, so clear in Frank's mind he hardly even needs my urging. But then Mama gasps and I open my eyes to see Jim standing in the middle of the room, arms loose at his sides, jaw set.

Frank cries out at the sight of his brother, the sound something between an exclamation and a plea. "Please, Jim, please," Frank says, dropping to his knees. "Forgive me. Forgive me, Jim."

Mama looks at me sharply, and I nod. I was sure before, but now she knows too.

"It was that little bastard's fault," Frank says, his voice hardly more than a sob. "It was him. He told me—he told me you were sleeping with Marlene. He said he saw you together. That was the final straw. After all you've done, after all you've cost me . . ."

Damn it, Jesse. That's what this is all about—Jesse's stupid lies.

"Why would I sleep with your wife?" Jim says, standing

over him, arms crossed over his chest. He looks more threatening than he ever did in life, like his anger has given him weight and power. "Why would I do that?"

Frank's face turns from fear to rage again, in the blink of an eye. "You slept with Shirley, didn't you? Right under your best friend's nose. And you were always looking for a way to hurt me. It wasn't enough for you to be a lazy drunk who got Daddy killed. It wasn't enough for you to be so sorry and so useless you couldn't watch him for one day, make sure he didn't choke on his own vomit for one goddamned fucking day."

"I made a mistake, and you never let me forget it. I made one mistake," Jim says.

"A mistake? A mistake?" Frank bellows. "He died alone and in pain and probably terrified. And yet Mama forgave you, Mama made me try to forgive you. But you knew I never could."

"You spent your whole life looking for a reason to hate me, Frank. Daddy's death just gave you cause. But you got your revenge, didn't you? You bashed my brains in. Aren't you happy now?"

Frank's face twists in despair. "Why else did you stick around? You wanted me to hurt you. I know you did. I didn't pay you shit, I gave you all the worst jobs. But you stayed." Frank glares up at his dead brother. "You sonofabitch, why did you stay?" he roars. "You knew I was going to kill you one day. You knew it."

Jim shakes his head. "Even this—even this you're blaming on me."

Mama lets out an anguished sob, and Jim glances at her,

regret in his eyes. "I'm sorry, Shirley." Honey holds out a hand toward him, her expression lost and frightened. Her lips form the word "Daddy," but I don't hear it over the fiddle.

"Turn Honey away from this. Don't let her see." Jim stares at Mama until she turns around, hiding Honey's face against her chest.

Jim returns his eyes to Frank, and there is no pity in his ghostly gaze. There is only triumph. Frank was right—Jim has been waiting for this, even if he had to die for it to happen. There's so much to people we never see, never even guess at.

"You know why I stayed?" Jim says, his voice terrible. "I stayed because after all those years of torment, all those years of being kicked like a dog, I wanted the whole damn town to see you for what you are. I wanted them to see you for the hateful, jealous, spiteful bastard that you are. I knew you would show your true colors eventually . . . though of course I didn't know it would be because you killed me." He chuckles darkly, running a hand over his stubble. "And it was worth it. It was worth having my head bashed in to spend these weeks haunting you, tormenting you, the way you've been torturing me all my life."

Frank raises the gun and points it at Jim, the rest of us forgotten.

Jim laughs. "You can't kill me now. But you know what you can do with that gun? You can turn it around and put an end to this. Shady was right when she told you I'll never leave you be. I won't—I'll haunt you until you can't sleep or shit or eat or do anything without hearing my voice in your head."

The distant scream of sirens floats in over my music, and

every head turns toward the windows. Red and blue lights flash from the road.

"What about Jesse?" I ask, hoping to distract Jim and Frank until the police arrive. No matter what Frank has done, I don't want to see him shoot himself. I don't want Honey to go through that, or any of us. Jim ignores me, so I pitch my voice louder. "You were willing to sacrifice Jesse for your hate too?"

Jim doesn't even look at me. His eyes are locked on Frank's with a fervent gleam. "I already told you your brother deserved jail, Shady," Jim says. "I'm the second person that little shit has gotten killed. But even so, hell yes, I'd sacrifice him."

My blood runs cold. Jim doesn't have any reason to lie. Frank is completely in his power.

"Do it now, do it before they get you," Jim says as the police cars speed down the driveway. He puts his hand on the gun and begins to turn it toward his brother's face.

This is what evil is—not some unnatural force, not demons or devils. It's this right here—a man clinging so hard to hate it's worth dying for. Worth risking the lives of his wife and his child. Worth seeing a bullet fly into his brother's brain. Worth everything.

As if in answer to my thoughts, I feel the shadow man slithering around me again, insatiable, eating up my fear and anger with a hunger so big the whole world's pain couldn't fill it. I recognize him now—I know who he is. But I'm powerless against him. Like Jim, I'll risk anything. I'll offer up anything in this world to keep playing my daddy's fiddle. I'll offer up myself.

Yes, play, play on, the shadow man whispers, his voice

filled with malicious glee. I do, pouring every ounce of agony I feel into the song.

Jim bears down on Frank with merciless hands, bringing the gun only a few inches away from his brother's sweating, anguished face. Frank's arms tremble with the effort to hold the gun steady. Why are the police taking so long?

I squeeze my eyes shut tight and wait for the sound of a bullet. Instead, I hear a honey-gravel voice that pierces straight to my heart. It's right close in my ear, so close I can almost feel the tickle of his stubble on my cheek. I don't dare open my eyes.

Shady Grove, you're stronger than this. You're stronger than the shadow man. You're stronger than your grief. You're stronger than I ever was, baby. Stop playing now. Stop playing before you tie yourself to that fiddle so tight you'll never be free

I know I lied, I know you don't have any reason to trust me now. But I made that fiddle with all the hate and the pain and the grief in my heart, and because of it I lost my life, and all the things I loved most in this world. I lost you and Jesse and your mama. I even lost music, Shady Grove. That fiddle don't make you play with all your soul. It eats your soul. It takes everything that's good in you and turns it to pain and hate and rage. Stop playing now, baby, before you lose everyone you love. Before you lose yourself.

His hand closes over mine, and his fingers feel so familiar I gasp. He doesn't make me stop drawing the bow across the strings. He holds my hand in his, and lets me choose.

I draw the bow away from the strings at the same moment

a gunshot explodes in the air. The final note of "Omie Wise" fades with the sound of the bullet. Frank is on the floor, bleeding from a wound in his shoulder. Jim is gone, and so is Daddy, if he was really here.

Then police officers are rushing into the room. They kick the gun away from Frank and survey the house, checking for more dangers. Everyone is alive and whole, even Frank, who groans loudly on the floor, still swearing at his brother's ghost. "I killed you, I killed you, Jim. I won. No matter what you do now, I won. I killed you. I got my revenge."

Mama rushes across the room and throws an arm around me, crushing Honey between us. Aunt Ena follows, burying her face in my hair. We're safe.

But whatever's left of Frank's life belongs to Jim now. He'll never be free, but neither will Jim. They've bound themselves together in hate.

TWENTY-NINE

The story of Jim's murder unravels bit by bit. Jesse really did tell Frank that Jim slept with Marlene—he was pissed at Jim and wanted to get back at him. Well, he'd always been pissed at Jim. But he didn't plan on Frank's decades-long grudge turning murderous, or on being framed for the crime. He didn't plan on Frank threatening to kill everyone he loves if he told the truth. He didn't plan on Jim's haunting and Frank's descent into madness. Of course, he didn't plan on any of that because he's Jesse, and being reckless and selfish is all he knows.

But he's getting out today and coming home to us. Mama asked if I wanted to go with her to pick him up, but I said no. Even though all I wanted was to get Jesse out of jail, I'm so angry at him that I can hardly bear it. He didn't kill Jim, but he still played a role in his death. His lies cost Honey her father, Mama her husband. I don't know if I can even look at him, after all he's put us through. And what else is Jesse capable of?

What else has he hidden from me? Jim claimed his was the second death Jesse caused. I don't want to think too hard about Daddy and what Jesse might have done to hurt him.

At least Frank's going to prison, and justice is shaking itself out, bringing everyone some closure. I do wonder if Frank and Jim could have reconciled—if they could have gotten past their petty squabbles and the divide their daddy's death made between them, could all this have been avoided? Could Jim still be alive? A part of me thinks Jim was in denial about why he stayed near Frank all those years. He didn't stick around to see Frank slip up and show his true colors—he wanted to be punished for their daddy's death and he wanted Frank to make him suffer. Like Jesse choosing to stay in jail for Jim's murder.

All the other stories that have unraveled are just as bad as Jim's death and Jesse's imprisonment. Brandy and the wasps and my grandfather—that secret makes me shiver every time I think of it, and feel a strange shame burning in the center of my chest.

Yet the story I'm most stuck on, the one that keeps me awake at night and sends me into the woods with a fiddle case I'm barely able to keep closed—that's Daddy's. He made this fiddle—not the instrument itself, but its heart, its soul. His grief made it capable of summoning ghosts and shaped it into a doorway for evil. I'm trying to hate him for that—trying to summon up a righteous anger for his lies and his weakness.

But I feel the same thing I've always felt for Daddy—kinship. We are the same. I know we're the same because I can't give up this fiddle. No matter how many people it has hurt, no matter how much danger it has put me in. I can't give it up.

That's why I'm in the woods now, kneeling on the warm pine needles with my hands hovering over the fiddle's case, midmorning sunshine filtering across my skin. After a long moment, I open the clasps and stare into the open case. The trees sigh around me, the ghosts stirring in their branches. They are waiting for me. I know now they've always been waiting for me.

I've somehow managed to keep the case closed these past three weeks, left the fiddle lying against its green velvet. I know this isn't what Daddy wants for me, I know the shadow man will kill me if I keep playing.

Daddy said I was stronger than he was. He said I could let it go. But he was wrong. I will stare this rattlesnake in the face until its poison stops my heart.

Because there's one more ghost I have to raise, no matter what it costs me.

Mama went to pick up Jesse from jail over an hour ago, and once he's here . . . This might be my last chance to raise Daddy's ghost. I waited all this time because I wanted to be sure I could do it, sure I wouldn't mess up. And maybe deep down I was afraid to call Daddy's ghost, afraid that if I saw him again, I'd never get over my grief.

I pull the fiddle from the case and ready my bow. Fear and love battle inside me, making my hands tremble. I touch the bow to the strings, and while I've never done drugs, I imagine this is what it feels like when you press down the plunger on a syringe, sending heroin into your bloodstream. A release.

I let "The Twa Sisters" pour from my fiddle, dark as river

water, deep as my grief. Almost immediately the shadow man's pull begins, a heavy blackness just at the edges of the music.

"Shady," someone says behind me. I swivel, and there's Jesse standing among the trees, his eyes on me. I didn't think he'd be home this soon. After weeks of bureaucratic processes I don't understand, I thought his release today would take hours. Or maybe it was hours, and I just lost track of time. Either way, he's here now. He's home.

"Shady, put the fiddle down," Jesse says, walking slowly toward me with hands outstretched, as if I'm a feral cat he's trying to tame.

A surge of anger floods me. I don't play, but I cling tight to the instrument. It seems to cling to me too, desperate to hold on to me.

This is the moment I've been waiting for—Jesse's release. It's what I've been fighting so hard for. But I don't feel happy or even relieved. Because he's going to take this fiddle from me. And it's going to be like hearing Daddy was dead all over again, like having my heart ripped out a second time. And if he takes it, I can never ask Daddy what happened to him the day he died or learn how Jesse was involved.

"Shady?" Jesse says. "I'm home. You brought me home."

Another voice whispers in my mind, seductive and sure. *He killed your father. He's the real reason your daddy's dead—not the fiddle. That's why he kept the fiddle from you, so you'd never learn what he did.* I shake my head, trying to dispel the shadow man's voice. It's impossible to believe Jesse could do such a thing, but I can't root out the thought. Not after what he told me at the jail, not after what Jim said.

Jesse kneels beside me. "Put the fiddle down. You don't understand how powerful it is, what it did to him."

I push away from him and stand. "What did *you* do to him, Jesse?" I hear myself say.

Jesse stands too and cocks his head. "To Daddy?"

I only stare at him, so Jesse reaches for the fiddle. Before I know what I'm doing, I've drawn back my hand and slapped him across the face. "Don't you dare."

Jesse reels away from me, holding a hand to his cheek. I put my burning fingers to my mouth, shocked by what I've done.

"He hit me like that once too, you know, when I tried to stop him from playing the fiddle," Jesse says.

"You're lying," I answer, another crack running through my foundation.

"He wasn't perfect, no matter how much you wanted him to be. You act like he was God's gift to the fucking world, but he wasn't. He loved those ghosts and that fiddle more than he loved us." Jesse's concern for me is quickly turning to anger.

"That's not true," I say. "You don't know what you're talking about." Maybe it was the shadow man acting through Daddy, whispering to him the way he does to me. The way he's whispering now.

"When I decided to stop learning fiddle, he wouldn't talk to me for weeks. I was a child. And he gave me the cold shoulder."

I don't know what to say to that. Jesse presses on, relentless. "He kept playing even though he knew it was hurting you. After I told him about the little girl who was haunting you."

Shock grips me like a cold, dead hand. I guess I should have put it together before now—

Daddy knew his fiddle playing was hurting me, but he kept playing anyway. His need for the fiddle was bigger than his desire to keep me safe.

I push the hateful thought away. "How much do you know about the little girl?"

"I know you were having nightmares about her, that you were seeing her all over the house. You used to cry and say there was a dead girl in your ceiling. Then there were the wasps."

I shudder, remembering their wings brushing my skin, the promise of their stings.

My eyes fill with tears. "She was his sister. Brandy. His and Aunt Ena's. And their dad is the reason she died."

"What are you talking about?"

"Aunt Ena told me. That's why Daddy was so obsessed with the fiddle. He was trying to hold on to his sister." Some distant part of me, which the shadow man can't touch, whispers that I'm doing the same thing—clinging to the fiddle to keep Daddy close to me.

Jesse's face has gone pale, but he shakes his head. "Fine. Whatever. His dead sister. We were his living children, and he chose her over us." He crosses his arms.

The shadow man's voice whispers again, sending chills through me, and before I know it, I'm hearing his words leave my mouth. "That's why you killed Daddy," I say, "because you thought he didn't love us enough?" I didn't mean to say it, I'm not even sure if I believe it, but it pops out like a cork from a bottle of cheap champagne.

Jesse's mouth drops open. "I didn't kill him. I . . . All I

ever did was try to protect you. Take care of you," he says. "I didn't mean for him to die, I swear. I just wanted all the ghost stuff to end. I wanted you to be safe. I was only thirteen years old, Shady, and I already felt like I was halfway to my grave. I wanted to spare you."

"Spare me?" I laugh. "What have you spared me from?" Not from Daddy's burden. That's what the fiddle is, however much I might love it. It's my burden now.

"I didn't kill him," Jesse says, his eyes desperate, pleading. "I took the fiddle when I went to stay with a friend by the lake—because I didn't want him to play while I was gone. Because I wouldn't be there to make sure you were all right."

He's a liar. Remember how he lied to Frank about Jim, how he lied to you? the shadow man whispers.

I shake my head, gritting my teeth. I feel like I'm being torn in two. "You're lying," I say to Jesse. "You wanted to destroy it. You always hated it."

Jesse stares into my eyes, and whatever he sees there makes up his mind. "I won't let you die for this fiddle. Not like he died." His hand shoots out and he grabs the fiddle from me, ripping it out of my hands. "I should have destroyed it then," he says, backing away. "If I had, maybe Daddy would still be alive. But I'm going to destroy it now."

And then he's running.

I leap to my feet and chase him through the trees, and I know exactly where he's going. My fractured rib feels like it's on fire, but I ignore it because my life is being carried away in my brother's arms, carried away to be drowned.

If he wanted to destroy it, he could smash it against any of the hundreds of trees zipping by our running bodies. But he's going to drown it, *the way he drowned Daddy*. I see that now.

I run and run and run, my body screaming at me to stop, my mind screaming at my body to keep moving, to keep putting one foot in front of the other.

I break through the trees into the marshy area that surrounds the lake just in time to see Jesse draw back his arm and throw the fiddle high into the air. It spins out over the water and then plummets down, far, far out into the lake.

"No!" I scream, and the pain in my rib is nothing to the stab of panic that shoots through my heart. I leap into the lake fully clothed, swimming as hard as I can, but I'm already gasping, the water dragging at me like quicksand. I dive down where I saw the fiddle fall, and my descent to the bottom is an echo of my last dive. But when I touch the silt this time, my fingers find the hard wood of the fiddle. I shoot upward and surface with a gasp, the pain in my rib blinding. As soon as I get a gulp of air, I'm underwater again, fighting against the pain in my chest and the weakness in my limbs. The shadow man seems to laugh inside my head.

"Shady!" Jesse screams. He splashes toward me. He reaches me quickly and begins to tow me toward shore, while I kick and hit at him, thrashing with all my might to get away, to keep him from the fiddle. I'll drown before I lose it.

He drags us both to shore and I lie in the grass, clutching the sodden instrument to my chest. "Please, Jesse, please," I cry, "I need it."

Jesse gets to his feet and stands over me. "You could have died, Shady, just like he died. All for this fucking fiddle." His voice breaks into a sob.

He's right—the fiddle has too much power over me. The shadow man won't stop until I'm lying belly-up in this lake. But that doesn't change the fact that Jesse caused our daddy's death. Jesse's the one who needs to answer for what he's done, not me.

"What did you do? How did you make him crash? I know you did something to make it happen. There wasn't a deer in the road," I yell, clutching the fiddle to my chest. That's why Jesse let himself be framed for Jim's murder. Because just like Jim's ghost said . . . he was owed punishment for something else. Jesse almost admitted as much when I visited him in juvie. He said he'd caused enough trouble and pain for one lifetime, that he had done something I'd never forgive him for.

"You're . . . right, there wasn't," Jesse says, struggling to push down his sobs. "I—I made it up. I wasn't even in the truck. I never told anyone, not even Mama. I was too ashamed."

I gaze up at my brother's anguished face, anger turning to dread in my stomach. "What happened?"

Jesse finally gets his tears under control. "Daddy came to my friend's to get the fiddle back. And my friend was kind of high and his parents weren't there, so I was on my own. And Daddy was so mad at me for taking his fiddle. We argued, and I got scared and I grabbed the fiddle and ran. I tried to stay in the woods along the lake, but when the trees thinned out, he spotted me, and then there was nowhere to go but the water.

"He was still driving at the edge of the road, yelling at me from the window, begging me to get in the truck. Begging me not to hurt the fiddle. He said it would kill him to lose it. Said if I loved him at all I should get in the truck and give him back his fiddle."

"You should have," I say.

Jesse shakes his head slowly, fresh tears running down his cheeks. "I wish I had. I swear to God, every day, I wish . . ." He takes a shuddering breath.

"How . . . ?" I whisper, unable to say the words.

"I ran out onto the dock, and then I heard his truck hit the water. He must have sped up and lost control trying to get to the boat ramp, and the truck rolled over the bank. And then it was sinking. And then he was dead—all for that stupid, god-damned piece of wood."

Jesse wipes his eyes again. His voice is hoarse. Now that he's talking, he can't seem to stop. "I dropped the fiddle on the dock and ran to the truck. I waded in and tried to pull open the door, but I couldn't. But his window was down, so I put my head down in the water and looked in. He was already dead. The water was red and he was kind of floating upside down."

A sob wrenches itself from my chest.

"I'm sorry." Jesse reaches for me but pulls back, like he's not sure if he's allowed to offer me comfort.

"Then what?" I ask, my voice hardly more than a croak. "Did you pull him out?"

Jesse clenches his jaw like he's fighting back nausea. "I reached in and pulled him by his shirt, got about half his body out of the truck window. There was blood everywhere."

Jesse's eyes are wide with fear, as if he's seeing Daddy's body for the first time, right here in the woods. "And he was dead, the kind of dead you don't come back from. Eyes open and staring, more blood out of him than in."

"What did you do?"

"I ran. I ran all the way back to my friend's house, and we called the police. I lied and said I was in the truck with him, that I swam out the window. I was soaked and covered in blood, so they believed me. They thought I was lucky.

"But I wasn't lucky. I . . . I think we're all cursed, Shady."

I hear an echo of Mama's words from a few weeks ago, saying she thinks maybe she's cursed because her husbands keep dying.

I close my eyes, but all I see is Daddy's body in its coffin. The unnatural-looking suit, dark against the white pillows. How much smaller his body seemed. I couldn't bear to look at his face, so instead I looked at his hands. The hands I had spent so much time watching play the fiddle, clean fish for supper, dig into the deep, dark earth in the back garden.

"We have to destroy it," Jesse says, ripping my thoughts back to the present, to the fiddle clutched in my hands.

All I feel for Jesse in this moment is hate—for taking Daddy, for trying to take my fiddle. The image of Daddy's body floating open-eyed in the red water sears itself into my mind. Twice now, I could have joined him.

"Let me take it," Jesse says. "I'll do it for you." He comes near and puts his hands on the instrument. My arms are so weak, he pries it from my grip without effort.

As soon as the wood leaves my hands, I feel an unbearable hunger to have it back. "Please, Jesse, please. I'll die if you take it. I'll die, Jesse," I sob out. "I'll die just like Daddy did, and it will be all your fault." Didn't Jesse just tell me Daddy said the same thing—that it would kill him to lose the fiddle? Well, Daddy was right.

Jesse stiffens as if he realizes it, too, but then he turns away, carrying the fiddle back toward the trees.

"Wait," I scream, and he pauses, still turned away. "Let me play it one more time. One more time, Jesse, that's all. I'll raise Daddy's ghost and you can see him again. He'll make everything all right. And then you can do whatever you want. You can drown it or burn it or smash it to pieces. Just let me play one more time. Don't you want to see him? Don't you want to tell Daddy you're sorry?"

Jesse turns, anguish carved into every line of his face. "Do you promise? One more time?"

"I swear," I say. "I swear." I don't know whether I'm lying or not, and neither does Jesse.

"Now?" he says. "Here?"

I shake my head. If I played the fiddle now, with my grief thrumming through me, filling up my body like the water that drowned Daddy, I'd wake every ghost in this wood. It'd be too much for the shadow man to resist.

"I'm too tired now," I say.

We stumble back through the woods, Jesse's hands tight around the fiddle. "I'm going to keep the fiddle then. Until you're ready to play it for the last time. I won't lose you the way I lost him."

The walk is endless and agonizing, but we finally break through the trees into the yard outside our trailer. Mama's rental car is there; I'd forgotten she brought him home. Jesse stops outside, like he's afraid to go in and face her twice in one day.

I push past him into the trailer, and Mama looks up, her eyes widening at the sight of my drenched, dirty form.

"Mama," Jesse says, coming inside with me. His face crumples. "I'm—I'm so sorry. I should have—I should have said it earlier, but I'm—" His voice breaks.

She crosses the room and pulls Jesse into a hug, crushing him against her. She holds him to her like he was dead and came back to life and she's never gonna let anything happen to him ever again.

"I'm sorry, I'm sorry, I'm sorry," he sobs into her shoulder. She shushes him like a baby and holds on, rocking him gently while the grief pours out of him, unstoppable, seemingly endless. She holds on while his tears and snot cover her blouse, while his body shakes like he's frozen all the way to his bones.

But finally she pulls back and puts her hand on his face. "I don't blame you, baby. Maybe you done wrong, but you didn't throw that hammer. It's not your fault."

I want to ask her if she knows he's the reason Daddy's dead, but I can see in her eyes she knows everything. She knows all that Jesse's done.

And she forgives him.

She'd forgive me too, if it had been me.

But it wasn't.

I climb to my feet, walk to the bathroom, and slam the door behind me.

THIRTY

The next morning, golden light falls across the green fields down the road from our trailer, making the wildflowers along the barbed wire blaze. The sky looks like somebody took a bite out of a Georgia peach, the orange fading into pink at the edges. I don't know how the world can go on being so beautiful when all this horror keeps unfolding in my life.

I came out to the fields to see something twisted and dark, something like the grief and anger wrapped around my insides. Isn't a lightning-struck oak tree the perfect companion for a girl whose daddy's food for worms, whose family's secrets keep rising out of the ground like locusts? A girl who might murder her own brother to get the fiddle he's trying to keep away from her? I almost feel capable of it. The shadow man whispered all night in my dreams, and twice I nearly got out of bed to take the fiddle from Jesse. I forced myself to lie still, to obey Daddy's wishes.

Now my feelings are going in so many directions. I don't

know what's true anymore. Jesse's the reason my daddy's dead. If he hadn't taken the fiddle, Daddy would still be here with us. But if he did it for me—even partly for me—maybe I'm the reason too. Maybe nobody's innocent. Not Mama, for refusing to see, refusing to know. Not Aunt Ena, who kept Daddy's secrets even after he was gone. Daddy's guiltier than all of us, for letting his grief rend the veil, opening a hole ghosts can flit through and creating a space for the shadow man to fester and haunt us. After all, he kept playing even though he knew it brought my nightmares, even though he knew I was in danger. That's hard to forgive.

When I reach the oak, it doesn't look like the twist of misery that's inside me. Instead, it's glowing in the morning light. I slide down its rough bark to the grass. In the quiet of the field, away from the fiddle's pull, I almost believe Daddy's words. He said I was strong enough. Strong enough to choose the people I love. I hope he's right.

I don't want to be like Jim and Frank, chained to grief and hatred and a deadly grudge. And even though I loved Daddy more than anyone else in this world, I don't think I want to be like him either. I don't want to sacrifice my family, my very existence, to the fiddle's magic. I want more—I want love and life and beauty. I want to glow like this lightning-struck oak tree in the day's first light. No matter how much it hurts, it's time to let the fiddle and its painful past go.

Holding my decision close, I get up and go home and make my way to Jesse's room. When he doesn't answer my knock, I stick my head in.

"What?" Jesse groans from underneath his pillow, his voice groggy with sleep. He's always slept with his head under a pillow, which I've never understood. Maybe he got in the habit from trying to block out Daddy's nightly fiddle playing.

"Get that pillow off your head. We've got things to do today," I say, my voice determined. "Some ghosts to lay to rest."

Jesse's face appears. His sleepy eyes are full of fear, but he nods. "Okay. Let me get dressed."

As I sit on the couch waiting for Jesse, I think about calling Cedar or Sarah or Orlando. I think about asking my whole band to come. They'd be here in a heartbeat, and they'd make it easier for me. But this feels like something Jesse and I need to do on our own, something only we can share.

"Where to?" Jesse asks once we're settled in the cab of Jim's truck.

"The lake?"

Jesse is quiet for a long moment, but then he shakes his head. "He's got no reason to stay there. That's not where he'd be."

"You sure?"

"Aunt Ena's," he says, starting the engine.

The fiddle lies on the seat beside me, and Jesse glances at it every few minutes as we drive. He's afraid I'm going to snatch it up and jump out of the truck. I can't say the thought hasn't crossed my mind. But I'm resolute. I've made up my mind to be rid of the thing after its final performance.

When we pull onto Aunt Ena's road, Jesse starts drumming the wheel with his fingers.

"You've never been back here," I say, realizing why he's so nervous.

"Couldn't. Not without him here."

Or is it really because he'd be too much here? Hints of him in every room, memories crowding around every object? The atoms of his grief in every breath we take?

I know now where Daddy's true pain lives, and it's in Aunt Ena's attic. This is where everything started—Brandy's death, Daddy's grief, Ena's trauma. And all it led to: Mama's affair, Jesse's pain, my unbearable loss. It makes sense that this is the place it will end, or at least where the fiddle will play its last desperate notes.

Aunt Ena opens the door, the cuts on her face almost healed. If she's surprised to see Jesse standing on her doorstep with Daddy's fiddle in his hands, she doesn't show it. She steps back to let us in and then trails behind us up the stairs. But she hovers at the threshold of my old bedroom while Jesse and I move the dresser to uncover the attic door. One arm is wrapped around her stomach, and one shaking hand covers her mouth.

I'm surprised again by how small the attic door is—it looks like a place a child would sneak off to play. Instead, Brandy was sent up here to die.

"Are you ready?" I ask Aunt Ena, as gently as I can.

Her eyes seem to plead with me, not to make her go up those stairs, not to make her walk back into the past. But her feet carry her to us, and she hands us our flashlights.

We go single-file up the stairs, Jesse in the lead. The attic looks the same as it did when Cedar and I came up, though now that I know its full history, the room feels darker and smaller and more frightening. Aunt Ena lights some candles she brought up, and we turn off our flashlights. A soft, flickering light fills the room.

We let the silence settle around us for a little while, our nervous breathing the only sound. I listen for wings, but there's nothing living up here, except the termites boring their way incessantly through the wood. It's a rotten room with a rotten past.

Aunt Ena starts speaking as if continuing an earlier conversation. "We got word he died the year you were six," she says. "I remember because you were doing a family tree project at school and kept asking who your grandpa was, and we were glad to be able to tell you he was dead. Then you left it be."

I remember the way Daddy held me tight and wept into my hair the night his father's ghost came, how he clutched me to him like I was the most precious thing on earth. I can't imagine being so afraid of my own daddy.

I take a deep breath and bring the fiddle up.

"Can you play Brandy's song?" Aunt Ena asks.

"I'll try." I know now that's what Daddy's song was—a lament for Brandy. I close my eyes and look down into myself, down into my deepest, farthest memories. A haunting melody floats up to meet me.

After a few moments, I feel the air begin to stir, a welcome chill entering. I almost expect to see Brandy herself, eternally young, traumatized by wasps, but it's Daddy who appears.

He is exactly the way I remember him. Dark hair, dark eyes, and a sad, lopsided smile.

"Shady Grove," he says, eyes locked on my face like I'm the most beautiful thing he's ever seen.

"Daddy." My heart fills with an ache that's part joy and part grief, the two almost too close to tell apart. "Jesse's here."

"Hey, Dad—Daddy," Jesse chokes out. "I, oh my God, I'm so sorry for what I did."

Daddy shakes his head. "You did right, son. You always did right."

"But you're dead because of me," Jesse says.

"No, I'm dead because of myself. Because I couldn't let go of the past. I don't want the same for you two. I want you to be free of all this." He gestures around the room.

"Will," Aunt Ena whispers from her corner, and he breaks into his first true smile.

"Ena," Daddy says. "I—"

"Where's Brandy?" she asks, interrupting his joy. "I thought she'd be here." There's so much longing in her voice.

Daddy shakes his head. "Brandy didn't have any reason to stay up here. Her conscience was clear. She left as soon as she died, as the innocent always do."

"But what about my dreams?" I can't help but interrupt. "With the little girl and the wasps? I think my little sister Honey dreamed about her too."

"Those are because of *our* father," Daddy says. "That trouble only started after he died. That man's become a thing of nightmares, worse than he was living. A black pit of despair and self-loathing and hate."

"Shadow man," I say, shuddering. "It's him, isn't it?"

I knew it on some level, but could never completely admit it to myself. All along, it was my grandfather haunting me, as the shadow man, with the rattlesnake and the alligator, even with the little dead girl in my ceiling. He used his own daughter's death—her murder—to torment me and then my baby sister. He whispered in my ear, making me think my own brother killed Daddy.

Daddy nods. "I thought you'd be free of him after I died. But when you started playing "The Twa Sisters" in the woods, he saw how like me you were—how you opened yourself to the music. He knew your grief and pain could make him strong again. That's why he led you to the fiddle."

My fingers tremble, making the bow squeal. *I'm* the one who drew the shadow man here. With my grief and my pain. I let him back into our world. "What does he want from me?" I ask. "To kill me?"

"Baby, I'm not sure he even knows. I think he wants to cling to this family, to keep on hurting us, even in death. Maybe because of what he's become he can't do anything except try to destroy what's good and pure. There's no saying what a twisted heart like his is after. I don't know what he wants, but he's not going to get it. We're not going to let him."

"Daddy," I whimper, my terror overtaking me. Believing the shadow man wanted to kill me was bad enough, but not knowing his true motives is somehow worse.

"Don't be scared, Shady Grove," Daddy says. "We're here

now. Your family. We won't let him take you. We'll help you."

His eyes blaze, kindling a final ember of courage in me, pushing away my terror and my guilt. When he sees it start to burn in my eyes, he nods. "Baby, I think we've all had enough of that song. Enough of that grief. Play us something with some joy in it."

It takes effort to stop playing "Brandy," like that's the one song this fiddle was really made to play and it's not ready to give up its purpose. I see now why the shadow man taunted me with this song—he's the one who killed Brandy, the one who caused all my daddy's pain. I have to yank the bow away from the strings, plunging the attic into a sudden silence. I know better than to give the silence hold, though.

Without thinking, I start playing "I'll Fly Away," which is a strange choice for a family that's not religious, but it's got joy and hope in it, which is mostly what we need.

Daddy smiles sadly for a minute, but then he starts singing, his voice the honey-on-gravel I remember. Aunt Ena joins in, a little off pitch, but that never hurt anyone. I look over at Jesse, and even he's singing, or mouthing the words anyway.

The attic, this place of torment and shame, this sealed tomb, fills with my strings and their voices, and a rising hope.

I'll fly away
When I die, hallelujah by and by
I'll fly away

I suppose that's what we all want, someday, to fly away from all this suffering and this pain. Most people don't get to fly away until they die, until they're released from the flesh that binds them to this earth. But there's a deeper hope in the song, I think, the hope that we can leave the shadows and the pain here on earth, while we live.

That we can fly toward life instead of death.

That our lives can be more than a slow descent into the grave.

That we can *fly*.

I think of Cedar, Orlando, and Sarah, of Mama and Honey, of Jesse and Aunt Ena, who sing on either side of me. All the people I love most in this world. The ones I have left.

So when I feel the shadow man creeping around us, his soul buzzing with wasps, his mind as rotten as the wood of this attic, I don't let myself feel afraid. He's drawn here, perhaps against his own wishes, perhaps knowing his dark will is weakening. But he's here all the same because we are, because Daddy and Aunt Ena have held space for him all these years, letting his poison infect Jesse and me too.

Everyone stops singing, but I play on, my hands steady.

Our lack of fear seems to anger the shadow man. The room fills with the sound of rain, lightning and thunder striking overhead. His voice whips around us like wind through the pines, deep and chilling. "You've always been a liar, William. Why don't you tell your children what really happened—what you did and who you blamed?

"I know every thought in your head, every shadow in your heart," the shadow man says. "You poured it into your fiddle, feeding it right to me. I know what you are, and it's you who should have gone to prison, not me."

Fear creeps over my skin like the feet of a hundred wasps. What's he saying? Was Daddy involved in Brandy's death after all?

Of course not, I realize. The shadow man is a liar, a manipulator, and I shouldn't trust a word from his mouth.

"Isn't that what all your songs have said?" the shadow man asks, and then pitches his voice into a mocking imitation of a child's, pitiful and afraid—"*My fault, my fault.*"

Suddenly I'm not playing "I'll Fly Away." Daddy's mournful old song for Brandy pours from my fiddle again. As the music builds around us, the wind and rain pick up, lightning forking on every side. And then we're not in the attic anymore—we're somewhere else, in a memory, or inside the song, I don't know which. It feels like dreaming.

It begins with a scream, a long, endless scream—agonized and unbearable. It goes right through me, searing its way into my bones. The scream that started my family's history.

And then there is a little girl's body on a table, covered all over in wasp stings, her long, blond hair the only beautiful thing left. Daddy's mother throws herself over the pale and bloated body, and little William's face is hard and set, a dark, miserable hate forming in his breast—hate for himself, and for his father. He clenches his small fists by his sides.

My fault, my fault, sings the fiddle. All along, that's what the music was saying, wordless but clear. *My fault*.

Here in the attic, Daddy's jaw tightens. He looks just the way Jesse did when I asked him what he'd done to deserve jail. Angry and ashamed.

"It was you who took the cookies, not Brandy," Aunt Ena says to Daddy, but her voice doesn't hold judgment, only surprise and pity.

Daddy nods and forces himself to speak. "She was too scared to take them on her own. I—I didn't think anyone would notice. I wanted to make her happy. Instead, I got her killed. I should have said something, I should have stopped him." Daddy's voice breaks, and the sound wrenches through me. All these years, he's blamed himself for Brandy's death. All these years, he's carried that weight, that shame. I can't imagine holding all that inside me.

Sensing he's losing our attention, that we feel sympathy instead of rage toward Daddy, the shadow man changes tactics, drawing us back into the past. The memory shifts from the house to a field, where lightning flies down, striking an enormous oak tree. William runs to it, his pull to share in the violence and devastation so great we can feel it now, in the room. As the inside of the tree burns molten, he feels his own rage burning just the same—hot, unbearable, searing.

A huge branch flies off, one of the only pieces not destroyed. William picks it up and holds it tight to his chest, letting it singe his skin, relishing the hurt. He promises himself that he'll pay and he'll make his daddy pay—if the man is sent to prison, the moment he gets out, William will burn him like this oak tree. Until then, he'll carry the flames inside his heart and in this wood.

The fiddle in my hands grows so hot I can feel the molten wood it was made of, the hate that shaped and formed it and made it what it is. Aunt Ena said Daddy made this fiddle from grief, but he made it from hate, too, and shame. It's a thing of fear and loathing and pain. It's the literal embodiment of Daddy's heart.

But I've seen what that tree became, and it's beautiful. Maybe this fiddle can be made beautiful too. "Daddy, it wasn't your fault," I say, pitching my voice above the fiddle and the storm. "You have to let what happened go. Your father's the only one to blame."

Daddy's tears break, flowing like vapor down his ghostly cheeks.

I lean toward him. "Blaming yourself for Brandy's death is like Jesse blaming himself for yours—it's not fair. You don't hold Jesse responsible for your death, so how you can you hold yourself responsible for Brandy's? Your little sister died knowing you loved her, just like I know Jesse loves me."

I can see the moment my words hit home. Daddy's face fills with relief, and he falls to his hands and knees, all the guilt and pain breaking free from his chest.

The storm-swept field is an attic again, the shadow man's hateful power almost gone. He has played his last card, and it's not a winning one.

I thought if I ever made up my mind to face down the shadow man, if I were ever brave or strong enough, I would somehow rip him apart with my music, grind him to dust and let him drift off on the wind. I imagined a violent struggle, bloodless but wild as any war.

But that's not how you kill a shadow man.

I see now, you can only destroy him by letting him go.

I wrench back control of the fiddle and begin playing "I'll Fly Away" again.

In the candlelight, I watch Daddy's and Aunt Ena's faces as they struggle through their fear and their hatred, their love and their longing.

I know what to do now; I know how to cut the shadow man down to size. "Say his name," I tell them. "Make him take his true form." We've got to make him just a man again, take back the fear that feeds his shadow form.

I expect Daddy to speak, but it's Aunt Ena whose tremulous voice names the shadow man. "George," she says. "George Stephen Crawford. That was his name. But we called him Daddy."

The shadow man, too big for these tight quarters, stops his shifting about.

Aunt Ena speaks only to him. "You were our father and our tormentor, and you were the reason my precious sister died."

"But you were just a man," my own daddy says. "A sad, pathetic man. You don't deserve to cling to this family. You have no claim on us."

The shadow man's form seems to be clearing, lightening. Daddy's and Aunt Ena's words, spoken openly, are unveiling him. And then he's the man I recognize, a ghost who shares my surname, who once shared my blood.

George turns his head, and his eyes settle on Daddy. "You here to forgive me?" he says, his sneering voice carrying the hoarseness of a smoker's.

"There's no forgiving what you done," Daddy says. "But

hating you's not worth what it costs my family, so I'm letting you go. To heaven or to hell or to darkness, I don't care, but you've got to go. We're done letting you haunt the living."

George turns to Aunt Ena. "And you, Ena, after all I took from you?"

Ena's got murder in her eyes, a look I've never seen there before. She wants to wrap her hands around his neck and choke him, but she can't. He's dead, beyond the hurt her hands can do.

"You didn't take as much as you thought you did," she says, her voice trembling but resolute. "And you don't get to keep any of it. I'm going to wash this house of you. I'm going to erase your memory from this earth. I hope you turn to nothing on the wind, I hope you float into the atmosphere and burn up in the sun. I hope there is no afterlife for you, only nothing. Less than nothing." Aunt Ena crosses her arms. "I'm done entertaining your ghost."

George has lost his darkness and his wasps, and what remains is pitiful. A sad, empty old man, hardly worth the word *human*. He turns his eyes on me.

"I never meant to be a monster," he says.

I can see a tiredness at the center of his soul, a weariness—of himself and of this world, of all these old griefs.

"Then stop being one," I say. "You've done enough harm here, so why don't you try to undo some of it. Go on now. Go on back to your rest, if there's any rest for a man like you."

George nods, all the fight gone out of him. He never really had any power of his own—only what we gave him, with our hate and our fear, our bottomless grief. He doesn't even have the strength for a farewell speech. He's there and then he's gone, like a candle snuffed out.

Aunt Ena begins to weep, the sobs pouring out of her like there was a weight on her chest, and now she can let out the breath she's been holding for thirty years. Daddy nods, his eyes sad and solemn. I wonder if he has fully forgiven himself. Can a man who turned an ordinary fiddle into a ghost magnet from sheer grief let go of his oldest, deepest pain?

I transition from "I'll Fly Away" into a song I hope will make him smile, the song that gave me my name. I want to hear him sing it one more time.

He doesn't disappoint. His eyes light up just the way I remember. And then he's singing with the most beautiful voice this world ever held, at least as far as I'm concerned. The voice that made the sun rise in the morning, the moon shine at night. The voice that bookended every day of my childhood. The voice that made this earth seem like a place worth loving.

He went away four years ago, but it's only now that he's really going. For the last time, never to return.

So I drink in his voice and his joy, the love he presses into every syllable of this song. When he's done singing, I stop playing, because this fiddle's dark magic's almost spent. But I can tell Daddy's spirit won't disappear right away. He's got a few minutes left.

I reach out and feel his hands in mine, cool like any other ghost's but otherwise just as I remember. His eyes fill and brim over, but not with grief. With pride. With love.

I look over at Jesse, the brother who loves me as much as my daddy does, maybe even more. I won't have him left out in the cold, wondering if he's forgiven. "Come here," I say. "Tell Daddy goodbye."

Jesse joins us, and then Daddy takes us in his arms, the way he did when we were little and fit better. He holds us close against his chest and looks across the room at Aunt Ena. "Bye, baby sister," he says.

"Bye, Will. I love you," she replies, her voice hoarse and sweet at once.

Daddy pulls back so he can look at us, and I feel like the last four years never happened, like he never died and I never grew up, like Jesse never went to jail, like I never had to find out my family's secrets or face the monster they made. I'm a little girl in my father's arms, safe again.

There are so many things I want to say to him, so many questions I want to ask. But he's already slipping away from us. He's finally laid his burdens down.

"We love you," I say. I want him to go with his heart both light and full. "You gave us everything we need."

"I love you both," Daddy says, one last time. "With all I am."

Then I say the words my father taught me when I was six years old. "Go on home now, go back to your rest." And I add, just for him, "We'll keep you in our dreams."

EPILOGUE

"Please welcome to the stage Wind in the Pines," the announcer roars. The audience cheers in the welcoming way bluegrass fans always do, and Cedar leads us out, smiling his rodeo boy smile, Sarah blushing behind him. Then Kenneth, Rose, Orlando, and finally Jesse and me.

Jesse is second fiddle in our band now, playing on my old pawnshop violin. Daddy's ghost-raising fiddle is just a regular instrument now, its haunted heart gone. I offered to drown it or burn it for Jesse's sake, but he told me to keep it and play it for the living. He said I should make our family's darkness into something beautiful. And then he surprised us all when he asked to join the band a few weeks ago.

It took the rest of us ages to choose a name. Kenneth's first suggestion was the Ghost Whisperers, which made Cedar smack him on the back of his head. Orlando nominated Longwing Summer, for the Florida state insect, the zebra longwing butterfly. Everyone agreed it sounded nice, but Rose thought it was stupid. Actually, Rose thought all the names were stupid. We almost had to choose one without her.

In the end, Sarah came up with the name after we held a band practice in the woods, sitting out under the trees, the pine needles glowing gold around us, the whispers of the ghosts drifting through the trees.

"Oh," she said, out of nowhere, and everyone looked up from tuning their instruments to stare at her. A slow smile spread across her face, making her dimple sing. "Wind in the Pines," she said, eyes all bright. "For our band name. Let's call ourselves Wind in the Pines. It's perfect."

Rose laughed. "That's the first name that hasn't made me want to lose my mind. I vote yes." Then she kissed Sarah on her cheek, right over that heart-stopping dimple.

Rose and Sarah had officially started dating the month before, finally brave enough to try again, after their first disastrous attempt three years ago. Rose doesn't mind that Sarah never puts herself out there, because Rose is always out there, so a person's only other option is to run away.

And Sarah didn't run away. Instead, she fell in love.

"Wind in the Pines," Cedar repeated, smiling. "It's perfect."

The rest of the band agreed, so now, months later, we're standing together on a stage for our first big show, at the county fair. Cedar'll be showing off a prize cow or something later, but for now he's here with us, mandolin in hand, cowboy hat, Wranglers, and all.

I love our name, Wind in the Pines, not only because it

describes the woods that mean so much to me but also because it reminds me I let go of my shame. I let people into my life, let them see who I am, trailer and all, ghosts and all, broken family and all. If I learned anything from my weeks of ghost raising, it's that shame is what makes secrets so dangerous, shame that keeps us tied to the darkness.

"Hey, y'all, we're awful glad to be here," Cedar drawls into the microphone, playing up his accent. "We're going to start out with a bluegrass favorite, "Shady Grove," which also happens to be the name of our pretty little fiddle player here." He smiles at me, little red hearts floating over his head, and I can't help but smile back. The crowd loves it—we haven't even played a note and they're already whistling and stomping.

Once we start playing, I scan the crowd, looking for my family. I spot Orlando's parents first, sitting with Cedar's mother and Sarah's father. Mama, Aunt Ena, and Honey are in the third row, and Honey's sitting in Mama's lap, singing along, her eyes locked on me. The seat next to them is empty, and though I know he's gone on to his rest, I imagine Daddy sitting there, his eyes teary with pride, his honey-gravel voice mixing with our music.

Daddy's absence is a hole in the world, and it's always going to be that, no matter how many years go by. His memory is starting to bring me more comfort than pain, though, like the music he taught me to play.

Bluegrass lyrics are almost always about death, loss, and unrequited love, but the music—the noise we make with our banjos and our fiddles—is joyful. The dead are always with us, even after their ghosts move on, but it's the life pulsing through our veins that makes the music.

The fast, bright, twanging noise of bluegrass comes from Sarah's shy dimple and Cedar's sly smile, from Kenneth's raucous nonsense and Rose's sailor-worthy swearing. It comes from the wonder Orlando feels when he holds a butterfly in his hands, lovely and delicate as a dream. And today it comes from the joy that surges up in me as I watch my baby sister's golden hair swirl in the Florida wind, her eyes as blue and bright as the September sky, her whole life stretching out before her.

Bluegrass might be full of ghosts, but it's the life in it we love.

ACKNOWLEDGMENTS

Getting a book published in today's crowded market involves a mysterious combination of talent, hard work, and good luck. Much of it boils down to connecting with the right people at the right time. I've been so fortunate to connect with some incredible people, without whom *Ghost Wood Song* would only be a file on my computer.

First, I have to thank my literary agent, Lauren Spieller, and my editor, Alice Jerman, who both helped shape this book into what it is today. Lauren, you are a fierce champion, and I'm so honored to have you in my corner. Your nitpicky line notes nearly killed me, but they made this book shine. Alice, your enthusiasm and love for *Ghost Wood Song* made slogging through those last rounds of revisions totally worth it. Thanks also to Clare Vaughn, Megan Gendell, Alexandra Rakaczki, and the rest of the HarperTeen team, as well as everyone at Triada US Literary Agency.

The person who did some of the heaviest lifting on this book is my Pitch Wars mentor, Lisa Amowitz, who convinced me to gut the whole manuscript and rebuild it into something much stronger. Lisa, thank you for believing in my writing and for giving so much of yourself to bring *Ghost Wood Song* into the world. Thanks also to my Pitch Wars 2017 class, for your camaraderie and excellent advice.

Many brilliant, big-hearted people offered me encouragement, help, and insight on my publication journey. I'd especially like to thank a few professors who made a difference in my life: my mentors and friends, Rickey and Anna Cotton, as well as Dr. Sandy Hutchins, who believed in my creative abilities before I did.

So many friends, family members, and fellow writers have read and provided feedback on *Ghost Wood Song* and my other manuscripts. Thank you to Lauri Sellers, Kara San Joaquin, Cayla Keenan, Kit Rosewater, Wendy Heard, Melinda Waters, Kathy Orzechowski, Jane Beasley, Anne Alesch, Chandrika Achar, Em Shotwell, Hannah Whitten, Allison Ziegler, Christine Doeg, and Candice Conner. Thanks also to my Nashville writer pals Logan Malone and Anna West, who make sure I leave my writer's cave at least once a week. A special shout-out to Rob Jackson, who helped me track down exactly the obscure old murder ballad I needed for an important scene. If I listed everyone else whose help I'm grateful for, I'd run out of pages. So if you are one of those generous people who has offered me your time and insight, thank you.

I have to give enormous thanks to my spouse, John, who not only patiently talks me through my plot problems, but also makes sure I have health insurance. Thank you for giving me the space, time, and encouragement I need to make books for a living. I love you.

Finally, I want to thank my parents. Daddy, you were always so proud of me and I hope you'd be really proud of this book too if you were here to read it. Momma, your example of strength and persistence helped me to become a person worth being proud of. Thank you for my life and for all your love.